BEYOND

PETER GULGOWSKI

Gulgowski, Peter

Beyond / by Peter Gulgowski

Summary: In a near-distant future, a teen uncovers the
truth behind the mysterious walls surrounding his town
and their other-worldly origins.

ISBN-13: 978-1-0879-4587-3

10 9 8 7 6 5 4 3 2 1

First Edition Hardcover Printing, January 2021

For my grandmother who thought this book would be 'the one', but would not get to see its completion.

In loving memory of

Barbara Gulgowski

1935-2020

BEYOND

PART ONE
RISE

PROLOGUE

The last day of life outside River Ridge was quiet and unknowing. The heat of the late-August sun hung low to the ground, and in the fields that circled the small town, the steady hum of cicada and swishing of tall grass carried on the lift of the breeze.

Up the curved road, leading towards distant farmland, a five-year-old boy—thin and long, blonde and narrow-faced—sat curbside.

Splotches of mud caked his jeans, and his T-shirt was dyed with sweat around the neck, but Victor Winslow reveled in the summer heat. He leaned back onto his forearms, smiling mistily to himself.

He'd been playing only a few-hundred yards from his home, alone as usual. Over time, one curious object of nature pulling his attention after the next, he had made his way further from home.

Now resting, his fingers brushed the grass as he raised his hand, greeting the older children riding bicycles past him, back towards River Ridge. After the dust had settled from their tires, he found his hand still raised absentmindedly.

He pushed off the ground, standing still on the rough terrain. Dusting off the back of his jeans, Victor moved further down the road, the pull of curiosity his fuel.

In the final moments before his life would forever change, the way he'd see the world forever skewed, he nearly tripped on a loose shoelace. Lowering to a knee, he looked up when, from across the field, there was a deafening whoosh. He covered his ears, but by the time his hands had cupped them, the sound had already fallen silent. Looking up, what he saw next sent a swift rush of air into his lungs, a gripping knot into his belly.

A tall figure, cloaked and hooded, was moving towards him through the field. The cloak, made of a pale brown burlap dragged behind him. The Stranger, as Victor would forever remember it, carried a long, wooden staff with a small sphere of orange light glowing bright above it.

Victor rose, leaving his shoe untied. As startled as he was in front of the Stranger, he was also in awe of its great presence. In awe of its power.

It seemed the figure didn't notice him. As it grew closer, Victor could make out the face beneath the cloak: deathly gray, matte and devoid of any traces of hair. Black, vacant eyes—almost lifeless—stared forward, fixated on River Ridge behind him.

The Stranger's stride didn't falter as he pressed through the grass. He continued towards the boy, swift and determined, until he reached him, stopping a few feet away. Victor's eyes briefly narrowed before he spoke, inspecting the figure up and down wide-eyed. "Are you a—a giant?" he asked.

The Stranger did not respond, but it now looked down, and met his eyes.

Above the pair, the sky had dimmed with a sudden arrival of clouds that were not there a moment ago. As they moved in, they dropped, pulling close to Earth's surface. Victor cast his eyes around, looking past the Stranger to the sky which was turning a shade of emerald. He'd never seen the sky in such a state. Winds from nowhere began tearing across the fields, and for the first time, Victor was now frightened.

The figure above him pulled back the drooping sleeve of its cloak, exposing a withered, mangled hand. Its fingernails were yellow and sickly, long and jagged. The Stranger's fingers reached out, touching Victor on his bony shoulder. Held there for a moment, Victor shuddered beneath its great power, its coldness slicing right through to his very heart.

With his hand still on Victor, the Stranger raised his staff to the sky. The sleeve of his cloak slid back, revealing more of its sickly, purple-veined arms.

Heart drumming wildly, Victor squirmed within the giant's solid grip, but something held him in place. Feet frozen in the ground, as though nailed into the dirt and surrounded by concrete, he couldn't do anything but shake his shoulders. The Stranger continued to disregard the boy.

To it, Victor was as insignificant as the blades of grass that surrounded them. Merely an obstacle in its way.

But suddenly within that moment, deep beneath his feet, the Earth began to shudder and move.

The trembling grew heavier and bolder. It was as though Hell itself was a ship lost to the sea, rising to the surface to reach daylight once again. Victor grabbed the Stranger's hand to free himself, but felt an immediate scorching heat on his palm. He yanked it away, pulling it close to his chest.

Looking to Victor now, the Stranger began to speak in a language not of this Earth. From low-grumbles to mere hisses, phrases were long and rhythmic. Victor looked up to meet the eyes of the Stranger, but when he did, a splitting pain exploded within his brain, as if it would tear in two, pulled apart by two giants. Victor grabbed his head, pressed inward, and rubbed his temples.

Anything to make the pain go away.

And within that moment, that was when the visions appeared. At first, quick and scattered, they slowed to a rate he could comprehend.

Victor saw illness; saw death. Bodies everywhere, smoke billowing. He could feel the stinging in his chest, the burning in his throat of swallowed ash and smoke. His eyes were blinking rapidly now, and he lifted his hands to his face, wishing for everything to stop. He tried to call out, but found his voice paralyzed in fear.

And then came the bombs. Unable to escape the theater of his mind, he saw the people huddling together in the shadows blown away, engulfed like leaves; bodies charred and then blown away as if they were never there.

The trembling in the ground grew stronger, winds grew fiercer. Victor could feel it in the distance and within his bones. He struggled to shake himself free from the Stranger's grasp, but its binding hold wouldn't give.

Finally, Victor found his voice, and he screamed.

He screamed a primal roar, a shattering cry of despair, of torture. He screamed until his throat went raw and no sound could come. The Stranger didn't so much as even flinch.

From a place deep and sacred, the Earth split with rapturous force. The Stranger shoved Victor to the side as a massive shape tore free from the broken ground. Shadows grew and blanketed the town. From what he could see behind hands raised in defense, it was a wall made of steel, intricately detailed from base to top with illuminated designs and patterns. Dirt continued to spill off the top, collecting in piles along the base of the rising structure.

Breathing the dusty air, sight became veiled by the brown haze. Hidden in the dust, Victor now only saw the visions the Stranger *wanted* him to see, the knowledge *meant* for him.

Victor covered his eyes, begging for it to stop. He called for his mother and sister. As he did, he saw slivers of the aftermath; saw clusters of survivors taken out by something his mind couldn't understand. It was dark, it was powerful, and it was not of this Earth.

But no matter how much he tried to fight off the visions—the horrible visions—they wouldn't stop. Nothing could stop them, it seemed. Tears fell from his eyes to the ground, watching as the Stranger continued chanting to the sky.

Now towering above River Ridge, the rising wall slowed, but from behind it, something he hadn't seen emerged. It was clear, glass-like, and glistening against the sky. In silence, it rose and curved above them. Behind it, the sky remained emerald green, but the winds stopped. The trembling grew softer and eventually to nothing.

Masked in shadow, the figure reached out its hand to Victor. Of instinct, he feared being singed again, but of impulse, he took it. When he did, a searing jolt surged through his arm and sent him skidding across the dirt.

The boy's lips trembled, muscles went rigid, as the figure stepped back. Its eyes focused upon him. Clenching his eyes shut, Victor was helpless to think of anything but the pain ravaging his small frame. When he opened them again, the Stranger had vanished.

He lay still for a few moments, trying to hold on; fight back tears like his father would want him to. But he was slipping. He knew it. Victor's vision was tunneling and closing in. Not more than a few seconds later, just as he knew it would, the emerald sky above went full dark.

When he woke a week later, the walls and dome were still up, and the sleepy, little town of River Ridge was in full panic.

But despite the despair, despite the terror, came a tunnel of hope—a way out of the darkness. The Stranger had showed him the way.

He was the chosen one.

And now, the fate of River Ridge and its occupants lie solely in him

Victor saw the path clearly, and even in the days that would pass, he'd still feel the great power running through him.

Death was the beginning, but it didn't have to be their end. The nightmares, however, had only just begun.

ONE
73 YEARS LATER

In his seventeen years, Blaze Davies found himself content only when he was in motion. Today was no different. The wheels of his bike rolled over the long-abandoned walkway, scattering dust and rocks in his wake. Wind rushed through his chocolate brown hair as filtered sunlight within the woods highlighted the small marks of adolescence on his face.

"C'mon, Aurora. Keep up!" he called back, taking a sudden detour off the path.

Behind Blaze, his best-friend and perhaps someday, girlfriend, Aurora—four months younger, enough to make her sixteen—peddled behind.

"If you weren't shooting all this dirt in my face, it'd be easier to," Aurora yelled over the wind.

"That's your problem," Blaze laughed to himself. "Should've taken the lead when you had the chance!"

In response, Aurora gave him the middle finger.

Fair enough. I earned that one.

They continued down the new dirt path and snaked through a densely-forested area. The overgrowth of trees and forgotten shrubs made an interesting obstacle course. Sunlight from above sifted through the trees and cast various arrays of designs on the damp, moss-covered earth.

Peddling slower now, Blaze came to a near halt. He planted both feet firmly on the trail.

"Need a break now, do you?" Aurora asked between breaths as she came to a stop behind him. She sat up, pushed back her dark-red hair behind her ears. "We're close to no-man's-land, you know?"

"Yeah," replied Blaze, "we're close." He leaned over his handlebars before stepping over and off.

The corner of his mouth curved up as he set his bike down beside the trail. Blaze reached behind his back and grasped his drawstring bag. Setting it down on a pile of leaves, he pulled the bag open and reached his hand into it. He pulled out a mason jar of water.

"Ladies first?" he offered, unscrewing it and extending it out to Aurora.

"You know I hate that phrase, right?" Aurora quipped, raising her hand. "But I'm good. Thanks."

Blaze took a swig. "Can't say I'm not a gentleman."

"Doesn't mean I don't appreciate it."

He raised the mason jar to his lips again, took a few more sips. Blaze wiped the back of his hand against his mouth and exhaled. His eyes cast upward, looking through the overgrowth. Through the curtain of nature, steel—clean and seemingly untouched by the grit and patina of time—stood tall into the sky. Lined with faint blue patterns, an unbroken array of designs of circles and squares, lines curved and straight—made up the entire surface of the great wall. Blaze and Aurora looked up, their mouths widening as they skimmed the surface. It was as impressive today as it was when they first saw it up close.

Climbing high up and splitting the canvas of sky, it seemed to go on forever. And as the sun continued its daily descent, the shadows grew longer and darker.

"They say there was once a dome," said Aurora.

"I know." His voice softened in interest. "A dome for what, though?"

"We might never know. Sad but true."

"But the wall remained." Blaze knelt down, working his hands along the dirt before the line of demarcation began. For him, he wished he could sift away some dirt and find the wall's origins just beneath the surface. He wished it were as simple as stepping onto an archaeological dig where most of the work had already been done.

Even without the obvious shimmering air in front of him, between them and the surface of the wall, he knew where he couldn't cross. A line of bird and tiny rodent skeletons, bones spread far and wide from where they'd died, created a line a small distance from the wall.

Aurora stepped forward, leaning down with her hands on the tops of her thighs. "It protects us. From what? Maybe it's best we don't know," Aurora said. "But you know what they say, we shouldn't get too close. We shouldn't even be here. They patrol the area."

"Yeah, at night," Blaze dismissed, pressing off the dirt floor. "We're good for another hour or two."

"Sure, but do I really want to be hanging out here and get caught? No, I don't think so." Aurora stepped back, lifting her crimson bike off the ground, brushing the left handlebar off with her hand. "Besides," she continued, "you know how Winslow is about people getting too close."

"So, he's a neurotic freak and scared of his own shadow. What else is new?"

"Blaze..."

"I know," he exhaled. "You're right. But it's cool, isn't it?"

"It is," Aurora agreed. "But we can always come back It's not going anywhere."

Blaze walked back to his bike, lifting it up and swinging one leg over the side. "Think we'll ever know what's behind it?"

"My parents haven't, so I doubt I will."

"That's negative," Blaze said, turning to her. "Gotta have a little hope. A dream? But I'm with you. I'm not holding my breath."

This time, he let Aurora take the lead to guide them out of the overgrown greenery along the wall. He followed behind, breathing in her sweet lavender scent that still lingered even after a day of exploring.

"Where to?" she called out into the wind.

He thought, then answered, "Home, I guess."

More time with Aurora was always desired, but it was getting late and his parents would want him home soon.

After they had left the forest, and the sky had darkened a few more shades, they were passing through Main Street.

Aurora and Blaze hopped off their bikes at the fountain that hadn't run in decades. Rumor had it that it had stopped when the walls rose, but that was just their friend, Forrest Kremer, talking. Blaze could only take Forrest's word so far.

They passed some townspeople as the streetlamps were lit with candles beneath the overhangs of the store fronts. Across the way, Blaze noticed his neighbors, Mr. and Mrs. Nyman walking. Mrs. Nyman carried her patchwork bag with some groceries from the town's garden and pantry.

"Getting chilly tonight," said Blaze.

Aurora turned to him, slipping off her flannel shirt and leaving only a thin, spaghetti-strap tank-top beneath.

"Here you go, wimp."

His brows netted together. "Rory, no," Blaze said, refusing to take it.

"Come on. You're cold, I'm not."

"No, this is my punishment for not wearing an extra layer. I keep feeling like it should be warmer at night, but it's September now. Can't be expecting it to stay warm in the evenings anymore."

"Stop overthinking and just take it." Aurora said, extending the shirt towards him again. "Go on."

"Aurora, I'm not taking it."

"If Forrest was here, you'd take his."

"He's a dude, though."

She recoiled her hand, slipping her flannel back on, buttoning the buttons. "Oh, I see," she cooed. "You do realize it was my granddad's, right?"

"I know. It's just me. Thanks, but no thanks."

"Last time I offer you anything."

As they passed Kremer Hardware, Blaze stopped and peered in the window. "Wonder if Forrest's working tonight?"

"It's Monday, he probably isn't. Hadley might be."

Either way, it was worth a shot. Besides, Blaze enjoyed seeing new tools or gadgets from the old-world Mr. Kremer had for sale or even better—for loan.

He pulled a hand through his hair, catching his reflection in the store's window. They walked to the front door, pulled it open, and stepped in. The air was perfumed with wood and metal, of old wax and age.

Like everything in River Ridge, nothing was new. From the floors to the clothing, everything that was in the town had been there before the walls.

Anything new had to be built by hand. Cut off from the rest of the world, nothing came in and nothing went out. Clothes were recycled, passed from family to family. If Blaze wanted a new shirt to wear, it was required that he donate one shirt. And sometimes, you were just better off with what you had.

Citizens were allowed ten shirts, five long-sleeved and five short-sleeved. You could have one winter jacket, one spring jacket, and ten pairs of pants. Shoes were getting harder to come by as the years had gone by, and shoemakers were a dying breed in River Ridge.

As they stepped in further, Blaze looked down the length of the various shelves, seeing them to be barren, with items pulled to the very front.

Scraps of wood stuck out of a thick cardboard box. Tools, rusted and chipped, sat under yellowed plastic cases locked with a small padlock.

As Aurora and Blaze moved in, a swift motion behind them startled them.

"Stalking me at work, I see," said the smooth voice of Forrest Kremer.

Aurora spun around. "It's Monday, what are you doing?"

"Hadley's *sick*." He motioned with both hands, index and middle fingers flexing. "So, my dad asked if I could chip in some. Only working until nine."

"And homework?"

"Already done," Forrest said, looking at his hands and wiping something off on his canvas apron. "Slow night tonight. Any way, what brings you both here?"

"We went to the wall, felt like seeing if you were in on our way back," Aurora said. "Well, he also probably wanted to see if Hadley was in. I just wanted to stop in and say hi to whoever was here."

Forrest shook his head, sending his curly brown hair back and forth. "I love you, buddy, but stay clear from my sister. When I said she's sick, I should have said she's got bad diarrhea, as in *explosive, window-shattering* diarrhea."

"A visual I never wanted to have and never want to again," Aurora said. "Thanks for that, Forrest."

Blaze smirked. "I know you're just making that up, so it doesn't bother me."

"Nasty. You're a freak." Forrest laughed. "So, anything new at the wall? We still locked in? Winslow still paranoid?"

"Obviously," Aurora said. "That wall isn't coming down anytime soon."

"Too bad," Forrest said. "You guys going to the community gathering tomorrow?"

"Kind of have to, don't we?" Blaze asked.

"Yeah, but it's nice to pretend we have a choice once in a while. Winslow likes to keep us close. I think it's so he knows what's going on. He likes the gossip."

"I doubt that's it," said Aurora. "It's tradition, you know. Checking in on each other, offering support; it's what communities do."

Forrest scoffed at this. "Yeah, close ones."

Aurora shot him a stern glare. "I'm just saying, I think it's nice."

"It is. But since Winslow suggests it, the rebel in me thinks it's stupid. If anyone else said it—nice. Winslow? Stupid."

Blaze checked his watch. It was getting close to seven, and he knew that he should get home soon. Even if he had missed dinner, his parents would want to see him for a bit before bed.

"Am I boring you, buddy?" Forrest asked.

Blaze shook his head. "No, man. Just have to get going. My parents will kill me if I'm not home soon. Wish I could stay."

"Parents can be like that. Yeah, you best get home. Aurora, you can chill here. Not much to do. If I wax the floor anymore, all that'll be left will be the foundation."

Aurora shook her head. "Blaze and I are a package deal tonight. Where he goes, I go. Besides, I actually hung out with our friends at school during lunch. I didn't do my homework, so I have to do that."

Forrest reached over, grabbing a broom resting against the front counter. Distracted, he balanced it on the bristles, cupping his hands in the air around the handle as though he could keep it suspended by sheer thought alone.

"We'll see you tomorrow," Blaze said, stepping out of the door.

"Sure. See you later. Have a good night. Don't get abducted on the way home."

"They won't be able to take us far," replied Aurora. "See you, Forrest."

He raised his hand, returning back to his balancing act as the two stepped out of his father's store.

Both retrieved their bicycles leaning against the storefront and continued walking down the pathway, turning into their subdivision and eventually parting ways where the way to their respective streets were no longer on the same path.

When Blaze had put his bicycle in the garage, he went in through the garage door and into the kitchen. Lit by candles and smelling of toast and eggs, his father stepped around the corner leading into the hallway.

Anton Davies stiffened his stance. Blaze's father — in his mid-fifties with the physique of a Marine—eyed his son down. His peppered hair was mid-length and wind-swept to the side. His beard and mustache complimented his sharp jawline. There was a faint film of satisfaction across his face, but no warmth. He cocked his head to the side, studying his son.

"Sorry. Aurora and I took a detour the wall."

"I've told you to stay clear of that place. You know they patrol the perimeter."

"Not until after dark," Blaze said, remembering his conversation with Aurora earlier.

"It's sunset. Do you know what comes after? I'll remind you: dark." He threw out both hands. "You could've gotten lost. You step into no-man's land and you're dead."

"But I didn't get lost, and last I checked, I'm not a ghost," Blaze replied stiffly.

"Watch it, son," Anton warned.

The two remained looking at each other. Over the years, Blaze had learned to mask his fear of his father. It seemed Anton could see right through the facade, though with each piercing glare, he chiseled away at an already-damaged exterior.

Anton relaxed. "Come. It's time for supper. Mom saved you some since you were out exploring."

"Good. I'm starving."

Wordlessly, Anton followed Blaze behind as he walked into the kitchen. A plate was set out on the countertop. Blaze lifted it and walked to the wood-burning stove where a pan with scrambled eggs sat cool, no longer steaming. He scooped some up, placed it on his plate.

Blaze went to sit down at the table, and much to his surprise, his father and mother, Lorna, sat down with him.

"How was school?" she asked, skipping right over the fact that he'd been out much later than they had wanted.

"School was good. Then Aurora and I went to the wall."

"I know," she said, annoyed. "I heard."

"And putting himself in danger. Fun, fun, fun, right?" Anton said, putting his elbows and the table and pressing his fingertips against each other as he looked at Blaze.

Quickly, Blaze set his fork down. "Just drop it, Dad. The wall is not this dark, scary place. It's actually pretty cool."

Lorna's eyes lowered. "Can we not get through one dinner without an altercation?"

"I didn't ask for one."

Lorna's eyes lowered. "When you open your mouth about things we agree not to talk about, you're asking for one, Blaze. And not just with us. You know how it is here."

"That's 'cause you let Mr. Winslow and his cronies bully you both into submission by—"

"*Enough,*" Anton hissed through gritted teeth.

"Okay," Blaze said, taking a breath. "I'm sorry. All I'm saying is I wish the adults in this town would grow a set and stand up to Winslow and demand to know the truth."

Lorna slammed her fork and knife down onto the table. "The truth, Blaze, is that the walls were built almost a hundred years ago to protect us from a failing society. The townspeople of River Ridge built the walls to protect its descendants from the damage the others were inflicting," said Lorna. "Anything else is urban legend."

"Have you seen the walls?" Blaze asked.

"Of course," she replied quietly, looking out the window over the sink. "Every day."

"No, up close," Blaze continued.

Lorna shook her head dismissively. "I've stayed away from it. They told us to."

"Well, I have, and I'll tell you that either we were extremely advanced before they went up or we didn't build them. One or the other. There is no in-between."

"After the walls rose, the war took out everything, Blaze," Anton said. "Databases, technology, everything was wiped back. We're lucky we've come this far in the century. We still can't figure out some things our ancestors created. Don't be so sure of yourself."

"Yeah, yeah, but we weren't *that* advanced," said Blaze. "The walls haven't aged in a century—"

"Were you there when they were putting them up?" Anton asked.

"They have strange designs and writing."

"They call it graffiti," retorted Anton.

Blaze leaned back in his chair. "Dude, can I finish?"

"Don't call me 'dude', Blaze."

Blaze looked at Anton, exhaling through his nostrils.

Anton motioned with both hands. "Go on."

"The walls aren't from us—our people—our ancestors."

"That's what we've been told," said Lorna.

"And you believe it?"

"I struggle to, but it keeps me sane," she replied.

Blaze turned to his mother, surprised. "So, you don't?"

Lorna shook her head, as her face paled. Her lower lip quivered momentarily as she spoke again. "But you know what they are capable of to anyone who questions them, don't you, Blaze?"

Blaze lowered his gaze to the table. "I'm not a fool."

"Neither are we," she continued. "But we go with what they want us to think because it's easier than going against them. They'll silence anyone who goes against. That's why we get so angry when you press us because someday that mouth will get you in trouble with the wrong person, and it won't end well. Your heart's in the right place, but let's face it—you're a smart-ass."

"Don't knock it. It's my best trait somedays," said Blaze. "But, in all seriousness, I'm careful."

"Careful isn't enough. Thinking before you speak isn't either," she continued. "In our world, you need to stop before you even think anything different than what they tell us."

"Are you just saying all of this because of Winslow's town meeting tomorrow?"

"*Blaze!*" Lorna yelled. "Knock it off! This is serious."

"Sorry, sorry."

"You need to promise us that you'll stop going to that wall."

"You know I'm not going to agree to that."

Anton leaned back in his chair, crossed both arms. "What's so great about that wall? What's so fascinating? Enlighten us, please. Do those designs change? Do they perform a light show we've missed? What's the deal, Blaze?"

"How brainwashed are you both? God, I hope I'm not like you when I get old. Start thinking for yourself and stop letting Mr. Winslow tell you what to think."

"Bedroom. Now!" Lorna said.

"Fine, but I'll never stop asking questions about the wall. So, sorry in advance." Blaze took a bite of his toast.

"Yeah, I'm sorry, too," Anton said, shaking his head. "Because when they come for you for going one step further, just pressing a little extra because you could, we'll be the ones at your funeral."

"If that's what it takes to get you both to see the truth, then that's not a heavy loss."

Lorna pressed away from the table, pushing her chair back in. "I can't even believe what I'm hearing. Like Dad said, one day you will step out of line, open your big mouth, and get yourself killed. And guess what? We'll be left to pick up the pieces."

Blaze scooped up the last of his eggs, took a final bite of his toast. "Don't worry. Inside the walls, they won't go far."

But Blaze realized he'd pushed his mother to the edge. But instead of killing him, she cried. Within an instant, the stinging, pitting sensation of regret came over him and took him with crippling force.

" I—I know. Sorry, I went too far."

"You always do." She took heavy breaths, pressing her trembling fingertips against her temples, rubbing them, soothing them. Her lower lip quivered as she tried to speak, but his father chirped up, his face firm and unwavering.

"Go upstairs now," Anton said. "You've caused enough drama for one night."

"Mom, I'm sorry. Please—"

"*Now!*" boomed Anton, slamming his heavy fist on the table. It rattled Blaze's plate and fork, and he stood up, pointing down the hallway. "Look what you've done."

Blaze got up, lifting his empty plate and putting it in the sink. He hurried past his father, whose hand was still pointing down the corridor Blaze had walked every night to go to bed.

He climbed the creaky stairs, reached his bedroom, and shut the door. Blaze laid down on the bed, cupping the base of his skull with his hands. He felt the cool wind of looming autumn across his bare legs, and watched dark clouds twirl above the town, illuminated slightly with deep purples and pinks.

Blaze wondered what a sunset really looked like. He imagined it to be how it was when the sun rose or fell past the crest of the wall, only it was ground instead of steel.

But as close as it was, the experience of seeing daylight fall beneath the horizon of faraway lands would be something much different.

Laying there, he heard a rustling outside. But then he heard a tiny pebble bounce off the siding of the wall outside his bedroom followed by a sharp hiss.

"*Blaze!*" called out a voice.

Quirking his eyebrows, he wondered if it was his imagination playing tricks on him.

But it sounded again.

"*Blaze! Down here.*"

He sat up and crawled on all fours to the window near the foot of his bed. Blaze leaned his head towards the open window to spot a familiar pair.

Forrest—surprisingly off from work before nine—and their other friend, Ahmed.

"If you hadn't answered, I would've moved up to a bigger rock. Come hang out with us," said Forrest. "I got off work early."

"*Guys, I can't come out,*" Blaze whispered back through the screen.

"*Why not?*" Ahmed asked.

"*Er—I think I'm grounded.*"

"*What'd you do?*" continued Ahmed.

Forrest elbowed him in the side. "*You don't ask what he did, you tell him that his parents aren't being fair. Geez, do I need to teach you everything.*"

Blaze leaned back in, holding in a smirk. "*We can try to hang tomorrow after school. If I'm not grounded, that is.*"

"*You said you were,*" Ahmed countered.

"*Think I am. Not positive.*"

"*Just crawl out the window. Ahmed wants to see the wall. He hasn't been.*"

Blaze shook his head, pointing outward to the sky. "*It's dark. We can't see in the dark.*"

"*Problem solved. Flashlights,*" Forrest said, raising two above his head. "*Gotta live a little, right?*"

"They patrol the area," Blaze said, no longer whispering.

"*Keep your voice down!*" Forrest hissed. "*Besides, it's just a volunteer group of old men with nothing better to do than walk around a perimeter.*"

Now, Blaze let out the laugh he'd been holding. Forrest wasn't wrong, and now, having heard that, it seemed foolish that he was afraid of being caught. What would they do to him? Bring him back to his parents? Big deal. They'd have to try harder than that to spook him.

"Sure, I'll come," Blaze replied.

"*Just stuff a pillow beneath your blanket. They won't bother you then,*" Forrest said.

Blaze reached forward and with his fingertips, pulled in the clasps keeping his screen down. He lifted it slowly, pausing for any signs of movement outside his door.

No movement. Just the soft murmur of distant chatter wafting up the stairs and beneath the crack of the door.

He scooted back and reached down, slipping his shoes on and lacing them tightly. Taking Forrest's advice, he grabbed one of the decorative pillows on the floor and placed it beneath his gray comforter. He grabbed the knit blanket that sat at the foot of it—the one that usually ended up there during the course of the night—and draped it over. Careful to ensure it wasn't too smooth, he stepped back, admired his sculpturing work, and pulled himself out the window.

He stepped onto the narrow, sloped roof, mindful of the missing shingles that could cause him to slip. He steadied himself against the side of his house, listening once more for any signs of his parents.

At this point, he wasn't even sure of what use it would be. He was already out of his bedroom and standing on the rooftop, ready to jump down. His parents weren't dumb enough to disregard this. They'd know he was trying to escape even though Blaze was still unsure if he was actually grounded.

Blaze released his hold of the house, lowered himself to a crouch and moved down the slope of the roof towards where he knew his mother's rose trellis was.

"Am I good?" he asked, inching his head over the edge.

"Yeah, a little to the right," replied Forrest. "Don't step on your mom's pretty flowers. It'd be a shame."

"Not much choice. I can't jump down."

"Sure you can," Ahmed said. "You won't die from that height. Twist your ankle? Probably. Break a leg? Maybe."

"I'll stick with the trellis."

Blaze turned around, placing one foot down onto the first rung, testing its strength by pressing down slightly with his foot, apply a little weight.

He knew it wouldn't hold long, if at all. Blaze would need to move fast, even jump once he was half-way down.

He swallowed a firm lump, and lowered his second foot to the next rung down.

The wood bowed and crackled slightly.

Quickly, he lowered himself, grasping the gutter with his hands. He felt it flex beneath his weight, so Blaze grabbed the trellis again, which proved to be a mistake when the first rung he grabbed cracked.

"Screw it," he said and jumped down.

He fell hard and landed on the backs of his feet. The vibration burst through the soles of his shoes and up through his spine. Blaze nearly stumbled backward, but it was Ahmed who hurried up to him, grabbing him around the sides to stabilize him.

"I'm good," replied Blaze. "Thanks."

"You sure?"

Blaze nodded, exhaling a breath. "Er—Yeah."

"Nothing broken?"

"If anything was, he'd be on the ground crying and we'd be dragging him back to his mommy and daddy," Forrest replied. "But Blaze Davies is a tough guy. He's good."

The cool air of early nightfall bit into Blaze's skin as he walked past Ahmed and Forrest towards the street.

Blaze cleared his throat. "All right, geniuses, how are we getting there?"

Forrest pointed to his and Ahmed's bike lying on their sides in the street. "Bike, of course."

"No good. Mine's in the garage," said Blaze.

"Yeah, looks like you're riding passenger."

Blaze shook his head. "Sorry. Not sitting on your lap."

"Nope. No lap-sitting. Perks of having a BMX bike, buddy. I've got pegs on my back wheel," replied Forrest. "Hop on."

TWO

The three boys rode the twisting roads towards Main Street where glowing, candle-lit streetlamps illuminated their path. In the distance, against the dark canvas of steel, the walls climbed tall and mighty, emphasizing the great size in contrast to the miniature houses built beneath its great shadow.

Their bikes carried them, with Blaze holding onto Forrest's shoulders, all the way through, until they reached the cusp of the forest.

It wouldn't be long now. Blaze had never gone into the forest in the dark. As much of a rebel as he had become in the last year or so, this was still something he'd yet to conquer. He'd heard of others doing it, but often questioned whether they really had or not. Nevertheless, he would be doing it now; tonight.

Forrest came to a screeching stop. The tires skidded, and Forrest wiggled his handlebar left and right, struggling to regain traction. Blaze released his grip on him and jumped back, unsure if it would help Forrest or just send him speeding further down the slight decline.

But Forrest remained upright and came to a halt. Ahmed was already leaning his bike against a tree, seemingly unfazed by the near accident.

"You guys ready?" he asked the two, without skipping a beat.

Forrest nodded, but turned to Blaze. "Dude, you can't just jump off. Tell me when you're about to do that. It shifts the weight around."

"I'll remember it next time we're skidding down a hill," said Blaze.

"We were fine, man." Forrest stepped off and leaned his bike against another tree. He shook his head. "At least no one got hurt."

"Yeah, try explaining this to the person who'd find you, if you had," replied Ahmed.

Blaze knit his eyebrows together. "But I'm sure you'd sneak us out with no one finding out."

Ahmed let out a laugh. "Drag you both? Yeah, no."

"Good to know who our friends are," Blaze replied, somewhat miffed.

He shouldn't have been too surprised, however. Ahmed was nearly two years older than them. They'd grown up on the same block until Ahmed's family moved closer to Forrest's. In the years since, their friendship had fallen a few levels, and occasionally debated with himself if they were more or less just acquaintances at this point. Ahmed had come into the picture and as childish as it was, some days it felt like Forrest's friendship had become a competition between him and Blaze.

Nevertheless, Forrest liked him, so it was better to play along and stay on Ahmed's good side, even if it was just an act sometimes.

Ahmed pulled off a cloth bag, twisting it off his shoulders and into his grasp. He opened it slightly, reached in, and withdrew a large flashlight. The rechargeable power cord for the generator was still connected, and he removed it, sliding it back into the bag.

"And let there be light," said Ahmed, flipping the tiny switch at the base of the plastic case.

The intense beam of light bounced off the bases of the tree trunks, lighting them and the bugs swarming within the cool, musty air. They started forward, into the brush, scanning for any signs of the patrol force.

Blaze found himself peering around, keeping close to the other two. There was no scenario in which a forest at night wasn't creepy. It was what you didn't see that spooked him. It was the fear of what lurked just beyond the reach of light, watching and waiting. Blaze tried to distract himself, thinking of what he'd do tomorrow. He could feel the trickle of adrenaline emptying into his stomach. He steadied his breath, keeping his eyes forward, trying his best to pretend to be nature's greatest hunter.

What could hurt him if he was at the top?

Needless to say, it didn't take.

A dark forest was a dark forest, and he wasn't a hunter, nor at the top of the food chain. As much as he'd argue it, he knew he was probably on the prey side of things.

"Shouldn't be too far," Ahmed said.

"Follow the designs," Forrest replied, pointing ahead. "I think I caught a glimpse of it, right Blaze?"

"Not sure what you saw, but it should be there," Blaze replied. "It gets harder to see the deeper we go in. Once we reach the no-man's-land, that's where it opens up again. Nothing lives beyond the line."

"Yeah, and I'd rather not cross it," Ahmed said. "Has anyone ever tried?"

"Not sure if anyone ever tried," said Forrest. "I think the burial zone is enough to convince people to keep their distance."

"But you both go close," Ahmed replied.

"Close, not through," Blaze corrected him. "Big difference."

Ahmed turned to him. "I see."

"Why are we heading down here, anyway?" asked Blaze.

"The designs at night," Forrest said. "I wanted to see them at night, since I never got the chance. I've seen it, obviously, but not up close."

"Me neither," Blaze replied, turning to Ahmed. "What about you?

"Once, I think. It was late sunset, so technically not pitch black, but dark enough. Like you guys have seen, it lights up like a Christmas tree. But we'll have to be careful. They're already patrolling."

Blaze nodded absentmindedly. "We'll be quiet."

Forrest turned to him. "Even with your loud mouth?" he laughed softly.

"Yeah," Blaze agreed. "Even with that."

They proceeded forward, pushing through the dense woodland. Fallen logs and tree limbs were strewn across the area. Wind swept through the canopy, lifting the sweet, mossy scent of untouched earth. The boys stepped over a log when they came to a tiny creek.

Stepping through, feeling the frigid water slosh over their feet, the boys stepped around a row of great pine trees and found themselves standing in the clearing.

There, as it had stood for seventy-three years, the wall of River Ridge—well, one of the four—climbed high, bursting through the expanse of a cloudy night.

Ahmed crossed his arms, shook his head. "There she is."

"*She?*" Forrest questioned. "I'm picking up more masculine qualities."

"Regardless, it's a marvel," Ahmed continued. "And they told our parents that we built it?"

"Yeah," Blaze agreed, "I doubt it."

"Idiots," quipped Ahmed.

"If we didn't build it, who did?" Forrest asked.

"Aurora and I talked about this earlier," Blaze said. "Maybe it's best we don't know."

"But don't you want to?" he continued.

"Sure," agreed Blaze, "but once we know the truth, the mystery goes away."

Forrest stepped a few feet from Blaze, casting his gaze up. "And you like the mystery?"

"Keeps things interesting."

"Whatever it is," Forrest said, "it's more than just a wall."

Blaze turned his head as Ahmed shined his light on the wall, revealing scars in the strange metal.

"Look at those," he said quietly, pointing at the pits and gashes etched in the wall.

Following the beam of light through the thin, shimmering veil of no-man's-land, the light reflected off the steel surface, up the narrow lines, long and sprawling, as if inscribed by a giant.

Smooth and symmetrical, there were no end points of the lines. It was seemingly one line lasered in. Lines were parallel until they weren't, curving off into circles and triangles, until they went straight again. Within the etched engravings, a delicate line of silvery, ice-blue light beamed out, packing the space with illumination.

"Ever wonder if there's a door?" Ahmed asked.

Blaze surprised even himself and laughed. "I think they've checked over the years. If there were one, they'd have found it by now."

Forrest cleared his throat. "All right, hear me out. Y'all know I love a good conspiracy theory. What if they found it and hid it on us?"

"Hid the door?" Blaze pressed.

"They, who's they?" Ahmed asked.

"Come on. Who's the biggest nutcase in this whole city? Winslow. Who never wants us to leave? Winslow. If we leave, he doesn't have his story anymore. The wall is all he has."

"I think it scarred him for life," Blaze said. "My parents told me that back when he was a kid, he used to talk about it with the adults. One day, he just stopped. They shut him up."

"Yeah, because he was talking out of his ass. Now, he's got the whole town wrapped around his finger," said Ahmed. "Not sure why they suddenly believe him now, but didn't as a kid."

"Kids aren't inherently trustful," Forrest said. "Example: Why did my dad always think you were stealing from our store?"

"Because I'm not white?" Ahmed offered.

Forrest held his lips together, shutting his eyes. "Er, no. Because you were a kid..."

"A brown kid," Blaze joined in, chuckling.

Ahmed laughed, too. "Exactly."

"Dude, he's not racist. Just dull. Anyway, you're missing the point. Kids aren't trusted. Adults always think they're up to something."

Ahmed shrugged his shoulders. "Yeah, I suppose."

"Same applies to Baby Winslow. Now that he's Old-Man Winslow, everyone acts like he's the Messiah."

"He basically told my dad he was," Ahmed laughed. "But I see your point." He continued to cast his flashlight across the surface of the wall, when abruptly he shut it off.

Now, the only light remaining came from the wall itself, casting a blue hue across all of their faces. Blaze hadn't noticed until now, but he could see his breath in the air.

"Batteries die?" asked Forrest.

"*Shh!*" Ahmed whispered. "*I think I heard something...*"

"Relax. It's probably just a deer taking a dump," quipped back Forrest, hands on his hips and looking around. "We're in the woods after all."

But Blaze heard it too, just down the clearing a hundred or so feet from them: Crackling branches, pressing footsteps. All were signs that they weren't alone anymore. Then, from around a cluster of trees, the beam of another set of flashlights illuminated the path along no-man's-land.

"*Fuck!*" hissed Blaze. "*Company's here.*"

The boys set off, up the slight incline and into the brush. But as they did, they heard the distant shout of a deep, booming voice.

"Stop!"

They didn't listen, pressing through the thick forest. Blaze's heart pounded in his chest. He wasn't concerned about getting caught by the patrolling guardsmen as much as he was afraid of what his parents would do when they inevitably found out he'd been out after dark and so close to the wall—again.

"Go left!" Ahmed called out breathlessly.

Forrest countered, "No, right!"

"They came from the right," Ahmed spat. "We can come back for our bikes tomorrow."

"Are you kidding? They'll know whose they are!"

"I'm going left," Ahmed said. "You're making a mistake."

Forrest paused, pressing his hands against the tops of his thighs. In the distance, running, Ahmed turned on his flashlight, jogging away until neither boy could hear him any more in the midst of the dark forest.

"Are you with me or am I going alone?" Forrest asked.

"Sticking with you, even if we get caught," replied Blaze.

Forrest spit on the ground, taking a few deep breaths. When he rose, he slapped Blaze on the back of the shoulder. "Let's move."

Taking off, the forest became a twisting maze. Under the thick draping of nightfall, Blaze wished they could use their flashlights without giving away their location. Now without, he and Forrest were almost literally running blind through dense woods.

But right as they least expected it, through a narrow gap of foliage and up another slight incline, Blaze spotted a streetlamp, pointing at it with his right hand.

He pointed to it. "There! Look!"

Forrest took a breath, letting out an exhale of relief. "Finally. Thought we'd get lost in there."

And to their surprise, a flashlight lit up the pathway, bouncing slightly.

"Is that him? He made it to the bikes?" Forrest asked.

"We pretty much took a straight shot down. I wouldn't be surprised if he was able to loop around and out."

As they reached the top of the hill, their feet reached pavement right away. Standing beside their bikes were four figures. Ahmed stood with his arms out, facing the adults with his flashlight still on.

They could hear chatter between him and the other three figures. One of the men, wearing a dark, long-sleeved shirt, also wore a small badge. A gun rested in the holster on his hip.

Forrest, squatted down, stepping back into the shadows. "Great. Winslow's cronies. Let's just own it, and we'll get my bike."

Blaze lowered himself too. "Screw that, my parent's will kill me."

"Look, they probably got the serial numbers and will run it through the community database by morning. Either way, they're finding out. Owning it now means you get to control the narrative. Maintain the power, buddy," Forrest said.

Blaze sighed, looking away. *"Damn,"* he breathed.

"I know." Forrest turned to him, green eyes almost glowing near the streetlamp. "But if you want to leave, go for it. We only had mine and Ahmed's bike. No reason for you to go down, too."

He debated it for a moment. Forrest did have a point. There were two bikes. The guards were only expecting two bodies for them. He'd be the surprise. But he remembered what he'd told Forrest. He couldn't abandon him. Not now. That wasn't what friends did. He told him that if they got caught, they got caught together. He wasn't about to betray that trust or his friend.

Blaze turned back to him. "I'm sticking with you."

And though he wasn't positive, he swore he saw Forrest take in a breath of relief. The two rose to their feet, brushing their knees off from the dead leaves and dust.

"Ready?" asked Forrest.

"As I'll ever be."

They stepped out beneath the orange glow of the streetlamp, walking along the cracked pavement. The guard closest to them noticed.

"Stay there!" he ordered. The man was middle-aged with a large belly. The uniform shirt had clearly been a hand-me-down and didn't fit him well. The trigger-happy guard yanked out his gun, switching on the light on the barrel.

Instinctively, Blaze raised his hands. "It's us—the ones you were looking for. Look, we just went exploring."

Ahmed turned, walking towards them. "I'm so relieved to see you guys. I told you not to go running around."

"What are you talking about?" exclaimed Forrest. "You went down, too."

"Only after you," Ahmed said. He turned to the guardsmen. "I tried to stop them, but kids will be kids. I'm just glad they weren't hurt or worse."

"You're about to be hurt or worse," Blaze muttered beneath his breath.

But Forrest jumped into defensive mode straightaway. "He's lying. He was down there with us. He brought the flashlight, lit up the wall. Fuck, it was his whole idea to go down in the first place."

"T-That's not t-true. I told—"

"Boys!" exclaimed another guard, younger and possibly in his late thirties. He straightened his posture, calmed his voice. "Enough. Why were you down there? You know Mr. Winslow's rules—"

"Who made him the fucking emperor?" Forrest slammed.

"Language, Kremer. Look, let's not make more of this than necessary. Get your bikes and head home."

"And tell our parents?"

"Well, of course—" began the eldest, but stopped when the others turned to him. "Perhaps, we'll let this slide. It's for your safety you don't go down there."

"You walk around it all the time," Forrest countered.

"*Dude!*" Blaze hissed. "Drop it. They're letting us off."

Forrest nodded. "Sure. Understood. Thanks."

The three guards nodded while the eldest placed his gun back into its holster.

"Curiosity killed the cat, boys. Remember that."

Blaze turned to Forrest, catching the last roll of his eyes. "Thank you. We'll get home."

"Where's your bike?" asked the younger guard to Blaze.

"Didn't bring it. Rode on Forrest's pegs."

"His what?" asked the elder guard.

"Pegs, John," said one of the other guards. "They're for tricks, but kids can ride tandem on them."

Ahmed walked back towards his bike, lifted it up, and brushed off the seat. "Thanks for your understanding. I'll try to keep a better eye on them the next time I'm hanging out with them."

"Hear that? Next time?" Blaze grumbled behind Forrest.

Up close, the boys brushed past Winslow's guards, and Blaze waited for Forrest to retrieve his bike and walk it over to them. Once near Blaze, Forrest lifted a leg over and sat on the bike. Blaze stepped onto the pegs, much to the awe of the elder guard.

"Thanks," said Blaze. "Have a good watch."

And with that, Forrest pressed off the concrete and began peddling.

When Ahmed approached, pedaling quickly behind, he rang his bell multiple times. "Guys, wait up. I'm sorry. I didn't know what to do."

"And throwing us under the bus with a lie was the best you could come up with?" Forrest asked.

"I didn't throw you under a bus. I came up with a story that made it seem as though only two of us were breaking the rules—"

"Yeah! Us!" Blaze boomed.

"Hey, I had to think on my toes. I had three guys with guns circling me. Doesn't exactly start the flow of creative juices," Ahmed said, jumping his bike onto the curb and back down again onto the street.

"Should've thought harder," Forrest said. "You're lucky they're not reporting back to our parents, or I'd shove you off your bike right about now."

Ahmed shot him a dark glare. *"I said sorry."*

"And I'm still allowed to be annoyed."

"How long?" Ahmed asked.

"What? What do you mean how long? As long as I freaking feel like it. Go home, Ahmed. That was a shitty thing to do, man."

Ahmed grunted, pressing into his pedals with great force. He sped away on his bike, not looking back once until just before turning onto his street.

By the time Ahmed was fully out of view, Forrest was still seething. Blaze could feel it in the clench of his shoulders, the pedaling of his feet. He didn't press further, since he knew he'd be reopening a box he didn't want opened in the first place.

The boys rode in silence for the rest of the trip back to Blaze's home. When Forrest was near, he stopped two houses away. Blaze hopped off the pegs, landing squarely on his feet, and stepped onto the curb.

"Thanks for the lift," said Blaze.

Forrest nodded, offering him a salute. "Don't mention it. We'll deal with Ahmed later."

"We won't," replied Blaze, starting down the sidewalk. "Let's drop it."

Forrest kicked off the ground, riding on inertia alone. "What do you mean? He turned on us."

"Maybe he was right. Maybe it kept us out of further trouble," offered Blaze. "Not everything has to be sinister."

Forrest slapped his handlebars with both hands, throwing his arms outward. "Why are you defending him?"

Blaze stopped just on the edge of his neighbor's vegetable garden. He pulled back his flannel shirt that was about to get caught in metal rabbit caging. "Not defending him," he replied. "Just an idea."

Shaking his head, Forrest placed both feet on the pedals. "Well, I don't get it, but any way, I'm going to take off. See you in the morning. Night, Davies." Forrest said, pedaling down the street.

"See you later, Kremer."

He watched Forrest until he turned on the slight bend of the street. When Forrest faded from view, Blaze started forward. He looked around his yard, through the windows to see which candles were still burning: Living room and kitchen. The rest of the house was dark.

Blaze looked to the trellis, but shook his head dismissively. It wouldn't work. It was too fragile, and he was too heavy. He'd already broken one rung. Best not to ruin two. Besides, had he held on longer when coming down, he would have come crashing down unintentionally.

Blaze looked around to see what object could be a tool. Even if he placed their rusted patio chair by the side, it still wouldn't be enough of a boost to reach the rooftop. Frustrated, Blaze peered around the rest of the yard, trying to find another item that could possibly get him up to his bedroom again.

After scanning the entire yard, he came to the conclusion that he'd have to bite the bullet and just go inside. Sneaking up would be a failure, since the steps creaked with even the lightest of weight.

Blaze swallowed his pride, prepared himself for the official grounding he'd be soon under, and went to the front door. Twisting the handle, he was met with a sudden force from inside.

He opened the door to be faced with a new figure and one he knew quite well.

Victor Winslow.

Dressed in a black wool coat and black pants, patched on the knees, was an elderly man with a narrow, lined face and snow white hair. His glasses, round and made of thin metal, sat on the bridge of his nose. When he looked down to meet Blaze's sight, the man's thin lips flattened, twisting downward in disappointment as he shook his head.

But what caught Blaze's eyes, pulling them straight to it, was the glistening, brownish-red ruby that lie across Winslow's chest from a string. He'd seen it before, but only from afar. Even in the faint light, it seemed to shimmer a soft glow within the space.

Against the leader's outfit, it stuck out like a sore thumb. It didn't match, but likely Winslow didn't care. Fashion wasn't his strong-suit any way.

"Mr. Winslow," Blaze said. "What are you doing—" escaped before Blaze could stop himself.

"You've been playing where you don't belong," he said, without skipping a beat. "I thought your parents should know what you were up to."

"I'm sorry, sir. My friends and I were just exploring. We wouldn't go near No-Man's-Land."

"That's what they call that?" he asked, disappointed. "Exploring that area will only bring trouble, Blaze."

"I know the rules. And I'm sorry we broke them."

"Ah, but not as sorry as I was to hear of them being broken. I'll see you at the township meeting tomorrow, yes?"

"Of course, sir. Goodnight. It won't happen again."

And with a curt nod, Victor Winslow, the seventy-eight-year-old leader of River Ridge, started down the steps of the porch with determination.

Blaze didn't wait before entering his home with, "I'm sorry. I should've known better."

It was his father who met him first in the hallway. He grabbed him by the shoulder, dragged him further inside. "Foolish boys! How could you put yourselves in danger like that?"

"I know. Forrest and Ahmed—"

"We don't care about them, Blaze," his mother, Lorna said, joining them from the living room. "We care about you. Mr. Winslow came to tell us personally, for god's sake! How do you think that makes us look in his eyes, in the town's eyes?"

"He doesn't have the right to boss us around," countered Blaze. "Why do you care so much about him?"

"Because like it or not, he's the leader. We have to put up with him, follow his rules. He's kept us alive so far."

"No, we've kept ourselves alive so far. He's no more responsible than you both, grandma and grandpa, and anyone else who was alive when the walls rose."

"Honey, the walls rose seventy-three years ago. I know this may come as a shock, but I'm only forty," Lorna replied.

Anton folded his arms across his built chest. "Enough with this nonsense. Up to your room, now. I don't want to hear a peep out of you until morning."

"Yes, sir. Am I—you know—grounded?" Blaze asked.

"That's what you're worried about? What a stupid question to ask right now," Anton hissed. "Why? Do you want to be?"

Blaze pressed his lips together. "Not really."

Anton shook his head. "Just go upstairs. You're not grounded, but that doesn't mean we're not upset. You may be a kid, Blaze, and going on late night adventures is part of that experience, but not here. Not within these walls."

"I guess I'll have to escape then? Finish off my childhood right, you know?" Blaze said, climbing the stairs.

"We hope you'll get outside someday, just as our parents wanted the same for us."

Blaze stopped on the middle stair. "And what are my chances? Throw out a number for fun," he said.

Anton shook his head. "Just go to bed, Blaze. Goodnight."

Blaze pressed off the stairs, climbing once again. When he reached the second floor, he paused outside his bedroom door.

"We love you, Blaze. If we didn't, we wouldn't care what you did," called out Lorna from downstairs.

But he didn't respond. Instead, he walked inside his bedroom, closed the door, and threw the make-shift dummy—the pillow he'd stuffed beneath his comforter—to the ground and slid in.

Through the window, he looked at the walls in the distance.

Against the dark clouds, their ice-blue etchings indicated where the walls stood, even though he couldn't make out the dark shapes themselves. When the sun would rise, he'd only see the rising sun mid-morning when it had already been awake for a few hours.

It wasn't fair.

Someday, he'd find out the truth of what was out there, capture the sun just on the horizon of faraway lands, and explore the vast world forever with nothing stopping him.

But that would have to wait for now.

Tonight, he slept.

THREE

Hadley Kremer shook her head in disappointment. "I can't believe you got caught last night." With hands square on her narrow hips and brown eyes narrowed, it felt like a scolding.

Her brother, Forrest, shook his head. "They told us they wouldn't say anything. I bet it was the old one that ratted us out. At least we didn't get in trouble."

"What do you mean?" Hadley asked. "Winslow came to our house. I had to sit with him, mom and dad. It was awkward. His social skills are on par with a toothbrush."

Forrest smirked. "Insulting the dear leader, are we? Now who's gonna get into trouble?"

The three: Blaze, Hadley, and Forrest had stepped away from the community gathering in the town square. Tables, mismatched and uneven, were placed about the massive, stone globe that sat in the center. Daylight was fading quickly, and above, stars were already making themselves known.

Blaze let Hadley and Forrest go at it while he peered around, taking in the sights. His parents were talking to his neighbors, the Nymans. He looked over and saw a father showing his young daughter where River Ridge was on the globe—somewhere mid-center of the United States. He'd seen books that showed where they were specifically; some sector, called a 'state' in the old world, named *Illinois*. Strange word, he'd always thought.

As far as he was concerned, though, River Ridge was the world; his entire world. For many, it was easier to write off the rest, and while part of him enjoyed looking at old pictures before everything went dark, a piece of him—a seemingly stronger piece—grew very nervous and anxious. It was uncomfortable to see the other places, the other cities and their populations.

Blaze had explored all options. He assumed that there was a good chance that they were the last ones alive. As far as he knew, there hadn't been communication with the outside world ever.

River Ridge was fully independent. It had to be. Blaze's ancestors had done well establishing a communal approach to everything. Food was grown and prepared for the community in whole. Small amounts of power were supplied via windmills, reserved for only rare and special occasions. Water was gathered from fresh-dug wells around the town. Improvements were non-existent; they merely maintained now.

The first years were hard, Blaze had heard. His grandparents talked about the first decade being the adjustment period. But they made it work. Humans found a way to do with less.

Blaze felt sorry for those before him. They knew a world far different. For him, this was all he knew. Life in its entirety existed within the four walls. He couldn't miss what he never knew, and that was why he dreaded looking at historical photos. Blaze feared that the more he was exposed to them, the more he'd miss a life he never lived, places he never saw, and people he never knew.

As Blaze came back to the present moment, he noticed Aurora approaching.

"Hey," she greeted, voice softer than normal. "Winslow should be here any minute, give his talk, and then we're free to head out. Did you guys want to hang tonight? Study together?"

"I'm down for hanging out. Studying, not so much."

"So, are you grounded?" Aurora asked lightly, folding her arms across her chest.

"Not yet," Blaze smiled.

"I heard what Ahmed did. What a jerk," she replied.

Blaze shrugged his shoulders. "It is what it is. Either he did us a favor, or he screwed us over."

"I'll go with the latter," Forrest said. "Denial is Blaze's friend lately, it seems. He's defending him like mad."

Blaze twisted to look at Forrest. "How so?"

"You can't stand Ahmed. Don't pretend you do."

"He's not my favorite," replied Blaze.

Aurora lifted a brow. "Oh, please. You hate his guts. Have for a long time."

He turned to her. "Hate's a strong word," Blaze said.

"If the shoe fits…"

"I don't *hate* him. Forrest might after last night, but I didn't then. I don't now."

"Sure, Blaze. We'll go with that," she said.

He didn't respond. Instead, he looked back to the entrance of the courtyard where Winslow was speaking with another town leader—one less influential and overbearing than him.

Forrest pointed him out. "Guess Winslow's here. We better get back to our tables."

They each went in their respective directions back to their families. Anton was already seated, raising his chin once in acknowledgement.

"Saw Winslow. Looks like he'll be talking soon," said Blaze, pulling his chair out and sitting down. He saw his mother approaching. She offered him a momentary smile.

"Figured. Didn't want to just sit with your old man without a reason, did you?"

Blaze shook his head. "I didn't mean it like that."

Luckily for him, his mother sat down, wiping the tension away with a swiftness that only she could deliver between the pairing.

"How are your friends?" she asked.

"Good. We might hang-out after we're freed."

"*Released,*" Lorna corrected. "But good. Something to look forward to."

"Beats our monthly lecture," said Blaze, picking at some leftover corn on his plate from dinner.

"It's not that bad. It could be far worse," Lorna said. "Try a needle in your eye?"

"Most times, I'd pick the needle," said Blaze.

His mother didn't reply. She looked to Blaze's father. "What do you say? Is he good to go with his friends afterwards?"

"He's not grounded," Anton said plainly.

"Then it's settled," said Lorna.

When Blaze looked up, he saw a sudden rush of people standing, creating a line amongst themselves. Anton and Lorna stood up quickly. Blaze remained sitting until Anton yanked him up by the collar.

"Hands behind your back," he hissed through tight lips. *"Show some respect."*

Not wanting a fight, Blaze listened and looked across the way to see Forrest and Hadley beside their parents, and Ahmed and his father a bit further down the way. Aurora stood with her mothers. Catching glimpse of Blaze looking at her, she smiled slightly.

Every month, at each communal event Winslow attended, a receiving line created a corridor of well-wishers. They waited until Winslow passed through, usually without word, bowing their heads. A few brave souls would smile to the town leader, but Blaze usually kept straight-faced. Usually.

He found it mildly entertaining to watch people's reactions in front of Winslow. Some of his devout followers—those who thought the sun rose and set on the feet of Victor Winslow—would get emotional. It was clear the image he tried to project worked on them, but it hadn't on Blaze.

They stood in silence, waiting. A few beside him shifted in their feet. Forrest puffed out his chest, straightened his posture before looking down the line to see where Winslow was. Blaze leaned forward, too, seeing the leader moving forward, his body slightly hunched beside a bodyguard.

It was the younger one from last night. The one that had been kind to the boys. He couldn't have been much older than them, but Blaze liked him. Serving alongside Mr. Winslow was seen as a high honor. For someone in their twenties, he had to have been something special or his parents knew somebody.

They waited, and as Winslow passed, he turned to Blaze. Of instinct, almost kicking himself for giving into the image, Blaze bowed his head slightly. But, as usual with the other followers, Winslow didn't seem to pay it any attention, moving on as he approached his stage.

It was a minute or so later before Winslow climbed the steps with a little assistance from his bodyguard. Once on stage, he steadied himself, wrapping his hand around the metal railing before starting towards the wooden podium.

The groupings relaxed from their line-up and moved back to their tables. While the rest took their seats, Winslow pulled out a scrap piece of paper, smoothing it on the surface of his podium. He cleared his throat, rubbed his brow, and began.

"Good evening. I'm pleased we could all be here together. If we could bow our heads, express a moment of gratitude for the food we had, I would appreciate that." He stepped back, lowered his head.

The square fell pin-drop silent Not even a fork striking against plate interrupted Winslow's prayer. When he returned to the podium, he nodded once.

"To begin tonight," Winslow started, "I wanted to give thanks to Suzette and Paul Romero for tonight's feast. I know many of you contributed as well. Those of you involved know your names. I appreciate it, and your community thanks you. August was a busy month for River Ridge and progress was made on updating the—"

A sudden surge erupted in the distance, like a sharp, digitized scream. Long and drawn out, it turned heads.

Blaze kept his focus on Winslow, whose brows furrowed as his lips parted just slightly. He turned to see a pillar of fiery smoke and blue-tinted dust spewing up from behind the forest. There were a series of flashes, like rapid lightning, blinding all of the city for a moment.

"What was that?" Blaze heard his mother whisper.

"I dunno," Anton replied, twisting around to the other side.

Ripping across the town, another swoosh, another surge of sound came across them, and across the horizon—their horizon—a huge ball of multicolored fire belched into the sky, spherical and spinning. But along with the distant fire, a rush of light and color hurled towards them. The wave came in a flash of brilliant neon colors, spreading over the city, and then came the screams.

Blaze's brain sent him into survival mode, and he ducked beneath the table. His mother knelt, throwing herself over him. Anton stood up, grabbing a free-running child and pulled him to the ground.

In a terrible flash, the wave ran across them. Moments earlier, Winslow was speaking and now came the destruction, the crumbling walls of homes and surrounding buildings, the groaning cries of twisting metals and shattering glass.

Held tight within the grasp of fear, Blaze clenched his eyes shut, pulled his mother close and tried to protect her too. He counted to ten, wishing for everything to stop: the screams, the cries, the agony.

Thousands of pieces of glass shattered as the wave of color passed across them, but then their world went silent. Blaze could hear nothing but the sound of his own heart and that of his mother's. He opened one eye and saw chairs overturned, legs in the air, and debris of shattered glass and wrecked tables. Platters of food lie on the old concrete. But despite the scene, they were still alive.

Blaze peaked out and saw Hadley and Forrest stepping out from behind a pillar. Yet, in the silence of the wreckage, he had no idea what had happened. Blaze wondered what that was. Had something broken? Was there a bomb? He couldn't wrap his mind around what the town of River Ridge had experienced.

Then he looked to Winslow.

The town leader was being helped up by a few townspeople. When he stood, Blaze saw that the leader had a thin trail of blood coming from one nostril and a cut on his forehead. Turning, Winslow wiped it away with the back of his suit coat sleeve, but as quickly as it vanished, it appeared again.

He stepped towards the podium, but no speech came. Blaze looked around and saw the streetlamps had been extinguished and the city had gone dark. Had it not been for the gold stretches of sky, the colors of a fiery hearth and deep crimson sunset, the entire city would be in a sea of black. The velvety night would no longer be an escape, but rather a binding wrap of unease.

"Everyone, remain calm!" Winslow yelled, his voice gravely with a distinct rasp as he motioned with both hands. "We are okay. We're alive."

"What was that?" cried one male.

"Was this what happened to you?" another called.

Winslow continued to motion with his hands, stricken by shock and frozen on the edge of speech.

"What was it?" the male asked again.

Winslow could not reply. Turning to the others, as if they knew, Winslow continued to wipe away the blood onto his already stained sleeve.

Blaze watched a few citizens press their hands against their face, while a few cried.

But as Anton helped up the boy he'd protected, he cleared his throat. "Folks, if it had been dangerous, we'd be dead now."

"Good point," said another.

"True," Lorna said, crawling out from beneath the table.

"I say we go on as usual," Anton said, stepping onto an upright table, taking over for Winslow. "We can reset the generators, double check our connections, and we'll be fine."

Winslow was nodding in the background, finally finding his voice, cupping his mouth with both hands. "Very much so indeed. I wouldn't worry, my friends. We're okay."

As the citizens began talking amongst themselves, one of the patrolmen was rushing up to the community gathering.

A few turned, waiting to hear what he said.

"*Mr. Winslow!*" exclaimed the out-of-breath guard, wiping sweat away from his brow, bending over and placing his hands on his thighs.

The square went silent.

"Yes? What's happened?" Winslow asked, stepping forward.

"It's the wall, sir. P-Part of it has—er—I think—I think it's *collapsed.*"

Held on the edge of his next response, the entire town turned back to Winslow, surveying his people and casting a look of great concern.

"Everyone will return home," he said. "Patrol, you are to guard the area. Lethal force is approved."

"But sir?"

Winslow was shaking his head. "No one comes in, no one goes out. Repairs will begin in the morning."

"We don't have the supplies, Victor!" the guard replied.

"Well, we best find some. Until that breach is secured, River Ridge is at risk."

Citizens began calling out, dropping the gathering into a screaming match.

Blaze heard as one person called out, "At risk of what? You should know!"

Victor Winslow lowered his gaze, reaching for the ruby necklace hanging from his neck. He held it between his fingertips. "I'm afraid that after seventy-three years, I'm as unsure of what's out there as I was at five-years-old."

And it was from this that River Ridge lost all sense of control, of order. The citizens began rushing home; the chaos began.

But Winslow remained calm. He knew he had to present an image. Within, however, he was screaming. He'd tried to block out the nightmares. Over the years, they came less frequently, but when they did, they were as vivid as the day he was exposed to them—to the sights, the horrors.

He knew what was out there. He didn't understand it, however. But he knew the wall was breached, and they were coming.

For now, he'd try to keep them busy and distracted. It was the only way to maintain any sense of order. If they only knew what they soon would face.

Seventy-three years ago, he'd been shown visions—scenes and moments frozen in time. What had just occurred was the first of them. And as ready as he was, knowing with each passing day, they were inching towards their fate, it was still a shock.

The first vision marked the beginning of the Stranger's guide. The rest would follow quickly, it had promised him.

Victor Winslow decided long ago that he'd maintain the status quo, protect them until he could no longer. He'd fight the truth, knowing it was a losing battle.

He wouldn't tell them. It wouldn't save them now. Nothing could. Even a few days of unknowing were better than none, though. Standing still and looking across the frightened masses, he knew everyone in his plane of sight was already dead, including himself.

As of tonight, it was only a matter of time until death would find their little town.

FOUR

Morning found River Ridge in a new state of existence. What was supposed to be a quiet morning, was one that started at the break of day with heavy lifting and the thunderous drumming of repair.

Across the sky, thick clouds laid atop each other thick and flat, like a novice painter new to the delicate art and subtle skill of layering. Across the littered streets, a faint, early-Autumn haze clung to the streets, and the air was cool.

Work was plenty and not one hand was idle in the entire town. Some homes were untouched, others mere skeletons of their former selves. Walking through, Blaze could already sense the animosity towards those families who lost nothing while so many others had lost nearly everything.

Debris littered the sidewalks, with papers and photographs, clothes and shattered glass strewn about like confetti.

Beside Blaze, Aurora Elder walked with an intensity in her pace. She stopped at nearly every home where an owner was trying to save their life's acquisitions. She stopped, talked to them, and inevitably parted ways with a hug.

Blaze admired this. Even after all these years of knowing her, Aurora still hadn't changed.

Assigned to assess damage, report the greatest loss and most need, Blaze and Aurora each carried a clipboard with a few sheets of yellowed paper clamped down. They wrote addresses, names, and any additional notes they deemed necessary.

He felt awkward doing this. Who was he to decide whose damage was worse than the others? There were the ones where it was obvious, but for anyone who loses something, it's only natural to think their case is the worst and the others will be okay.

It didn't work like that; even Blaze knew this.

Forrest and Hadley Kremer were working in the pantry with their mother and a few others, making lunch for the community. Their father was busy in his hardware cache, handing out supplies and tools.

Jobs had been assigned quickly, and the town showed up for their assignments without complaint. As much as he disliked Victor Winslow, Blaze knew he ran a tight ship. They'd be okay in the end, though he hadn't seen the leader since last night.

Their final task was to go to the section of wall that had been damaged. Aurora was given a camera to photograph damage and bring it back for the town elders to assess.

Cameras were rare nowadays, and Aurora was excited at the prospect of using one. According to her grandparents, cameras were virtually non-existent by the time they were in their teenage years.

Photographs were taken on personal devices, which Aurora never had the opportunity to use. Blaze had seen one only once, but it was a long time ago and virtually useless now. When explained to him, he found the concept of talking to another person far away, like a radio, fascinating. It was a shame he never got the opportunity to try it with Forrest or his other friends.

Together, they moved through the town's streets in the wake of others curious to see the damage.

"What do you think caused it?" asked Aurora.

Blaze's shoulders shrugged. "Not really sure. I don't think anyone is. Forrest told me his dad went to the generators last night and they're fried. I wasn't supposed to tell anyone."

"I'm a one-way street," Aurora replied, unfazed by the news. "So, it's not looking good?"

Blaze shook his head. "Not now, at least. They hoped it would be a simple reset, but the whole system was destroyed. Maybe they'll figure something out. I hope so, at least."

"I'm sure they're trying whatever they can," she said. "They know a lot of people are counting on them to get the generators running, but if they don't, we'll adjust. We always do."

"Yeah. I don't even want to think about that now. That would be terrible."

Aurora waved to a passing child and offered a small smile. "At least no one was hurt too badly. That's the main thing. We're all okay, we have our lives. Some of us have our homes. All we had was a broken window. How was your house?"

"Untouched," Blaze admitted quietly, almost embarrassed.

"Don't feel bad. You shouldn't, at least. The others might try to make you, but you can't let it get to you. Bad things happen to good people. Not everything in this life is fair. It's just how it goes. It sucks, but it's the truth."

"Yeah," Blaze agreed. "Forrest's got it bad. Roof needs replacing, I hear."

"And they'll replace it, and they'll be whole again. Everyone will be okay, Blaze."

"Normally, your positivity would drive me bonkers. But today, I appreciate it," Blaze laughed. "I could tell you the world was coming to an end and you'd find something positive to say about it."

Aurora laughed, folding her arms across her bulky sweater, warming up her arms with her hands. "Yeah, you're probably right. It's my one redeeming quality."

"You have more than just one," Blaze said.

"Okay," Aurora laughed. "That and my killer hair."

"Sure, you can go superficial, but I like to go deeper than that," replied Blaze.

Aurora shook her head, trying to contain a smile. "Stop flirting. We're in a crisis."

Flushed with nerves, Blaze stifled a laugh and kept pressing forward. "I wasn't, but whatever you say, Aurora."

Though they both knew he was.

Continuing forward, they passed the long-abandoned homes. These were the houses that had been empty far before Blaze was born. They took the brunt of the blast, because he knew they didn't look this bad before last night. They were bad, but not in ruins.

But the line of ruins didn't last long before they reached the edge of the forest. Machinery had been brought to the edge, yet to be moved. Trunks, ladders, saw tables, and various garden tools were placed beside a pathway leading down.

There was something timeless about the mysterious place. It hummed with life around them, with sunlight breaking through the leaves and casting shadows on the dirt path ahead. They trudged through grasses, following the distant call of voices and idle chatter. The songs of birds came in bursts, transitioning with precision into silence. While beautiful, Blaze felt it had been ages since the forest of River Ridge presented itself in full glory. Thickly dense, it was overcrowded with ancient trees and twisting roots skimming across the surface of dirt the deeper they went in. Pressing inward, the canopy grew thicker and the air colder. Only the occasional streak of sunlight reached the floor now.

And then there was the wall.

Directly behind decades of animal skeletons, the wall sliced through the greenery. It's surface, silver and etched still looked untouched until Blaze turned to the cluster of townspeople along the surface.

Two stood near the wall, several feet into what had once been no-man's-land. The former shimmering barrier was no more. Now, uninterrupted, Blaze could place his gaze across the entire surface.

Blaze couldn't believe the barrier had vanished, but his focus was pulled through to the surface of the wall. Something had melted through—something massive— which made him step back out of instinct, to peer up, as if whatever had caused the melting of the wall would drip onto him. Blaze had to be sure. He kept his eyes on the wall, scouring over the intricate patterns and designs which looked like thick and deep scars now. Some areas were deeper, while others, where Blaze knew had formerly been traced, were slick and smooth. Along the base, a massive mound of molten metal had solidified into a solid mass. Aside from the heaping pile of molten metal, there were scorched holes blown in the wall around the breach point. Blue sky presented itself behind the opening.

Blaze looked and saw his father, one of the few standing behind where the line of division had formerly been. Old habits and fears drilled into him were tough to break. He spotted Aurora and Blaze and walked over.

"Aurora," greeted Anton.

"Mr. Davies. That's—well—something."

"It's something all right." Anton nodded, turning back to the breach. "We're still not sure what caused it. Don Engle, over there"—he pointed to a bald man with a thick white beard—"wants to test it, but we don't have anything for testing metal."

Blaze crossed his arms across his chest. "Did anyone touch it?"

Anton nodded. "A few of us did."

"You?" Blaze pressed.

"I did," Anton admitted. "Felt weird. Felt slippery and ice-cold. But it's definitely a metal of sorts. Not sure what kind."

"Has anyone climbed up?" Aurora asked, pressing through what she wasn't interested in.

"The ladders are there, but the guts aren't."

"But nothing's come through?" asked Blaze.

His father shook his head. "Nothing. It's been guarded since last night. Winslow said no one goes out, nothing comes in."

"Of course, he did," Blaze replied, regretting it the moment he said it. The words had slipped out before his mouth could recall them.

But his father wasn't himself. Not today, certainly. The response he would have expected did not come. Instead, Anton's brows lowered as he looked to Blaze. "This time, I agree with him."

"Right," Blaze said. "Of course. A lot of damage occurred from whatever happened."

Anton nodded, swallowing hard. "I heard he's on the way down to inspect the damage, assess the state of the wall and figure out where we go from here."

"Where do we go?" asked Aurora. "If the wall is breached, whatever it was protecting us from has an easier time getting in, now."

But they couldn't press the topic any further. The sound of fast-moving, rolling wheels filled the air as Blaze turned to its source, watching closely as a golf cart carrying Victor Winslow pulled up to an abrupt stop.

"Mr. Winslow," greeted Don Engle, offering a hand, "watch your step."

The town leader brushed it aside, stepping off the back step of the golf cart. He steadied himself on the uneven earth by holding onto the metal bracket of the golf cart. Instantly, Blaze could tell his eyes were taken aback.

The legend began here, at the wall.

Engrained in the town's history, like the etchings in the wall, Winslow had been an odd fellow for decades. For the longest time, he tried to talk about the event but found himself silenced by the adults. After a while, after much heartache, he stopped talking about the day the walls rose.

He had tried to warn them. Tried to tell them of what he knew, but they didn't listen; refused to listen. They made him feel like a fool, like he was lying. At times, they were so good at convincing him that he sometimes doubted his own recollection.

His conscience played tricks on him. Some days he would see entirely different scenes, remind himself he wasn't making anything up, and sooner than later, the memory— the correct memory—would present itself clearly.

Now, most of those he'd told had passed away. And in the years since, he'd remained silent. He was sure that rumors had gotten out, some quite near the truth, skimming just below the surface of truth, but he refused to speak on it. Now, all these years later, it was commonly known amongst the town that the topic was off limits.

Winslow approached the wall, stepping past Aurora and Blaze. "It's worse than I imagined," were his first words.

"Last night, the blast did a number. I'm surprised the town doesn't look worse," replied Don Engle.

Winslow was not happy to hear this. He shot him a stern glare. "It's a disaster, Don. No matter what. That's like saying a shipwreck only lost twenty lives. That's twenty too many."

Blaze turned to his father when he heard him clear his throat. He then looked to Winslow. It seemed the whole group was watching him, capturing the unease in the air.

"It looks like some sort of weapon has been fired at it from the other side, sir," said Anton. "Not sure what, but that's the impression I'm getting. It got rid of the force field— the barrier between us and the wall, too."

Winslow nodded slowly, patiently. He eyed the breach again. "And that's what the consensus is? A weapon"

"We think so. Ring any bells?"

Winslow's brows furrowed as he looked up, taking a slow and methodical breath. In exhale, Blaze could see how unsettled he was, standing there, swaying beneath the massive structure.

Jaw clenched, he said hushed, "Whatever struck the town caused this. There's no question." He lowered his focus to Anton. "Do you agree?"

"Yes, sir," replied Anton, "we're on the same page." Blaze could hear the worry in his father's voice. As much as he tried to mask it, the uncertainty of the situation could not be covered up.

Between a break in conversation, Blaze looked up. He could see Aurora was too. Afternoon sunlight beamed through the breach in the wall. Blaze had never seen the sun so low in the sky. Hidden behind the wall, River Ridge would already be cast fully in shadow.

Now, the beam of sunlight lit up the clearing and the tiny bugs flying around. The light shone onto the tree trunks and wildflowers, highlighting the footprints in the mud from the heavy foot traffic today.

Aurora stepped forward. "You were right, weren't you?" she asked.

The group turned to her. Blaze could see Anton exhale quickly.

Winslow, seemingly aware that it was meant for him, turned to her. "About what?"

"I believe you," said Aurora. "We didn't build this."

"Let's carry on," Don Engle interrupted, stepping towards Aurora. He placed his hands on her shoulders, continuing to walk forward.

"Don't push me!" she ordered, shoving him back. "Keep your hands off me. What did you see? Tell us, Mr. Winslow."

"That's all," Winslow replied. "I best be heading back. Maintain a tight patrol. No one comes in, no one leaves. Am I clear?"

"Please tell us!" Aurora begged. "Whatever built those walls, broke them down. I believe you!"

"That's enough or I'll talk to your parents!" hissed Engle, pushing her back, his hand twisting her forearm.

But Blaze was having none of this. Heat rushed through his blood and fueled him. "Look, man. Don't touch her."

"*Blaze...*" Anton breathed out in a hiss.

He didn't stop.

"Mr. Winslow, tell us!" Aurora said, trying to wiggle free from the man's grasp. "Why keep it a secret?"

"Enough!" Don Engle yelled, letting go and shoving her back.

Aurora stumbled, trying to find her balance again, but lost the battle. She fell to the dirt floor, skidding.

Blaze rushed in from of the elder, his chest pressed out, fists clenched and ready for a fight. "Big mistake," he said.

Anton sprung forward, grabbing his son. "Are you insane? Get back home, now! And take her with you."

Blaze reached down and extended a hand to Aurora.

"I'm fine," she said, refusing his hand. She pressed off the ground, wiped off her pant leg. She looked to Don Engle, who's face had gone stone white. "What a big man you are."

However, he didn't apologize, nor could he bring himself to look at Aurora.

Winslow stepped forward, lips pressed tightly together. "I'll be heading back."

"Nothing?" asked Aurora, wrapping some of her shirt around a scrape on her forearm. "You're offering us nothing?"

"I think now would be a very good time to stay very quiet," said Winslow while walking towards the golf cart.

"You can't hide from your past any more than we can hide from what attacked us last night," said Aurora.

Blaze was captured by her courage. Captured by her strength against the leader. He didn't know what to make of last night. Sure, the thoughts had run through his mind. Growing up, Blaze heard the rumors, the stories passed down through his grandparents about the legend of the Winslow boy. It was an experience shared amongst all children, a rite of passage of sorts.

Now seventy-eight, the Winslow Boy wouldn't budge an inch. He swore to silence decades ago and even the bravery of Aurora Elder wouldn't tear down his own personal walls.

But Blaze couldn't let her feel alone. Here, she was going all out for the greater good, and he wasn't even jumping in to save her.

As Winslow took a seat at the back of the golf cart, radio chatter sounded from the walkie-talkie on his belt. Muddled and static at first, Blaze could finally make sense of what was being said.

"...get up here when you can. They've found something—something unusual..." There was a break in the transmission; a moment of static. "...front yard, some sort of device...Nyman... Ruth found it sticking up....We've closed off access—"

Fumbling with the volume knob, Winslow was too late. The grouping had heard it.

"What'd they find?" asked Anton.

Winslow turned to him, firm-faced. "No idea."

Blaze cleared his throat. "Whatever it is, sir—whatever happened at these walls all those years ago—we can't run from it anymore. You know it, too. I can see it in your eyes."

Winslow took the walkie-talkie in his hands and ran his thumb against the holes of the speaker along the glossy black plastic. When he raised his gaze to the rest of the group, his eyes were glassy and his lower lip quivered on the verge of speech.

"We'll believe you," Aurora murmured. "You shouldn't have to hold it in anymore."

But Winslow shook his head. "It changes everything."

"It doesn't—"

"*Everything,*" breathed Winslow.

"So, what? We wait until it's too late?" Aurora countered. "We can work together, come up with a plan. We're a big town."

"Not big enough," Winslow trembled. "They're coming."

"Who? Give us something to work off of," Blaze said.

The others in the group focused on the town leader with unfiltered devotion. Everyone knew the events from seventy-three years prior were off limits. But they were as fascinated as Blaze was. As much as they feared confirmation of the legend, they were enthralled by the idea it proposed.

Blaze called out once more, an effort to try and pull even a thread of a hint out. "If they did it once, sir, they'll do it again. The force field, whatever you want to call it, is down. Now, it's just the wall between us and them, and even that's damaged."

"I know," Winslow said quietly, eying the battle-scarred wall up and down slowly.

Blaze's arms crossed his chest. "And when they come back, whoever they are, what do we do?"

"*What do we do?*" Winslow repeated softly, shaking his head with a trace of a smile.

Blaze nodded once, holding his eyes on the leader.

"We die, son," said Winslow. "We die."

FIVE

The entire way back to the heart of River Ridge, Blaze held onto Victor Winslow's words with adrenaline pumping through his veins.

Winslow left the breach point in his golf cart without further word. Those remaining in his wake were left speechless.

Blaze said goodbye to his father and then walked with Aurora all the way back, through the forest, towards home.

He'd heard the last name of 'Nyman' said over Winslow's radio, and there were only two Nyman's in all of River Ridge.

Gary and Ruth Nyman were childless, in their mid-sixties, and lived a few doors down from Blaze. He'd grown up spending summer afternoons with Ruth in her garden, and Gary in his small woodshed, where he'd build birdhouses and toolboxes for the community.

As Blaze grew older, so did the distance between visits. And eventually, visits became nothing more than a few kind words shared, a nod, and a wave.

Already, as they approached Blaze's street, he could see the large gathering around their home.

Ruth Nyman stood in her overalls, shaking her head in disbelief. Gary Nyman spoke with one of Aurora's mothers, Rachel, using a flood of hand gestures while explaining how this device was discovered.

"Winslow's already there," said Aurora, pointing to his golf cart pulled alongside the curb in front of their home.

"That's a shock," said Blaze.

Blaze quickened his pace as they approached, and beneath a massive oak tree, his mother stood on the curb, trying to get a peek.

"Mom!" Blaze called out.

Lorna heard him, turning to the direction his voice had come. Seeing him, she motioned for them to come to her.

Aurora and Blaze slipped through a grouping beside Lorna and stepped up, trying to see anything. It was of no use. There were too many people in the way.

"What is it?" Aurora asked.

"They're not sure. It was sticking out of the ground," said Lorna. "I saw it for a moment before they threw a tarp over it. It was long, cylindrical, and white."

"It landed there from last night?" Blaze asked.

Lorna shook her head. "Rose up. Ruth was helping next-door and when she came back to her yard, there it was sticking out of the ground."

"Any idea where it came from, though?"

"No. They don't know what it is or where it came from. Based on what I saw, I don't think it's—"

"From us?" asked Blaze.

She nodded once, clicking her tongue against the back of her teeth. "I don't think so, Blaze. How was the wall? Dad hasn't come back since he left at sunrise."

"There's a big hole," Blaze said simply, careful to keep his voice down. "Massive, actually. It looks like something melted it."

"Melted it?" challenged Lorna.

"Yeah," Blaze said. "There were holes beside the massive gash, too."

Lorna breathed deeply now, brushing the cleft of her lip with her index finger.

"It's all linked, Mrs. Davies," Aurora said. "We came from the wall, and Winslow was down there. I tried to get him to tell us what he saw."

"He doesn't talk about it these days," said Lorna. "Hasn't for years."

"I know," Blaze chipped in. "That's why she said she tried to get him to talk about it. It didn't work."

"Of course," Lorna dismissed. "Did he say *anything*?"

"Yeah," Aurora confirmed. "He did, actually. He talked about *them*, and if they come back to finish the job they started last night, we die."

"That's a bit of a revelation," Lorna said. "I'm surprised he'd even say that much."

"Mom, this isn't good," Blaze said.

Lorna reached over, placing her hand on his shoulder. "We'll be okay, Blaze. I won't let anything hurt you."

A small smile grew on Blaze's face, but his mother's words weren't enough. He looked up, through the canopy of the oak tree's leaves, unsure of how to respond.

He knew that whatever struck River Ridge last night was strong, powerful, and beyond the concepts humans understood.

A mother was supposed to protect their young, guide them, and keep them safe from harm. But Blaze knew deep down that even the strongest weapon of all—love—couldn't protect him or any of them from whatever breached their wall last night. There was so much they didn't understand about their world, and the mystery only grew from there.

There was a shift in the building crowd up ahead. Blaze watched as Winslow approached, crossing through the perimeter that had been quickly built with ropes and wooden stakes.

He spoke to Ruth Nyman, who nodded quickly in agreement with whatever he had said. Winslow placed his hand on her shoulder before proceeding further.

"Clear the way," said a male voice in the crowd.

A few others joined in.

"What is it?"

Another called out, "Show us!"

Winslow motioned for two of his patrol members to approach. They each held shovels.

Expecting for them to bury it again, Blaze watched carefully as Winslow directed them. One began to dig, the other pulled the tarp back.

And as the crowd began to move aside, Blaze caught a glimpse at what was beneath the blue tarp.

Like his mother described, it was thin and cylindrical, white and glossy. The device's surface had a sparkling sheen to it that gave it an extra flourish. But what caught his eye the quickest were the etchings and engravings into the surface. Patterns and designs matched those on the wall.

It was official. The two were linked.

Blaze started forward, pulled by the innate curiosity he had. Aurora followed him, quickly catching up as he slid through the groupings of citizens, pressing himself against the roped line.

The second man began to dig around the device, giving a foot of clearance beside it. Winslow stood a few feet away, his eyes intent and focused, hands clasped at his waist.

"What is it, Vic?" asked a female.

Winslow didn't budge, didn't turn. He kept his eyes on the device like he would a dangerous insect or a dog he didn't trust.

The younger of the two shovelers leaned over the device, hesitating before placing his palm on the surface of the top.

To Blaze, it looked like a smooth and rounded diamond with no sharp corners at the top or bottom. The top on the device was flat, parallel with the ground it had been buried in, and yet it was a blinding white, with not one trace of dirt on it.

Hand on the device, he began to wiggle it around. "Dig deeper," he said. "It's still in there pretty far."

The other man wiped a bead of sweat, pressing his boot against the lip of the shovel. "How far?"

"Let's go another two or three feet."

"Jesus," said the second.

Aurora turned to him. "What made it spring out of the ground? It's like it was on a timer or something?"

"What melted a massive gash in the wall?" Blaze asked her. "Nothing can be explained these days."

"But Winslow knows," she said.

But Blaze hesitated to agree with her on this entirely. "I wouldn't say he knows *everything*," Blaze countered. "He knows something, but based on his appearance right now, I'd say he's a bit perplexed by all of this, too."

"Could be acting," Aurora said.

"He's not acting. If he is, he should quit his day job and become an actor."

To Blaze's left, he felt a sudden nudge in the side. He turned to see Forrest and Hadley. Forrest stood beside him, raising his chin towards the excavation as opposed to pointing.

"What's this?" he asked, curious.

"They found a device," Aurora replied.

Forrest leaned in. "A bomb?"

"Probably not," Blaze said. "They've been playing around with it. If it was a bomb, I don't think we'd be here right now. They're trying to get it out of the ground. Sounds like it goes pretty deep?"

"Did something crash here last night?" Hadley asked.

"Nope. According to Mrs. Nyman, it rose up."

"Well, shit," Forrest said, almost sounding impressed.

Aurora turned to him. "We need to know what that device is. I think it'll have the answers to what happened last night."

"What do you think it is?"

"A weapon—"

"You said it wasn't a bomb!" Forrest said.

"A tool, a database," Aurora continued, listing off her thoughts, counting off with her fingers per idea.

"They're going to hide it," Hadley said. "You know they won't tell us."

"It would keep with the theme of today," Blaze said.

Forrest's brows twisted. "What?"

"I'll tell you later."

Aurora turned to the group. "Look, we should stick around and figure out what's next."

"What's next is we keep rebuilding our city," Forrest said. "Leave this to them."

As they continued looking forward, the two men withdrew their shovels from the deep pit. They each reached in, grabbed the shiny device, and lifted up. The device appeared light, and the men didn't struggle with it.

They set it down in the grass, stepping backwards slowly and carefully, admiring it from afar.

It was long as they expected, narrow and engraved from top to bottom. Winslow approached it, running his gaze across its surface.

"What does it do?" another voice asked needlessly.

Again, none of those closest to it replied.

"You can't hide it from us forever, Winslow," a male voice said.

Winslow turned to him, shaking his head a few times before returning to eye-up the surface. "This will be removed and disposed of," he said.

"Disposed of!" cried a different male. "How dare you? That's not yours to take."

"It will be taken and disposed of," Winslow repeated firmly. "Based on the events of last night, this is the safest option."

Blaze turned to Aurora, then Forrest and Hadley. "He's serious. He's going to get rid of it."

"We can't let him take it away. It's clearly from them," said Aurora. "He doesn't want us to know about them. His story never changed as a kid. He was telling the truth all along. And I think it's safe to say that the people who built the walls and dome around this town are the same ones who planted that—whatever it is—into the ground."

Blaze turned to Aurora. "Like you said, it's as if it were on a timer."

"And the clock hit zero," she said.

The two excavators lifted the device and placed it onto Winslow's golf cart. Draping the tarp over it, they lightly pressed the tarp around the edges to prevent scratching, and they wrapped a thick piece of rope around it to secure it to the cart.

"Guys, you follow the device," said Aurora. "Hadley and I will stay back and see if they find anything additional."

"Where are they taking it?" Blaze asked.

"Does it matter?" Aurora asked. "Follow them. Wherever they take it, get it and see what it is."

Forrest turned to him. "When they leave in that cart, we follow."

Adrenaline surged from the pit of his stomach. He liked a challenge, but this was one that would be for the ages— seventy-three years in the making.

* * *

Forrest and Blaze moved quickly along the concrete sidewalk, leaving the gathered crowd in their wake. The golf cart moved fast, but the boys were able to keep a good pace with the cart without losing too much distance between them.

"Where do you suppose they're taking it?" asked Forrest.

"No clue," Blaze said.

"Any inklings?"

Blaze shook his head. "No, but I wouldn't be surprised if they bury it again, wherever they take it."

"Why would he do that?"

"Whatever it is, he doesn't want any of us to see it up close or figure out what it is. When Aurora and I were with him at the wall, Aurora asked for him to tell his story of what happened when he was a kid."

"What messed him up?" Forrest added.

"Right. He said it would change everything."

"I mean, we all have heard what he saw. Why does he need to repeat it?" asked Forrest.

Blaze stopped at the intersection of the road, checked both ways and continued forward, quickening his pace. Winslow was leaving them in the dust now. "Because it's been passed down, lost in translation," he said. "We should hear it from his lips."

"But at this point, what difference does it make. If it happened, it happened. If it didn't happen, it didn't. Regardless, we still have the walls."

"Exactly. I believe something happened here a long time ago. I just don't know what."

Forrest nodded. "So that device might help us? Maybe we're supposed to place it on the wall."

"The hole in it is a bit bigger than that thing, Forrest. Come on, use your head." Blaze said.

"Not there. Somewhere else. Hear me out, call me an idiot—whatever. The shield that was between the inside of the wall and the forest failed last night. Maybe that thing they found recharges it?"

At first inclined to laugh, Blaze shrugged his shoulders. There was a chance he'd be right. It sounded stupid, but at the same time, maybe there was some truth to it. What were the odds that there would be a catastrophic failure in the wall and the next day, a device clearly linked to those who built it shows up.

The story was building itself.

"Maybe," Blaze admitted. "It's not outside the realm of possibilities. Stranger things have happened."

"Please," Forrest countered. "All of this is outside the realm of possibilities."

"I know," Blaze said. "But we've got to keep our heads screwed on straight. I'm not sure what happens next, but Winslow's scared. I could see it in his face. What happened is engraved in him, like the history of the walls are engraved in this town."

Their hearts pounded faster as they ran down the street. Winslow's cart pulled over directly in front of his residence. Immediately, those on it jumped off. Winslow spoke with the driver and passenger, pointing towards his home.

Blaze saw a nod of agreement between the three and Winslow walked up his driveway, unlocking his front door with a key and stepping in.

Forrest scratched his head. "They took it to his house?"

"I know. Doesn't make sense. Why would they not take it to an area separate from the town."

"Maybe it's not dangerous?" Forrest offered.

"How would they know?"

"They wouldn't. But if it were dangerous, they'd be dead by now. Maybe they're willing to take the risk."

"Or," Blaze countered, "he knows what it is."

Forrest nodded twice. "Yeah, I bet he does."

The boys stepped onto the curb, ducking behind a large tree that had grown out of the space built for it. Roots, thick and winding, broke through the concrete, and its branches stretched far out over the road and the debris-littered yards beside them.

The two men still at the golf cart, looked around and then proceeded to the back, releasing the rope from around the tarp.

Still keeping it covered, one lifted it up, like one would a child, and they moved quickly towards Winslow's residence, going through the same front door that the town leader had vanished behind only moments ago.

"Well, we know where it is," Forrest said. "Ready to head back?"

Blaze turned to him. "We have to get it. But not until he leaves."

"Break and enter?" Forrest questioned. "I want to know what that is as much as anybody, but you know we'll get caught."

"Now's the best opportunity to sneak into a place we shouldn't be. Power grid is down, security is focused on the wall on the other side of town. Winslow's distracted. Forrest, if we're going to find out, now is our window. Not now, now. But sooner than later."

"Like tonight?" Forrest asked.

"If the opportunity presents itself."

But Blaze stopped, noticing he was no longer paying attention. Forrest's gaze was directed just beside him.

"What?"

"By Winslow's window. Look."

Blaze did. Crouched by shrubbery below one of Winslow's first-floor window was Ahmed.

"He followed them, too. Or us."

Just as Blaze was going to ask if they should approach, Ahmed turned in their direction, keeping his eyes focused on the two boys.

Forrest raised his hand awkwardly in greeting. Ahmed kept his eyes intent.

"Come on," Blaze said.

"Don't make a scene, man. We'll get caught."

Blaze moved quickly onto Winslow's yard. Ahmed remained crouched, but adjusted his stance slightly, as if expecting Blaze to push him.

Steadied, Ahmed motioned with his hands for them to crouch. Blaze agreed this was best and did so.

"You followed us?" Forrest asked.

"*And you followed him,*" replied Ahmed in a whisper. "*Keep your voice down.*"

"Why?" asked Blaze.

"Why do you think? Why'd you follow him? You want to see the device as much as I do."

"Did you think we wouldn't share," Forrest murmured.

"First off, I didn't know you'd be coming. Second, I wouldn't put it past you to not tell me after what happened the other night."

"You ratting on us?" Blaze pressed stiffly.

"It would have been worse had they caught all of us—"

Forest held out his hands. "Worse for *you.*"

Rolling his eyes, Ahmed rose higher, peering into Winslow's home. When he lowered, he pinched his lips together, clenching his jaw. He drew in a breath, releasing an impatient sigh. "I would have done it again and again."

Blaze could feel the veins in his forehead begin to pulse as the length of his body tensed beside his former acquaintance. "At least we know where we stand," he replied in a low, fierce voice. He looked to Forrest, hoping for an additional voice to join in; however, he could see that while Forrest was upset over what had happened, he knew Forrest wouldn't say anything that would potentially harm the thin strings keeping them together.

Blaze knew he was alone now, and in defeat, decided to drop it for now.

"What have you seen?" Forrest asked, keeping the conversation moving forward. "Anything good?"

Ahmed turned to him. "No sign of the artifact. Look at his walls. I always told you he was a basket-case." He motioned for them to rise, lifting Blaze from beneath the armpits.

Blaze flung back his shoulders, shooting him a dirty look. "I don't need your help standing."

"Lose the attitude and look."

"At what?" Blaze snapped, feeling his pulse pounding in his throat.

"Cut the drama and look."

Blaze stood up, placing his hand on the wooded frame of the window. Beside him, Forrest also stood up, cupping his hands around his eyes to see in better.

It took a moment, but his sight began to focus, to adjust to the interior. He didn't see any movement, but inside, the table was covered with stacked books, messy and with no seeming order. Stuffed shelves lined the walls, but on the one wall without, was a massive collection of hand-drawn sketches. Done in graphite, the drawings were basic and of limited artistic ability, but Blaze could see they were done of the same person: a cloaked giant with a long stick of sorts.

To Blaze, it looked like a wizard without a beard. Blaze couldn't be sure if this was just due to the artistic abilities of the sketcher, but it seemed the man was slightly deformed. It was human in shape, but seemingly "off". The sketched cloak cast much of the figure in shadow, but what Blaze could see was unsettling.

There were hundreds of these, from floor to ceiling. Some appeared frantic and rushed, while others appeared to have taken a good amount of time to complete. Surrounding the cloaked figure sketches were several others of a different figure. It appeared to be naked, with internal organs visible as if the skin was made of glass and transparent.

"What the heck?" said Blaze, unable to filter himself.

Ahmed shook his head. "I told you he was a wacko."

"So, who're the people in the drawings?" asked Forrest.

"Probably the builders of the walls," Ahmed said.

"With a hammer and nails?" Forrest mocked.

Ahmed rolled his eyes. "Do you have a better idea? It's my best guess."

Blaze continued peering through the window, letting Ahmed and Forrest's talk between each other fade into mere background white noise. His eyes scanned the dark space, trying to capture anything additional. Near the drawings, Blaze observed a large cork-board with pictures and maps thumbtacked in. Narrow strands of crimson red string were pulled taut between the thumbtacks, drawing connections to people and places on the large board. Some of the faces Blaze didn't recognize, while others appeared to be mere sketches, like those of the cloaked man.

There were more sketches covering another wall. These appeared to be rushed, outlines with little shading or detail. Blaze could imagine Winslow sketching these in a hurried panic, trying to get everything on paper before he forgot. He imagined the leader to draw them in an altered state of being, unaware of what he was doing, and only guided by powers beyond what they could understand.

As he peered through the window, it was a crisp, whisper of a breeze that gently pulled him out of his thoughts. When Blaze turned, Forrest was crouched down beside Ahmed again.

"I doubt he's leaving today. Not after bringing that back," said Forrest.

Ahmed nodded. "He's probably in the basement, testing it and trying to figure out what it is."

Blaze looked down. "My money is on him knowing what it is. It'd explain why he snatched it away."

"I'm with Blaze, Ahmed. He knows what it is. I can just feel it."

"Then he won't give it up willingly," Ahmed said. "Look— we come back tonight, during dinner. If we find it, we grab it. If we don't get it tonight, we don't get it at all. Deal?"

"Option one is much more optimistic. Let's go with that one," said Forrest.

PETER GULGOWSKI

"I'm being realistic with myself. There's a good chance we walk away with nothing."

Blaze agreed with this. It was a huge risk attempting to sneak into Winslow's house. He couldn't imagine what the punishment would be if they got caught. If they were to do it, they had to have a plan, something in place, before stepping even an inch through the door. They'd have to have a strategy—a fast approach, and an even faster exit.

Thinking and planning while executing would only guarantee a failure. Sure, there was a chance it could succeed and luck would be on their side. But after last night, Blaze wouldn't put his faith in luck.

"So, is it a plan?" asked Ahmed.

Forrest nodded. "We meet here at dinner."

"Everyone think of a strategy before we get here," murmured Blaze. "This way, we can compare and decide from every one's ideas, pick the strongest—"

There was movement within.

Blaze dropped to his knees, instantly regretting it as a surge of pain sprouted from his kneecaps. His eyelids squeezed shut, his lips folded inward, pressing together, and his face contorted as he held in a cry of pain.

"That looked like it hurt," Forrest whispered, perking his eyebrows up and turning aside.

"We should go," said Ahmed. "There are too many lurking around here. Help him up when I signal to."

He stood up slowly, peeking just a sliver of his eyes over the window sill. Peering in, Ahmed held his breath.

"*Nothing,*" he said quietly. "Lift him now."

Forrest leaned down, reaching his arms beneath Blaze's armpits.

"I'm good, I'm good," said Blaze, slowly rising. His legs were stiff, kneecaps throbbing as he stepped onto the lawn. Blaze's first steps were slow, angled, and with a noticeable limp.

As Forrest and Ahmed joined him, it got better, the pain receded, and his walk became more normal.

"See you at dinner."

"Seven," agreed Forrest. "I'll make sure he gets home okay."

With a nod, Ahmed turned and fast-walked away, down the road, and turning towards his home. Now, Forrest stood beside Blaze.

"You sure you're okay?" he asked quietly.

"I'm good. I feel like I'm a hundred, though," laughed Blaze as they walked down the sidewalk.

"Think of it like this: you and Winslow can get along now."

Blaze shook his head, dismissing the joke. "Sure," he replied. "You excited?"

"About what?"

"The device?" said Blaze.

Forrest shrugged, taking a quick glance behind them. "I'm curious. Wouldn't go as far as saying excited. You?"

"Somewhere between excited and terrified."

"Yeah," Forrest agreed. "Between us, I'm a little scared, too."

SIX

At dinner, with the whole community gathered, the three boys snuck away. Both Aurora and Hadley knew something was up, but they didn't say. Blaze wondered if Forrest had told Hadley, who would only naturally tell Aurora.

But it seemed they weren't sure what was going on; only that something was *going* to happen.

Forrest and Blaze walked beneath looming nightfall with a quickness in their step. Fueled by the adrenaline and the nerves they refused to address, they moved down the old sidewalk in record time. By now, the streets were growing dark, long masked in shadow. But with the sky losing its natural, sunlit glow, there was little to keep them from feeling like they were walking to Winslow's blind.

Blaze had spent a good portion of an hour thinking of a strategy for retrieving Winslow's device. He knew it would likely be kept out of view, probably hidden, with some sort of security parameter in place. Now, without power, the extent of that security was limited. However, man-power did not run off of electricity. Blaze felt there was a solid chance that the device would be guarded by an armed guard—one of his patrolmen turned henchmen.

If there was a guard inside, it was all bets off. The search would be over, and there'd be no chance of retrieving the device. But taking it one step further, one step worse, if caught, Blaze knew that he and Forrest would be in trouble far worse than they could imagine.

They'd need to proceed carefully. Proceed slowly. Being mindful of their surroundings wouldn't be enough. They'd need to develop the powers of a psychic or the powers of X-ray vision. But, with a little luck, maybe they'd succeed.

Luck would carry them tonight. Blaze just wasn't so sure of how much faith he could really place in it. But tonight, it was all they had going for them.

As they entered Winslow's street, Forrest stopped, steadying himself on an old maple tree.

"See anything?" asked Blaze, stepping up beside him.

He shook his head. "Nothing, but wanted to be sure. Better to take in everything when you're not moving."

"Any sign of Ahmed?" continued Blaze.

Again, he shook his head. "No, but that's a good thing. He's hiding."

"Or," Blaze proposed, "he's not here yet."

Forrest checked his watch, holding it out for Blaze. "It's after seven. We're the ones that are late."

"Hadley's fault," Blaze said, starting forward again. "She wouldn't stop questioning you."

"I know. She needs to learn to mind her own business."

"It's because she cares," Blaze said, stepping over a large gap of missing concrete along the walkway.

Forrest shot Blaze a curious glance. "I don't think so, buddy. I think it's because she's nosy and wants in."

"Did you tell her?"

"Am I a fool?" Forrest stammered out. "Wait...don't answer that one. I may not like your answer."

"Probably wouldn't," Blaze replied with a soft laugh.

"Wow. Rude."

The boys stopped two doors down from Winslow's, peering around the street. Beneath the dark sky, it was hard to make out much of anything. Forrest took a few more steps forward, twisting his neck in all directions as he peered down the road.

"We should probably move into the grass. We're sitting ducks here on the sidewalk," he said.

Blaze agreed, stepping onto the neighbor's lawn without word. Motioning to the street, however, he pointed directly in front of Winslow's home. "Look," he said, "no golf cart."

"No golf cart, no Winslow. Besides, I saw him at dinner. But, I like a good sign when I see one any way. Good to have the confirmation."

"Increases the chance that there isn't anyone else here, right?"

Forrest laughed softly. "Wouldn't go that far. Time will tell."

They pressed through the lawns, stepping over debris littering the yards. Blaze was honestly surprised that

Winslow had allowed his own neighbors to not clean their yards. Most throughout River Ridge were somewhat tidy, given the circumstances. What debris could be saved had been moved back into the standing homes it came from, what couldn't be identified or properly returned had been brought back to a community lost-and-found at the school, and what had been destroyed was placed in piles at the edge of the driveway. There was a system put quickly into place. Blaze couldn't believe it hadn't reached Winslow's own street.

Against the inky sky, layered low with thick, unforgiving clouds, Winslow's home seemed darker than normal. Already painted gray, there was a haunted house aspect to it that Blaze knew was only his imagination's creation, but if the shoe fit, it fit. Forrest was first on Winslow's property, going to the window the three had been at earlier.

Blaze wasn't surprised to see that beneath the window sill was open space. No sign of Ahmed. He moved towards the backyard, careful and slowly, peered around the wall of thick pine trees.

No movement. No sound. No Ahmed.

He twisted around to Forrest.

Forrest knew straightaway that something was off. He lowered his gaze to the thick grass around their ankles, scratching the faint stubble on his chin. "I don't like how this is going?"

"Me neither," Blaze agreed, approaching Forrest, kneeling down below the windowsill. "And I don't think he forgot."

He shook his head. "And he didn't go in either, at least I can't tell that he did. So, what do we do?"

The options ran through Blaze's mind like a flip-book. He saw their next steps and the possible ramifications like a fast-moving blur. Staying and waiting was repeated quite a bit. It was logical, it was the option leaving the most trust with Ahmed. It was also the most dangerous. Staying on-scene meant that much longer they were around to get caught. Blaze let the choices continue again, peering around as he did. He slowed his thoughts, stopping on the easiest and most logical.

"Let's get out of here."

"You sure? This might be it. Might be our only chance."

Blaze took in a breath, held it, and exhaled. "Yeah. I don't exactly trust him after the wall fiasco."

Forrest stood up, brushed his legs from the old mulch stuck onto his pant leg. "Me neither. You saw it all along. I'm only now realizing it after what he pulled with Winslow's guards."

Blaze started off towards the sidewalk. "He's not a bad person. I just wonder what his ulterior motives are."

"I think he looks out for himself. Well, okay, I know he does. Look—I don't want to bash him. The evidence is just ramping up..."

Blaze could tell that pressing the topic further would not be of any use. He didn't like bashing people either, especially when they couldn't respond. As much as he wanted to see the good in people, there was a cynical side to him that had only recently developed within the recent years.

"You good?" asked Forrest.

"Just thinking."

"Shocking," he laughed.

But Blaze didn't pay it any attention. "Do you think we're going to be in trouble?" he asked.

"What do you mean?"

"I mean—do you think he ran and told them? Wouldn't be the first time."

"If he did, it's stupid because we need to get caught in order to back up his story. If we don't get caught, he looks like an idiot."

"And they all laugh in his face?"

Forrest tilted his head, "Or they hang him by his thumbs. That's how this city works, you know."

In the distance, a fast-moving shape startled Blaze. "Quick, tree," he directed with his hand.

Forrest, unsure, followed, quickly moving behind the large maple tree a few houses from Winslow.

"You could use your words, you know," he whispered.

"I saw movement."

But another voice called out in a loud whisper, "Guys!"

Blaze knew the voice, as did Forrest.

Ahmed.

Stepping out from the safety of the tree, Blaze swallowed a thick lump. "Ahmed," he greeted.

"A little cold, but I get it. Look, I didn't lose track of the time. I stayed back at the dinner to see what Winslow was doing."

"Lemme guess, he was eating. It was dinnertime for the community," Forrest said.

"With the artifact by him, smart ass. I knew he'd treat it like an infant," he said. "So, checking his house is a no-go, but we could use the time wisely."

"What do you mean?" asked Blaze.

"I mean we go to the wall. We're already out anyways. What's another mile or so."

"A mile or so," Forrest repeated unenthused. "We had a long day working."

"We can take bikes if it helps," proposed Ahmed. "We'll just need to stop at our houses. We go on foot, we go now."

"Because taking our bikes worked so well last time," Blaze replied stiffly.

"How many times will I have to apologize for that? I'm sorry. There, I said it again."

Forrest turned to Blaze. At first, Blaze figured that Forrest would ask him to bury the hatchet and move on, but instead Forrest asked simply, "Want to go?"

Blaze looked to the wall. Against the dark sky, the wall seemed a deeper, darker black. The gash—the massive chunk melted away—was lighter as the only thing behind it now was the expanse of cloudy sky. Ahmed had a point. They were already out. So, they get caught at the wall and not in Winslow's house. They'd still be in trouble, but Blaze figured that even in River Ridge, as medieval as their rule was, they would not see teens exploring their town as an equal offense to breaking and entering.

With that, Blaze nodded. "Sure," he said. "Let's go. No bikes."

Ahmed pressed his lips together into a faint smile. "Cool. Let's roll."

The boys ran beneath the veil of clouds, using shadow as their cover. Ahmed led the way and the boys followed with Blaze in the rear. Despite knowing dinner would continue for another hour or two, Blaze was still concerned. If they were skipping out, there was no reason somebody else couldn't be skipping out, too.

Ahmed guided them down a series of darkened, damaged roads. They ran past structures on the verge of collapse, ruins that looked ancient yet weren't. They ran past the junkyard where vehicles from the old world, ones that had been long-dead were placed to sit and decay beneath the elements.

Prior to being the junkyard before the walls and dome, it had been an old miniature, 9-hole golf course that used to be in the town. A few of the golf carts from it had been saved and were still in-use. Solar powered batteries were charged daily, replacing the need for alternative forms of power. The electricity from the windmills was a solid back-up, but they didn't like to rely on it, especially for something that wasn't a necessary need. The golf carts could hardly hold a charge after all these years, but it was better than nothing. The golf carts, however, were saved for the elite and elderly.

As they passed the junkyard, the next few hundred feet were clear and open before entering the forest. Blaze had never approached from this angle, and as far as he knew, he had never been to this wall before today. This one was the furthest from his home. A cul-de-sac ran right into it. Tall grasses broken free from the concrete sprouted tall and up. Ruins of a home were covered in greenery, while a tree grew out of what Blaze assumed was someone's old living room.

As they moved down the broken road, Blaze looked at all the abandoned houses that were in ruins. He imagined they left almost immediately after the walls rose. The people who lived there probably took what they could fit and fled into town to stay with friends. He didn't blame them for not wanting to be so close. The other three walls also featured a line of long-abandoned houses closest to them.

The trees grew thick almost immediately, and Blaze found his eyes were taking their time in adjusting to the dark.

"Don't get twisted around. It'll be hard to see the wall tonight," Ahmed said, slipping through two bushes.

Forrest followed, then Blaze.

"No blue light glowing through the leaves," Blaze said.

"Right."

"I thought you said to keep going straight," said Forrest.

"No, I was agreeing with Blaze."

"Ah, gotcha."

The coverage of leaves from above was pressing, like a blanket from Mother Nature, only she wanted to smother the three boys with it. Adrenaline trickled in, pulling from all the sources of fear: the wall, the dark, the forest, and the unknown. Blaze could feel his heart beating stronger now;

beating faster. It pounded to the beat of the forest, as he took in the great power around him.

"Almost there," Ahmed said from a distance. "I can feel it."

They moved quicker now, slipping through small breaks of the forest and climbing over fallen logs. They moved around a small build-up of rain water—a tiny pond of sorts— before breaking free at the other side.

There, tall and ominous, the wall stood almost scraping alongside the base of the clouds. A few dozen yards away, Blaze could see the reflective mass of what had melted away reflecting the glimmer of nightfall.

They moved down the clearing, doing their best to try and avoid stepping onto the bones of the dead animals that had passed through no-man's-land. For Blaze it felt strange. It felt foreign stepping where they couldn't only a day ago.

It was unsettling for him, knowing that he could lightly pass his hand over the wall and feel the carved engravings with his own hands. He often imagined what it would be like to touch the strange designs, what it would feel like. Now, with it right there in front of him, fear kept his hand trapped against his side.

"So, I should've asked this a while back. What are we planning on doing?" Forrest asked Ahmed.

Ahmed, keeping his pace up, turned slightly. "Looking to see what's behind it?" he answered, as if it were a stupid question.

"And how do you suppose we do that? The wall is over a hundred feet tall," Forrest said.

Still trailing the other two, Blaze shook his head. "He's going to climb the big mass and look through the big gash in it."

Forrest sighed. "We don't have a ladder."

"We don't, they do," he said. Relax, Forrest. I'll show you guys how it's done."

As they grew nearer, they slowed. Ahmed held out his hands, stepping further towards it and motioning for Blaze and Forrest to hold behind. They did, peering around for any signs of trouble.

Next to the mass, two guards were seated around a small fire. Eating sandwiches, Blaze could see they weren't overly focused on the wall; however, with them being right beside the gash, he knew they'd be a problem and one they needed to get rid of.

"Crap. So much for this," Ahmed murmured beneath his breath.

Forrest turned to Blaze, then walked up beside Ahmed. "I don't want to look. You guys can report it back to me, but I can go distract them?"

"How? You'll get in trouble," said Blaze.

Forrest clicked his tongue against his teeth twice, tilting his head in a smug glance. "Not so fast. I won't get in trouble if I don't get caught."

"What are you going to do?"

"Eh, I've got time to figure it out. I'll head across the way, get in place. I hope it'll distract them. You guys move into place. I can't give you a head's up or anything, so you'll just have to be ready."

"Works for me," Ahmed replied quickly.

"Wait, hold on. This sounds stupid. This isn't like a comic book. What, do you really think they'll get up and leave their position? Why wouldn't they call in backup to go investigate," questioned Blaze.

"Because there is no backup to call. They're all back at the dinner. These two just pulled the short stick," Forrest said. "Trust me. I've got this."

"I do. I just don't think this is the best approach."

"Well, what ideas do you have?" Forrest asked Blaze.

Blaze remained tight-lipped, darting his eyes left to right repeatedly hoping something would come into his mind. But before he could press on, Forrest crossed his arms against his chest.

"Exactly," he said. "Be ready to go."

Blaze watched as Forrest moved into the woods and slipped into the dark. He heard a few distant crackles of breaking twigs and crunching leaves, but he wasn't positive the sounds could be attributed to him.

Ahmed pointed down the clearing. "See the ladder?" he asked.

Blaze squinted. Illuminated by the flickering fire was a tall, steel ladder. He wasn't sure if it would be tall enough, but it seemed like it was all they were working with.

"I do," he replied.

"You help me set that against the wall. I climb, you hold."

"Great, so I do all the hard stuff and you get all the reward."

"I'll hold it for you afterwards," said Ahmed coldly. "Just be a good sport and do as you're told."

Blaze rolled his eyes. "Not sure if you talk to Forrest like that, but you won't order me around."

"I'm trying to create a plan here. Stop acting like a victim. It's not cool."

"No, you're treating me like a child."

Ahmed turned to Blaze. "Forgive me for being a leader and not a follower. It's about time you start making some decisions for yourself."

"You don't even know me. You've known Forrest for, what, a couple years? I've known him since we were babies."

"Look, I'm not interested in playing along with your childish game of who's known who the longest. Just shut up and help me and I'll—"

There was a high-pitched cry in the distance. Booming, screeching, and death-like. The two guards, distant enough from Ahmed and Blaze, stood quickly whipping their guns around, aiming into the forest.

Then another sounded.

"Show yourself!" called out one.

His response came from nature itself: chirping crickets, the soft lull of blowing wind, and the whispers of falling leaves.

The two guards moved forward, still aiming their guns.

"Come on," Ahmed muttered between his teeth.

Blaze held his breath as he watched them step forward, turn to each other, and then together, they pressed into the forest, vanishing from view. Ahmed was already darting forward by the time Blaze turned to look at him.

Footsteps pounded beneath his weight as they reached the gash. Blaze didn't even take a moment to look upward, knowing time was not on their side.

Another scream from Forrest called out, deeper and further into the woods.

Blaze grabbed the tall ladder with Ahmed, and they lifted it up. Against the wind, it swayed for a moment as they lowered it against the surface of the wall.

He couldn't help but feel the soft reverberation through the ladder and into his hands. The wall seemed hollow, casting a deep rumble through the surface and back into his wrist. Blaze also realized this was the closest in his seventeen years that he'd been to touching the wall.

Nerves and excitement ran through him as Ahmed started climbing into the dark unknown. Blaze cast his gaze upward, seeing that the ladder nearly reached the base of the gash. He'd have to stand on his feet, possibly hoist himself up, but it would be high enough.

Ahmed would see first what was behind the wall.

Blaze could taste blood in his mouth, and it was then he realized he was biting his lower lip. Ahmed was halfway up, halfway to seeing what was outside of River Ridge.

Adrenaline was bubbling up in his belly, breaths came quicker. He murmured to himself, "C'mon, climb faster. Climb..."

And Ahmed reached the gash in the wall. He paused, gazing his eyes across the surface. He slowly placed his hand against the surface, gently and quickly withdrawing it as if it were hot. Ahmed placed it against the surface again, and kept his hand there. He turned, smiling to Blaze.

"Go, look!" Blaze pressured, his voice raised in excitement.

Ahmed's shoulders rose and fell as he hoisted himself up. The wall must not have been hollow. Slowly, he leaned his head over, peering just beyond the surface.

And then he screamed.

Ahmed's voice came from deep within, as he cried out in terror. Blaze jumped back, flattening himself into the woods. "What!" he gasped.

"There are people! Hundreds!" he choked out. "Vehicles lined up. Skeletons, everywhere."

But Blaze couldn't press for further information. Ahmed was already mentally gone. His hands were raised, his body trembling atop the tall ladder.

"They were trying to get in. I know it!" he called out.

Blaze wanted to shush him, but it would be of no use.

"They're scattered all around—skulls—everything. They're all dead. Everyone's dead!"

But there was more sound, moving closer. Heavy boots against mud, crunching leaves, and snapping twigs.

Blaze slid back into the woods, watching as Ahmed continued looking out.

"Get down from there!" screamed a guard.

Once masked in the foliage, a sudden weight pressed down on Blaze's shoulders, and he gasped.

"It's me, it's me. What's wrong?" Forrest asked.

"I don't know. Ahmed saw what's out there—bodies, cars. People were trying to get in."

Ahmed was continuing to cry out as one of the guards began scaling the ladder, climbing the rungs with impressive force. When he reached Ahmed, he didn't wrap an arm around him to help him down. Instead, he used a set of handcuffs and cuffed Ahmed behind his back.

"Shit, shit, shit!" Forrest exclaimed.

Blaze stepped into the woods, pulling Forrest by his bicep. "We have to move."

"We can't leave him here. We have to help him," said Forrest.

Blaze realized Ahmed was right. He needed to be a leader, and now it was his time to prove it. He shook his head. "We don't know what they'll do. So far, they only know he's out tonight. We have to save ourselves."

Forrest grunted. "Save ourselves? We have to help him!"

"I know how it sounds, but if we get caught, it's all over. Come on."

Forest exhaled a shaky breath, but he nodded once.

As they left, Ahmed was continuing to cry, calling out slivers of sentences. But the impact had been made. They knew there were others, others who had tried to get in. Blaze didn't know how long ago it was, but there were others. People were trying to escape to River Ridge.

And ironically, it was Blaze that wished for nothing more than to escape the town.

They moved through the forest seemingly guided by instinct and instinct alone. Their footsteps were quick and spry against the forest floor. Blaze took the lead, moving through the thick brush with animal-like precision.

"We can talk about it later," Blaze said. "For now, let's just try to get out of here."

But Forrest didn't reply. Blaze turned to ensure he was still behind him. He was, but his expression was cast downward.

"We shouldn't have left him," he said finally. "They're going to punish him."

"It was his idea," said Blaze, not holding back. "Look—I know it may have been wrong, but we didn't ask him to go. He wanted to, he saw, and he made a scene."

"*A scene?*" Forrest repeated. "Geez, how would you react if you saw hundreds of dead bodies outside? Don't judge him for that. It's not fair. He wasn't expecting it."

Blaze nodded in agreement. A piece of him did feel bad for his ruthlessness, but he knew it stemmed from earlier.

"I just wouldn't have *screamed* knowing there were guards within an earshot," he said. "That's all."

"Easy to say when you weren't on that ladder. Let's just drop it and get home."

"Sure," murmured Blaze.

And that's all that would remain said throughout the rest of the woods. When they reached the streets of River Ridge, Blaze turned to his friend.

"I'm sorry."

Forrest twisted around, his lips flat and pressed together. "I don't want to talk about it."

"No, I was harsh. It came out wrong," Blaze said.

"Stop apologizing. You were right, even if it wasn't phrased well. Look, let's get home. Hopefully they'll just give him a warning."

Blaze nodded once. "You're good to get home?"

"I know where I live," Forrest said, brushing his wavy hair behind his ear. "See you tomorrow."

"Yeah, for sure," said Blaze, feeling a rush of nerves. "Forrest—if he talks, what's our plan?"

"We say nothing. We were each at home."

"And the wall?" Blaze asked.

Forrest raised a brow. "What wall?"

Nearly replying, Blaze caught the meaning in the words. "See you later."

And they each set off for their respective homes, down the shadowy roads. The distant rumble of thunder made itself known in the distance. Blaze could feel it in the ground beneath his feet. A storm was coming.

As he thought to himself, moving down the street, his mind led him to the dark side. Sure, a weather storm was coming, but he could feel another storm approaching at breakneck speeds. It wouldn't be long now. Someone had seen beyond the wall, the death that lay beyond. Winslow could no longer control the narrative. And if Blaze knew anything about Mr. Winslow, it was that he would always keep control.

Blaze quickened his step, rushing through the town. There were others out now, some in their yards talking. They noticed Blaze, but in a way, they looked through him. They wouldn't remember him if questioned. He was just one of the town boys that there were dozens of. But, knowing there were others outside, he knew that his parents would be home.

He had to find an explanation and stat.

The clouds had rolled in lower and darker by the time he reached home. Blaze practically swung the door of its hinges when he ran in, off the front porch.

It was his mother who met him in the dark hallway.

"Where the hell have you been?"

"No time, Mom. Did you tell anyone I wasn't at dinner?"

"A few asked. I said you probably weren't feeling well. Why?"

"Mom—Ahmed climbed the wall. He looked over the side of the gash."

Anton Davies' booming footsteps thudded against the wooden floor. "He did what? You didn't, did you?"

Blaze shook his head. "He got caught. Forrest and I escaped before they saw us. We left him, and they were handcuffing him."

Lorna raised her hand to her mouth. Anton pressed his hands deeper into his hips, then ran his hand through his salt-and-pepper hair.

"You foolish boys," he said. "What did he see?"

"Bodies. Skeletons," Blaze said. "He wasn't making sense. He was out of it, screaming. But I believe him. He said there were cars."

"How many?" asked Lorna.

Blaze shrugged his shoulders. "Hundreds, I think. Like I said, he wasn't making full sense. But I'm worried he'll talk and tell them about Forrest and I."

"Go upstairs. Get into bed," Anton said.

"But what if they come?"

"They might," he continued, "and we'll handle it. Go upstairs. Quickly."

Blaze took a look at his mom and dad, steadying his breath. "Mom...Dad...I'm scared."

"Just go, Blaze," said Lorna, shaking her head.

And he did.

He climbed the stairs quickly, hurrying into his bedroom. He closed the door, pulled off his pants, tossing them where he normally would, and slid into bed. The window was open and the cool air of autumn was especially crisp tonight. He pulled the comforter around his body and shut his eyes.

Against the pillow, he could hear his beating heart, like a loud drum in his ears. He kept his eyes closed, focusing on an imaginary scene he projected onto the backs of his eyelids, but no matter what, no matter how hard he tried to focus on his pleasant image, gasps of what Ahmed saw, or at least Blaze's interpretation of it, slipped through. He saw the long, blowing grasses, the rusted vehicles. And between gusts of the breeze, he saw the skeletons—women, men, children— all clamoring for the wall, as if there were a door leading in. He saw the huddled masses, spread slowly apart by Father Time. Blaze could see the decaying suitcases, personal belongings that the dead tried to save getting into River Ridge.

And just as he thought it couldn't get any worse, he saw the cloaked figure from Winslow's drawings, standing there, watching the whole time.

He squeezed his eyes shut, feeling the tension in his lids as he tried to force the sights away. He knew he should have never agreed to it. Blaze knew it had been stupid. But curiosity got to him. Curiosity was great for scientists, but not for seventeen-year-old boys who had a history of getting themselves into trouble.

Now, this was big. This was huge.

He wasn't sure if Ahmed had been the only person to see beyond the wall, but this was the only reasonable height in its history that someone could have climbed.

Rolling up the road, he heard a soft murmur of wheels against road. It stopped in front of his house, and he heard some chatter.

He squeezed his eyes shut, knowing it was them. They had come for him. It was all over now.

Would his parents protect him? Could they protect him?

He recognized the tone in their voice. But it was his father's, out on the street, that startled him. He couldn't make out what was being said, but it seemed lighthearted— a reunion of old friends. Then, he heard his name.

"Blaze?" his father repeated, distant and echoing. There was a pause. "Er—not since Mr. Winslow came by the other night. Why?"

The conversation started up, but he couldn't make out what was being said.

He steadied his breath, remembering it was his father who directed him to come up to his room. He knew they would come, and he wanted Blaze to pretend he was asleep. It was the oldest trick in the book, but it would work. It had to work.

The thump of the screen door told Blaze they were in the house. The several footsteps on the wooden stairs told him they were approaching fast.

"Make this quick. He's asleep. Wasn't feeling well," said his mother's voice from the other side of the door.

And then the door opened, and time froze still. Blaze slowed his breath, terrified they'd be able to hear his beating heart. Through a blurred gap, he slightly opened one eye to see three figures in black step into his room, only a few feet from him.

"See," Anton said. "Out like a light. He had a bit of a stomach bug earlier. Skipped out on dinner."

"I see," said one of the new voices. "The kid told us that both him and the Kremer boy were with him."

"Probably wanted to get out of trouble," Anton suggested. "A distraction? I mean, here you are, when you should be with the boy who was out there."

"A legitimate point, Anton, but we have to investigate it. It was a serious violation of rules. Winslow is furious."

The figures, including Blaze's parents, stepped out into the hallway, but Lorna kept the door slightly open.

"And the boy?" his mother asked. "How is he?"

"Distraught. It was a terrible sight, I can imagine, but he shouldn't have been up there to begin with. He's being held at Winslow's while we figure out what's next."

"What is next?" asked Anton.

"If you were anyone else, Anton, we wouldn't be telling you this. But if we let him go, he starts a panic," said the second guard.

"Right," Lorna agreed. "Maybe you can work out a deal where he agrees to remain quiet. A *gag-order*, I think they call them?"

There was a silence before the guard replied, "Mr. Winslow doesn't negotiate. You know that, Lorna."

"So, what happens to him, then?" she asked.

"Firstly, he lied. He falsely accused your son and brought him into this mess. Secondly, he's going to start a panic with his rule breakage. He starts a panic and all Hell breaks loose. You know, as well as anybody, that Winslow will not allow that to happen."

"So, what does this mean? For Ahmed?" Anton asked.

The first guard chuckled to himself. "I think Mr. Winslow will be making an example of him. Thanks for your time."

SEVEN

By the time he awoke several hours later, the storm had already passed. The rain had fallen, the thunder had boomed, and now, the town was quiet.

At home, Blaze's mother and father never came back into his room, even after Winslow's men had left. He'd been trapped in his room with a flurry of frenzied thoughts, fears, and regrets tearing through his brain. He stayed in bed until a little after two in the morning, where he desperately needed to use the bathroom.

Even then, it took a great deal of bravery to crawl out of bed, feeling that the guards would be waiting downstairs at the foot of the staircase for him.

"See! We knew you were out of bed tonight!" they would hiss at him in the dark.

But, instead, when he opened the door, peering down at the landing, there was no one there. The house was silent apart from his father's deep snores in the next bedroom over.

The cool air flowing from his bedroom window skimmed across the floorboards, over his feet, and down the stairs.

He steadied himself before moving into the restroom. When he was finished, he washed his hands and pressed some cool water into his face. He remained standing over the sink, looking into his reflection until he saw straight through himself. After a few minutes, he returned to his bedroom and slipped into the linen sheets, raising the back of his hand to his forehead.

He smelled the mint essential oil his mother had put into the soap and couldn't help but think back to the forest. The scent of the herb planted him right back into the shadows, watching Ahmed climb the ladder.

Thoughts slipped through his head until he turned on his side, slipping his hands atop his damp pillow case. He sat up, flipped it over, and relished against the coolness the other side brought him.

For the longest time, he tried to return to his mental happy-place, at the edge of a winding river just along the base of a great mountain. He'd seen the image in one of the old textbooks at school, and he found it beautiful and relaxing. Some days he would open the textbook, only to go to that one page.

Page 279.

For whatever reason, that one photo called out to him. Over the years, he made it his own, swapping out a few pine trees and angling some jagged boulders a little further out of the water. But it was his happy place. However, tonight, even the mountain range of page 279 couldn't save him from the demons he faced in his own head.

Eventually, he fell back asleep. But pleasant dreams did not wait for him. Instead, he fell headlong into a sea of nightmares he couldn't think away.

* * *

At daybreak, Blaze rose to crimson sky and dewy, moss-scented air. He laid in bed, half-asleep, listening to the sounds of a waking town. Like yesterday, there was already a clamor of hammers and thumping of debris being moved. Blaze had awoken much earlier than normal, and he felt that what happened last night was a dream.

It felt so real. Ahmed was climbing and looked over. The scream he let out was so real, so raw. It was of terror. The sound was stamped into his eardrum.

But as much as Blaze wanted for it to have been a terrible dream, he knew it wasn't. What had happened last night was real. Ahmed had looked over the breach in the wall and seen what was beyond it.

What Blaze was able to understand was nothing but sheer panic and terror.

There were bodies. Hundreds of them.

Blaze had no idea what to expect. Growing up, whenever he would ask what was beyond the walls, his parents would tell him that there was nothing. That's what they had grown up with and given the circumstances, it was the most logical explanation.

Some days, he wondered why they were chosen to be saved and why the walls were there in the first place. Though he knew no different, Blaze could tell that walls around a town were not normal. This was not how the rest of the world lives or had lived.

And as of last night, he knew there was truth to that. There were others out there in the world, at one point or another. And those people, those desperate people, had tried to get into the enclosed city. He wondered what they were running from, though inside he believed he knew the answer. They were running from whatever had launched the weapon at the wall.

Winslow was afraid, and now Blaze was too. He could feel it in the air, the sense of unease weaving throughout the town, between homes and past troubled citizens. Though the others he'd seen were trying to play it cool; act as though all was normal, he knew this was a front. They could pretend all they wanted, but good actors they were not.

Blaze breathed in, shutting his eyes for a moment as he pulled back the comforter on his bed. He swung his legs over the side, propping himself up. His legs were sore, and a dull ache ran the length of his calves—the only solid proof that he'd been down by the forest last night. Pulling on his pants, he buttoned them and pulled on his pair of socks before leaving his bedroom.

There was a quiet humming, that of his father's, downstairs. Blaze looked to his parents' bedroom door and saw it shut. His mother was still asleep. For a second, Blaze debated internally whether or not to return to bed. He was afraid of the wrath he knew he'd get. The other side of him told him that he'd have to hear it eventually, and that he couldn't stay in his room forever.

So, Blaze mustered up some last-minute courage and walked downstairs, entering the kitchen where his father was washing a pan in the sink. He looked up as Blaze entered, raising his head in a nod of greeting.

"Morning," said Blaze.

"Sleep well?"

Blaze took a seat at the table, placing his hands on the surface. He rubbed his fingers absentmindedly on some scratches in the surface. "On and off," he said, eyes lowered. "You?"

"Not well."

"I'm going to address the elephant in the room, okay?"

Anton looked up, pulled the pan out of the sink, and grabbed a towel from the countertop, drying off the pan.

"Go for it."

"Are you mad?"

"*Am I mad?*" Anton repeated stiffly. "What do *you* think?"

"I think yes."

Anton placed the pan down, flipping the towel back onto his left shoulder. "Mad is a fairly basic word, Blaze. How about irritated, furious, steaming?"

"Okay, I got it," Blaze said, pulling his hands back, crossing them beneath his armpits. "I'm sorry."

Anton moved to the table, placing both hands on its surface. He arched his back upwards, slightly hunched over the tabletop. "Don't apologize to me. Apologize to yourself.

You put yourself in such danger, Blaze. You know how this goes. You know what's next. I know you weren't asleep last night. You heard them, they're going to make an example out of your friend."

"Yeah, I heard."

Anton shook his head, exhaling. "I've told you to stay away. Why can't you listen."

"Because I need to know."

"There's nothing to know."

"There's *everything* to know," Blaze insisted. "You have to hear what you're saying. You can't agree with them, Dad. You have to want to know, too. It's human."

"What I don't know won't hurt me," said Anton.

"Oh, come on, Dad! Listen to yourself. You sound so weak. Really? Anton Davies is saying that. What happened to the Dad I knew, the man who wasn't afraid of anything?"

His father remained quiet, face blank. He returned behind the counter, drying more dishes he had laying out on another towel.

"You have to want to know, Dad," Blaze continued.

Anton raised his gaze. "Look, I don't fault him for looking. If I had the option, maybe, given the right circumstances, I would have looked, too."

"But saying what you don't know won't hurt you? The man I know wouldn't say that. The man I know would be screaming at me for going to the wall and then secretly congratulate me for going against authority."

Anton cracked a smile. "Yeah, I suppose so."

Blaze relaxed his hands. "So, what happened? Why the change in personality?"

"The unknown attacked us," said Anton. "Before, I wasn't afraid because I figured there wasn't anything out there. Then came the attack the—whatever they did to us."

"Do you think those people, the dead that Ahmed saw, were related to the ones who attacked us?"

"Doubt it," replied Anton. "Whatever did *that* to that wall is on the same level as the ones who put it up; perhaps higher, since they damaged it."

"Has anyone said anything?" asked Blaze.

His father shook his head. "No one knows a thing. But interestingly enough, Winslow asked someone about the device they found at the Nyman's house."

"Okay?"

"Asked before they found it," Anton clarified. "Meaning—"

But Blaze knew what it meant already. He didn't need it spoon fed to him. It was as clear as day for him.

"He knew they were going to find something," murmured Blaze beneath his breath.

Anton returned to the sink, dipping his hands into the water. "Right. Don Engle didn't want that getting out."

"Don Engle can go to Hell."

"Blaze."

Blaze stood up, throwing his hands out. "He shoved Aurora."

Continuing to wash dishes, Anton nodded. "I thought that was a poor choice, too. Look—and I mean *look*—"

Blaze turned to his father, their eyes locking together. There was fear in them, a dangerousness in his voice of caution, of warning.

"You can't go looking for that device. He's obviously going to protect it. He's been waiting for it for a long time, and if that goes missing, he'll kill every last one of us until he finds it."

"But if it's the only way?" Blaze pressed. "What if we're stuck here forever, with no idea of what really happened?"

"Then we just don't find out, and we deal with it. They have for generations, so why should we be any different."

Blaze stepped away unsatisfied with his father's answer. He looked back to him, still feeling the sense of fear emanating from his father's total self. Completely off the cuff, unrestrained, and non-filtered, Blaze shook his head.

"What would my old dad say—*you*—before all of this?"

Anton laughed softly, drying his last dish. "He'd tell you not to get caught." He turned to him, with a trace of a smile. "We can't save you forever, kid."

"I know. I'm not asking you to, but you have to trust me. Someday I'll find out for all of us."

"If anyone will, it's you Blaze. I trust that with my heart. But for our sake, I beg you not to."

* * *

Aurora Elder and Hadley sat beneath the shade of a great oak tree in Hadley's backyard. Forrest sat, plucking blades of grass out of the ground and examining them close, as if they were each totally unique.

Words between the two had been few but polite. Aurora had tried to ease the tension gradually, but Hadley had no time for nonsense. She brought it up right away, drawing attention to it with no hesitation.

"Look, you guys have to move forward. Blaze was right—you both get caught, all three of you were screwed."

"I'm not mad at him," Forrest replied reserved. "Honest."

Blaze sat back against the tree, bending a knee to his chest. "Convincing."

Hadley eyed her brother up and down, reading his expressions like a carefully detailed map. Her eyes scrutinized him until she relaxed.

"He's telling the truth. He's my brother. I'd know if he wasn't."

Forrest rolled his eyes. "Of course, I'm telling the truth. Blaze is my best friend. I'm worried about Ahmed, but what happened last night isn't anyone's fault; including Ahmed's."

Blaze nodded, relieved to be hearing confirmation that Forrest wasn't angry with him. The entire way here he was dreading that first, awkward meeting. But it went smoothly and without incident.

"It was stupid to go any way," said Aurora.

"Careful," Blaze cautioned. "Remember what we said. We're not saying too much out here. Possibility for others to be listening."

"Right, sorry," Aurora breathed, leaning back and arching her neck backward to look through the leaves.

Blaze found himself looking freely at her. There was something about Aurora, a slight confidence and inflated ego, that sent a burst of excitement through him. He knew there was something special about her—something that drove him crazy in a good way.

When Aurora looked down, she caught Blaze looking at her. "What? I said I was sorry."

"Not that," he laughed, blushing. "Just was thinking."

"Zoning out? About what?" she asked.

Blaze changed the topic, knowing it was getting dangerously close to uncharted territory. "Something my dad said about the thing found you know where."

"Finally had 'the talk' with your old man? Proud of you, buddy," Forrest said, patting Blaze on the back.

Blaze swatted his hand away. "Not that thing. The thing at the Nyman's," he said quietly.

"The thing the important guy took away?" asked Blaze, keeping the cover of the conversation going.

"Can we just spit it out? This is painful to listen to. What did your Dad say?" Hadley said forcefully.

"Winslow knew the device would be found. He asked about it before it went up in the Nymans' yard."

Aurora's brows pressed in. "I was with you. He said that when he was at the wall, the first he heard of it was there, on the radio."

"Yeah, well he lied," Blaze said. "Surprise, surprise."

Aurora shook her head. "So, he knew it would rise. What's next?"

"Seems like only Winslow knows," said Forrest. "I've said all along he knows more than he lets on. This just proves it."

"Well, it proves he knew about the device. Maybe one of the people from his time buried it?" Hadley suggested.

"*His time?*" Forrest scoffed. "Geez, Had, you make it seem like he's three-hundred years old. He's not a vampire, you know. There are others who are still alive from before the walls."

"You know what I mean, Forrest."

"Just giving you crap. I guess it's a possibility, but I have a feeling the others would know about the device they found, had it been that. I think he knew that it would come out of the ground when the explosion happened. Maybe the device holds the next clue."

"What were the other clues?" asked Aurora.

"Okay, good point. Maybe it holds the *first* clue," Forrest corrected.

Blaze turned aside, casting his gaze across the Kremer's yard. He thought of Ahmed and what happened the night prior. He turned to Forrest.

"You heard about Ahmed, right?"

Forrest nodded gently. "My mom filled me in. When they came looking, she told me. I'm worried about him."

"What happened?" asked Aurora, pressing herself vertical, crossing her legs.

"They brought him to Winslow's house. That's the last anyone has heard," said Forrest. "I doubt they released him."

Aurora sighed. "You guys didn't say that. Just that he got caught."

"Yeah, sorry, it's worse than that," Blaze said. "I heard one of Winslow's guys say they were going to make an example of him."

"You heard that?" Aurora asked, eyes wide.

Blaze nodded firmly. "Couldn't get it out of my head all night."

"We have to do something," said Hadley. "We can't let them punish him. We should find out a way to sneak him out."

"And hide him where?" Forrest snapped, throwing out his hands. Hadley was startled, sliding back a foot. "Toss him over the wall? May have not noticed, but we're kind of locked in here."

"I know," Hadley said. "All I'm saying is if we leave him, he's good as dead."

"And if we go in and try to save him, we're good as dead. We sneak him out and they find him, they punish him worse. They catch us? Boy, it's game-over."

Aurora cleared her throat. "So, what's next. For us?"

"We lay low, recalculate our options once we know what Ahmed's punishment is," said Blaze. "I doubt they're going to do anything dramatic. Everyone is already on edge these days. They won't want to add to it."

But Forrest tilted his head, "Er—I'm not so sure about that, buddy. Ahmed snuck up to the wall, right under Winslow's direct order not to leave. He's rebelled in the worst way. And if one did it, another could. I mean, we almost did, right? If he feels Winslow thinks he's losing power, he's going to show his strength in another way."

Blaze wrapped his arms around his bent knees, nodding in agreement. "You're right. He's going to show he's not messing around."

"And you said that he said he was going to make an example of Ahmed?" Aurora asked.

"No, the guard sent to check on us did."

"They wouldn't have said that had they had other plans for him," Hadley said. "I—I think they're going to do something. Something big."

"Something dramatic," Forrest agreed. "Sorry, man, but I think your no-drama idea is out the window. They're going to go all out. Scare us into obeying."

Blaze looked away, watching a rusted lawn ornament slowly turn, grinding at the rust. He knew they were right, but he desperately wanted them to be wrong. The more right they were, the worse he felt about leaving, about ordering Forrest and him to get out of the area. They could have saved him, but Blaze knew in his heart that there was no way Ahmed could have been saved. If they were to make an example of him, they would have made an example of all three. Blaze and Forrest were lucky. They made it back to their homes. Anton and Lorna covered for Blaze, risking their own safety. He assumed Forrest's had done the same thing.

Missing the last pieces of conversation, Blaze was yanked back into the present when the screen door of Forrest and Hadley's patio slammed shut. He turned, seeing Forrest's mother, Jenna, in the doorway.

"Kids, we have to go to the town center."

"Why?" asked Forrest. "Dinner isn't for another few hours, right?"

"This isn't dinner. Mr. Winslow called a town meeting."

Aurora was the first to stand. "Is it about the device they found?"

Jenna shrugged her shoulders. "I'm really not that sure. They didn't give details, only saying that we had to be there or there would be repercussions. Dad's already locking up at the store. I told him to tell your parents that you guys were with us if he runs into them."

Blaze looked to his three friends. "We better get down there, too. Maybe we'll find out what happened to Ahmed. He might be with his dad already."

"Yeah, fingers crossed," Hadley agreed, helping Forrest up.

"If he's alive, that is," said Forrest, wiping the back of his pants.

"Yeah," Aurora agreed. "A big if right now."

"Don't even talk about that," Blaze said. "Let's stay positive."

A short few minutes later, Blaze was walking with the Kremers and Aurora with a drive in his step. The other neighbors, residents of River Ridge, were moving down the road in groups and pairs. It seemed the general consensus was that no one knew what this meeting was for. Blaze looked at the houses as they passed, admiring the hard work that had been put into the city clean-up. While some homes were still badly damaged, repairs were already underway, lawns were clear of debris: old shingles, scraps of wood, aluminum siding.

As they approached the town center, Blaze could already see a well-established crowd. In the center of the space, separated from the citizens by large, wooden crates beside each other, was a large stage. It had been constructed quickly, with little planning it appeared. Various pieces of wooden planks—different lengths, types, and conditions—made up the structure. There was a large rising beam with another section that branched out over the stage.

But dangling from the horizontal beam—the part that was over the stage—sent a stinging sensation through Blaze's blood.

Hanging from the wooden beam was a long piece of rope. At the end of the rope, a large loop—a noose.

Blaze turned to Aurora beside him, but she was already pressing her palm against her forehead. He turned to Forrest who was tight lipped, but his eyes were glassy. Hadley turned to him, taking his hand.

"Sorry," she whispered.

And it was in there, the sense of finality set in.

He turned to Aurora. She looked back to him.

"We can't save him now," she said beneath her breath, taking in a deep inhale.

"No," Blaze agreed. "We can't."

It wasn't long before the entirety of the town was gathered in the square. By the looks of it, most of the faces were firm and unwavering in expression. When two of

Winslow's patrol team appeared, they were pulling a figure with a potato sack over its head.

Blaze knew from the walk of the figure it had to be Ahmed.

The men set him in place on the platform, lifting the bag up. It confirmed the identity beneath it.

Ahmed.

Immediately, from down below, a voice called out.

"Tell them! Tell them you were making up tales!" cried Ahmed's father, Fadi. "You were trying to joke, yes?"

Tears were streaming down Ahmed's face as she shook his head, biting his lip.

"I can't, Abi," he said. "I know what I saw."

Only the wind across the space broke the silence. No one spoke a word. Blaze caught a glimpse of his mother and father a few rows ahead. His father had his hand around her, watching Ahmed just as everyone else was.

When Winslow climbed the steps onto the structure, there was a noticeable chill that fell across the space. He approached slowly and methodically, holding the handrail the entire way up. His steps were loud against the silence.

Ahmed turned to him, the tears streaming faster. But through the tears, Blaze could see it in his eyes that he was broken. He had led a rebellion—*the* rebellion. He defied the rules of Winslow and saw for himself what was behind the wall. How many could say that? In a sense, Blaze could see bravery that he hadn't seen before. Despite the tears, he bore a firm expression. He was resolute in his decision, and it was very clear there was no going back now.

"Good afternoon, everyone. As you may have heard, there was a serious breach of the town's rules. This was not the first rule breakage for Mr. Ahmed Naser, but it will be his last. As he was brought back to my residence for questioning, he yelled that he climbed the wall and saw what was behind it. He put on quite the show, calling out to a few citizens what he saw. I want you to know that what he said was a lie."

"It was not a lie!" Ahmed cried. "I saw it! I saw the bodies! Hundreds of them. They were there for years. Skeletons everywhere—"

"SILENCE!" Winslow boomed. "Hook him up now!"

Winslow's men moved quickly. One held Ahmed, guiding him up onto an overturned milk crate while the other lowered the noose around his neck. They tightened it, stepped away.

"Tell them you made it up!" Ahmed's father cried again, his voice breaking. "Please, son! You were telling a story!"

But with the rope around his neck, Ahmed shook his head. "I can't. I'm sorry, Abi." He turned to Winslow. "They deserve the truth. You can't hide it from them forever."

Winslow said nothing in response. He turned to the guard who stood near the milk crate Ahmed stood upon, and simply raised his eyebrows.

In a swift motion, the guard kicked his foot at the milk crate. It flew out, and the rope tightened as Ahmed fell the short height.

Blaze couldn't shut his eyes fast enough. Below the stage, Ahmed's father cried pure pain. From his mouth, a cry so raw tore across the space, so full of agony that even the winds seemed to pause. He pressed forward, grabbing onto the platform as his son hung, twisting before him.

Winslow stepped forward, looked down. His expression was enigmatic, devoid of feeling, of emotion. In one moment, Winslow flared his nostrils and in the next, his boot came stomping down once on Fadi's hand. "Get back or you'll be up here next."

Instantly recoiling it, Mr. Naser burst into a sob, burying his face in his hands. Around him, other citizens surrounded him, placing their hands gently on him.

Blaze felt the back of Aurora's hand grace the back of his. He took it, turning to her. He didn't realize but his own eyes were blurred, layered in tears. Aurora's were red. She widened her eyebrows, breathing deeply, trying to hold in her emotions.

"This won't work forever," Blaze got out. "He can't hang all of us."

Aurora looked down, squeezing his hand. "But he'll try. I know he will."

When they looked up, Ahmed's body had gone still, swaying gently in the wind. Blaze wanted to look away, but felt doing so would be dishonorable to his memory. Though in the last year or so they hadn't seen eye to eye, Ahmed wasn't a horrible person. He'd have to let the past remain in the past.

No matter how much Winslow and the other devout followers of his would try to persuade them that Ahmed was lying, he knew the truth. The others knew the truth. There'd be those who'd refuse to listen to reason and reject his truth out of fear, but there were those who would accept it.

On the platform, Winslow's voice carried. "Let this be a lesson to all of you not to play with the fire. This young man, here," he said softly, gently placing his hand on Ahmed's back, "wished to start a panic. He climbed the wall and then, as a joke, wanted to scare you. He needed to be punished."

"This is wrong, Victor. If the boy was telling the truth, we must face it with courage," called out one female voice.

Winslow turned to the source, his eyes narrowing. "I'd mind your mouth, if I were you."

"Listen to him. He knows," replied another voice, defending Winslow. "He was here when the walls rose. He knows what happened."

"So was I," another voice replied, older and gravely. "I was here, too."

"Quiet," Winslow warned severely. "I ask that you all get back to work. I thought it was necessary you saw this."

"You thought we needed to see a teenager be hung?" replied the older male again. "You're losing it, Winslow."

Blaze realized then and there that there would be those who sided with Winslow—the façade, and those who would side with Ahmed—the truth. The town would be divided soon enough. Like he had thought, Winslow couldn't hang everyone who went against him.

It wouldn't work. This scare tactic's reach was limited. He'd run out eventually.

Now, in the clearing of the town square, Blaze knew that time was running short for a town at peace. Soon, there would be the switch, the others would turn on him, and there'd be full-on chaos.

And if Blaze had learned anything about their leader in his seventeen-years, it was that Victor Winslow would keep order, no matter the costs.

* * *

When Blaze arrived home a short while later, both Lorna and Anton Davies were sitting at the kitchen table illuminated by the faint glow of late-afternoon. The air in the kitchen was stale, though the windows were opened. Two mugs of water sat on the table, hardly touched.

He came in the front door alone, slipped off his shoes, and went into the kitchen.

Lorna stood, rushing to him, wrapping her arms around him. She pressed her chin into his shoulder blade, holding him tightly.

Anton rose, stepping around the back of his chair, and wrapped his fingers around the backing. "This is why we tell you to watch yourself," he said.

"Dad, I don't need a lecture. I wasn't reckless. We had a plan."

"And the plan backfired. Severely."

"Anton," Lorna said, stepping back. "Breathe. Relax."

He listened, shutting his eyes and leaning his head back. "You're right. I'm sorry."

"Blaze, why did you go down there?" Lorna asked.

"We were curious. We wanted to see. Ahmed did and here we are."

"Look, if you're going to do these sorts of things, you can't get caught. You need to be more practical. This is your life we're talking about," Anton said.

"This doesn't sound like a 'don't do that again' type of speech," Blaze said. "What gives?"

"The tides are turning. You saw it in the crowd, you felt it in the air. He did, too. The town is growing divided by the day. Soon, there won't be much left keeping us together. Soon, the last thread will break. Then, it's anyone's game."

"So, what are you saying?"

Anton stepped around, approaching Blaze. "You want to explore, explore. But you're going to do it right. You're going to learn to protect yourself, your friends, whoever. You want out? You can get out. They can't rebuild the wall, since we didn't build it in the first place. Blaze, the next few days are crucial. Winslow knows something's up; something will happen soon. He's scared to death, so that means we need to exploit this. Use it to our advantage."

Blaze looked to his mother. "What's he talking about."

"Just listen," she said, her expression severe. "He's serious."

"I am," Anton said. "We both decided that they may be able to trace you and Forrest being out there yesterday. They may figure it out. We want you prepared to run, to get out of here if you need to."

"And escape? What are you saying? This is—"

"*Insane?*" proposed Anton. "Yeah, I know."

"You're scaring me, Dad."

Anton put out his arm, grabbing Blaze on the shoulders. "You'll hear me out. I'm going to train you, show you what supplies we have. It's not much, but when the time comes, you'll need to move fast."

"And get over the wall? And go where?" asked Blaze.

Shrugging his shoulders, Anton shook his head. "I don't know. A major city. There might be others out there. I really don't know, Blaze."

Lorna took his face between her hands. "You need to live, Blaze. You can't suffer the same fate as Ahmed."

"What about Forrest?" asked Blaze.

"It's up to his family to prepare him. If they're not reading the writing on the wall; if they're blind to truth, that's their problem."

"Dad—he's my friend."

"I can prepare you and only you," he replied. "It's up to them to take care of their son."

Blaze nodded. "What makes you think they'll piece this together?"

"They didn't buy the story last night," Lorna said. "The way they phrased certain sentences, looked at us, at you. It's clear they knew something wasn't right."

"Winslow doesn't need proof. Why didn't he just take me, like they did Ahmed."

"Because he knew there would be resistance to them taking Ahmed. If they took all three of you, it would've been full-out war. If they decide to come for you and Forrest, they're going to wait it out. They're in no rush. They think you're stuck in here with them. Like us, you're in the snake pit."

He wasn't sure where all of this had come from. Ahmed's death—the public nature of it—must have spooked his parents. They saw Blaze's face on Ahmed and it scared them terribly.

"When do we start this training?" asked Blaze.

Anton reached over, patting him on the cheeks twice with his hand. "Now, Blaze. Let's move."

EIGHT

Downstairs, the basement felt like a bunker, of endless concrete, shelving, and a plethora of canned goods. The air was musty and cool. The softened echo of footsteps brought forth a claustrophobic sensation in the compressed space. With each step, the dust-laden air swirled in their wake.

Rotting beams along the low-hanging ceiling held the floors above. Windows, thin and narrow, dusty, and discolored, allowed for tinted light to enter the space.

Anton motioned with his hand for Blaze to join him beside a plain bookshelf lined with stacks of canned goods— tomatoes, jams, applesauce cans, beets. With summer having come to an end, it was full and ready for the approaching winter.

"Stay back a couple feet. Mind your toes."

Anton leaned his head to the left side, closest to the wall of the basement. He slid his hand back, gliding it along the side of the shelf, and Blaze heard a clicking sound of metal against metal.

Anton leaned down, crouching slightly, doing the same action just a few feet below. Again, Blaze heard another click and in one, solid sweep, Anton pulled back the shelf, swinging it open like a door. Blaze heard the soft roll of a few hidden wheels below the base shelf, assisting his father.

Despite its otherwise untouched appearance, the shelf revealed its age, creaking and groaning, until Anton released his hold of the shelf, revealing a small opening into a space Blaze had never seen.

Awe cast itself across Blaze's narrow face, brightening his brown eyes.

"Come in," Anton said. "Do watch your head, though."

Blaze followed his father through the small opening in the wall into a tiny, darkened room.

"No lights, no power," he said, "but I have an old cigarette lighter in here. That should work."

Blaze waited in the partial dark, steadying himself against the archway of the opening.

Anton reached down, and by memory, he grabbed the lighter where he'd likely last left it, flicked on the flame, and illuminated the space with a soft orange glow.

It was smaller than Blaze imagined. Consisting of concrete blocks that did not match the rest of the basement, the space had a few wooden shelves. There were more jars of preserved foods, gallon jugs of water, first aid kits from the old-world. But most eye-opening, almost gleaming in the flickering light, were three rifles and a pistol.

Weapons were practically extinct nowadays. There had been a gun confiscation some years after the walls rose. Blaze had heard about it from his father. Weapons were required to be turned in and were later hidden away. The fact that there were four weapons that survived, let alone were in his own basement, was a wonder.

"Whose are these?"

"Great-Grandpa's," Anton said coolly. "Grandpa built this after the walls rose. Figured the town would panic, loot, riot. He thought ahead and dug this space out, and sealed it within a week. With the town in shambles, he did it all right under their noses. They were too busy to notice."

"So, who knows about this?"

"Me, Mom, and now you."

Blaze felt the gravity of it strike him. "And you want me to hide in here if they come?"

Anton whipped around, putting the lighter near his face. His brows were quirked, lips twisted, as he shook his head. Blaze felt a little stupid now. "No. We're not playing that game. This is our emergency supply closet. It's for when we're in a crisis. Mom and I feel that we're going to be entering a crisis sooner than later. Blaze, this is going to get worse before it gets better and you need to be prepared."

Blaze nodded. "So, what's next."

"I train you on basic hand-to-hand combat, introduce you to weapons, basic survival skills." With his free hand, Anton placed it onto Blaze's shoulders. "The tides are turning, son, and the water's about to get deep. We're not letting you drown."

Blaze cast his gaze across the supplies in the room. He knew in this moment that there was no going back. There was no old-life. His first step into the secret chamber was his last step of childhood. His parents could no longer protect him from the brewing storm. Their shelter was leaking and they knew, as well as he did, that it would be breached anytime now.

He shut his eyes, breathed deeply. Anton remained quiet. Blaze took a swallow, shook his head slightly, and nodded. "Let's do this."

Anton pressed his lips together. "Proud of you."

But Blaze's mind was already elsewhere. No matter how much he wanted to be ready and learn from his father, he knew he wasn't. He didn't want to let go of his life, but within, he knew he didn't have an option anymore. The time to act was now. And that time was running out.

* * *

An hour had passed. The two had moved back into the main part of the basement, savoring what remained of daylight. Anton had shown Blaze an old backpack—one Anton had used as a kid. He took out the objects, taking his time in showing Blaze each tool or gadget inside, it's purpose, and with what he had laying around the basement—which wasn't much—how to use it.

Blaze fought hard to pay attention, focus intently, and learn. But he knew he would forget certain things when the time came. His father would recap, and Blaze found himself just staring, not soaking anything in.

Anton read this, and in his usual fashion, called Blaze out on it.

"I see it in your eyes. You're not paying attention."

Blaze looked up. His father's expression was firm and severe.

"I am. It's just a lot."

"This isn't that hard. You need to try harder."

Flushed, Blaze shook his head. "It's not just the tools. It's everything: Ahmed, the wall, this—*everything*."

But Anton's expression was unwavering. "Enough with the drama. Enough with the excuses—"

"Drama? Excuses? How heartless are you? They hung Ahmed! Do you have any sympathy at all?" Blaze yelled. It came from deep down, an explosion of steam that burned on the way out; burned his father.

Anton sat back, tossed the backpack aside. "You want to be done? Let's be done."

"It came out wrong. I'm sorry," Blaze said. "You're not heartless. That was anger talking, not me."

Anton stood up, zipping-up and putting the backpack back into the secret space. "I'm not the enemy here, Blaze", he said, his voice distorted in distance.

"I don't think you are."

Anton walked out of the darkness, leaned against the bricked archway. "Look, my job as a parent is to protect you, to guide you, but let you make your own decisions; even the stupid ones. I'm trying to do the first two, but if you'd rather take the punches as they come, I can't stop you. But I can't protect you from them either."

"Dad, I want your help."

"You don't. If you did, you'd pay attention, ask questions. You're sitting there, catching flies in your mouth. I feel like I'm talking to myself. Surprise, I know how all of this works! I know how to stay alive. I don't think you realize what's in store for you. If you have to run to save yourself, Mom and I aren't coming with. You're on your own. I didn't want to say this, but I will: I'm scared to death for you, kid. To be frank, based on your attitude and resistance to all of this, you're fucked."

Taken aback, Blaze swallowed his pride and took the verbal punches with both cheeks. He knew his father was right. He heard the anger, the pressure in his voice. As frustrated as he was at Blaze, he was more frustrated at the events for putting them in this position in the first place.

"Yeah..." Blaze agreed.

"Stop agreeing and fight for this, dammit. Show some passion, some drive! This isn't some fairytale adventure where the bad guys are chasing after you and you can take them down with a few kicks and punches. The town is under attack by some—some *force*, there is a lunatic running this town, and he's going after anyone who wants to learn the truth of why. Both you and Forrest are his next targets. I need to prepare you to stay alive."

"Dad—I get it. I'm sorry. Can we continue?"

"No." Anton shook his head. "Not now. I need to cool down. Go play with your friends. We'll continue another time."

"I'm seventeen, we don't play. We're practically adults."

Anton closed up the bookshelf, locking it into place. He turned to Blaze, lifted his chin upward. "If you're practically adults, then you better start acting like it."

Blaze nodded.

Anton exhaled through his nose. "There you go, agreeing with me again. Dammit, Blaze! Are you dense? Do I need to hammer this into your thick skull? You won't last ten minutes out there!"

Blaze rose to his feet, slamming his hand against a concrete block. "Then help me!" The rage pooled around his frame, escaping in bursts.

"I'm trying to, don't you see? Mom and I are terrified. We want you to be safe, but we can't save you from them. This is the only way I can help you, and you're fighting me every step of the way."

Even in the dim light, Blaze could see tears in his father's eyes. He'd never seen his father cry, not even when his own parents had passed away.

"I'm sorry," Blaze said gently. "When you're ready, we'll try again."

"Don't apologize to me. Apologize to yourself. That's the only person you're hurting now. At this point, when Winslow comes for you kids next, I pray he shows you some mercy."

* * *

Afternoon came and went. Blaze and Anton had returned upstairs in silence. They had not spoken to each other aside from a few exchanges of small-talk.

Lorna had tried to ease the tension, smooth it with her tender approach, but she knew it was of no use. As with any argument between her boys, she knew only time would heal.

They ate lunch at the town center, acting as if all was normal. Beneath the shadow of the podium where Ahmed had died and still hung, Blaze found himself unable to look, staring off into space, letting his mind wander everywhere but here.

When they returned home a short while later, Blaze had gone to his bedroom to sit at his desk and read some old magazines that had been handed down to him.

Midway through his fourth, a soft knock tapped on the closed wooden door. He knew it was his mother's touch.

"Yeah?" said Blaze, turning to face the door.

But he had thought wrong. Instead of his mother, it was Aurora.

"Hey, stranger. What was up at lunch? You didn't even come over and say anything to us?"

Blaze shrugged his shoulders. "Just tired tonight. A lot to process."

Aurora walked in, straightened a framed painting print on the wall, and hopped onto the foot of his bed. She crossed her legs beneath her. "I hear you. Forrest is making jokes like crazy, an obvious distraction. Hadley's keeping him grounded and checking in on him. But I wanted to see how you are."

"I'm fine," Blaze said, a little too eagerly, trying to cover his emotions. She didn't buy it.

Her brow lifted. "It's okay to not be."

"I know," Blaze agreed. "It hasn't hit me." There was some truth to this, he felt. He wasn't fully lying.

"Want to walk?"

"Where?"

Aurora rolled her eyes. "Seriously? Is it a deal-breaker? Does it matter?"

Blaze laughed. "I'll grab my shoes."

Once outside, Blaze savored the fresh air. He breathed it in, held it. His time in the basement had soured his senses. The stale, stagnant air of his home didn't help either, and now, he was free.

He felt free to think. Free to feel.

Beneath an autumn sky, Blaze walked in step with Aurora, looking to her every few minutes. She was thinking. He could feel it. Her silence was telling.

"What's on your mind?" asked Blaze, diving straight in.

Aurora furrowed her brow, lips pressed firmly together. "I've been thinking about the device and Ahmed. We—uhm—look, I don't think we're going to find out what's going on. Do you?"

Blaze turned to her, watching her dark red hair blow past her shoulders. "Doubt it," he said frankly. "This town is all he has. Those walls, as scared as he is of them, are his safe-zone, his protection from the unknown. He's not letting anyone take them away. It's like a kid with a sleeping blanket."

Aurora agreed. "He's losing his control of the situation. He thought nothing would threaten his power. I think whoever built them has a sick sense of humor."

"So, who do you think it is?"

"Our ancestors."

"Aurora, you're with me. You don't have to tell me what they've shoved down our throats—"

"Not those ancestors," she stopped him. Pausing. "The ancestors that go back. Way back."

Blaze smirked. "Not aliens?"

"Aliens?" Little green men with big eyes?"

"Who said they had to be little and green?"

"Blaze..."

"Sorry. I'm just saying it's a possibility," he said, stepping over branch in the road. "At this point, any door is open in the hallway."

"Whatever it is we're hiding from, it meant to hurt us," said Aurora. "That wasn't a greeting. That was dark; an attack, like your dad said."

Blaze nodded. "But we won't get any closer to the truth without exploring more and finding out what that device was that Winslow took. That holds the key."

"How do you know?" Aurora's tone changed suddenly.

"What do you mean?"

Her quiet green eyes were focused, darkened. "You saw as much of it as I did. What do you think is on there? A full explanation of what happened etched onto the outside."

"Maybe?"

"Blaze, be serious."

"I am. You never know."

Aurora stopped, turning to face him. "You saw what happened to Ahmed. You and Forrest went looking, but the only difference is that you both didn't get caught. I'm not losing you, too."

"But it's the only way. We have to at least try," replied Blaze. "We give up now and we never find out."

"I'm up for the adventure, but at what cost? Is it worth it? We don't know if it has any value."

"Winslow—"

"Blaze, keep your voice down," snapped Aurora. "He has eyes everywhere."

"*He* knows what it is," whispered Blaze. "I know it."

Aurora moved from the road and up onto sidewalk. "Based on what? Him taking it? When has he not taken what he wanted?" she asked quietly.

"You know it, too." Blaze paused, focused deep upon her. "I can see it in your eyes."

"No, what you're seeing is your reflection, Blaze. Don't cast your suspicions onto me. I'm not getting involved in this. You saw what happened to Ahmed..."

"That's why we need to keep digging. We're getting close. We do nothing and his death is in vain."

Aurora bit down on her lip. "Blaze, you have to let this go. I'm serious. It'll get you killed."

Tapping his fingers against his upper thigh, he raised his hand to scratch his head. "What happened to the girl I rode bikes with? The girl who went into the forest with me at night; the girl who lived for adventure?

"Blaze, this isn't a game!" Aurora slammed, cursing beneath her breath before continuing. "This is dangerous, this is real, and believe it or not, I care about you—a lot."

A flush of adrenaline tingled through his body, rising from his core. He tried to hold back a smile, staying cool. "This is the first I'm hearing of this."

Even beneath nightfall, Aurora's face brightened. "Yeah, well, I'm a good poker player. Never reveal your hand."

Blaze gave her a wink, a playful smirk. "Speaking of hand." He took it, wrapping his fingers around hers. "I care about you, too."

"And you never made a move?" she asked.

Blaze shrugged. "I thought you would. You're independent and don't need a man, which is good." He laughed. "Didn't want to interfere with that."

She rolled her eyes, shook her head.

He laughed, pulling at her waist. Their eyes locked as he tightened his hands around her. His lips played into an amused smile. Blaze took the moment, their moment, to study her. He wanted to remember this, savor it, and treasure it. He raised his thumb, tracing the pout of her lower lip.

She closed her eyes, exhaling a shaky breath. "Just kiss me already—"

Far above and full of power though, a cry of thunder roared, stretching across the sky. It pulled Blaze and Aurora's attention away from their moment. He felt the trembling deep in the ground making him stand unsteady.

But as their eyes linked with the sky, their breath, their connection, was stolen by a mind-bending sight. Fast-moving clouds rolled in dark and ominous. They covered the city, snatching what little amount of afternoon remained in the sky. In a few seconds, a massive shadow covered River Ridge, hanging low, as if blanketing the earth. With the clouds came powerful winds. Long-fallen leaves, damp and stuck to the roads, lifted from the pavement, scattering in the air and away.

Aurora turned to Blaze, her dark-red hair billowing behind her. "We've got to get indoors. Something is happening."

Blaze nodded, pressing his lips together, having noticed his jaw was slack in wonder as he kept his focus on the sky. Their eyes met, glimmers of fear igniting in hers. Blaze took her hand, but quickly she withdrew it.

"You don't need to be my knight in shining armor. I'm not a damsel in distress. You be brave, I'll be brave."

He smiled slightly, as they moved towards the center of town. "I should've known. Old habits."

Aurora leaned into him, kissed him on the cheek. "Let me slay my own dragons, fight my own fights. We're partners. Equal partners." Her attention lifted. She paused, pointing to the sky. "Something isn't right."

Pointing, Aurora pulled Blaze's attention also to the sky. Swirling and rotating, the sky above had taken on a green hue, the color of an emerald caked in mud. The darkness came strong and dangerous, pressing in on them and their entire world. Within it, the streets and standing structures took on shades of gray. It took what little color remained of their world and replaced them, layered them, in paralyzing fear. It surrounded anything and everything within the confines of the walls, swallowing anything in its path without mercy.

Blaze quickened his step to match Aurora's. He found himself lifting his gaze, watching the sky because he knew it could change at any moment. Like a wild animal, he didn't trust it. This was new and unfamiliar. The winds were howling now, brushing through the abandoned facades of the harder hit homes from the blast. It pressed a cold breeze into their skin, bit in, and would not let go.

They covered a lot of distance moving amidst the sea of shadows. They passed homes, destroyed remnants of lives. Blaze watched as slacked-jawed citizens stood at the edge of the street, stone-white faces lifted sky-bound.

A large gathering was moving towards the center of town. Aurora turned to Blaze, as they both overheard them mentioning Winslow's name.

"He'll know what to do," murmured one.

"He won't know shit," said another. "But he was there. He lived."

Blaze turned to Aurora. "Town Square? Guessing that's where they're going."

She nodded. "Besides, if this gets worse, we won't make it home in time. Hey—" her tone suddenly changed "—I see Forrest and Hadley. Guys!"

Forrest was the first to hear Aurora's call. He twisted around, raised his hand. Hadley started towards Blaze and Aurora first. Forrest followed.

When they were within a few feet, Hadley pointed up to the sky. "This looks bad."

"Bad is putting it lightly," Forrest said, hands on his hips. He went in to give Blaze a side-hug. "You doing okay?"

"As good as I can. You?"

Forrest swallowed hard. "I've been better." He paused and took a breath. "It sounds like everyone is heading over to the center of town. From what I've pieced together, Winslow's down there. I guess he's spooked."

"Let's walk and talk guys. From the looks of it—" Aurora peered up, fidgeting with her necklace "—time isn't exactly on our side."

Without further word, Aurora started forward and Hadley moved beside her. The boys turned to each other, shrugging their shoulders.

"Guess you guys are leading, eh?" Forrest asked.

Hadley twisted her head around, brown hair blowing in the wind. "I didn't see either of you stepping up to the plate."

"Hey, no hate. I like the change," replied Forrest.

"Oh, please, Forrest. Go be macho another time, someplace else. It's not cute."

"Well good thing I'm not trying to pick you up," Forrest said.

Hadley rolled her eyes. "Don't be disgusting."

Beneath the covering of the darkened sky, the four followed the fast-moving groups. The closer they got to the center of town, the more other groups joined them. Entering the plaza, there were a few hundred gathered around the large globe at the center. Blaze peered around, catching glimpse of Aurora's mothers, of Forrest and Hadley's parents, and then his own.

They didn't see him, though, their attention focused at the center. Anton had his arm wrapped around Blaze's mother, her head leaning against his chest.

"I should go tell my parents I'm here," said Blaze.

"Yeah," Aurora agreed. "They'd appreciate it. I waved to one of my moms, just now. We'll be here."

Blaze wove through gathered, huddled groups, weaving around them and through to his parents. When he approached, his mother's eyes widened.

"Thank God you're here," she said, moving forward to Blaze and wrapping her arms around him. Anton approached too, placing his hand on Blaze's shoulder.

"I was over there. Any idea on what this is?"

"Not a storm," Anton said. "That much we know."

"Yeah, no shit."

"Watch your mouth," Lorna scoffed.

Anton pressed onward. "My dad talked about the sky turning colors when the walls rose. Maybe another set will rise or the others will fall?" Anton said. "It's a toss-up."

"Are we in danger?" Blaze asked quietly.

Anton pressed his lower lip against his top. He turned around, looking to the gathered masses. "Not sure, Blaze. I'm not sure."

Blaze turned, looking through the blank faces around him. Against the old market, still standing, was where they hung Ahmed. Swaying in the wind, his body hung as a reminder of what happens to those who disobey. Blaze turned swiftly, seeing the state the body was quickly falling into.

Winslow, suited in a green tweed suit, patched at the elbows and one knee, stood motioning for the panicked followers of his to calm down, lower their voices. Blaze couldn't make out what the town leader was saying, but Blaze could see the tension in his eyes, the subtle hints of fear seeping through unmasked and unfiltered.

Blaze found himself moving away from his parents. He turned to see Aurora following. Forrest and Hadley hung back.

"Where are you going?" asked Lorna.

"I'll be back in a second," said Blaze.

As they approached, Winslow's snow-white hair took on a shade of sea-foam green beneath the sickly sky. His face, already narrow and lined, appeared more gaunt and pallid. Sweat lined his brow.

"Mr. Winslow," Blaze said.

The elder turned to him. "Stay calm. We're fine." Already, his attention was drawn to another panic-stricken citizen.

"When are you going to tell us?" pressed Blaze. "Tell us what you saw, what you experienced. We've all heard it—the rumors. Might as well tell us now."

"Don't speak to him like that," spat a middle-aged woman.

"He ought to cut out your tongue for your cheek," an older male—mid-fifties—hissed.

But Winslow held out a hand. "I don't know what you're talking about."

"Oh, that's rich," Aurora said, stepping forward towards the leader. "Everyone knows at this point. Just tell us. We can handle it."

Winslow slipped through, steadying himself on a small wall made of bricks. Behind his thin-framed, round glasses, his eyes narrowed. "I suggest you be very quiet now. There's already a panic."

"Because we've heard the rumors. All of us. Just own it."

Winslow swung his arm from his side, pointing a narrow, bony finger at Ahmed in the distance. "I've already made an example of him. Need I make one of you two?"

"You're sick," Aurora said. "You probably like this, don't you? Having everyone clinging to you for support and wisdom."

Winslow's lips curled up into a wicked smirk. "Guilty of what you criticize, aren't you? Asking me for my story or does that not count?"

"Because you know what happened. The last time this happened, those walls rose out of the ground. Within the last days, we had an attack at the wall and an artifact was located. Now this? Something is happening, something is changing. And you know what it is."

Winslow shook his head.

"Don't shake your head," Aurora said. "Just tell us."

"I've had enough of you," Winslow hissed at her. "Back at the wall, now here. Little girls should be seen, not heard."

Blaze gritted his teeth, seething at the seams. But he remembered what she had said. He needed to let her fight her own fights and slay her own dragons.

"*Little girls?*" Aurora asked, stepping forward.

Winslow stiffened his posture. He pointed at Ahmed again. "Don't make me do something I'd rather not do."

"Put your hand down, you little man," Aurora spat. Others turned to her. "You might scare them, but you don't scare me. I'm not a little girl. I won't be silent. You want to hang me, make an example as you phrase it? Go ahead, but they'll only turn on you faster, the few that haven't already."

A bolt of lightning ripped through the darkened, inky-green sky. Around them, a few dozen screamed as it tore across the canvas. The thunderous warning, as usual, came one moment too late.

It sent a few ducking for cover. As the shake trembled in the ground, Winslow steadied himself again. The few who'd gathered around him, lowered, kneeling around him.

Aurora shook her head. "You like this. You thrive on it."

Winslow's face lost what little remaining color remained. His chest rose and fell, his narrow frame suddenly seeming weaker. "I was destined to protect them," he said, meeting Aurora's gaze. "It's my duty. I won't let anything happen to this town."

Blaze stepped up beside Aurora. "Whatever's next, even you can't control it."

"You say that as if I don't already know that," the leader said.

Again, another bolt of lightning sheered through the sky. Winslow shuttered beneath it, shutting his eyes. Blaze turned upwards to see a clearing, a momentary clearing of brilliant blue light, like a spotlight, beaming down into the crowd.

The next moment, a massive thud sent shockwaves through the space. A few lost their balance, including Blaze. Instinctively, he covered his head. Around him, the winds began to pick-up, swirling around a single space. Blaze felt his own world starting to spin. He felt sick, squeezing his eyes shut and covering his ears. Aurora lowered next to him, and he reached out, pulling her to him.

But as fast as it came, it stopped. The winds ceased, but the sky held its sickly appearance. As the spinning stopped, Blaze's attention was pulled forward by an audible gasp from those around him.

Knelt down in the center of an impression in the pavement was a broad-shouldered figure. Head lowered, still in a kneel, it was draped in a thick burlap material. Slowly, the figure rose, towering above all who'd gathered in the square. It wore a cloak over its head, which cast much of its face in dim shadow. But from what Blaze could see, it had silver skin and long, mangled fingers that slipped out from the sleeves of the cloak. In its right hand, it held a long staff. A glowing orange orb seemingly floated between curved pieces of shiny metal at the tip.

Winslow moved in front of Blaze and Aurora, holding out his arms. River Ridge was silent. Held on the leader's next words, the figure remained standing, staring.

Winslow held his breath, didn't blink. But no words would come yet. He lowered his hands, dropping to his knees. "No!" he cried, his voice breaking in terror. "No! Leave us alone! Leave us be!" He grabbed for his chest, pulling out the ruby necklace he always wore, holding it out, face turned aside, as if the figure would be afraid of jewelry and listen to Winslow's request.

But the towering figure stared at Winslow. It was in this moment that Blaze knew that this was the man from Winslow's drawings. The obsessive sketches, drawn in frantic, frightened hurry, were of the man—this being—standing directly in front of them. Blaze had heard the rumors of the cloaked man, but now to see it made the reality of their situation that much more real.

He could feel the terror. Could feel the fright.

Whatever happened to Winslow all those years ago was here now. He'd hid from his demons for over seven decades, but he had to of known he'd be found again. He couldn't hide forever.

Blaze's eyes bounced back between the two, pulled to Winslow's ruby. It seemed to illuminate slightly, but Blaze figured that with his own imagination.

As the figure approached Winslow, the rest cleared a space as they stepped back. Winslow remained on his knees, lowering into a bow before the massive figure. Closer, Blaze could see the figure had a human face—somewhat. A nose, two eyes, and thin lips. Its expression was flat, an expression that Blaze could interpret in any number of ways. It took on whatever the viewer projected upon it like a film screen.

The figure lifted its hand, pointing to Ahmed.

"You?" the figure said, it's voice gravely and filtered.

Winslow burst into a sob. "I've done nothing wrong!"

"*YOU?*" it repeated.

Again, Winslow cried. He raised his hands to his face. But the figure approached quickly. It leaned down, scooping Winslow up in one swift motion by the collar of his dress shirt, moving up to his neck. The figure's strong hands clamped around the leader's throat. The few nearest him let out soft whimpers, cries, and a few gasps. The figure paid none of them any attention, however.

As it lifted Winslow up without any signs of struggle, a cold wind swept past Blaze. It sent a tingle across his skin. He shut his eyes, unable to watch Winslow's frantic kicking as he hung suspended by the figure's tight grasp. Blaze could see the darkness blooming around the edges of Winslow's vision, closing in on him. Blaze turned aside.

But when he opened his eyes, Blaze heard the sudden sweep of looming rainfall. He felt the cool rush of air that would carry it. Winslow gasped for air, prying at the cloaked man's long fingers. Its long, yellowed nails carved into the leader's neck, digging in and latching on. Frantic in death, Winslow wasn't giving up. He wouldn't let go of his power.

The old man had a bit more fight left within him.

Rain poured across the walled town. Muffled, the effects of the sudden rainfall against pavement silenced Winslow's struggles for life. Amongst the crowded square, the rain and the darkness only amplified the sense of emptiness that hung across everyone.

But from nowhere, the figure released its grip on Winslow, and he fell.

Crashing to the ground, he curled up and took several gasping breaths. The figure's hand remained in the air for only a moment more before it lowered, retreating back into the sleeve of the cloak.

Rain continued to fall across River Ridge. All eyes remained focused on the towering man and what his next steps would be. Carefully, with determination and a clean movement of the hand, the figure raised his staff into the air.

A great bolt of blue energy shot from the tip and into the sky. And as quickly as it had come, the rain stopped. The sky lost the green hue that had woven itself through the clouds, and then the clouds in their entirety merely vanished.

The bleeding sunlight of looming dusk lit the space. It illuminated the droplets of rain that clung to the leaves and blades of grass. It glimmered off the droplets on Blaze's skin, and lit the pavement like thousands of tiny diamonds embedded into the uneven surface.

Blaze wanted to pull his shirt away from his skin, but it held tight, like a second layer. Looking down, he watched Winslow who remained curled in a fetal position beneath the drenched, towering figure.

Then, in another swift movement, the figure pointed the orb of his staff at the distant damaged wall. Another beam of energy, this time a pale blue—almost white—rushed out from the glowing sphere. In mere moments, the wall that was missing a massive chunk was made whole again. As if in reverse, the melted blob rose up the side, repairing the surface it skimmed across. As it reached the top, the etched lines in the surface were crisp and strong. Blaze figured if it were night, the wall would be illuminated once again.

A few voices chirped up. Others near Blaze pointed.

"Look," one said. "It's back. The wall is back."

Blaze turned to his side and Forrest and Hadley were now beside them, only mere feet from the strange man. Though he'd performed miracles, seemingly appearing from the sky, the four were not afraid.

As the figure continued to peer across the gathered townspeople, Winslow slowly rose to his feet. He pressed off his thighs, straightening his back, and pushed back his hair that was strewn across his forehead and brow.

"I ask that you leave," Winslow cooed. "Please. I've kept them safe for this long."

The figure turned to Winslow. "You've done nothing," it said, deep-voiced and guttural. "You know what your task was."

From deep within, from the center of Blaze's core, tingling sensations ran from his stomach upward. He felt the shallow pinch of sweat rising from his pores, the beat of his heart increasing. Blaze knew this man—this *whatever*— would have answers.

It was clear that the man behind the walls was the cloaked figure. He would know the history of them and the truth that Winslow feared.

Blaze cleared his throat. "Who sent you?"

He felt dozens of eyes shift to him.

Winslow hurried over to him. "Don't speak to it! Don't you dare." Spittle landed across Blaze's face.

Looking past his shoulders, Blaze saw the cloaked figure approach. He reached out his pale hand and placed it on Winslow's shoulder, then he yanked him back. The leader flew backward, brushing past the figure's cloak and landing atop the hard pavement.

"The others," answered the figure, smoothing out its cloak.

"The others?" Blaze asked, avoiding direct eye contact.

Up close, the figure appeared to be less human. The expression, the dead eyes, made it seem as though the figure had attempted to mimic humans, so they would not fear it as much. Masked within the shadow of the cloak, the figure's skin—what little Blaze could see—was stone gray. It cocked its head, revealing black eyes that shimmered beneath the sky. It considered him, as if deciding whether or not to answer more questions from the human child. But Blaze couldn't help but wonder if this was a peaceful being or a killer.

The obvious answer, at least in Blaze's mind, was if this being was a threat, they'd already be dead. Why else would it have repaired the wall or cleared the frightful storm? Blaze decided he would keep going, press deeper, until he met resistance. Regardless, it was clear the figure hated Winslow. Maybe they were more alike than he thought.

But Forrest would be the one to take over, clasping his hands in front of his waist. "You say the others. Who are the others?"

"The Council," the figure said silkily, turning to meet Forrest's gaze. "Some of them did not want me to come back. They did not want me to return after all these years."

"So, it was you who came here all those years ago," Forrest said, motioning to Winslow. "You came to him when he was a child."

"Enough!" Winslow hissed, now standing again but keeping his distance.

The figure slowly rotated around, likely staring the leader down into silence. It worked. He turned back to Forrest, nodding gently.

"Yes," it said. "And he failed my order, my directive, of how he was to prepare your people."

"Prepare for what?" Aurora asked.

Eyes switched over to her.

"Your survival," said the figure. "There are some who wished for your species to die. Others like me, others like the Council sought to protect you. The Creators sought to destroy you."

"So, these Creators tried to break the wall?"

"They did break the wall," the figure said. "They broke through to scare you, to torment you. They wanted to lure us back."

"Obviously it worked," Forrest said.

Blaze crossed his arms across his chest. "There was a device planted in the ground. When the wall was damaged, it came up. Do you know anything about it?"

"It was planted by the Council. It's a piece of the information you need to survive. It contains what I showed your leader; information he was supposed to divulge years ago."

"You knew?" Aurora asked, looking to him.

Forrest shook his head. "He's held it over us all these years."

The figure held his hand up into the air. The sleeve his cloak slipped back revealing the thin, bony arm. Deep purple veins ran the length of it into his hand. As the figure's hand continued to hold in the air, Blaze watched a faint ripple in the air near his palm. There was a swirling motion as dust in the air pulled towards the figure's hand. Then, in a swift swoop a shape tore through the sky, just barely skimming above the heads of the gathered townspeople. A few ducked. Others covered their heads.

Blaze watched as the artifact flew directly into the figure's hand. And it stopped moving immediately. It took the large relic between both hands, twisted it. He pulled off the two ends, threw them onto the ground, and revealed a smaller cylinder.

It held the device out to Blaze. "I leave this in your possession. Follow the directions if you want to live. They found you once. They'll be back to finish the job."

"What about you?" Blaze asked, taking the device. Absentmindedly, his thumb traced over the etched carvings in the side. As he did, the device's carvings illuminated beneath his touch.

"I will not return. Not again. The survival of your town is upon you—all of you. May the Creators take mercy upon you."

The figure raised his staff into the air. There was great power in the air. Energy flowed through the wind, gathering at the single point of the orange orb. The figure's cloak began to billow as he lowered into a kneel.

"How much time do we have before they come back?" Aurora asked quickly.

The figure was already beginning to disappear amidst a shimmer of light. But it looked up to meet Aurora's gaze once more, eyes glowing brightly even bathed in white light.

"You don't," it replied. And in an instant, the figure vanished into the clouds.

When Blaze looked up, the sky was already clearing into pale pinks and crimson reds. But his world seemed to darken even further around him.

Still holding the device, he looked around. All sets of eyes were on him now. He looked to Winslow whose face was stone-white, eyes hollow and dark.

Blaze turned to Forrest, to Aurora, to Hadley.

Forrest placed a firm hand on his back. "So," he murmured in a near-whisper. "I guess you're the new Winslow."

PART TWO
FALL

NINE

Anton Davies kept a solid grasp of his son as he and his wife hurried back to their home. Forrest, Hadley, and Aurora were following. And so were others.

Hundreds of others.

River Ridge had erupted into panic. Hundreds of voices spoke, no clear direction of intent. Some wanted Blaze to open the device straightaway and reveal its secrets. Others wanted him to give it back to Victor Winslow.

The town leader was following them, too.

"We're not going to be able to hide you," Anton said into Blaze's ear. "Either you open it now or never. You have the power. You have a secret they want. As soon as it's revealed, they don't want you anymore."

But in the hurried panic, Blaze didn't reply though he agreed with his father. From behind him, he heard a familiar, aged voice.

"Don't do anything you'll regret, son," Victor Winslow said, brushing through a gathered group of the followers—his followers. "Hand it back at once. Give me that container."

"You kept it from us. Kept it from the town," Forrest said. "He wanted Blaze to have it."

"Don't speak about it as if it's a man," he spat. "He's not one of us! He sent the others to attack us. I'm the glue keeping this town from falling apart. They'd have found us sooner if I didn't do what I did. Now, listen to me, Blaze. Hand it back."

Blaze shook his head. "No," he said, stopping. "I'm not letting you keep more secrets from us. You're not keeping one more secret. We're getting the answers we need; the answers we deserve. We can't figure out what's next unless we know what we're dealing with."

Aurora stepped beside Blaze. "There's more out there than just this town, Mr. Winslow. And that scares you to death. There has to be others, sir."

But Winslow was gritting his teeth together, fists clenched at his side. "There's nothing left! I promise you! Everything is gone!" he screamed. "There hasn't been anything for seventy-three years!" Tears came faster, breaths harsh and gasping. "Everyone is dead. You think that thing—that whatever it is—will save us? Have you gone mad? Gone insane? Everyone is gone!" The town leader buried his face in his hands. "I've spent my life trying to protect you from everything I've seen."

"What have you seen?" Aurora asked. She stepped forward.

"The nightmares," he said simply, shaking his head and wiping his right eye with his hand. "They came in the middle of the night, after the walls went up. Infected everyone. By the end of the first week, millions were dead. I saw the piles of bodies waiting to be burned. Saw the numbers scrawled in blood. They couldn't burry them, not like normal. They started with pits, but even digging the holes took too long. Eventually, they gave up. The bodies were rotting in the streets. Then they came back for round two, set off bombs that wiped out the damned few who didn't die in the first round. We were the only survivors for whatever reason. I tried to tell everyone, tried to warn them, but they laughed it off. Some believed me, but who would believe some kid? I wouldn't have. But I saw it as if I experienced it. And I experienced it as if I had lived it. Even if there is something out there, it's the closest to Hell on Earth I can imagine. I've lived with the horrors of the truth, and tried to protect you all from them. I tried to keep you from ever having to see what I saw. And here I am, the monster."

She stepped back. "We need to work together. We can figure out how to save ourselves."

Winslow pulled back his hands, looked up. "Please, no one can save us from them. No one."

"We have to at least try, sir," Blaze said, pulling the leader's attention. "Even if you don't think anything will work. If we don't try, we'll never know."

Shaking his head, Winslow wiped his eyes with the edge of his tweed jacket. "Please, I beg of you. Do not open that."

Blaze held it, rotating it in his hands. In his grasp, it felt so smooth that he worried it would slip out. While scanning it, he observed a small notch in the top, where it appeared something else could be connected to it.

"Are there more pieces?" he asked.

No one replied.

Blaze started moving again down the road that led to the wall. The townspeople continued to follow; however, he now noticed a few of Winslow's devout followers were armed with weapons.

Time was ticking, and if he were to act, he'd better do it soon.

Taking the device in both hands, gripping the ends, Blaze turned to Winslow. "Are there more? Tell me or I open it."

Winslow eyed to his side. "Don't you dare."

"I have nothing to lose and everything to gain," Blaze said. "I'd think wisely."

"You'll wish you hadn't said that," Winslow said. He looked to his side, to his men. "Get that object from him!"

A few around Winslow pressed off on their feet, running forward. Blaze shot a last glance to Aurora as she pointed down the street.

"Run!"

He shot forward, legs pumping pure adrenaline. He felt his muscles burn as he ran hard, ran fast. Blaze's arms swung rapidly beside him, with the mysterious device held securely in his left hand.

Looking behind, he saw that he had a good head start. The others Winslow had sent after him were older and slower.

But they had heavy weaponry. Rifles dangling from around their necks swung wildly in front of their torsos. A few—the smart ones—grabbed the weapon, ran with it in hand.

Blaze dipped off the road and into the forested area. He made his way down a slight embankment, jumping over a decaying wooden bridge that once covered the now-dry creek bed.

He moved beneath the cover of leaves and into the shadows. Even with his heightened senses, Blaze underestimated the blackness of looming nightfall in the woods. He thought the trees would be black trunks against cobalt sky, paths would be a lighter shade of earth, leaves serving as murky path lights. Instead, he was met with pure darkness. He felt it press into him from all sides and wanted to stop and get his bearings. But his brain screamed for him to run, to continue forward.

Move, Blaze, move!

Heart pounding, blood pumping, he took a few breaths and tried to find some sort of direction or order within the tangled woods. He focused. Light was still light; dark still dark. But he couldn't surrender to his fear. He had to find a way to see in the dark.

But Blaze was called from his head when he heard his name being called in the distance.

He kept moving. They were further back than he had thought.

"*Nothing to lose, eh?*" called out Winslow, his voice straining to be heard through the brush.

Then he heard a woman scream, a man shout.

"Don't come back, Blaze! Run!" the female voice cried out before being muffled.

It was his mother.

Blaze spun around, pressed back through the trees towards the road. He could feel the darkness pulling into him, pressing and suffocating. Adrenaline fueled him, propelled him. He should've known there was nothing off the table when it came to Victor Winslow.

The packed trees loomed high above him, but he saw light at the other end. He heard the collected crowd and their softened voices against the brush.

And he stepped back into society, the relic still in hand, but his heart nearly ruptured.

Blaze's eyes widened with fear to see his mother and father kneeling upon the asphalt surface, hands atop their heads.

Winslow paced in front of them, hands clasped at his waist. He was facing the opposite direction of Blaze when he said, "Didn't you say you had nothing to lose? Hear that, Mom and Dad? What a son you have."

Lorna shook her head, squeezing her eyes shut. "I told you not to come back."

"Silence!" Winslow hissed. "Don, please."

Don Engle pressed the barrel of his rifle to the back of Lorna's head, held it there as if toying with her.

"If you're going to kill one of us, make it me, Victor," said Anton. "Leave my wife out of this."

"Don't tell me what to do. Your son is harboring crucial technology that could put all of us in danger; holding it for hostage or ransom," he said stiffly. "Two can play at that game."

"Look, don't hurt them. I'll give you what you want, on one condition," Blaze said.

"You aren't really in a good place for negotiation, Mr. Davies," said Winslow. "But I'll humor you. What?"

"You tell me what you know," said Blaze. "Tell me why this is so important—"

"It came from the Stranger—from the being you saw. That's why it's important. It could be a weapon," said Winslow. "We can't trust it."

Blaze was beginning to step back following the edge of the road. Behind him, the wall was towering above, the pale blue lights lining it having come on while he was in the woods. The pair had separated from the remainder of the group.

It was Blaze and Winslow, now, in the clearing.

"What does this do?"

"I don't know," said Winslow.

"Liar."

"I said I don't know. That's why we need to investigate it."

But as Winslow finished his sentence, there was a rumbling beside him. In a swift eruption, a narrow white pole erupted from the ground. Blaze turned to it, looked back to Winslow.

A glowing blue button was on the top. Had there been some sensor between it and the device in Blaze's hand? There had to have been.

The light illuminated Blaze's side.

"Don't you dare!" said Winslow.

Blaze looked to the device in his hand and then to the button on the box. It was now or never. He slipped the artifact inside his pocket.

"Sorry, sir," said Blaze. "It's our destiny."

He slammed his hand onto the button.

"Fire! Fire!" screamed Winslow.

The two gunshots tore across the space, and though Blaze's heart lurched, sound from behind him grabbed his attention.

Solid, swooping quakes rocked the earth below. Blaze felt everything deep within, far beneath the base of his feet. Before him, there was movement. The panel of wall began to separate. As it moved, dust shot out around the cracks at the surface. Plumes of dust rose, masking the seemingly ancient, yet surreal, carvings.

Blaze turned around. Winslow stood at the front of several dozen too curious to stay away, too fearful to step nearer. A few with weapons adjusted their grips. He saw his parents lying on the asphalt, and felt the tension grip his throat. He turned back to the wall, unable to look at his parents any further and looked skyward, tracing the top of the wall with his focused gaze. The gap was widening, but slowing. The trembling softened, lessening into a barely noticeable tremor.

And then nothing...

Silence.

The whirl of wind, gusts of air from the outside world, rushed past the trio. Blaze stood strong in its presence, watching as the thick dust continued to dissipate into the sky.

Forrest and Aurora raced up to stand beside him. Aurora took hold of his hand.

Blaze noticed, only then, that his grip on Aurora's hand was vice-like and tears were stinging his eyes. But she held it and didn't complain. He turned to her as every fiber of him wanted to run, to take her with him and retreat to safety. But Blaze was rooted to the ground, much like the ancient walls had been. The veil of dust was rapidly disintegrating, fading into dark blues as sky became visible behind. Wind from the outside world continued to push through the newly-opened gap, from across the distant plains, pressing into the soil and whipping old forest decay around them into a small vortex.

But as the dust continued to rise, vanishing nearly entirely, the three stepped back.

They weren't alone.

Standing before them was a group of three others—others like them.

At the front of the three, stood a woman. Though crowned with thin lines—almost like the etchings in the wall—her dark eyes were lively, skin bronze-brown. A scar stretched around the right side of her face, from the edge of her eyebrow down to her lip. It was old. Decades old. Even the aging effect of time had met the scar with its relentless touch, merging into the canvas of her face with lines curving around it, from it.

Beside her, to her left, stood a tall, olive skinned boy— thin and lanky—with chocolate brown eyes widened in curious wonder. His brows were thick, yet groomed, and his hair, russet brown, was short and curly. Stern and angular features were accented by a strong jaw and a thick lower-lip.

The third stranger was a second, younger female, porcelain skinned with blonde hair pulled back into a tight bun. Her features were soft, warm and welcoming, eyes bright green and kind.

The two females wore clothes of mismatched styles. The male, however, wore a tight-fitting black T-shirt, dark charcoal military-style tactical pants, and dirty, old boots. A Navy-blue flannel shirt, two sizes two big was wrapped around his waist, the arms hanging freely at his sides. The two females wore more colorful attire, patched like an old quilt in spots.

"It's about time you guys breathed some fresh air," said the elder female. "Don't be afraid. We're like you."

Blaze tried to speak, but grief-stricken, no words came. He turned to Aurora, to Forrest, before looking back at the strangers.

"How'd you find us?" Aurora asked quietly, reserved.

The tall male, perhaps only a few years older than Blaze, chuckled, smirking. "Hard to miss these enclosures. You can see them for miles. When we saw the storm appear and disappear, we figured there was activity behind the walls." He looked past the three to the gathered rest behind them. "Looks like we have a bit of an audience. Hello," he said, raising his hand in greeting, raising his brows.

"Don't mock them, Donovan," said the eldest woman. "I'm Nori. Nori Kouma. Smart-mouth, here, is Donovan. And this—" she gestured towards the blonde-haired girl— "is Amelia."

Donovan stepped forward towards Blaze, reaching out a strong hand. "You are?"

"Er—Blaze. And this is Forrest and Aurora."

"Blaze, friends of Blaze—good to meet you. Nice change? Meeting others from the great beyond, I mean?" he laughed.

Sensing movement behind him, he turned. Approaching slowly was Winslow.

"I ask that you close the wall and leave us in peace."

"We came in peace," Amelia said. "Jesus, I sound like one of the Council or something."

Nori stepped forward, readjusting her grip on her rifle.

"Is that necessary?" Winslow asked, motioning with a trembling finger towards the firearm.

Nori quirked her scarred brow. "I don't know? *Is it?*" She motioned to the bodies of Lorna and Anton. "And you're afraid of us? We're the monsters? The demons?"

Winslow's lips pressed together, shaking his head. "Why are you here?"

Nori swung her rifle around to her back, wiping her hands on the fabric of her pants. "We should be asking why you haven't joined the rest of us in the world. It's about time. You're fifty-years late."

The citizens of River Ridge turned to him, analyzed his every movement. He was treading water, about to drown. The waves were growing stronger, the tides turning on his reign.

"My town was safer behind the wall. We learned how to be self-sufficient, protect ourselves and our land."

"You say that as if we had a choice to leave," Forrest said. "Did we?"

Winslow looked to him, face firm in expression. "After time had passed, yes.

"You conniving piece of shit!" Forrest shot forward, grabbing a hold of Winslow's sweat-stained, buttoned collar. His fingers wrapped around it, face contorting in fury.

"Forrest!" Aurora boomed. "Enough. Let him go."

Nostrils flared, Forrest squeezed Winslow's collar once more, twisting the weathered fabric within his grasp before letting him go. The town leader stepped back quickly. A few surrounded him as he smoothed his shirt, fixed his hair. Forrest turned around, shut his eyes; breathed.

Forrest turned to Aurora. "He's not worth it."

"Right," she agreed. "He's not. We can't change the past. What matters now is the present and the future it leads to."

But Blaze wasn't ready to let this go. Not at all. He looked to the leader, taking breaths, steadying himself. He needed to approach this carefully. Wisely. There was one chance—only one.

"What do you mean after some time?" he kept his voice cool, restrained despite his hatred for the man and for what had just happened. His voice darkened, trying to maintain his restraint as he continued. "Could we leave the whole time?"

Winslow breathed loudly threw his nostrils, shifting in place. As his lower lip lowered, revealing his yellowed, horse-like teeth accented by recessed gums, he cleared his throat. "I knew we had to be secured for twenty-five years. The wall would not open, under any circumstances, until that time had passed."

"Twenty-five years after they rose?" asked Blaze.

Winslow nodded. Several around him, seemingly having been protecting him, stepped back with faces suddenly empty of color, hurt reflecting in their eyes.

"So, I take it he's this town's chosen one, right?" Amelia asked, taking the pressure off Blaze of needing to respond.

"Chosen one?" questioned Aurora.

"The one the moon walkers, sky people, aliens— whatever you've decided to label them as—picked to share information with the rest of y'all."

"*He never shared shit,*" Forrest quipped beneath his breath, pressing a closed fist against the cleft of his chin.

But Amelia must have heard him, for she replied, "I'm getting that vibe, too."

"I saw it when I was five-years-old," Winslow said quietly. "I've lived every day since with his image burned into my mind, his words and images stamped into my skull. Everything I have done for this town—for these people—has been done as a result of what I saw."

"Keeping everything secret? Keeping us locked in here?" began Forrest. "Face it, Winslow, you did it for the power. You liked keeping people guessing, bowing to your feet. If you shared what you knew—everything you knew—you'd have lost your adoring followers. You became a church of yourself. Quit acting like you don't love all of this attention, especially nowadays."

"You think I asked for this? This may be a stretch for you to understand, but I wish it had picked someone else. I didn't want this life. I had no choice. He picked me, destroyed me, and left me to pick up the pieces."

"Looks like you've picked them up pretty well. You seem pretty content," said Donovan, crossing his arms across his chest. "To be honest, there are very few of you left. Chosen ones, I mean. We've only met a few. From what we've seen, they didn't usually pick children. They picked adults, so I'm not sure why you got the short straw. On another note, the others that couldn't cope usually didn't last long. So, I think you're exaggerating a bit. The real 'broken' ones took blades to their wrists, pills to their mouths, guns to their temples. You're a dying breed, old-man," he said.

Winslow did not reply.

Forrest was next to speak, changing the topic from Winslow back to the present—to what mattered now. "So, what are you here for? You want in?"

"*In there?* Lord no," Nori said. "We've come to take anyone who wants to leave to a safe place, a place where other survivors—'*Reapers*' we call ourselves—live, breathe, and survive day after day."

Blaze turned around expecting to see a group of citizens approach the line of division between the two groups, but no one came. Everyone remained still, firm-footed on the old earth.

"Boy, what a turn-out," Donovan replied. "Let's try that again. Do you want to continue to stay her with him?" She paused, pointing to Winslow. "Or do you want to leave with us? Come on guys, don't get too excited, now."

Again, they were met with total silence. Blaze peered around, running his sight across the collection of timid and fearful faces.

He didn't blame them, for this—what existed behind the wall—was new. New often meant scary, a stepping out of one's comfort zone was never supposed to come easy or without great effort. As much as the citizens of River Ridge likely wanted to get out, now that the moment was here, they feared it. In fact, they possibly hated themselves for ever wanting out.

Even the sliver of sight through the wall and behind the three strangers—Nori, Amelia, and Donovan—was enough, like putting one's toe into cold water. They weren't ready to jump straight in, but nor was Blaze. Nor Forrest or Aurora.

But someone would have to do it. There was always a first and somebody would have to be that first.

With thoughts, quick and unfiltered, rushing through Blaze's brain, it didn't come easy to latch onto a solid one, hold it close and really decide what his next choice was. How could he stay back? Stay where his mother and father had been killed? How could he go forward? Forward, where his mother and father had dreamt of stepping foot into, without them?

It wouldn't come easy leaving them behind. River Ridge was the only home Blaze knew. Stepping out meant he was leaving everything behind, everyone he knew: friends, neighbors, teachers.

But it meant he would be living, moving forward, for his parents and with them by his side in a new way.

When it came to death, Blaze didn't see it as the end, but merely a change. Maybe he was a fool? Maybe there was nothing. Perhaps it was just lights out? But he longed for something more. It brought him comfort. Brought him peace. Even after their death, he knew his parents were with him, just in a new way. He could still talk to them. Could still feel them. Death was a change, but never an end. He intended to believe that for himself and for them.

To remain in River Ridge was to maintain the status quo that Anton and Lorna had always encouraged him to challenge. To stay here made their deaths, and what they sought to protect Blaze from until the very end, a waste.

Tears held at the corners of his eyes, and breaths came shallow and shaky. He knew what he had to do, though the realization seared through every vein like fire.

Twisting around to face those behind him, he peered through the crowd, past Winslow; past everyone. He saw himself as a child running through the streets, playing catch with his father. He saw himself walking, waist-high, beside his mother to the town farmer's market to collect fresh vegetables and rare fruits.

He imagined his home. He pictured the yard, his kitchen, and the conversations held within its four walls. Though the memories would remain, he couldn't help but feel he was losing everything.

But he loved his family and the values they taught him. The pep-talks he received from both had prepared him for this moment. If he loved them, he needed to let them go. And before he could stop himself and retract his offer, Blaze raised his hand.

"I want in."

Forrest placed his hand on Blaze's back. "Me too."

"Dude, you have people here. Family that loves you," said Blaze. "Stay with them. I have no one left. It's okay."

"I know," Forrest replied. "But I'm your family now. That's why I'm coming, too. We've been brothers from the beginning, and you're not doing this alone."

Aurora stepped forward. "Someone has to keep you both on a leash," she laughed softly. "I'm coming with, too."

Nori nodded firmly. "If you're coming, we leave now. Anyone else."

Forrest turned, searching the crowd. "Hadley?"

But Hadley stood back behind a group of others. She moved through the gathering, covered her eyes as she passed Blaze's parents.

"Forr—I gotta stay back with Mom and Dad. Come back for us, and we'll go."

"Leaving me to test the waters?" he asked, sniffling a laugh. Blaze could see the hurt in his eyes.

"Someone's gotta do it," Hadley said. "Aurora's going to keep you both on a leash. I'll keep Mom and Dad on theirs. Good luck. You'll see us later."

Forrest took a breath.

Blaze put his hand on the top of Forrest's shoulder. "She's right, you know. You'll see them soon."

But Forrest kept his head lowered, eyes focused on the old asphalt below their feet. Leaves from the outside world blew in. Identical to those within, but at the same time there was something different.

"*I'm not so sure about that,*" Forrest murmured beneath his breath, soft enough that only Blaze and he could hear. No one else.

"We will," Blaze said firmly.

Forrest turned to him, forced a pressed-lip smile. "Even if you're wrong, I appreciate hearing that in the moment."

"I believe it," said Blaze. "Just think of it as scoping out the horizons. An adventure, like we went on as kids."

"I think this'll be a bit different, Blaze. But again, I appreciate it," he smiled.

But ahead of them, Nori was growing impatient, shifting her weight on her small feet. Her larger frame rocked back and forth, and as she folded her arms across her chest, she cleared her throat. "We're losing daylight fast. We need to make it back to the Haven. So, say your goodbyes, convince any others to follow—whatever. Regardless, we leave, with or without you, in two minutes.

And two minutes started then.

Forrest and Aurora said their goodbyes, gave their hugs. They said what needed to be said, shared parting words and dreams of the future together. Blaze stood in place, unable to bring himself to look to his parents. He couldn't say goodbye. Not like this. From behind the group, a few called out telling them not to go.

'It wasn't safe,' they repeated over and over. And while a part of Blaze wanted to believed them—a tiny part actually did—the rest of him couldn't move past the reality of what River Ridge had become in the past week.

He couldn't brush past Ahmed, nor his parents. River Ridge was safe for some, but not for him. Not anymore. And it wasn't for Forrest or Aurora either. If it was, he seriously doubted they'd join him, regardless of the *brotherhood* status he and Forrest shared. Even the strongest of bonds could be broken in times of desperation or of logic.

It was stupid to leave, perhaps even childish. Why go with strangers when you could stay with a town older than your family, with neighbors whose ancestors were friends and neighbors with yours? The reasons of why to go were drowned out by the reasons why not. But at that same time, Blaze knew he couldn't stay. He simply couldn't.

As Forrest and Aurora parted ways with their families, they turned, didn't look back, and approached Blaze. No one else had come.

Of the whole town, the remainder wanted to stay with Winslow behind the walls.

"You're making a mistake," Winslow said stiffly, stepping forward from the group of collected citizens. "Going with them is walking to your deaths. I told you once, I'll tell you again. There's nothing else out there."

"How do you know that, old-man? Like you've been out? Taken a risk? We come from outside. There's something out there, or else we wouldn't exist," Donovan said.

"Quiet down," Nori instructed him. "You won't change their minds. As silver-tongued as you are, Donovan, you can't pursue the firm-brained. And frankly, I won't waste my breath on relics of a by-gone era, who use violence to intimidate."

"I reject that," Winslow said, raising his voice. "I think you know better than anyone that living here wasn't a punishment. Sure beats the wrath cast upon the outside world."

"Buddy," Donovan said, walking forward with long legs leading his stride. "We're all in Hell. We just have different versions." He stopped beside Aurora, eyed her down and extended a hand. "Ready, gorgeous?"

Aurora rolled her eyes. "Not for you."

Blaze tried to hold back a smile. As handsome as Donovan was—older, too—he was elated to see that Aurora held her ground. He should've known better than to think she would suddenly go after him just because he was good-looking, built, and tall. What he and Aurora had was special; years in the making.

Blaze reached down to his pocket, and skimmed his hand across the surface. He could feel the device secured, pressed deep into his pocket.

Satisfied, he stepped forward, taking that solid step onto the path that was his new life. The dirt, freshly uncovered and damp, shifted slightly beneath his feet. He could feel the tremble through his thin, narrow frame. He moved past Donovan, past Amelia and Nori, and took his first steps beyond.

Aurora and Forrest also joined him, trailing in his wake. As Blaze turned, he was silently heartbroken to see they were alone. Though, any other belief of others joining them—a mass exodus from River Ridge—was merely a far-reaching fantasy.

Forrest craned his neck around, turned to his family who were holding back tears. Aurora turned back, too, taking Blaze's hand and squeezing it. But it would be Winslow who would speak again, ruining this final moment shared.

"You leave, you don't come back. That's how this works. Think wisely," he said, several dozen feet away from the perimeter.

"You can't keep us from returning, Mr. Winslow. This was your town, but it's not yours anymore," Aurora said. "These walls have officially decided that River Ridge is ready to be shared with the world. We'll be back when it's time. We might bring supplies, knowledge…"

"No, I assure you, you won't."

From his pocket, Winslow withdrew a small white device of his own that appeared to shimmer beneath the early-afternoon sun. It was small, fit nicely in the palm of his knotted hands. He ran his thumb across the top of the surface before suddenly pressing down firmly.

"To answer your question, Blaze, yes there were other objects."

The trembling began again. Blaze's eyes widened in disbelief.

"No!" Hadley cried from the crowd, hurrying forward. But Mr. Kremer grabbed her, yanked her back.

"The whole time?" Blaze called out over the roar of the closing wall.

A smirk grew across the leader's narrow face. *"The whole time."*

The dust rose again, this time more subdued, as the wall closed. Forrest stepped forward, stopping just feet from the track the wall would follow. His voice remained silent, though Blaze could see his back rising and falling quickly, fists bunched at his sides.

Aurora moved forward, steadied him as the wall shut fully.

Blaze stood still, eyes cast downward again upon the fresh earth. Wind rushed through the tall grasses around them, swirling them in disorganized chaos.

Amelia walked to Blaze, took his chin and raised it with her gentle fingers. "Hey, keep your head up. You might be able to come back, might not. We don't know that much about these walls. They kind-of have minds of their own, you know. Organic lifeforms, almost like their makers. They've opened for us in the past, so in a few weeks, a few days, they might open again."

"And he'll shut them again," said Blaze.

"That may be," Amelia agreed. "I'm not going to bullshit you. You all have been through enough. We're about transparency and honesty. We don't have much going for us out here in the wasteland, but those two things maintain some sense of order."

"How bad is it?" Blaze asked, silently wondering if maybe he'd been wrong to take this chance. He wanted to keep his mind distracted from his parents, keep the questions coming, the answers flowing. Silence would give him time to think.

"It's fine and at times, not fine. But we have a good group. You'll be safe, fed, protected—"

"Given that you contribute," Nori interjected. "No one gets a free ride, especially out here. There are other groups; some that fight others for limited supplies. There's violence, but mostly at night. It's best you don't go out after dark."

"You're not really helping solidify our decision to leave River Ridge," said Forrest.

Donovan crossed his arms across his chest. "It's not our job to do that. We're all nearly adults here—apart from Nori who could be our mother, maybe grandmother—"

"As if I haven't heard you use that in the past?" quipped Nori.

Donovan's brows lifted. "Look, Forrest, you made an adult decision. Made the right one, in my opinion, but it was your choice. You want to be coddled? You're not in the right company. But we'll help your lot find your way. This is an opportunity for growth, to spread your wings and fly. I suggest taking it."

Forrest nodded, running his hand through his wavy hair. Blaze looked to Aurora, unsure of where to go next with the conversation.

She took the hint and took over.

"Our friend, Ahmed, saw behind the wall a few days ago, after there was some sort of explosion."

"Explosion? They said to be honest," Forrest said. "Say what it was."

"We don't know what *it* was," Aurora said. "Not for sure."

Forrest shook his head. "You guys know anything about that?"

"An explosion? Here, at the wall? No," Donovan said.

"What about part of the wall melting?" he pressed.

Donovan's brows lowered as he raised his eyes to the sky momentarily. "Look, let me save us the game of twenty-questions. We don't know anything about any explosion, damage, or breakage in the wall. Does that help?"

"Clears things up," Forrest said.

Aurora turned to him "Can I have the floor back?" she asked.

Forrest motioned with his hands, stepping aside. "All yours."

She cleared her throat, waited a few moments before continuing. "He claimed he saw vehicles. Saw bodies. I wasn't with him. They were."

"Then maybe they should be asking the question?" Amelia offered.

"Maybe so," Aurora agreed.

"I don't know what the question is," Nori asked. "Sounded like a statement."

"Are there bodies?" Blaze asked.

"Sure," Nori said unfazed. "A bunch of cars and trucks. Look over there, through the grass. There are skeletons. Mostly separated by time, settled into the dirt. But you dig, you'll find something—or someone."

"How did they find this place?" Blaze asked.

Donovan sighed, clenching his square jaw. "You say that as if it were invisible," he jeered acridly. His posture stiffened. "It's as visible now as it was then. If millions—fuck, billions—were dying around you and you saw some new, high-tech enclosure miles away, I'm sure you'd make an attempt to get in, too."

Nori raised fingertips to her brow, shaking her head. "Enough with the smart comments, Donovan. It's understandable they ask questions, even ones you think are dumb. We'll talk as we walk? Deal?"

"Deal," agreed Blaze, moving forward onto the ruined streets of the world outside.

"I warn you," Nori said carefully, "you might not like what we tell you next."

"Honesty and transparency, like you said," Aurora replied. "We're ready for it."

"Doubt you got that back there," Donovan said.

Pressing forward, Aurora lifted her brows. "I don't think we ever got it."

Forrest started, "Nora—"

"My name is Nori, not *Nora*."

Forrest shook his head quickly. "No—No offense. Sorry. I—I like that name. Didn't mean to offend you."

"Nora's a nice name, but not mine. Start over."

"Nori—" Forrest was sure to enunciate, to be deliberate. "How did it all begin?"

"Turn to your religious text for that," Nori said, checking across the street both ways. "If you want the last seventy-years, I can help you with that."

"She was there for it, too," Donovan quipped.

"Silence, Smart-Mouth, or I'll talk to your granddad."

"What's he gonna do? Hit me with his walker?"

Amelia sighed loudly. "Donovan, shut it."

Nori slowed her stride letting Donovan take the lead. "You want the short answer or the long answer?"

Forrest shrugged his shoulders. "How far away is your home base?"

"I'll give you the long answer," replied Nori.

Blaze increased his pace, stepping beside Forrest. Aurora did too, moving beside Nori. Amelia trailed in the back, rifle held across her chest, with both hands cupping it to her breast.

"I don't want to overwhelm you, kids—"

"We can handle it," Aurora said.

Nori turned aside, shooting a watchful eye at her. "Please, allow me to finish. I don't want to overwhelm you, but I'm gonna be honest. I tell the truth. It's not pretty out here, even now. It was worse then. By the end of this, you may want to return back home, but I warn against that."

"That bad?" Blaze asked.

Nori ignored him. "God—no matter how many times I tell this story to others we rescue, I never figure out a good way to tell the story. Where do you even begin?"

"The beginning is always a good start," Donovan suggested over his shoulder.

"Mind your mouth," Nori spat. She paused, breathed, turned back to Forrest and Blaze, then to Aurora. "I don't have the answers. The more we come into contact with others like you, we're putting the story together. The gaps in the story close in, loose-ends tie up. We're continuing to learn, so don't think this is the full story. This is just what we have now, at this moment."

"Starting with the walls, then. What do you know about them?" asked Blaze.

"Not much. You probably know more about them than we do. At the beginning of the Illness, they rose just before, along with a dome. The dome vanished shortly after. None of it was man-made, we know that. You probably figured that much, too."

"We put one and two together," Forrest agreed.

"Good. At least you weren't in denial," Nori said. "Walls go up, domes go up. Silence within your world for the next seventy-plus years, right?"

Blaze nodded. "Right."

"Well, wrong on the outside, though. When your walls went up, our world fell down. The Illness was some sort of virus—a contagion that spread. It spread fast. Spread quickly. By the end of the first two-weeks, millions were dead. Society fell apart practically in two nights. First started the riots, the looting. Medical services were overwhelmed and swamped. There was nothing they could do for the damned."

Nori took a breath, wiped sweat from her scarred brow. "The media tried covering it up—television, news, Internet." She looked to the three, saw blank looks on their faces. "Those were things people watched and listened to for entertainment and information," she explained. "People were connected across the world via the Internet—"

"Remember who you're talking to," Amelia offered quietly, interrupting her leader. "They don't know what any of this is."

"We're not idiots," Forrest said.

"So, you know what it is then?" asked Amelia.

"*Not exactly...*"

Amelia stopped in her tracks, running her hand through her hair. "First rule, don't lie to impress. It isn't cute and makes you look like an insecure fool. Just don't do it," Amelia said.

"Noted," Forrest replied.

"The Internet was a database, like a massive digital book that contained unlimited information, connected people all across the world through computers, devices, even cars near the end," Amelia said.

"Are you telling this story or am I?" Nori asked Amelia.

"Sorry. Your stage. Go for it."

"All right, so, the media covers it up until they can't. Body count rises quickly and it, like everythin' else, overwhelms the world. This wasn't exclusive to us. It was going on worldwide, at the same time. The idiots in charge were playing politics, blame games; trying to put on happy faces while the rest of us were dying. When they tell you not to panic, that's when you panic. No one was safe from the Illness, either. Rich or poor, if you were gonna die, you were gonna die. That's just how it went. By the end of the second week the President was dead, her Vice-President was dead, and three people down the line of succession were dead. By then, it was already game-over anyway so it didn't matter who was next in line."

Blaze asked, "How many died by the end of it?"

"Next to everybody. They lost track really early on. Some estimate it as high as eight billion by the end," Nori said. "We never got a solid number. All my mother told me was that, close to home, they couldn't burn the dead fast enough. She didn't like to talk about it. Haunted her 'til the day she died."

"And how long did the Illness last?" asked Aurora.

"Until it took everyone it wanted," Nori said. "As simple as that. About a year and then it went away."

"Went away?" Blaze shook his head, keeping his sight forward, piecing together the story in his mind. "Was there a vaccine for it?"

"Get real. It took out the scientists as fast as the rest of us. They couldn't have figured one out if they tried. One day it just—you know—*vanished*. The immune didn't realize it until years after. Why we were immune, don't ask. I don't know."

"Are we immune?" asked Blaze.

"Like I know that," Nori replied coolly. "You were safe behind the wall while the rest of us were out here fending for our lives. The others inside were, so I guess you're lucky, too. Not sure why you needed the wall though. It's a bit of a mystery."

"We don't know why, either. *Sorry*," Aurora said.

"I don't blame you," Nori said. "Just doesn't seem fair only a few thousand were fully protected. I shouldn't criticize you though. I wasn't even alive for most of it. I was here just for the scarred remains of what the Illness and bombs left for us."

Blaze cleared his throat. "So, after it went away, after the bombs went off, then what? What takes us to this point? To now?"

"You want seventy-years in one answer?" asked Nori, but before Blaze could clarify, she began. "The rest of us were left to pick up the pieces of a world left behind. Some couldn't handle it—the pressure, the reality of what was left. I'm guessing some, like my granddaddy, put a pistol in their mouths. They couldn't cope after a while. Positivity died when the rest of the world did. I guess it weeded out the weak ones. Only the fighters kept going and kept fighting. So, I ask you, are you going to be fighters or should we drop you off here? I have no patience for weakness, for those who won't carry their rightful weight."

"We didn't come this far to be paperweights," Forrest said. "We're not here to take up space. We want to help, and we want to start over."

Nori nodded slowly. "We've been promised empty words before. We'll give you the benefit of the doubt, though. You seem like good kids. Come from good families."

"Tell us how we can help you," Blaze said.

Donovan stopped, turned to the three. Both Nori and Amelia did too. Dust blew aside in their wake.

"You can start," said Donovan, "by telling us about the capsule device that was located in your town. What do you know about it?"

"How do you *know* about that?" Forrest asked.

"Please, you're not the first group we've rescued from the walled-in cities," said Donovan. "We're helping you, you help us."

Blaze turned to Forrest. They nodded in mutually understood agreement.

"Not much," said Blaze. "We're not really sure what it was. What it was used for."

"Liar," Amelia cursed.

Nori swiftly spun around, shooting her a severe glare. "You don't know that. Don't accuse the innocent."

"Someone used it," said Donovan. "Amongst the rest, it led to the wall opening up. Do you know who activated it?"

Blaze swallowed firmly, steadying his breath. They were too new to share everything. He had to play this carefully, be mindful. He shrugged his shoulders to Forrest, turned to Aurora. "I—I don't know. They never said. Guessing Winslow?"

"What's Winslow?" asked Nori.

"Our leader."

"And it's with him?" asked Nori.

Blaze nodded. "Last I saw," he lied. Meanwhile, he felt the device pressing into his thigh. Even through the layers of fabric of his pants and underwear, he could feel its icy touch splitting through straight to his spine. Blaze could feel trickling sweat on his brow, fearing they'd attribute it to his own budding nerves.

"And that's all you know?" Nori asked carefully. "Nothing further?"

Blaze swallowed, pressing his lips together tightly. He wasn't lying when he shook his head. *"Nothing,"* he murmured.

With a nod of agreement amongst them, Nori, Amelia, and Donovan seemed satisfied for now. They started forward again, down the abandoned ruins of roadways of the outside world. Blaze turned to Aurora, to Forrest. They didn't meet his gaze. Not once.

Satisfied was the best way to phrase it. He'd given enough information—as little as it was—to satisfy the craving. An offering of sorts to the three strangers. All was fine now, for now.

TEN

Blaze wasn't sure how long they had been walking, but day had turned to night, light to shadows. One foot in front of the other, over and over again.

Along their path, neighborhoods stood in ruins. Homes were dirtied. Windows not boarded up were broken, shattered long ago. Shrubbery surrounding the homes was overgrown, though Blaze could imagine the yards to have once been neatly groomed, homes freshly painted and maintained. Vehicles sat upon cracked concrete driveways, their tires flat, paint burned white by years of sun exposure.

But most disturbing was the silence, the whistling down the streets and through the covering of overgrown curbside trees.

Aurora stepped beside Blaze, leaning her head. Through the corner of her mouth, she said, "I hate this. It's a ghost town."

"Just shows the reality of what happened," replied Blaze. "Seems like no one got out unscathed."

Forrest slowed his stride, turned to Nori. "What happened here?"

"I don't know what happened *here*," Nori said, almost annoyed. "It's no different than anywhere else, though. The riots led people to board up their homes and hide inside. By then, they were probably already sick and dying. The survivors, like us, went in and took what we needed. Didn't come easily, though. Felt terrible breaking into people's homes, but the dead didn't need the supplies. We had to keep on living. Supply has dried up, obviously. We've become more self-sufficient in the years since, thank God, but there's still some supplies out there if you look hard enough."

"I can imagine you guys fight over what little remains?" Aurora said.

Amelia turned. "Not within our own group," she said firmly. "We're not animals, but there are other groups that act like it. Groups that feel they're entitled to an unfair share. This is survival. We will protect our supplies no matter what."

"Other groups?" asked Blaze.

"We're not the only ones left, man. Obviously," Donovan replied. "Communication is limited, but frankly we're not that friendly with them. They don't like us, we don't like them."

"You call yourself the Reapers," Forrest said. "What do you call them?"

"Enemies," answered Donovan. "We're not that creative, as you can tell."

They continued forward in silence now. While Blaze's head was filled with questions, the last thing he wanted to do was to annoy the new group. He figured there would be plenty of time to get caught up on the last seventy-plus-years.

Eventually, Donovan consulted with his map, then with Nori. They turned at an intersection and led them for another few miles before reaching an on-ramp to a large highway.

Abandoned vehicles lined the on-ramp, askew and staggered in ways that Blaze wondered if they'd somehow been moved after running out of gas. Some were burned-out, charred remains. Others had been left to the outcome of time. Some trunks were open with debris scattered about on the roadway and within, the interiors caked with dead leaves and dirt.

As they passed them, Blaze wondered where the drivers had gone. Had they run out of gas, like he thought? Had the occupants decided to try their luck on foot for safety and survival? Were they lucky?

He imagined they were desperate leaving their vehicle behind. They likely wondered if they'd ever come back to their vehicles or their home. Blaze hoped they found some form of safety, in whatever form it would come, yet his mind explored the much darker fate they likely faced.

Gazing straight ahead, a tiny pinhole of movement interrupted the still picture ahead. Moving fast, tiny and black, it approached quickly. Seemingly without awareness of the six lined in its path, two lights—high beams—illuminated, identifying the shape as a vehicle.

Bubbling up, anxiety flowed through Blaze's veins. He felt it knotting up his stomach, like a giant fist squeezing his guts, twisting them around in circles. He felt he'd be sick.

Aurora cleared her throat. "Should we be hiding? We've got company."

Donovan paused, steadying himself on the shell of a burned-out vehicle beside them in the furthest left lane. He motioned with his right hand for the rest to stay back.

"Hold on…" he murmured quietly to himself.

"Friend or foe?" Nori questioned.

"Hold on. Still determining that. Patience, please."

From within the fast-moving vehicle, probably only two-hundred or so feet away now, a shape extended out of the driver's window. Thin and narrow, Blaze squinted hoping to be able to make out what it was.

But as the truck approached, something unfurled itself from the narrow shape: loose, waving fabric—a flag. As the vehicle approached closer, slowing in speed, Blaze observed the flag was really a section of a white bedsheet attached to a wooden dowel, knotted to the wood at the corners of the thin fabric.

Regardless, it was effective.

A sign of peace or surrender.

Blaze was able to relax. To breathe.

Plumes of dust rose in the vehicle's wake, and the six remained still, watching as the truck came to a slow, wobbly stop. The figure within the vehicle was obscured behind a tinted windshield. It pulled in the flag, set it aside.

The truck was a Jeep, rust-red and heavily aged. But Blaze was stunned to see a vehicle from the old world running and running reasonably well. The engine was loud, more of a roar than a gentle purr.

Donovan stepped closer and aside as the door opened, and then moved even closer. Nori motioned for the three to follow her and Amelia. Blaze took the lead, curious to learn the identity of the driver.

When he turned the corner, the driver was deep in conversation with Donovan. Hunched over the steering wheel, resting his forearms on the top, was an old man with a fringe of gray-white hair around his balding scalp. The man wore large glasses, masking many of his wrinkles behind the impressive frames. Jowls sagged at the corners of his lips. His expression was stone firm, eyes laser focused. He looked up, met Blaze's gaze, then looked to Donovan.

"Who's this?" asked Forrest from beside Blaze.

Donovan turned to the three, rubbed sweat from his left brow. "My grandfather. He's gonna give us a lift."

"Where?" asked Blaze.

"Home," he replied. "Unless you'd rather walk?"

* * *

Previously bumpy and curved roads became short and perpendicular the closer to the city they got. Blaze found himself studying the scenery, making a mental map of where they were and where they had come from. Though it wouldn't save him in the slightest, maintaining some sense of awareness made him feel at ease in the presence of so many new faces.

Though the strangers' intentions seemed genuine and of care, Blaze knew at least one of them—among him, Aurora, and Forrest—would need to be mindful and not let the new people in too far. At least not yet.

"We didn't get your name, sir," Aurora said softly, clasping her hands in her lap from the third row, beside Blaze.

Nori, sitting up-front, turned and quirked a brow. "Honey, you're gonna have to speak up. Carl's a bit hard of hearing."

Donovan shifted around to face the three. "Good guy, but doesn't say much. I s'pose eighty-something years on Earth do that to a person. Especially eighty-something in *this* world."

"So he was here for all of it?" asked Blaze.

Donovan nodded, turning to face his grandfather for a mere moment. He turned back to Blaze, pressed his lips together. "Yeah," he said quietly, voice lowered. "He was old enough to understand what was going on, too."

Aurora breathed out her nose, shaking her head in empathy. "Talk about pulling a short stick."

Donovan's brows raised as he laughed softly, tilting his head. "No kidding. Not many are left to remember it. They're dying by the day, now. But don't get any ideas," he warned, "my grandfather doesn't do interviews. He doesn't talk about

PETER GULGOWSKI

the past, and he's in a good place," he said flatly. "Took him years to work past the horrors he lived through. I want to keep him there, and I intend to protect that."

"Having an open dialogue might help him. Avoidance works, I suppose. But it doesn't heal," Aurora said.

Donovan's eyes went cold, his expression hardened. "So you're a psychologist, now?"

"I'm just saying—"

"Look, you don't know what you're talking about," he said icily. A vein twitched in his forehead. His tone darkened as he said, "Like I said, I will protect him. He's in as good of a place as he'll get. Don't you *dare* mess that up." Donovan then turned back to face the front of the vehicle.

Aurora sat back, biting her lower lip. She turned to Blaze, raising her shoulders briefly in defeat.

But Blaze felt a tightness in his chest. He felt the need to defend Aurora, though knew she could handle him on her own. He tapped on Donovan's shoulder.

He craned his neck around quickly. "What?"

"She didn't mean to upset you. She didn't know."

Aurora sighed. "I don't need you to defend me, Blaze."

Donovan shifted around in his seat. "Look—this isn't comfortable, sitting like this, so I'm gonna make this fast. You three are new to this world. Don't pretend like you know how our world works when you've been hiding behind walls your whole lives. You've been sheltered from the truth and sheltered from reality. Our reality. Am I making myself clear?"

204

"You act as if that was a choice," Aurora sighed, turning to look out the window.

"Don't give me that playing-the-victim bullshit," Donovan shot back. "That man has seen more horrors than you ever will—"

"Really? We watched one of our friends get hung in front of our whole town," Aurora argued. "He saw his parents get killed right before you showed up. Don't act like tough shit is an outside-the-wall exclusive. Because I've got news for you, it's not. No one makes it out of this life without getting hurt. Not one of us doesn't get singed or burned—"

"Watching billions of people die around you is—how'd you say it? Getting burned?" Donovan questioned.

Forrest turned to Aurora. "You're not going to change his mind. Just let it go. Pick your battles."

Amelia, seated beside Donovan, turned around in her seat now. "It's not a battle. It's a discussion."

"An unhealthy, heated one," countered Forrest. "It's useless. No one is going to change hearts or minds."

"Look, I see both sides," suggested Amelia. "She means well, Don. She's not the enemy. Relax."

Donovan looked to her, and his expression softened. "Right. She's not." And he turned around once again.

Amelia offered a nod of content to Aurora, lifting the corners of her lips just slightly.

But Blaze wasn't satisfied. It wasn't sitting right with him. "Are you going to apologize?"

Aurora elbowed him in the side. "Shut-up, Blaze. What'd I just tell you?"

Donovan already was turning around to face Blaze. "I'm dropping the topic. That's as good as you're gonna get tonight."

Blaze swallowed hard, nodded once, but didn't reply. As Donovan spun around once more, Blaze looked to Aurora who shook her head at him, rolled her eyes.

"Just trying to help," Blaze said.

"Always are," Aurora replied, still annoyed.

They drove for another fifteen minutes in silence. Total, absolute silence. Nori looked back from her seat several times, having left the younger ones in the back to fend for themselves. Blaze kicked himself for not letting it rest. He knew breathing air on hot embers never ended well. He should have known better. Should've listened to Aurora the first time.

He'd stay quiet. So did the others.

Not too much longer, they reached the city—Chicago—it was called. And for seventy-plus-years, it had become only a mere facade of what it once was.

Buildings stood, still tall and mighty, in defiance of the occupants who'd been long dead. After decades of weathering, looting, and destruction, there was hardly anything organic left to greet them. Nothing but a jungle of weathered concrete and steel.

Decades ago, the streets had been full of people and cars. A city that never slept, Nori explained as they passed through. Buildings and the light they produced illuminated the sky in a halo, but had since gone dark. Cars of the dead remained parked where they'd last been left, searched and gutted for parts. Forests and greenery had moved into the former urban sprawl, sprouting small vines across the facade of the abandoned skyscrapers.

Along the sidewalks, trees had erupted and broken free of their enclosures, breaking concrete and the containers that previously held them. Mother Nature always would find a way to reclaim what belonged to her. In the decades following her demise, Chicago had become a living, breathing lesson in ecology.

Blaze could imagine the former life the city held. He could picture it being quite nice in its glory days—full of character, of thoughtful architecture, and of life. He wished he could have been there before.

In many ways, it was much like the abandoned sections of River Ridge closest to the walls. It was similar enough not to be jarring to him. But Blaze wasn't a fool. Chicago was an entirely different world within itself. As they passed through, Blaze found his chest tightening, his eyes widening, and his heart beating faster.

This was new. This was uncomfortable.

But he'd have to get used to it, because the base of the Reapers was here, in the city.

Very soon, this—all of this—would be his new home.

* * *

He'd fallen into a dreamless haze, just on the verge of sleep and wakefulness. It was that middle-land, where thoughts became odd, peculiar, and yet at the same time, strangely clear.

The rolling road had a lulling effect on Blaze. If he'd believed in hypnosis, this would be his prime example of it.

He had seen the last week of his life in one solid sweep of memories, pressed together like a well-sewed, colorful tapestry. His brain had taken him on a journey for reasons unknown.

Blaze saw the attack on the wall, from forces still unclear. If he'd only known then that this was the beginning of the end. Looking back, he knew there was a different person who existed back then. The last week had been one of growth, of change. He was no longer a naive child, but was unsure of what he was now.

Like the haze he'd fallen into, he was in a middle-land of his life. Transitioning into something new was scary and full of unease. He couldn't control what would come in the next hours and days, but knew full-well that it would all shape him and sculpt him forever.

The slow rumble of applied brakes startled him, brought him back to the present.

He sat up, straightened his shirt and smoothed out his pants. Turning to Forrest, he received a nod of greeting.

"Asleep?" he asked.

He stretched his neck, craned it left and right. "In and out," Blaze said.

Amelia turned around, placed her hand on the worn headrest behind her. "We're here. Stay close. Stay vigilant."

Carl turned off the ignition and removed the key, putting it in the pocket of his flannel shirt. He opened the door, fumbled with his seatbelt, and slipped out, steadying himself on his left knee with a firm hand.

Nori hopped out, opened the truck door for Amelia. Both her and Donovan got out, stepping up onto the curb.

Aurora sighed, reaching over Forrest to adjust the seat so the three could get out.

He reached out to the latch, pulled it towards him. There was a click and the back seat slid forward just enough for the three to slip through and out.

As Blaze exited, he stepped onto the concrete curb, felt the sensation of solid ground beneath his feet. He peered up.

Darkened in shadow, the Chicago skyline towered above them. The roads seemed strikingly narrow with the towers piercing through the thick overhang of clouds. As he swiveled around, peering up in all directions, he saw countless broken windows, sides streaked and in need of cleaning. Canvas overhangs, long faded by sun exposure, were torn in places and free-hanging in others.

The streets were dark and he could feel a chill in the air, the wind strong against the nape of his neck.

Lowering his gaze street-level, he turned to face the building the others were looking at. Brown-bricked and three levels, the building was oddly short in comparison to its neighbors. It was rectangular and used as much of the plot of land as possible.

Chipped concrete steps led up to a barricaded door. Above, letters—with a few missing—spelled out the name of a dead president from decades prior. But Blaze recognized this was a school—or had been one, at least.

"Welcome home," said Nori.

"A school?" Forrest asked.

Donovan slid past him. "The skyscrapers were already taken," he said coolly. "No, it was a strategic move," he said. "High enough for a good view. Low enough to escape and flee—if we need to, of course."

Aurora looked around, brushed her hair behind her ear with her fingertips. "Looks well-protected," she said. "How many are in there?"

"A few dozen," Amelia said. She raised her hand to point. "First floor is basically empty. We planned it that way, of course. Second and third floors are the heart of our operation. Sleeping quarters are tucked away on the third floor, along with our arsenal of collected weapons. No one is gonna get to us before we're already up and ready. We've blocked off access stairwells, created a few of our own. There are ladders through holes in the floor, dead-ends. We've planned for an invasion we pray won't happen."

"An invasion from other survivors?" Blaze asked.

Donovan turned. "Like we said earlier, we're not the only ones. Times are desperate, people are desperate. Not a good mix."

"Desperate times call for desperate measures," Forrest agreed. "I hear you."

"Thanks for the support. Didn't need it," replied Donovan. "Look, let's get you guys in. I'm gonna pull the vehicle around into the garage. Nori, Amelia, and Granddad will get you settled."

"They can. I'm going up to take a nap. You try driving two hours," said Carl to his grandson.

"I offered to take the wheel," countered Donovan.

"And you drive for crap, so that was one offer I wouldn't take you up on." Carl reached into his chest pocket and removed the set of keys. "Try not scratch her. She's vintage."

"I'll do my best," Donovan said."

Carl tossed the keys in the air, and Donovan snatched them with a quick hand.

"See you guys inside," he said before moving around the front of the truck.

Nori stepped ahead, turning to the rest of them. "Ready to go in?"

Blaze nodded. "I think we're in need of a nap."

Carl shook his head. "New kids are beat already? Your lot aren't gonna make it. Promise you that, if you can't make it through a simple car ride."

"*Carl*," Amelia said, voice firm but polite. "They're guests. Give 'em twenty-four hours, at minimum, before you skewer them."

"Twelve. Take it or leave it," he said, pressing forward and hobbling up the steps. "Lucky they get that."

Behind them, the engine of the truck started and Donovan pulled forward and around the building.

Nori watched until it vanished, then turned back to the building and waited until Carl was a few steps up and already huffing and puffing, cursing beneath his breath at his bum knee.

"He's a real softy once you get to know him, I promise," she said. "Deep down, he cares and wants us to be okay."

"He's seen a lot," Forrest agreed. "I don't blame him for being a bit bitter, resentful, even downright mean."

"Mean is a bit of a strong descriptor, so I wouldn't go that far," Nori replied. "Tough? Difficult to impress? Those I can agree to."

"We'll convince him we're worth the effort," Blaze said.

Amelia looked to him. "If we didn't think you could rise to the challenge, we would've left you in your little town."

Nori's gaze lifted skyward. "Let's get in, get you settled. I see a storm coming tonight."

"Do you mean that as in weather-wise or unwanted company?" asked Aurora with a slight, nervous laugh.

Nori tilted her head and quirked a brow, but her lips remained neutral. "Not sure. Haven't decided yet," she replied. "Hopefully the first. The garden needs a good rainfall."

Stepping forward, Blaze cleared his throat. "Either way, we're ready."

Nori looked them over, shook her head in disagreement. "No, you're not," she replied flatly. "Not for them, you aren't." Her voice lifted as she said, "But kudos for the positivity."

* * *

Nori and Amelia would show them to the sleeping quarters on the third floor. Carl left them, nowhere to be seen. If Blaze were being fully honest, he'd say that he didn't mind his absence.

If Blaze had ever pictured a post-apocalyptic, citizen-army base camp, this is exactly what he would have envisioned. But growing up, he'd never had the vision nor had the need to imagine a life outside the walls of River Ridge.

His parents hadn't left. Why should he? Even as a child, Blaze preferred to deal with the real-world. He wasn't much for daydreaming or concerning himself with anything but the facts; the actual reality of their situation.

Now, was no different. He knew this would be a challenge and one he'd need to step up to the plate for with both feet, solid and grounded. He hoped Aurora and Forrest would approach this the same way. He wasn't worried about Aurora as much as he was concerned for Forrest. After all, Forrest had always been more of a free spirit. It was something he'd never grown out of. It was part of his essence and his charm. With his head in the clouds, Forrest always saw beyond the wall.

Maybe Forrest had been right to see and think that way. But maybe—at least as far as Blaze saw it—maybe it had just been a lucky guess. Had it not come true, it would have been a mere crazy thought.

Life beyond the wall? Yeah, right.

Nori guided them up a shadowy corridor. Steps lined with warped vinyl climbed into the shadows. Muggy air remained bottled up in the narrow stairwell.

They passed boarded-up windows as they climbed the stairs. Generator power lit a small lamp without a shade. The bulb was exposed, protruding from a shiny silver base. It lit the space with a harsh blue light, casting shadows across the floor and up onto their faces.

Stepping closer, now onto the third floor, Blaze noticed large, irregular holes in the walls on both sides. Lights from behind the other side of the wall illuminated exposed piping, wiring, and wooden framing.

Forrest pointed out the damage. "Is this strategic too?" he asked lightly.

Amelia sighed. "No, that's called years of water damage without maintenance."

"Ah." He took in the sight once more, then eyed her. "Makes sense."

With them now on the third floor, Nori turned, her umber-brown eyes reflecting back the light. She slipped a curious glance to Amelia.

"Think anyone's asleep?"

"Possibly third-shift crew? Most should be up now for dinner, though."

Nori bobbed her head, giving a half-smile. "True. They had all day to sleep. They can deal with it."

And she turned, pressed forward down the dark hallway. "When we get in there, pick a cot, lay down, and take a nap. Want someone to get you for dinner?"

"Please," Forrest answered. "I'm starving."

Nori continued moving quickly, footsteps drum-like against the floor tiles. "Okay. And you two?"

"I could eat if you put food in front of me," said Blaze.

"Me too," added Aurora.

Nori smiled. "Settled then. We'll grab you in a few hours, okay? But do me a favor, don't expect a feast."

She approached the door at the end of the hallway, turned the handle, and opened it.

Streaked across the scuffed floor, moonlight entered through two long and narrow windows. A slim figure was standing at one, just finishing pulling the drapes open.

As the three entered, Blaze took in the new surroundings. A line of cots with mismatched blankets—some torn and ripped—were made. The one closest to the window was still unmade, the thin pillow still molded in the shape its occupant had made.

From the window, the figure turned, walked towards them.

"Newbies?" he asked, voice a bit groggy.

"Yeah," replied Blaze.

He couldn't have been much older—if at all—than the three. Still left with a lingering boyish charm, dark eyes were wide and curious. He had a clean-shaven square jaw with dark, wavy hair.

"Trent," he greeted, approaching Forrest first.

Forrest extended his hand, took Trent's, and shook it firmly. "Forrest."

Trent flashed a genuine smile. "Cool name. I like it." He bit down on his lower lip, turning to Aurora. "You?"

"Oh—er—Aurora," she said, lifting a hand in a swift wave.

He returned the wave, laughing. "Cool name, too."

"Thanks," she said.

"And last, but not least?"

"Blaze." He took Trent's hand, shook it.

"Well I got the lame name of the group," said Trent. "So, what brings you to the Reapers?" he asked, sitting down on the unmade bed, smoothing out the blanket with his hands.

"Your people," Forrest said. Trent turned his attention to him, nodding slightly. "They came, the wall lowered, and off we went."

"Just like that?" asked Trent, raising a brow.

"Just like that," agreed Forrest.

"Impressive. Usually most struggle leaving the walled-in cities. So, what did they tell you?"

"Who?" asked Forrest.

"Nori," replied Trent. "I heard her voice outside as she brought you here."

Forrest brushed past Aurora and Blaze and sat down on the bed beside his. "They filled us in on what we missed. The plague that ravaged the country, the immune, and what came after."

"Must've been quite the car-ride."

"Most of it was done on foot. Carl only got us for the final push into the city."

Trent nodded, looking to Blaze and then Aurora. "Is that how it went?"

Blaze smirked. "Pretty much. Covered the basics."

Trent shook his head. "I wasn't clear. I said that more in surprise. Look—whatever they told you is probably true. But they always leave out the true motive of why they grab you guys from the cities. Every time, without fail. Makes me sick."

"What do you mean?" asked Forrest, his voice deepening.

"Let's just say in our world it's best to always maintain the upper-hand. Don't trust without verifying, don't trust blindly. If you do, people will think you're a fool, and I'm guessing you don't want me to think you're a fool, right?"

"Right," Forrest replied.

Aurora shot him an annoyed glare.

Trent fought a smile, twitching a lip. "What I mean is they think you know more than you're letting on about the people who built the walls."

"But we don't know anything!" Forrest exclaimed.

"Jesus—want to get me in trouble, too?" Trent asked. "Quietly, quietly," he expressed with smooth hand gestures. "Look, I hear you. I was in the same boat. My parents were in one of the cities. Even after the walls lowered, we stayed put. I wasn't alive yet when the walls lowered, but the Reapers still thought we knew more. Wasn't true, of course, like you guys. But they kept pushing for info we didn't know. Eventually they gave up, but haven't stopped going for others."

"Sounds a little scary," Aurora said.

Trent nodded smoothly, pursing his lips. "I'm not trying to scare you. I'm not. Just be mindful. If you do know something, I wouldn't share it right away. Keep that upper-hand strong, right?"

Forrest raised his arms and flexed his biceps. "Strong like bull," he laughed.

Blaze looked to Aurora, she too him. "Don't mind him. He always gets a bit goofy with new people."

Aurora agreed. "Yeah, it'll pass once you get to know him."

Trent's lips turned up into a smile, shoulders relaxing as he leaned back onto his palms. "I don't mind it. Some life around this place is much needed. You do you, Forrest. And you both let him, okay?"

"As long as you're good, we're good," laughed Blaze.

"You do realize I'm right here," said Forrest. "Wait until I'm gone to bad mouth me or to talk about me," he chuckled.

"We're not bad mouthing you. Just trying to save you from yourself," Aurora replied. "We know you. He doesn't."

"But I look forward to getting to know him," replied Trent. "And all of you. You guys gonna take a nap, I overheard?"

"Yeah. They're gonna get us at dinner," Aurora said.

Trent nodded. "We eat by seven. I work night-shift, so that's why I was just getting up when you got here."

"And what do you do?" Forrest asked.

"Forrest, let's get some sleep. We have later to catch up,' Aurora said, picking out a cot. "I'm not trying to be rude, I'm just beat."

Blaze agreed. "Yeah, we'll be up in a few hours. We'll talk more at dinner."

Forrest shrugged. "Guess it's my nap-time," he replied. "See you, Trent."

Trent extended his hand. "Nice meeting you. Have a good sleep. And Forrest, if you want to talk, I'll be downstairs. We won't bother them then."

Nodding, Forrest shook his head. "Appreciate the offer, but we'll meet-up later. I probably shouldn't pass on some much needed shut-eye."

"Sounds good. I'll leave you all to it," he replied, shutting the drapes once again. "But before I go—back to what I said— they're looking for some gadget from the *others*," he said firmly, his dark silhouette against the gray light seeping around the edges. "Each city had one planted somewhere around it. If you know anything about it, don't talk. If you know where it is, don't say. And if it's on your person—or in your pocket—I'd find a hiding spot before they look. And yes, they will check."

Blaze turned to Aurora, feeling the weight of the device against his thigh. How did Trent know? Did he see or have one from his own town at one point?

Aurora looked to him from the corner of her eyes. Blaze saw her focus, steady her breath.

Trent pressed his lips together, gesturing with his strong hands. "Just saying. This conversation stays in here, and I'm a one-way street. You're safe with me. G'night."

ELEVEN

He was falling through the darkness.

Bone-chilled, the grasp of sleep pulled on him hard, yanked him down by his feet. Blaze felt as if he were being pulled through a deep, dark, and dangerous ocean—one where he knew he couldn't see beneath him.

He kept falling, fading.

Breaths came fewer, further in between, shallow and unsteady. Blaze felt the weight of oblivion press in on him, around him. He felt the weight on his chest, on his ribs. He felt the pressure steady around his fingertips that were extended far above his head. Long arms were weak and flowing through the upward current

But Blaze knew what was happening—his unconscious self that is. He wouldn't remember this when he woke, as no one ever did, but now—in this moment—he was present. He felt it clearly. Felt every muscle relax into sleep. And he felt the sacred, nightly transition, between conscious to unconscious. He surrendered to the freedom of the abyss, savored it.

He felt the current of the dark slide across his body and slip between his fingertips.

And then he hit solid ground.

Still suspended in darkness, yet firm-footed atop whatever was beneath him, he found himself again and steadied his breath.

He was aware. Oh, yes, he was aware.

Blaze was aware of the doorway that suddenly appeared standing directly in front of him: Plain, white with four carved rectangles on its surface. A smooth, rounded knob of silver reflected invisible light. And he was aware where he was, just on the cusp of reality and not.

He stepped forward, feeling only mild resistance against the dark. He kept his feet planted firmly in the substrate of sleep, stepping with conviction and determination. When Blaze stood in front of the door, he reached out, grasped the knob with his hand, and he hesitated.

As with each time he dreamt, Blaze's stood unsure of whether to open the door. He didn't know what lie beyond it, what stood just behind. He felt a surge of courage build from the deep pit within himself, yet excitement brewed within rapid torrents of thought.

Then again, Blaze often mistook his anxiety for excitement. Same biological response, different outcome.

From within, he listened to the voice in his head. He was aware, he knew this much. He could have some control on his dream—not necessarily what lie beyond the door, but how he responded. Like life, his dreamscape was often unpredictable, but when lucid, he knew he had some control.

Blaze adjusted his grip and twisted the door knob. He heard the clicking, pressed forward a bit and stopped. Bright light shone around the edges, like a border between dark and the unknown.

But the unknown was better than the dark, and so with a firm swallow, a focused breath, he stepped forward into that unknown.

With his head lowered, gaze cast downward, he watched as his bare feet stepped forward onto thick, long grass. The rest of his body appeared from the dark. He was clothed in a long-sleeved, white linen shirt buttoned to the second-from-the-top button. He also wore long and flowing linen pants with the legs rolled up to the center of his calve muscle.

Blaze rotated his arms around as if discovering his body for the first time. And when he was finished, he looked sky-bound. Dark fast-moving clouds were rolling across deserted plains. He turned around, saw the door behind him to be missing. He stood alone, feeling the crisp air of an approaching storm-front press against warm skin.

And yet, even in the silence and solitude, he was not afraid.

He stepped forward a few steps, feeling the prickle of grass against his bare feet and the blades brushing against his exposed legs. He moved with determination, as if he were being pulled forward by bravery and courage alone.

Blaze did not know where he was going, but that was okay.

Grass was taller now, and in one moment further, he was entering a corn field, like the one he had passed back in River Ridge upon leaving. Blaze found himself easily maneuvering through, weaving in and out, while pushing aside the leaves and stalks of corn with extended hands.

He continued forward like this for another dozen stride lengths until he stepped into a clearing.

In the center stood the Stranger—the Man—the Alien. Blaze had yet to settle on how he identified the hooded and cloaked figure.

It stood taller than he remembered, basked in gray light that matched the fabric of its cloak.

Blaze stood before the figure, eyed him up and down. "Please, tell me what to do. I need your help."

But the figure didn't reply.

"Please..." he begged.

The figure tilted its head, eyed Blaze up and down now. "You've come this far. A bit further and you'll find the truth."

"But what is the truth?"

"Ah," the figure cooed, voice lowering, "but isn't that the question most sought?"

The figure vanished, fading from the clearing with a sudden whoosh. Blaze felt anger flow through him, down to his fingers which curled into tightly held fists.

"Not useful. Not at all," spat Blaze.

But as he finished speaking, hearing the distant echo of his voice in the dreamscape, the scene began to change. The clouds began to roll across the slick canvas of sky faster and faster. The stalks of corn began to bend, flowing with the sudden change of wind. Beneath his feet, the dirt floor felt unsteady, wobbling beneath him as if he were standing on a narrow beam atop one of the skyscrapers of Chicago.

He lowered to the ground, placed a hand atop the dirt. And as he did, his hand was swallowed. A wave of fear ran the length of his body, but what happened next occurred too quickly to process. Pulled through the dirt, he fell back into the darkness once again.

Headlong, he found himself falling at a faster rate than before, feeling a surge of icy air rush past him. Losing all sense of up and down, he started to feel as if he were spinning. His mind went blank, his stomach rose into the hollow of his chest.

Blaze squeezed his eyes shut, begging for it to stop. Begging to find solid ground again and something to grasp onto. At this point, he'd take a nightmare over this.

And just when he thought he'd get sick, the motion stopped, and Blaze found the solid ground beneath him once again. This time, it came in the form of damp, ice-cold concrete.

He was on his stomach, hands outreached. Clothed in a flannel shirt and patched jeans, he remembered this outfit. It wasn't any special one, so he brushed the curiosity of its importance in this dreamscape aside. Frankly, it wasn't. Blaze figured his unconscious merely went into the mental wardrobe of memories, picked the closest outfit hanging on the hanger.

His sleeves were rolled up to his elbows, and his exposed skin felt dewy and clammy to the touch. Still rolling, his stomach took a few more moments to settle. Blaze kept his eyes shut, feeling exhausted from his fall, until he felt a cool, gentle hand press against his forehead.

He opened his eyes, saw the back of his mother's hand. Blaze tried to sit up straightaway, but he felt another hand press against his shoulder.

"Easy now, son," said a deep voice belonging to his father.

Blaze pushed through the resistance, twisting to sit on the concrete floor. He recognized this space immediately. It was the basement of his home.

"Mom, Dad," Blaze said, nearly breathless, "there's so much to say—"

Lorna was holding a hand out, offering a gentle smile. "Blaze. Nothing was left unsaid. We heard it all. It's okay."

Tears built at the corners of his eyes, like a chisel against granite. But this chisel was solid and strong—stronger than the medium it was carving into. Blaze didn't want to cry. Not now. He was afraid he would wake himself, and he didn't want them to go.

"I couldn't stop them," Blaze said, voice breaking. "I didn't even try. I—I should have known. I could've saved you."

But Anton, dressed in his favorite dark-green work shirt shook his head, ran a weathered hand through his thick, medium-length black hair. Even from behind his beard, Blaze saw the familiar coy smile of his father.

"Blaze—son—there was nothing you could've done. Nothing."

"I can't," Blaze replied, tears breaking through, the granite wall failing.

Lorna stepped forward, lowered onto both knees. She placed her hand on Blaze's head, ran her fingers through his hair. She leaned down, kissed him on the top of his forehead, cupped his face in her hands, and wiped his tears with both thumbs.

"We can't prevent what we can't predict. It's just a fact of life. Blaze, do us a favor and let go of your guilt."

"It's not that easy, Mom…"

Lorna shut her eyes. "I know, but do it for us. You can't lie down and die now that we're gone," she said.

Blaze nodded.

"The best way to honor us is to keep on going. To keep on fighting. To keep living."

"But I'm not ready. To be honest—" his voice broke, "I wish I had gone with you both. I want to go back to how it was," Blaze said continuing to tremble in his mother's grasp.

Anton placed his firm hand on Blaze's shoulder, squeezed it with his thumb and fingers. "You know you can't do that, Blaze. You were always so good at dealing in reality," he smiled. "You're fine. Everything is fine. You have friends that love you, a good head on your shoulder, and a strong heart. You're more than ready."

A short laugh escaped from Blaze. "Dad, you never were much for sentimental phrases. I think you've lost your touch."

Anton smiled, wrinkles crinkling at the corners of his eyes. "You needed it. I'm not entirely heartless, you know."

Blaze nodded, taking his hands and wiping his own eyes. "Is this real? Are you both real?"

Lorna looked to Anton, he to her. Lorna cleared her throat. "We're with you, always. Never forget that."

Blaze shook his head. "But is this real. Are you?"

Anton cupped the back of Blaze's neck. "If you believe we are, then we are."

Blaze nodded, knowing the truth of the dream. Though his heart sank, he looked to both of his parents. "Please, come back. Don't let this be it."

"Are you going somewhere that we're not going?" Lorna asked. "Trust me, Blaze, we're not far. We're never far."

But as Blaze turned to his father, there was no one there. He looked back to where his mother had been kneeling.

She was no longer there.

It was just Blaze in the center of his basement, in the shadowy lighting.

Light cast in from the window along the ceiling. But slowly it transitioned. Blaze held himself still, afraid he would fall back into the darkness, but instead, the light through the window changed—darkened.

It swiftly turned into a deep shade of crimson. Filling the room with a red glow. Blaze shrank into himself, feeling so small in the vast, dark space. Now, unlike the plains outside, he felt solitude wrap its tight bindings around him, heard it's dark laugh, and in the shadows, saw its devilish grin as it overwhelmed him.

Tears turned to sweat. The basement grew hot, as if moved onto hot embers. Beads of sweat rolled from his hairline, past his brow, and down his cheek. Too afraid to move, he remained still, and focused on the scene.

Though part of him wanted to leave, something—some unusual curiosity—kept him grounded, held him down. It worked alongside the darkness, the solitude, the fear.

Blaze closed his eyes, counted to three.

When he opened them, standing directly before him, basked in the illuminated, crimson glow gleaming through the window, stood a shadowy Victor Winslow.

Blaze fought away a gasp, watching as the elder stood almost motionless, eyes focused outward, as if skimming just above Blaze's head.

But in a swift swoop of a moment and blur of motion, Winslow was directly in front of Blaze. His eyebrows were curled down, hair manic and sweat-streaked.

"GIVE BACK THE DEVICE! YOU DON'T KNOW WHAT YOU'RE DOING, FOOLISH BOY!" he hissed through yellowed and gritted teeth.

Blaze smelled his breath, his foul breath—a scent of decay and death. Too frightened, Blaze found himself unable to breathe or think. His eyes widened, though he desperately wished they'd shut.

Winslow placed his hands on Blaze's shoulders, shook them with a horrific force. "This is all your fault! *ALL OF THIS!*" he hissed, voice crackling like burning timber. "What happens next is on you, boy!" He turned aside facing the crimson light. *"Should've listened, should've thought through,"* Winslow murmured beneath his breath, turning back to face Blaze. "You thought you knew best. I should have taken you out, too. I saw what lies ahead, boy! They're not our friends, you know. I protected you, and all you've done is expose our town!" said Winslow, voice lowering.

"I—I didn't know."

"Of course you didn't," Winslow sneered, lips curling into a foul smirk. "Best of intentions right?" He raised his brow, ran a hand through his slick, damp hair.

Blaze didn't answer.

Winslow pursed his lips, chortled a laugh deep within his throat. "Isn't that how it goes? The worst things done have been done with best of intentions? Yeah, that's usually how it does go..."

"What do you want, Mr. Winslow? Want me to give you the device?"

Blaze found himself no longer in control of his dream. He found his voice speaking for himself, and he was merely observing from within.

Winslow's grip tightened on his shoulders. A sharp hiss escaped—no, a *sizzle*. In the fear of the moment, he didn't realize his own shoulders were being burned, scorched by Winslow's grasp. Winslow's neck began to tremble, to bend and twist. His face began contorting into inhuman positions. Muscles quirked, lifted and lowered, and then, as if built within from solid ash, Winslow's face began to peel away, rising into the air and vanishing. Behind the former facade of the manic Victor Winslow was a mass of dull, gray ash in the form of a human..

"*It's too late, boy...*" hissed the town-leader, soot falling to the ground..

And just before the form of Winslow was about to fully collapse onto the concrete floor of his basement, Blaze felt another violent shake.

"BLAZE!"

A rush of cool air filled his lungs. Blaze sprang forward, sitting up.

"Jesus!" escaped a startled voice.

Blaze opened his eyes, realized he was in a dark room. A small light in the corner was lit, and sitting at the foot of his bed was Aurora. Above him, with a steady, firm hand on his breast bone was Forrest.

"Man, you were talking in your sleep," said Forrest softly, brows lowered in concern.

Blaze swallowed hard, chest rising and falling quickly as he caught his breath. He raised the back of his hand to his forehead, held it there for a moment. *"Oh—er—Sorry."* he said between gasps.

Forrest shook his head. "It's fine. Don't apologize, buddy. Nightmare?"

"Yeah," he said, opening his eyes. "Something like that." He reached down the side of his mattress, and slipped his hand beneath. He felt the cool touch of the artifact right where he had left it. The others didn't notice.

"You want to talk about it?" Aurora asked. "We're all ears."

But Blaze shook his head, pushing back matted hair along his forehead. "I'm good. I'll forget about it soon enough. Just gotta catch my breath."

Forrest nodded and stepped back. "You look like you need a shower. You're drenched."

Blaze twisted around, saw the sweat on the pillow case. He looked down and pulled the back of his shirt away. It was clinging to him, so he held the fabric and fanned himself, savoring the cool air against his body and wished he could hold it there.

"I'll be fine. Is there a—uh—sink?"

"In the bathroom—er—*obviously*," Forrest said, snickering lightly. "Shocker right? Want me to go with? Make sure you're steady?"

"I'll be good," Blaze replied.

"*Forrest,*" Aurora said firmly, "go with him."

Forrest pressed his lips together, held his hand out to Blaze. "You heard her, boss."

Blaze shut his eyes and tried his best not to smile. "Why are you difficult?" he asked Aurora.

"Because I care," she said. "It's my job to be difficult."

Pulling back the blankets and swinging his feet over the edge of the bed, careful not to kick Aurora, Blaze looked up and took Forrest's hand. "*Thanks,*" he murmured in defeat.

Forrest helped him up, lowered his brows as he focused on Blaze. "Damn, buddy. Was someone kicking the shit out of you in the dream? You look rough."

"Nah, just a bit of a fright," replied Blaze.

"Gotcha," said Forrest. "You good to walk or you want me to help you?"

Blaze turned to Forrest and rolled his eyes. "Forrest, I'm fine. Thanks."

"Bathroom is down the hall, second door on the left," replied Forrest.

"Go with him," Aurora said again, annoyed.

"And what?" countered Forrest. "Watch him while he pees? He had a nightmare, not a surgery. Besides, you heard him—he's fine."

"If he falls down the stairs, it's on you," said Aurora.

"If he falls, it's his own fault," replied Forrest.

Aurora shrugged, waving off Blaze. "We'll be here," she said. "Yell if you need help."

Blaze laughed. "Thanks, but I'll be good. Promise. Besides, calling for help in the bathroom is honestly the last thing I really want to do. I'd rather die there than die of embarrassment. I'll be back."

"Back in a flush?" Forrest laughed, much too amused at his attempt at a joke.

"On that note, bye!" Blaze set off forward, leaving the two behind. As he exited the sleeping quarters, he opened the door to see Trent behind it, hand raised about to knock.

"Oh—er—hey," replied Trent awkwardly. "Guess you beat me to it. I was just gonna get you guys up."

"Eh, I've been up for a few minutes. And don't worry, I already woke them up," said Blaze, starting forward again.

Trent stepped aside, allowing Blaze to pass, before entering in his wake.

As Blaze moved down the corridor, he saw a short figure with wide eyes peering at him from behind a wall. He stopped, questioning his own sight for a moment, before hearing a muffled laugh come from the child—a young boy.

"What?" asked Blaze, just outside the bathroom and in no mood to entertain a child.

But the boy leaned back and returned into the room he had been peering out of. Blaze brushed it aside, and though in a bitter mood, smiled absentmindedly, happy to see a young face for the first time in a long while.

While in the bathroom, Blaze ran the old faucet for a few moments while waiting for the nuke warm water to cool. It never got ice-cold, but anything was better than the flush of heat across his body.

He held out his palms, collected a small pooling of water, and dunked his face in. In momentary gasps of memory, he felt himself falling through the darkness again, but in his conscious mind, didn't understand what that familiar sensation was. He figured he was just dizzy and still a little disoriented.

"Good?" asked a voice.

Blaze shot up, startled. Water flung from his palms and streaked the mirror. The rest splashed back into the porcelain basin.

Donovan.

Blaze lowered his palms, but he kept his head down, looking up into the mirror after a moment to meet the watchful gaze of Donovan.

"I'm fine," he replied.

Donovan's eyes remained focused. "Sound pissed off. You sure you're good?" he asked coolly.

"I said I'm fine. Why?"

Waiting a moment, Donovan then nodded and crossed his arms across his chest. "Dinner's ready."

"I know. Trent came to wake us up. I beat him to it."

"He's down there with Aurora and Frank."

"Frank?"

"You're other friend," Donovan replied coolly.

"You mean, *Forrest?*" pressed Blaze.

"Shit—yeah—*Forrest*. Never been good with names."

"What's my name?" Blaze asked, lifting his brows. *"Inferno?"*

"Nah, you're Blaze. That one I remember," he said. "Look, I wanted to talk to you real quick—one on one."

Blaze reached down, lifted the bottom of his shirt to meet his face. He dabbed it gently, knowing there'd be water splotches but it was better than going down with a soaked face. "Shoot," he replied.

"About earlier, I was stressed about a lot of things, pissed that I was being challenged."

"Well, it's not me to apologize too, it's Aurora. You didn't insult me."

"I know," he admitted. "I talked to her, apologized—*twice*. I think that's a record for me," he laughed softly. "She forgave me, but Forrest was there. I didn't want you to think I was a— you know—*dick*."

Blaze shrugged his shoulders. "It's all good. Is that it?"

Donovan's thick brows lowered. "Er—yeah. Anything you want to talk about?"

Shaking his head, Blaze stepped forward. "If anything comes up, I'll know to ask you."

234

Donovan uncrossed his arms, gave a thumbs-up with his right hand. "Cool. Sounds good. I'm here if you need me."

And with that, the two exited the bathroom. Once in the hallway, of curiosity, Blaze turned and looked down the length of the hallway. Half-expecting to see a child's face peering around the corner again, he found himself almost disappointed to have been wrong. Blaze shrugged, looked back in the direction he was walking, and together, the pair headed downstairs for a communal meal.

* * *

Long, narrow tables were set up in the vast room that had always been the cafeteria. It was funny how some things never changed.

Of the hundred seats available, only a little over a quarter were taken.

They were spread out, and as Blaze entered, he figured if everyone was lumped together, it would have been even more unsettling to see how few there were in such a big space.

Donovan pointed to a table where Forrest sat beside Trent, Aurora beside an empty spot, and beside Trent, at the end of the table, was another empty spot.

Blaze moved towards the table, took the seat beside Trent. Sitting across from him was the young boy from the hallway.

"We meet again," Blaze said, offering the boy a mere smile of the lips.

The boy met Blaze with wide, green eyes. He looked from Blaze to Trent.

"What? He won't bite," said Trent, taking a woven bowl of fresh baked rolls, selecting one from it, and taking a bite.

Blaze turned back to the boy. "He's right. I won't. Am I scary or something?"

"I don't know?" the boy replied softly, a bit timid. "Are you?"

"He can be," Forrest said breaking through the ice. "Should've seen him wake up from a nightmare," he laughed, taking a sip of water from a bright green cup.

"Honestly, Forrest," Aurora said, shooting him a dark glare. She turned back to the boy. "My name is Aurora. What's yours?"

"Aiden," replied the boy meekly.

Blaze looked at Aiden, studied his small, rounded face. Thin blonde hair hung across his forehead down to the top of his patchy brows. Freckled below the eyes, the boy was thin, lanky, and on the edge of a growth spurt.

"How old are you, Aiden?" asked Aurora.

"Eleven," he replied.

Trent held out a roll to Aiden. "Want one?"

Aiden shook his head.

"*Eleven,*" Forrest said, sounding impressed. "That's a good age. After twelve it all goes downhill, so enjoy it."

"Traumatizing him as we talk to him for the first time, right?" Aurora asked, eyes widened, lips pursing at the conclusion.

"Gotta learn the truth sooner or later. Let Uncle Forrest deliver the message with style, right?"

Aurora shook her head, rolled her eyes. "No. Not right. Blaze, save this kid from Forrest."

He eyed Aiden, ran through a list of questions in his mind. He knew it was odd that he found such trouble finding conversation starters for a child, but he wasn't around them that often. Much of River Ridge was older. Pregnancies came in waves. The last few years, in fact, had been dry-spells. The kids just a few years older than the trio, would be the next round of parents.

So Blaze went to the basics; tried-and-true topics. "Do you have any hobbies?" he asked.

"Hobbies?" Aiden clarified, confused.

"Things you like to do," Trent said.

"Oh—uhm—I like exploring, when they let me. I like to read my comic books. I like playing games, too."

"What about your drawings?" said Trent. "You like to do that, don't you? You should show them your pictures sometimes."

"Yeah," answered Aiden. I—I changed my mind. Can I—er—can I have a roll?"

"Of course," Trent said. "Don—pass the bowl back." He waited until it was extended out to him. He took it, reached in. "Which one?"

"The one by your left hand. It has my name on it," said Aiden.

Trent reached in, took it lightly and held it out. "Need me to cut it in half for you?"

"I got it," said Aiden, taking the dull knife beside his chipped plate.

Aurora looked to Donovan and leaned her head to the side.

Donovan cleared his throat. "You sure, buddy? It might be tough to do."

"I'm fine," Aiden said.

"Chill man. Leave it," said Trent. "Remember—we don't baby them."

Donovan looked to Aurora. "He's right. We don't."

Blaze looked down the length of the table. Walking through the narrow corridor, Nori approached wearing a ripped and torn shawl over her broad shoulders. She saw Blaze, raised her hand in a quick glance of a wave before approaching closer.

"You guys good? Food should be out soon," she said, pulling her shawl around her, tying it across her chest at the ends.

"Thought this was it," Donovan laughed, taking a bite out of his roll.

Nori looked to him. "Watch that sass or it will be the only food you get tonight, my friend."

Aurora twisted around to look to Nori. "Any plans for tonight?"

Nori pulled back the baggy sleeve of the fisherman's sweater she was wearing. Rolling the cuff behind her wrists, she exposed a gold watch with a brown leather band. She brought it closer to her face, eyed the time. "Old eyes," she said absentmindedly. "Well—erhm—we planned on doing some basic combat training in the morning, but I s'pose, if it was good with Carl, we could start tonight? Aren't you tired though? Dinner and sleep probably would be best for you kids?"

Aurora turned to Forrest, then to Blaze. "I'm good. What about you guys?"

"I mean, I'd pick sleep—but then again, I was a koala in another life," Forrest said. "I'm game. You teaching us combat, then?"

"Please," Nori quirked her brow. "I supervise, honey. You're sitting beside your teachers."

Forrest looked to Aiden. "You didn't tell us you taught combat?"

Trent laughed, nudging Forrest in the side. "You goof. It's Donovan and me, tonight."

"Cool," replied Forrest, "but to be honest, Aiden, you could probably take me in a fight."

Aiden smirked and looked to Nori. "Miss. Nori, can I watch?"

Nori dropped the sleeve and lowered to a knee. She stabilized herself on the sturdy bench they were sitting on. "If Mr. Carl is good with it, I can see if he'll let you watch. But you need to stay out of the way. Keep to yourself, okay?"

"I can do that."

"Well, do it and do it well," Nori said, rising to her feet once again. "One peep from them about you getting in the way, and you'll be off to bed quicker than you can say sorry. And for the rest of you—I'll talk to Carl and see what he has to say. If he approves, then it's settled. Good?"

"Sounds good to me."

"Do I get a say?" asked Donovan.

Nori looked to him, shrugged. "No."

"Cool."

Nori took an exaggerated breath. "What is it, Donovan?"

"Look, if you want to do it, better let me talk to Gramps. He's been in a mood since we got here. There's at least a fighting chance if I can convince him."

Nori looked down the length of the corridor where Carl was seated at a table with a bowl of some liquid—likely homemade soup. "I see your point. He is usually a bit ornery—"

"But that's part of his hospitality," Trent chirped in. "Don't take that from him. It's all he has."

Donovan struggled to maintain a firm expression. "Trent has a point, but I'll work my magic."

"With a wand?" Aiden asked genuinely.

"No wand required, little man," Donovan replied, scratching his chin. "It's all about the delivery. It's called charm and style. Like the Illness, either you have it or you don't."

Nori snorted. "Yeah, okay. When you find that, let me know. I'll find you a medal—shiny and golden."

"Like my heart," Donovan replied.

"I thought it was black and coal-like," replied Trent, smirking.

"Depends on who you ask. I'll be back."

Blaze watched Donovan step out from the bench and move quickly down the corridor. He looked back, pulling up his tactical pants that hung on his narrow hips. In a fluid motion, he tightened the old belt. He sat down beside Carl, folded his arms on the table.

"He's a good guy, in all honesty," Nori replied, watching from afar. "A bit of a mystery, borderline socially awkward, but has a good heart. He'll work his magic, like he said. Worst-case scenario is we train tomorrow. I wanted you guys to go on a supply run, so if we get some basic combat out of the way tonight before bed, it saves more time for preparation and scouting tomorrow, and for me, heartache and worry while you're out and about. What are your thoughts, Trent?"

Trent shook his head, widening his eyes. "About what?"

"What I just said..."

"Care to repeat? Wasn't paying attention."

Dismissive, Nori sighed and took a seat. "At least he's honest," she said to the rest of the group. She turned back to him, focused for a moment. "I was saying that if Donovan doesn't, as he called it *'work his magic'*, we train tomorrow. I want-slash-need you guys to go on a supply run tomorrow, so getting some training out of the way tonight opens a wider window for you guys to scout locations."

"Ah," Trent nodded, pursing his lips. "For sure. Either way, won't take long. Amelia and I found an apartment complex last week, so we figured we'd try there first. Looked pretty untouched, too."

Nori looked aside, brows centered, narrowing. "How well did you already scout it? How long was your surveillance?"

"I mean we didn't camp out there all day," Trent replied coolly. "Long enough to see it was quiet. We slip in, snoop around, take what we need, and slip out."

"Where is this place?"

"Few streets down. Still our neck-of-the-woods, right?"

"Please, we're lucky if this is our neck-of-the-woods," Nori replied. "All I'm saying is I don't want you leading them into danger."

"They don't have to come," Trent proposed. "Probably should get acclimated anyway. They can come next time."

But Nori was already shaking her head. Blaze looked aside, disappointed. Though a part of him wanted to stay back where it was safe in their new 'normal', the rest of Blaze longed for adventure, to see a former major city, explore its alleys and abandoned roads.

Nori cleared her throat. "They're not children. They need to learn the rules and keep to 'em. Chip in or you're out."

"They've been here for three hours," said Trent. "Give 'em a break."

Nori nodded twice. She raised her hand to her face absentmindedly and touched the long scar on her face, as if discovering it for the first time. "I'll talk to Amelia and see what she has to say about this complex—"

"She'll tell you the same thing I did, Nori. It's untouched."

"I don't trust anything. Not saying I don't trust you. There's a reason it's untouched. Be careful," she warned.

Trent nodded, taking another roll out of the woven basket and took a bite. "Always am," he said, voice muffled by chewing.

Nori pressed away from the table, rising to her feet. "That's promising she said. I'm going to go check on Carl and see if Donovan has driven him mad yet."

Taking another bite, Trent forced down a laugh. "Think you're eighteen years too late for that one, Nori."

"Good point," she agreed.

As Nori walked down the narrow passage between tables, Trent looked to Blaze, then to Forrest. "If she's good with it, you guys want to go tomorrow?" he asked. "Amelia would probably come, too."

Forrest nodded. "Of course. Would love to help out."

Trent reached over, patted on Forrest on the shoulder. "Good to hear, friend. You, Blaze?"

Blaze quickly agreed. "For sure. I'd like to do some exploring."

"Eh, not exactly exploring, but I hear where you're coming from. I guess it's exploring, but this is more-so of a mission. Think of a military mission—you know—with a set-goal, mission parameters. We don't go into this lightly. We plan ahead, look for any obstacles or road-blocks that'll get in our way."

"Do you draw maps?" asked Aiden.

"You've seen what we do, Aiden," countered Trent. "Sometimes yes, sometimes not."

"I know what you do, but they don't though."

Trent nodded. "Ah. I see what you were doing. Good point. Sorry."

Aiden shrugged as Blaze looked aside to see Donovan approaching with a widened smirk on his face.

"Good news," Donovan said, once he was close enough to hear. "Potatoes and vegetable medley for dinner tonight."

"Yum," Trent forced through tight lips. "What about tonight, tonight?"

"Oh," Donovan said dismissively, "that. Yeah—we're good to go for tonight."

"Seriously?" Forrest asked, excited.

Donovan nodded. "Yep. After dinner. I told Nori. She seemed relieved. I rubbed it in her face that I got the unmovable force of nature to bend."

"Probably broke him while you were at it, too," laughed Trent.

Donovan looked to Aurora. "Whatever it takes, right?"

Aurora raised her brows and smiled with her lips, though didn't reply.

"Damn. Tough crowd," replied Donovan. "Anyways, we eat and we train. Got it?" He looked to Blaze, then Forrest. He waited another few moments before asking again, "*Got it?*"

Blaze and Forrest looked to each other, then back to him. "Got it," they replied in unison.

They didn't wait much longer for dinner to arrive. When it finally did, the group dug in, savored each bite. Blaze hadn't realized how hungry he had actually been until now. He held onto his self-control with a firm grip and didn't let go. It would be so easy to scarf down everything, but he knew he needed to make it last—for at least a few minutes more.

In the silence, his brain explored the realm of his emotions. He felt the excitement and nerves in his blood.

There was a certain anxiety milling about, one that he could feel in the beat of his foot tapping against the solid floor.

He thought of his father, Anton, who had wanted to teach him combat but never got the chance to. Instead, Blaze got the survival talk—supplies and how to use them. Equally useful, but so very different.

He looked to the table, spotted Donovan looking to Aurora. When Donovan caught Blaze's gaze, he looked to him, then back down to his food.

Blaze followed, taking another forkful of baked potato and placing it in his mouth. He held it there, didn't swallow for a few long-held moments.

"You'll be fine," he heard the voice of his father say. *"Two ears and one mouth for a reason. Listen and focus, study hard and try your best."*

Though he knew it was likely from his imagination, the words brought him comfort and that desperately-needed focus. He dug deep and planted the words into the solid bedrock of his mind.

He *would* be fine.

He knew so.

So Blaze decided then and there that he would take on any challenges, any new experiences, with an open mind and a willingness to learn. After all, at this point, it was all they had.

And by making peace with his thoughts, he noticed the tapping of his feet and bouncing of his thighs ceased, the rhythm of his heart softening. He returned to his dinner ready for whatever tonight would throw at him. Blaze was ready to listen, to focus, and to try his best, as his father had said.

Even in death, they were with him. He could feel it.

TWELVE

Blaze looked at the stack of cleaned and dried plates that he and Forrest had worked through after pitching-in for clean-up duties.

"Not bad," said Blaze.

"Next time, let's offer to sweep or wipe tables," Forrest said. "Not the biggest fan of dishwashing."

It was only the two of them in the old kitchen. The stainless-steel tub was filled with water that hadn't stopped steaming. An old bar of soap—one meant for one's body in the old world—sat on the lip of the sink, and Blaze took hold of it, dipped it in to rinse, and set it back down on the small plate it sat on before. He then reached in, a bit deeper this time, and pulled the drainage plug. Instantly the water began to swirl down the drain, pulling the floating bits with the flow.

He stepped back, admired his work again, drying his hands on the already soaked dish towel.

Behind them, the door to the kitchen clicked, and standing in the doorway was Aurora holding a bright, neon orange bucket that had maintained its color over the years. She entered, squeezing a dirtied rag into the bucket and draped it over the edge.

"Hope you both didn't get into anything while I was gone," she said. "How was it?"

"Fine," Blaze said, folding the towel over the edge of the sink. "How was table duty?"

"Fine," she said. "I would have been fine with either. I like the instant gratification of dish washing. You know, not clean to clean. Just like that. But table duty was fine, too."

Following behind her, Donovan stopped in the doorway. "You guys nearly finished?"

"Just wrapped up," answered Blaze.

"Good," Donovan said. "Trent and I are ready downstairs. I'll lead you down."

"And what do I do with this?" Aurora asked, pointing with her free hand to the bucket.

"Pour it down the drain, rinse it? What did you think we'd do? Save buckets of dirty water?"

"Wasn't sure. I know supplies is tight."

"Gross," Donovan laughed, scrunching up his face. "We're not that desperate."

Aurora went to the sink, dumped the bucket over the lip, and set it into the sink. She twisted the glass knob of the faucet, filled the bucket halfway, and swirled the water around a few times before emptying it down the drain. She rinsed the rag, then hung it beside Blaze's towel.

"And there. I'm ready to go," she said, drying her hands on her jeans.

"Cool," said Donovan. "Follow me."

He led them out of the kitchen and through the dining room. A few unknown faces were lingering at the tables, midway through another story or conversation. They were focused, seemingly unaware that they were going to be all alone. Blaze figured they didn't care.

As they left, a few lights were on in the first floor hallway. The ones furthest down the length of corridor were off. Blaze figured the rooms down that far were unused, and nothing went to waste here. The Reapers were a wise group. He also figured that strategically, they wouldn't want occupants on the outside, perimeter rooms. It was dangerous out there, and they wouldn't want to take any chances.

Donovan turned at the corridor, where a double-door stood at the end of a short hallway. A single lamp with an exposed bulb sat on the ground in the corner. Blaze looked up and saw old florescent lights along the ceiling that would have previously lit their path.

Donovan reached for his pocket and pulled out a small flashlight. "Mind your step," he said. "It's dark in here, but downstairs, we have it well lit. "Hold the railing and you'll be fine."

As Donovan passed through, Blaze eyed the staircase directly before them. Three narrow windows allowed pale moonlight to illuminate tiny slivers of space in the area. The

Reapers hadn't bothered to board them up, as no human could fit through the narrow panes of glass.

Blaze grabbed the handrail, felt the textured metal that had been painted over several times. He went behind Donovan, Aurora behind him, with Forrest in the rear.

"Anyone else joining us?" asked Blaze.

"Er—yeah, sorry. Not private lessons."

Aurora replied, "We'll manage."

"Makes sense. Get everyone on the same page," said Blaze.

"Right. Can't waste good opportunities like this. Trent's very good. Learned from his dad, who learned from his dad. I taught myself, since I never knew my dad. Then again, my mom could have taught me, I'm sure."

"Is your mom here?" asked Blaze.

Donovan waited a moment. In that, Blaze already knew the answer. "She died a year ago. Got a bad infection that we couldn't stop. Even with the medical gear we've built up, it wasn't enough."

"I'm so sorry," Aurora said.

Donovan kept his gaze forward on the next illuminated steps. "Thanks. It sucked, and I'm not really over it, so I'd prefer if we didn't talk about it."

"Yeah, no one's ever over it," said Forrest.

Blaze tried his best not to think of his own family, of his mother and father. He didn't bother bringing it up, as it wasn't relevant.

"At least I have my Granddad," said Donovan. "He won't be around forever, though," he added quietly. "But, that's why we're a close knit family, here at base. We might not have our families, but we have each other. We've become a family and we'd do anything for each other. I hope someday you'll see that for yourselves."

"Definitely," replied Blaze. "I bet we will. We already see how tight you guys all are."

Donovan stopped, turning around. "Yeah, but there's always room for more here, so that's why we try and find you guys."

"And we appreciate it," said Aurora.

Behind the two, Forrest cleared his throat. "Dumb question."

"Short trip," Aurora replied, chuckling.

"But a serious one," added Forrest.

Donovan continued forward, stepping down the stairs. "I'll try to answer it. Go for it."

"You guys were outside of the walls. How long had you been there?"

"Waiting?" Donovan asked quietly.

Forrest replied, "Yeah. A few days?"

Donovan laughed. "A few minutes," he replied. "Remember how we told you guys that you weren't the only ones from the walled cities, right?"

"Yeah," Blaze said, joining in.

"The same thing your town-leader had is something we came into possession of. They must be on the same frequency or something, 'cause, Nori pulled it from her pocket, once we were outside your town. She clicked a button, and voila, a couple moments later, down comes the wall and out you guys come."

Blaze looked to Aurora. "I wonder if that's what rose the final button out of the ground. I hit it and the wall opened. I don't think Nori opened it. I think she activated the exit button, though."

Donovan nodded. "Interesting. So you hit something inside?"

Blaze nodded. "Yeah. It was a post with a button on it. I hit it, the wall began to move."

"Makes sense. I'll have to let Nori know there is more to it than we thought. Thanks for filling me in. You guys were—as far as I know—one of the last groups to leave the walled cities. Your leader kept you in there, like pigs for slaughter."

"We'll never know why," Aurora said.

Donovan stepped down onto a landing, stepping against the wall and twisting on his feet. He motioned for them to pass.

"Of course we know why," Blaze replied firmly.

"It's probably more involved than we think," said Forrest. "Winslow was a dick, but he wasn't that simple-minded."

Blaze turned to him. "It was that simple. You saw him, he was terrified when they came in. The guy was scarred of his own shadow—"

"Look," Donovan replied, "there's probably truth on both sides. Not that I know the guy, but it wouldn't be that far off from other people's experiences. Whatever these chosen ones were shown when the cloaked man appeared messed 'em up pretty damn good, scrambled their brains, you know. Don't discredit fear. It may be basic, but it's damn powerful."

Forrest nodded. "Don, I was—"

"Donovan," he corrected.

"Sorry—*Donovan*, this device. Where is it?"

"Honestly, I don't know. Nori and Granddad know, for sure. He gave it to her. Not sure if he knows or remembers, but Nori would, since she had it earlier today, obviously."

"We could go back and help the rest of River Ridge," Aurora replied.

Blaze turned to her. "They had every chance to come with us. They picked Winslow over us."

"They didn't know he'd shut them in again, I bet," said Aurora. "I could get my parents, bring them back here."

"Well, we're not going back anytime soon," said Donovan. "I'll keep this short and simple. I agree with Blaze. They had the chance and blew it. Only three out of however many were there is pretty pathetic."

"Someday we'll go back," Forrest said. "Once we've built up some more supplies and found our way. Then, we'll go back. I promised my mom and dad and Hadley. I'm a man of my word."

Donovan stepped in front of a door, turned the knob, and opened it. Instantly, bright lights blinded the four as they stepped into an open space.

"Welcome to our school gym. It's not much, but the school was pretty well equipped. Hand weights over there," pointed Donovan, "some old machines needing oil there, and our mats here."

The room was lit with dozens of exposed bulbs along the ceiling. They had obviously been installed by the Reapers, but they looked good—certainly better than the random, old lamps placed around hallways upstairs.

Blaze stepped in and looked around. Mats were adhered to the walls with a bright orange-and-black striped tiger mascot. The words, *'Go Tigers!'* were written in bold lettering, curving across the width of the mats.

On the floor, mats that had been intended for wrestling were worn and damaged in spots. Foam chunks were missing from areas, but Blaze was grateful for any padding at all if they were to do combat training.

In the center, Trent stood with his arms crossed against his chest. He had changed into some Navy-blue shorts and wore sweatbands around his wrists.

He raised his hand, waved to the four.

"And we'll call it a party," said Trent to the three others in front of him, including Amelia. "Come on, gang. Take a seat."

The three stepped away from Donovan and sat down around the others. Donovan walked around, slipped the flashlight back into his pocket.

"Mind if I go change real quick?" he asked Trent.

Trent smirked. "Yeah, I think I can handle them."

Donovan pressed off, and left the room.

"Cool," said Trent, looking over the group, "well first off—welcome. Glad you guys could make it. I know you four are veterans, while you three—", he motioned across Blaze, Aurora, and Forrest, "are brand new to this, right?"

Blaze looked to Forrest, knowing neither of them had been in any fights.

"Right," Aurora answered for them. "We're total beginners."

"Speak for yourself," Forrest replied.

Aurora turned to him, parted her lips. "Oh, care to fill us in on your fight stories?"

Forrest went silent. Blaze held in a laugh.

"That's fine," said Trent. "No need to feel bad that you haven't been in fights. I see that as a plus, in general. Means you can hold your temper. But what we're going to cover tonight is some basic maneuvers. Sorry, Veterans, tonight will have to be a refresher."

Blaze looked to the group closest to Trent. Amelia had her hair tied back into one, long braid down the center of her back. The others—a female likely in her mid-thirties with a bit of belly yet muscular, and a darker skinned male with a short, cropped haircut. He had to be in his late-twenties.

"So, once Donovan gets back, we're going to link up and I'll go over some moves with you all. In the meantime, introduce yourselves. Amelia, you go first."

"I'm Amelia," she replied, raising her hand.

"And say something interesting about yourself. Don't be awkward," said Trent. "These are friends."

"They know me already," Amelia pressed.

"Barely," he replied.

"I'm Amelia, and I'm decent at drawing portraits. It's how I photograph moments or people important to me. If you're lucky, I may add you to my portfolio."

Blaze raised his brows, impressed. "That's cool," he said.

"Now, you, Blaze. We'll go back and forth," Trent said, eying the door Donovan had vanished behind.

"Er—I'm Blaze. I'm seventeen. I like to ride bikes and I—erhm—yeah—guess that's it."

"Blaze the Bicyclist," said the dark-skinned guy. "Easy to remember. Double 'B'."

"Hey, whatever works. So, Elliot, you go then."

"I'm Elliot. I'm good at trapping wildlife for food. And before you ask, yes I'm humane about it. My mom is Nori, who you guys met, and I can play the piano."

"Do they have one here?" asked Aurora.

"They do," replied Elliot. "Way out of tune, though. Humid summers and icy winters battered the hell out of it."

"Bummer," Aurora replied genuinely.

Elliot nodded. "With you on that," he said.

"Forrest?" asked Trent.

Forrest raised a hand. "Yeah—uhm—Hi, I'm Forrest. Like Blaze, I also like to ride my bike, but I worked with my dad at the hardware store in town. I became a pretty good woodworker, so if you guys have any construction projects, I'm your guy."

"Noted," smiled Trent. "And you, Rose?"

Rose sat up a bit straighter, offering a wave to the group. Beaded bracelets, of different colors and designs, slid down her wrist and onto her long-sleeved shirt. "Hi, guys. I'm

Rose. One of my hobbies is free-running. It has different names, too, but Chicago is a free-runner's dreamland. Lots of buildings to scale, alleys to explore. As I'm getting older, it's a bit tougher, but it's a good skill when escaping enemies. Other than that, I'm fluent in Spanish and am in the middle of learning French."

Trent nodded, crossing his arms again, widening his stance. "Merci, Rose," he replied in French. "Aurora?"

"I'm Aurora and I like to try new things," she replied, shrugging her shoulders.

Trent waited, brows lifting slightly. "Er—okay. Short and sweet. Nice."

"What about you, Trent?" asked Forrest. "What's your fun fact?"

"All right," he smiled, nodding. "Fair enough. Er— okay—I'm Trent, and I'm a skilled marksman and good enough at hand-to-hand combat."

"Ever used either?" asked Forrest.

"More often than I'd prefer."

Across the room, Donovan was approaching. Like Trent, he too was wearing athletic shorts. His socks, older dress ones, were mismatched shades of blue.

"Good timing," said Trent.

Donovan waved a hand in disregard, "Eh, I didn't want to share my fun fact, too, so I waited a bit." Without skipping a beat, he continued, "Okay, I need a volunteer. Anyone?"

Blaze's eyes shot to Aurora, impressed, as she raised her hand high and proud.

"I'll volunteer," she said, standing up. Immediately, Aurora removed her flannel shirt, wrapped it around her waist as she approached.

"There are some rubber bands for the ladies," said Donovan, pointing to a pile at the corner of the mat.

Aurora bent down, picked a rubber band up and quickly tied her hair back into a ponytail. She stepped beside Donovan.

"You sure you're down with this?" he asked, his voice lowering. "I was thinking more along the lines of another guy."

Aurora put her hands on her hips. "Will the enemy not fight me because I'm a girl? Or are you just afraid to hit one?"

Forrest clapped. "You tell him, Rory."

She stretched her arm across her chest, held it. "God, I hate that nickname," Aurora said to Forrest. "How many times have I told you that?"

"A few dozen," Forrest said, his lips curling into a smile.

"Clearly hasn't stuck, has it?" she sighed, stretching her other arm.

Donovan's stance went solid. He eyed her up and down, shaking his head. "Look—I don't want to hurt you."

"Then I should defend myself. For both of our sakes. Besides that, you were a jerk earlier in the day, so why stop now?"

Forrest leaned into Blaze's ear. *"Damn, she's on a roll. Kicking ass, taking names..."*

"I already apologized about that," he replied, voice heating with each syllable. *"Aurora,"* he softened his voice. "I'll try not to hurt you, but I can't promise anything."

"That's fine," she said. "Just tell me what I need to do. I know what I signed up for."

"Impressive," he said. "If I awarded points for this and there was some prize or something, you'd definitely be getting some bonus points."

"Enough flirting, more teaching," said Aurora. "Tell me what to do."

"All right, that's how we're going to play this." Donovan cleared his throat. "Trent?"

"We're going to start with a basic stance. Literally the basics. Aurora, I see you're right handed, so I want you to turn slightly so your right leg is back, your left leg is forward—yeah, like that."

Blaze turned to her and saw her already in position, hands raised at chest level.

"Now, Donovan is going to be in the same position. Hands up, Don. Yeah—that. Okay, so this is your basic position when you're in a fight. Now obviously, when shit hits the fan, rules don't apply, but try to always keep yourself in this position. Organs face away, and you have the power to pack in a good punch. Easy enough?"

The group nodded.

"So, when you're going in for a punch, you pivot on your hips, while keeping your left arm raised in defense. Don't lower it, because if you need to use it, best to have it ready to go. So you pivot, and with your strength, thrust it forward via your fist into your enemy. Now, I say go for the head, but it's a small target and easy to move. For a safe option, go for the abdomen since it's soft and full of sensitive bits. Now, if you're really in trouble, go for the heart. A knee to the groin is a cruel move, but a good tool to have in your toolbelt. Guys are especially susceptible to this one, as you can imagine."

Trent looked to Aurora. "Now, in slow motion, show me the move if you were going in for a punch."

Aurora steadied her stance, raised her arms slightly. She squeezed her fists tighter, leaned back, just slightly, before slowly moving her fist through the air towards Donovan's side."

"Nice. Solid and smooth," replied Trent. "You went for the side, which was the smart option, especially for a beginner. You go for the head and it's a gamble. You miss, and you're at the disadvantage. Best to play the safe odds. Nice."

Forrest raised his hand, clearing his throat. "I have a question. Can Aurora demonstrate the classic, knee-to-groin maneuver. We could use a refresher."

Donovan flashed Forrest a dark glare. "No, we can all use our imaginations," he replied.

"So, I'm not going to have you guys repeat that. That one is easy. But let's move into our next topics: take-down maneuvers and escape maneuvers. Sounds good?"

When no one objected, he nodded. "Great. Link-up."

Aurora remained with Donovan, while Rose and Elliot paired together. Amelia approached Blaze.

"Partners?" she offered.

"Of course," he replied.

Trent approached Forrest. "Looks like you pulled the short stick," he said.

Forrest laughed softly, smiling. "I'll take it."

And with the pairs together on the mat, they looked to Trent and Donovan for further guidance.

"All right, guys. Let's do this," said Trent.

For the following hour, they practiced a whole slew of combat maneuvers. Starting with the basics and working their way up, the pairs practiced everything. A few times, Amelia grew tired of the slow-motion aspect and went a bit faster, with a bit more force. Blaze bit his lips and refrained from complaining.

"Listen and focus," he heard his father repeat.

This was good for him, and it would pay off.

Donovan and Trent showed them how to get out of a hold and how to escape someone on top of you. As Blaze watched, studying the motions intently and imagining himself to be in the place of the victim, he realized how much of this came down to one simple idea. This is life or death.

Fight and you live. Surrender and you die.

The simplicity of it was terrifying, the acidity of truth scarring.

He knew that in a fight to the death, it came down to skill and who wanted to live more. Once you were at this point, there was no bargaining or pleading. You fight or you die. That's it.

The hour passed quickly. By the end of it, Blaze could already feel his body growing sore from the few accidental punches that had slipped through. He could feel the tension in his hips and the tightness in his abdominal muscles— ones he didn't use too often, if at all.

Donovan looked across the group, checking his watch. "Damn, it's nearly ten. Let's call it a night. We can do more tomorrow or the day after. Deal?"

The groups relaxed their postures, and Blaze turned to Amelia.

"Sorry about the punches," she said genuinely. "Didn't mean them."

"It's all good," he said, rubbing the forming bruise below his lower rib. "I can heal from this. A real fight might not end so well," he said.

Amelia smiled with her lips, nodded once, and walked over to Donovan.

Forrest approached and placed a solid hand on Blaze's shoulders. "Good?'

"Been better," replied Blaze. "How about you?"

"I'm doing great," said Forrest. "Feeling good, but that might be the exhaustion talking. I'll sleep like a baby tonight. That's for sure."

Aurora approached, putting her flannel back on and buttoning a few of the buttons. "Aiden never showed."

"Probably past his bedtime," Forrest said. "It's late. When I was eleven, my folks put me to bed practically at five. Probably just wanted me to shut up," he laughed.

"Yeah, I can see that," replied Aurora. "I'll remember that one."

Blaze looked to Donovan. "Are we good to head back up?" he questioned.

"Oh, yeah. You know the way, right?"

Blaze nodded. "We do. Thanks for your time. You too, Trent."

"Sure. See you up there later," replied Donovan.

Trent raised his hand. "Bye, guys."

"Nice meeting you all," said Forrest.

"See you later," said Elliot, offering a wave. "Tonight was fun. We'll do it again."

Together, the three left the gym and climbed the staircase in the dark. They made it up the stairs and all the way to the sleeping quarters. Now, a few of the bunks were occupied by sound sleepers. Blaze picked the one he had slept in earlier, pulled back the blankets and slipped in. He felt for the artifact from River Ridge, pressed his fingers against the surface, and relaxed. Forrest and Aurora got into the bunks beside his.

He could feel the drumming of his heartbeat in his head against the pillow. He swallowed a firm lump in his throat, breathed. He closed his eyes and pulled the blankets up to his chin.

"Night, guys," said Blaze.

"Night," they replied softly.

Within the span of a minute, Blaze fell into sleep. A dreamless sleep with no nightmares nor visions of his parents. Just pure, mindless sleep.

And for that, he was grateful.

* * *

Blaze awoke to a gray sky morning. It was just before dawn, or so he figured. Deep gray light slipped through the narrow gaps of curtains, illuminating tiny specs of free-floating dust.

There was a soft hum throughout, a chorus of those still in deep sleep.

He lay there for a moment on the fence between rising and going back to bed. It had always been a struggle for him, since he was never a morning person. Blaze envied anyone who could open their eyes and spring out of bed. No matter how hard he wished for that to be him, it simply wasn't. He was a night owl, through and through.

Blaze raised the back of his hand to his forehead, held it there for a few seconds while listening to the soft lull of his breath, the gentle beat of his heart. He turned his head, felt the tightness in the muscles, as he sighed.

He lowered his hand atop the blanket before grabbing for the edge and pulling it off. He slipped out of bed, pulled on his pants that he'd neatly folded beneath the cot, slipped on some socks, and put on his shoes, tying them tight and snug.

Holding onto the lip of the thin mattress, he sat there, illuminated slightly by the light of early dawn, basking in its pale glow.

"Come on. Now or never," he pressured himself as he pressed off carefully, rising to his feet.

Blaze steadied himself, waiting for the light-headedness to pass. He looked over, saw the crest of Forrest's head peeking out from beneath the blanket. Aurora slept on her side, facing Blaze, her hair still tied back from hand-to-hand combat training last night.

Carefully, he wove through the cots, trying to keep his eyes focused on the ground so he wouldn't step on anything. As he did, he heard a soft rustling beside him. He paused, stepping slower.

"Getting up?" asked a soft, gravelly voice.

Blaze looked down and though his dark, wavy hair now covered his forehead instead of being slicked back and to the side, he knew it to be Trent.

"Er—yeah—sorry for waking you."

"It's fine. I was off tonight. Figured I'd catch up on some sleep. Need any help?" Trent continued. "I don't mind."

"I'm good. I'll wait up for the others. Thanks," whispered Blaze back.

Trent took a breath, nodded once against his pillow. "Cool. See you in a bit."

Blaze gave a thumb's up, but by the time his fist was already raised, Trent was already back in Dreamland.

When he got to the door, he reached for the handle and carefully turned it. He waited for the soft click before gently pushing it forward and stepping out through the narrow gap he left for himself.

The hallway was much darker. In the corner, a small lamp sat in the corner. He used the light and all of the shadows it cast, and made his way to the stairs before descending down to the main floor.

Creaking stairs kept the element of surprise to a minimum. If anyone else were awake, they'd know they weren't alone anymore. He made his way down quickly, gliding his hand along the metal railing of the staircase.

He wondered how many students went to the school before it became the Reaper's home base. He imagined dozens of bodies crammed together trying to scale the stairs to get to their next class.

Now, in the silence of a morning seven decades later, it was only Blaze, and he wasn't sure where he was even going.

His steps became louder once on the tiled floor of the school's corridors. He moved down them quickly, seeing more gray light down the hallways.

Blaze followed the path taken last night, heading towards the old cafeteria. He felt it would be a good place to sit and wait for the others. If there were more awake, he'd probably be able to sit and talk with them until breakfast, if breakfast was going to be served.

Blaze stopped in the bathroom and used the limited amount of light inside to look at his reflection and fix his hair. He brushed his fingers through and slicked some behind both of his ears.

Letting out a yawn, he stepped back a foot and placed both hands on the edge of the white sink.

"This is as good as it's going to get," he told himself. "Enjoy it."

And he released his grip, scratched below the cleft of his chin, and walked the short walk to the cafeteria.

When he arrived, he was met by the bloom of early light from the skylights. Unobstructed, it was nice to see windows in their entirety, not boarded up.

The long tables were empty, and as Blaze moved further in, he thought himself to be the only person up. But then he saw a small figure sitting alone at a table beneath another skylight.

Blaze paused, focused in. He realized in an instant it was Aiden. He teetered on the cusp of approaching or trying to slip out.

Poor kid was probably bored out of his mind. Part of Blaze felt it was too early for conversation. He didn't feel on his game until at least nine on a good day, but he couldn't just leave him. Not like this.

His footsteps must've given it away as Aiden turned, almost instantly, when Blaze approached.

"Up early," Blaze commented.

Aiden looked down for a moment, his hair tousled and in need of a comb. "I get up early," he said very matter-of-fact. "Why are you awake?"

"Same reason you are," answered Blaze. "Couldn't sleep."

Nodding, Aiden gestured for the bench. "Want to sit down? I can show you my comic books. They were my dad's."

"Definitely," replied Blaze. "Thanks."

He walked forward and took a seat, swinging one leg over at a time before plopping down onto the wooden bench. He rest his hands on the table top.

Spread out across the surface, were several comic books. A few were stacked in a small pile in the corner. Aiden held one in his hands, carefully turning the yellowed pages.

"Those are your dad's?" Blaze asked. "Did he collect them?"

"My grandpa did. They're older than you and me put together."

"A lot of things are older than you and me put together," Blaze laughed gently. "Mind if I look?"

"Sure, but be careful. Please."

"Of course," said Blaze, taking the one nearest him and paging through it.

It had been a long time since he last saw a comic book. Blaze liked reading the short, bolded words and looking at the pictures, which were still bright and colorful. He paged through it, taking care with each page.

"Who's this fellow?" Blaze asked, pointing to a white-faced man, wearing a purple suit and a manic grin.

"Oh, he's the villain in a lot of these. They never die, so the fights are useless," replied Aiden. "I like him though. He's a good bad-guy. You can borrow one, you know."

Blaze smiled. "Maybe one day. I saw you didn't come down last night for training. Why was that?"

"I tried, but Miss. Nori made me go to sleep. The grown-ups don't realize that I just end up waking up really early when they do that. I'm not a baby, but they treat me like one."

"It's a grown-up thing," admitted Blaze. "Tell me if I'm ever treating you like one."

"I will," Aiden stated firmly.

"So—are there any other kids?"

Aiden shook his head. "I'm the youngest. A few are older, but they don't pay me much attention."

"And your parents?"

Aiden looked forward, lowering his comic book slightly. "My mom and dad died," he said. "The adults here, they take care of me. But someday I won't need to be taken care of. I try to prove I'm okay, but they keep babying me."

Blaze swallowed a hard lump. "Yeah, I get what you're saying. But you're only eleven. I know it seems like you're grown-up, but you're not. Not yet. Up until last week, I thought I was grown-up, ready to take on the world. Boy was I wrong. I'd give anything to go back before all of this."

"But you can't," said Aiden. "You can't go back."

"I know," Blaze said. "It's a—it's a figure of speech."

Aiden nodded, setting down the comic book entirely.

"My parents died yesterday," Blaze admitted, feeling the tension in his throat, the clench of grief squeezing tight and binding. "They—er—they were protecting me. I'm seventeen and they were protecting me." He could feel his voice wobbling. He paused, steadied himself and his breath. He blew out quickly, shutting his eyes.

"I'm sorry," Aiden said. "The hurt goes away after a little bit. It doesn't feel like it will, but it does."

Blaze looked down, kept his eyes closed. He breathed steadily through his nose as he held the tears in. "Yeah, I know it will. But you're right, it doesn't feel like it will. But I brought this up because of what you said. How you don't like the adults taking care of you. It'll sound weird, but I wish someone could take care of me. I know, it's messed up—"

But Aiden shook his head. It comforted Blaze, when he didn't think anything could. "I understand," said Aiden. "It doesn't sound weird. I—I think it'll pass, too. I don't know. I hope it will."

Blaze nodded. "Yeah...well—"

"Are you okay?" Aiden asked quickly before Blaze could carry the conversation elsewhere. "How are you doing?"

"I'm trying not to think about it. The less I think about it, the better I am," replied Blaze.

"I wouldn't keep doing that. I'd talk to someone. Your friends, Miss. Nori, me. If you keep it all inside, you might blow-up."

"You might be right."

"I am right," Aiden pressed back firmly. "Don't hold it in. Talk."

Blaze sighed, leaning on his elbows and raised his right hand to rub his temples. "It's not so simple."

"I know, but you have to do it. You just have to."

Blaze waited a moment, savoring the silence. Though he knew Aiden was trying to help, he was feeling a rush of anxiety, of frustration pent up. Maybe the eleven-year-old was right, but right now, Blaze didn't want to talk about his parents' death. He wasn't ready now, and he wouldn't be more ready later. He took a breath, remembered Aiden was trying to help, and pressed on.

"So, what is on your agenda for today?"

"You're running away from the problem," Aiden countered, sounding much older than his age. "Don't change the topic—"

"*Aiden*," Blaze replied firmly, "I don't want to talk about it. I know you're trying to help, but I need you to stop. Okay?"

Aiden lowered his chin into his small frame. He nodded quickly, eyes widened slightly. "Okay," he replied in disappointed agreement. "Sorry."

Blaze shut his eyes feeling a tinge of regret in his words, but knew it wouldn't have ended well had he allowed him to keep going, to keep digging.

Raising his hand slowly, Aiden cleared his throat.

"You don't have to raise your hand. Just don't talk about my parents. Not now, okay?"

"I won't, but if you feel bad, you should talk with someone you trust. It doesn't have to be me, but talk to someone. I did and it helped me a lot. There, I'm done."

"Aiden, when the time is right, I will. Sorry for snapping at you."

"It's okay. You asked what I'm doing today. Miss. Nori asked me to help prepare some meals for later in the week, so she's going to teach me in the kitchen. I heard you're going out for supplies. Do you know where?"

"Sounds like an apartment complex? Right, that's housing for a large amount of people?"

"Before they all died, yes," Aiden said. "You never saw one?"

"We lived in houses—individual families, you know."

Aiden nodded. "This," he motioned outward, "is all I remember. I was born here."

"It's probably nice to have a bunch of people around, right? Like a big family."

Aiden lifted a brow, contemplating. "Even with everyone around, they don't always play with me or talk to me. It can get lonely. Donovan usually will spend time with me. We read my comics. Elliot also does. He'll bring back things for me to play with."

"That's nice of them," Blaze said, hearing a distant tap of footsteps. He turned, spotted a thin figure wearing a baggy T-shirt and loose athletic shorts.

Trent.

Blaze raised a hand, pausing for a few moments before saying, "Good morning."

Trent smirked, also raising a hand in greeting. "You woke me up, and I couldn't fall back asleep. Figured you'd be down here. Aiden—you too? When I was your age, I slept in as long as I could."

Aiden shrugged, turning his attention to the loose comic books spread across the tabletop. He reached out, collected them, and began sorting them. Blaze assumed he was placing them in order, based on the large, bolded numbers in the corners.

Blaze cleared his throat. "Aiden was showing me his comics. Pretty cool stuff."

Trent took a seat and extended his hands out onto the table, tapping a soft melody into the wood with his palms. "Yeah, they're neat. He almost always has one with him." He turned his attention to Blaze. "Sleep well?"

"Passed out."

"Figured," he chuckled lightly. "You guys had to of been beat. New names, new sights, and adding combat onto it? Talk about a full plate of a day. Not sure if you have any room for desert."

"Desert was a solid night's sleep."

"You count waking up now as a solid night?"

"It's a start. I feel good, a bit sore, but I'm doing good."

Trent adjusted his position on his chair, scratching the back of his forearm. "That's good to hear. Today's going to be a bit of a busy one, but once we're done, we're done."

"Going out for supplies, you mean?"

"Right. We're probably going to split up groups, so don't be surprised if you're not with your buddies."

"That's fine," he replied. "We're not bound at the hip."

"Even if you were, that's cool with me. It's a lot of change to take on yourself, so I fully support leaning on your friends. But know you can make friends here, too."

"I'm feeling that already, but it's good to hear. Can I talk to you about last night, something you said?"

"When? During training?"

Blaze shook his head. "Before we took a nap, when you were getting up. You talked about the Reapers—"

"Walk with me," Trent said. "Aiden, we'll be back in a bit."

"I'll be here," said Aiden.

Trent rose to his feet and helped Blaze rise to his. They moved quickly through the cafeteria and Blaze followed, unsure of where they were going next. Trent wove them through the corridors, up the staircase—three flights— before they reached a door that read: *Maintenance*.

"Taking me to a broom closet?"

"There's a ladder up to the roof," Trent said coolly, opening the door with the twist of the knob.

"You really don't want anyone to overhear us," laughed Blaze.

Trent turned to him, eyes cold. "Would you?"

"Er—no, I wouldn't," answered Blaze, dropping the light-hearted expression on his face.

"Yeah, figured," said Trent. "Follow me."

Trent opened the door and entered a small, darkened room. Sitting on a foldable card table was a wide flashlight. He took hold of it, turned it on.

A few feet from them was a rust-colored ladder that rose into the darkness above.

"Hope you're not afraid of heights," said Trent.

"Want me to go first or you?"

Blaze shrugged. "Heights don't bother me. I can go first. Just keep the light pointed upwards."

Climbing into the murky dark, Blaze moved at a steady pace, reaching up and stepping up fluidly. He felt a soft vibration below him as Trent stepped up, still aiming the flashlight towards the rafters.

In the flickering light, Blaze spotted a square door in the ceiling directly above him.

"When I get to the ceiling, what do I do with the door? Is it locked?"

"Not locked," Trent called up. "Gravity is our lock. Get some inertia and push up. It shouldn't be too bad. If I can lift it, you can."

Blaze climbed the last few rungs, remembering the crucial rule not to look down. He reached his hand out, and in a momentary burst of light from down below, spotted the handle. Blaze wrapped his fingers around it, gripping the solid metal tightly.

He took a breath, gripped the ladder with his left hand a bit tighter, and sprung vertical, pressing up. The door lifted easier than he first thought it would. Instantly blinded by early morning light, Blaze squeezed his eyes shut, as he lifted through and let go of the door. It caught itself on a mechanism and the door hung, slightly angled, away from the opening.

Blaze climbed the remaining rungs quickly, hoisting himself up and onto the gravel floor of the rooftop. He scooted back and took Trent's flashlight, set it aside. Reaching out, Trent took Blaze's hand as he lifted himself out of the darkness.

"Better be worth it," Blaze said, rising to his feet and dusting the back of his pants off with his hands.

"It'll be what you make of it," replied Trent. "I don't have all the answers, but I pay attention. I listen," he said, rising to his feet now, as well.

The two walked towards the half-wall of the rooftop. Against early dawn, the concrete and metal skeletal remains of Chicago pierced the sky. Mere silhouettes against the rising sun, Blaze steadied himself on the wall and looked across the abandoned city, losing his gaze somewhere between here and there, across the distant ruins.

He listened to the wind, felt its presence on his skin. But in the silence, found it unsettling. Though he knew no different, he knew this wasn't right. It didn't make sense. Cities were meant to be loud. He was meant to hear traffic and sirens. Now, in place of all that, was only the wind.

Blaze turned towards Trent, who had joined him at the edge. "Not that you'd know, but how long has it been like this?"

"You're right," Trent agreed, "I don't know. Since long before either of us were alive. I'd say within a year of the Illness being released."

"Released? Sounds like a weapon."

"Piecing it together, it sounds like the cloaked figure you saw was protecting us from others like them—others that don't care for us, though."

"Have you seen one?" asked Blaze.

Trent stared ahead before shaking his head gently. "Only sketches from others. They all look the same. Hooded, gray figures. Human in form, but obviously not." His jaw tightened. "I'm glad I haven't seen one. They'd scare the shit out of me. What was it like, you know, to be in its presence?"

Blaze leaned his head aside, unsure of how to respond. "Not really sure. I didn't think much about it. Guess I just kept my focus and didn't let it bother me, you know?"

"Not really," laughed Trent. "If some lifeform from another world was in front of me, I'm sure I'd freak out."

"Don't get me wrong, it was something—it was special—but I think I was so desperate to ask questions, I forgot who I was talking to."

"Yeah, still struggle to believe that," Trent replied, "but I can tell you're telling the truth, your truth. What do you want to know?"

Blaze's brows knitted together as he turned to Trent, avoiding the harsh orange light of the rising sun, cupping the side of his face with his left hand. "You talked last night about the Reapers and not trusting them—"

"Didn't say that. No, I said to be mindful. The group wants to live as much as anybody. You wall-dwellers were protected, and I'm not sure why. No one really knows why. They think you guys know all the secrets, all the answers."

Blaze's mouth was slightly ajar, his weight shifting on both feet.

But Trent was holding a hand up, shaking his head. "I know," he replied flatly, "you don't know the answers. But they think so and that's what matters. Like I said, if you have anything on you, let me know. I'll help you hide it."

He was already shaking his head. At this point, Blaze knew he needed to commit. There was no going back now. "Nothing," lied Blaze.

Trent kept his eyes on Blaze's, studying him. He stood still, hair blowing in the Chicago wind, before he pressed a hand to his temple. "Okay," he replied, clearly not convinced.

"*I don't,*" Blaze repeated firmer this time.

"Not questioning you," said Trent. "But, let's say you *come across* anything, I'm here to help. I love my friends here, but if you need something to be private, I'm a one way street."

"I appreciate it, but I don't think this will be a problem."

Holding his gaze, the corner of Trent's lip rose, highlighting the dimple of his think cheeks. "I'll drop it."

Secretly, Blaze breathed a sigh of relief. He changed the topic, transitioned smoothly. "Do you trust them? The Reapers? Weird name for a group, to be honest," said Blaze.

Trent rolled his shoulders, squaring them as he yawned. "They weren't always that," he replied quietly, reserved. "Used to be called something else, but I can't remember what. But as for them, I trust individuals. I keep bits to myself, and I'm mindful of who I talk to, who I share with."

"Why do you talk to us?"

"Because you're not a threat."

"That's a lot of trust in a few people you've only just met," Blaze replied, lifting a brow.

"You're not. Even now, you may not realize it, but you're still in deer-in-the-headlights mode. All of this," he motioned to the distant city with extended hands, "is mind-blowing. You're too new to this to be a threat to me. Plus, I can see you guys are good. After today, I'll see if you're useful. That'll be the real test."

"What's planned for today?"

"Eat breakfast, load up, and go," replied Trent. He relaxed his posture, slouching over the half wall. Resting on his forearms, he took in a deep breath of the fresh morning air. "It'll go smoothly. I can feel it. For you guys, it'll be good to jump in feet first. Nothing to be afraid of."

"Any tips?"

"Yeah. Follow our directions and don't get ahead of the operation. Remember your place. You're new to this, but don't be afraid to speak up if something seems odd."

"That's fair," Blaze agreed, leaning down to match Trent's frame. "Anything else?"

"Sure, I've got one more for you: Tie your shoes tight and be ready to run."

"From what?" asked Blaze.

Trent turned, inched closer. "Anyone that's not one of us."

THIRTEEN

After breakfast, those going out for supplies today had gathered in the entrance hall of the school. There were only a few of them: Aurora, Blaze, Forrest, Donovan and Amelia, Rose, Elliot, and Trent.

Donovan stood at the head of the group with a canvas backpack slung behind his right shoulder. He held the strap away from his chest, his other hand over his hip, thumb lightly stroking a gun in a holster.

Trent stepped beside Donovan and turned to face the group. "Forrest, Rose, and Amelia, you're with me."

Donovan cleared his throat and raised his brows, eyes widening slightly. "And Blaze, Aurora, and Elliot, you're landed with me."

Blaze looked to Forrest. "Guess this is where we part ways," he said.

Forrest shrugged. "Eh, you'll both be fine. Besides, abstinence makes the heart grow fonder."

"That only applies if we're dating," Blaze said. He lifted his left hand, showed his ring-finger. "Last I checked, no promise ring," he laughed.

Forrest's skin flushed as he stifled a laugh. "Good one," he said.

Aurora stepped a foot closer. "I think a little break is what you both need. Especially after that."

Elliot stood beside Forrest and planted his large hand on his shoulder. "They wanted to get to know you better anyways."

"What about us?" asked Aurora.

Elliot scrunched his lips, lifted his brows. "Eh—" he broke off with a laugh. "Only joking. They picked. Not us. They'll keep him safe and return him in one piece."

"You better," said Aurora, "who else will I get to use my quirky, know-it-all, motherly lines with?"

"Me?" asked Blaze.

Aurora smirked. "You don't count."

Behind them, the door to the cafeteria opened. Nori stepped through holding several bags in hand. She walked to Elliot first. "Here, take these. Pass them down."

"What are they?" he asked his mother.

"Granola bars. Had some left-over granola, made some peanut butter, added some flour. Should be edible. Not great, but edible."

"That's the least we can hope for," replied Elliot, taking the bags, choosing one, and passing the rest to Rose.

"Don't be a smart-mouth, child. I brought you onto this Earth, and I can take you straight out."

"*Woah!*" exclaimed Elliot. "Fighting words. You guys hear this?"

Donovan shook his head rapidly. "Nope! Not jumping into this one. You're on your own, friend."

"Thanks, man. Appreciate the support."

Nori tilted her head, focused her glare upon Elliot. "Just be grateful for the treat. You'll need your energy today. All of you."

Blaze raised the bag. "Thanks."

"Yeah," agreed Forrest. "Thank you."

Nori waved her hand dismissively. "Don't mention it." She turned her focus to Trent, to Donovan. "What's your plan?"

Donovan shrugged, rotated his palms to face the ceiling. "You know how we do things, Nori. We play it by ear—"

"Great," she sighed. "That is code for, 'We have no plan.' Just what I wanted to hear." Nori shut her eyes, found her focus. "That's not good enough. I want plans, I want times."

"Since when?" pressed Elliot.

"Since today. Activity's been increasing in the area. Daylight, nighttime—doesn't matter. The other groups are spreading out, reaching further towards us and our space."

"And we're going deeper in. You know how it is. The good stuff—the quality loot—is all inside the city."

"And so are the enemies," Nori reminded them. "Don't forget that."

"We're careful," replied Elliot.

"That's not good enough. Jesus, child. You need to do better than that. Need to try harder than that. One bad choice and you're good as gone. Ashes to ashes, dust to dust."

"You know a little optimism wouldn't hurt, Mom," said Elliot.

"I'm serious, Elliot James. You need to be careful, plan things out. I want to see you guys with maps and time frames. I want to know things to a tee."

"And how is that useful?" Donovan asked. "You know how it goes, Nori. Nothing is planned, nothing ever works out the way you hope it will. It's probably best we don't have a plan. We'd be more likely to try to stick to it at all costs, even when it's not safe, just to say we followed the plan," he said. "This way, we're responding to immediate, timely information and nothing is out of date. Besides—Maps? Really? They're decades out of date."

"The streets are the same," countered Nori. "Have you seen a construction crew designing and building a new road in the last seventy-years? No? Didn't think so. Don't knock the power of a good map. You'd be surprised."

Trent twisted his wrist in front of him, pointed to an imaginary watch with his other hand. "Boy, look at the time. We better head out. Wear your gear with pride and congratulate our new friends on their first venture into the city."

A few—Rose, Elliot, and Donovan clapped. Forrest joined in as well, quickly remembering the applause was for them.

But Nori maintained a stern expression on her face, and her brows lowered. "I'm not joking," she said, "I want specifics."

"Why are you being like this?" Elliot asked. "You never cared before."

She turned to him. "Well, I do now."

Elliot sighed, dug his hands into his hips. "Either of you guys know?"

Trent looked to Donovan. "I thought we had agreed on the apartment complex."

"I thought we had, too," replied Donovan. "It's a few blocks east. Can't miss it."

Nori's eyes fell to meet the worn flooring. She crossed her arms, pressed her fingers into her thick arms, and made tiny indents in her skin. "Okay, and how long are you planning on staying out?"

"We have a curfew now?" Donovan asked stiffly.

Nori turned to him. "How long?"

He didn't dare return her tone. "A few hours. Back by early afternoon, I'm guessing. As long as it takes."

Satisfied, Nori dropped her arms, smoothed out her shirt and picked free a piece of lint. "Very good. You be back before dusk. If not, we aren't coming looking for you until morning. You know the rules…"

Forrest raised his hand slowly. "Er—what are the rules?"

"We don't go out after dark," she said coolly. "You'll see why soon enough."

"The others?" asked Blaze.

She nodded. "Not a pretty sight. Some people need order. Helps to keep things in line. Keep them in check. You can imagine what happens when there isn't law and order for decades. It's every man for himself."

"And that's why we go out, too," Trent said. "No one cares if we live or die. But between you and me, I don't have a death wish. We're smart, and we're respectful of others we come across. Respect gets you far in this world. Don't forget it."

"Are others respectful of you guys?" asked Forrest.

"Not always," Trent replied. "But we won't worry about that until there's reason to be worried. You guys ready?"

Blaze looked around, as if a line of speech would be written in graffiti on the school walls, and when read, would be a sure way to get him out of it. As excited as he had been, he could now feel the pull of dread guiding him back to his corner of safety, of security. He knew he would need to press through. After all, he wasn't doing this alone. He was with friends—old and new. They wouldn't steer him down the wrong path. But no matter how much he thought of this in his mind, it didn't help.

Blaze looked to them, and his expression relaxed. "I'm good. Are you guys?"

"Ready as we'll ever be," Forrest replied.

Trent looked to him and smiled. "That's what we want to hear." He looked to Nori. "We'll be back—"

"Before dusk," reminded Nori.

"Before dusk," Trent agreed.

And with a wave of the hand, a dismissal, she waved them off, free to head out into the world. Nori turned and walked back where she had come from.

Awkward silence hung over them, crushing and heavy for the next few seconds. There was an uncertainty—an uncertainty of what comes next and of who's in charge. But there wasn't too much uncertainty for long, however, because Donovan stepped forward, pulling his backpack onto both shoulders. He even went as far as to connect the two parts of the buckle that hung on woven straps dangling from the main straps.

Donovan cleared his throat "All right. Stick to your groups. We'll reconvene at the fountain a few streets away. Be back there by two-thirty, three at the latest," he said firmly.

There was a unanimous agreement and understanding. No one would dare press their luck and show up beyond the limits of the wide time frame. Blaze looked over to Donovan, spotted the dull, chipped wrist watch that clung tightly to his wrist. Two-thirty was fair. It allowed for several hours to explore and left plenty of time to re-group should they be separated.

Donovan walked forward towards the entrance doors. They were well-barricaded with chains, deadbolt locks, and boarded-up windows closing them in and away from the outside world. School desks were stacked against the front wall. A few were pulled aside to allow for a narrow gap that led to the door.

Sitting in a chair, with their feet on a desk, was a tall, pixie-haired female. She looked up from the old fiction novel she was reading, bending a corner at the top as a bookmark. The OCD in Blaze cried out within, slamming against his gut and forcing him to look away for a moment.

"Heading out?" she asked, voice disinterested and forced.

"We are," answered Trent. "Four with me, including me. Four with Donovan, himself included."

The female sat up, looking over the group. "Copy, four and four." She jotted down notes on a piece of notebook paper. "Have fun," she said, nearly mockingly.

Donovan reached for the deadbolts and unsecured all of them. He pushed aside the loose-hanging chains, hung them up where the female would be able to secure the door again after they left.

He turned to the group, looked them over. "Fountain by two-thirty," Donovan said flatly. There was no inclination of an offer or alternative. Set in stone, two-thirty was it.

A unanimous nod came from the others.

Trent straightened his posture, pointed to the group assigned to him. "We'll go first," he said.

Donovan nodded, lifting a solid metal bar that lay across the door. "Be my guests," he replied, opening the door to the outside world.

Morning air, damp and cool, pressed into the small, darkened space. Blaze took in the scents of abandoned Chicago with stride, imagining a world that no longer existed, but reminded himself to focus on the mission ahead.

What captured him most, however, was the silence. The silence of death was loud and powerful. He felt it, drum-like, carried down the streets on the wings of the dead. He felt it in his head. Felt it in his heart. And if Blaze listened closely, he swore he could hear the despair in the wind.

Waved forward by Trent, Forrest was the first to follow. Then Amelia and Rose.

"See you guys later," Blaze said, offering a hand of farewell.

Forrest's lips pursed together, curling up at the corners. "Yeah, see you, Blaze. Remember to be on your best behavior," he added.

Blaze swallowed a laugh. "Yeah, you too, my friend."

And without a moment for hesitation, Trent led the three others out into the world, leaving the remaining four in the shadows.

"We'll just give 'em a minute," Donovan said, turning to face them and leaning against the wall beside the opened door. He lifted his right leg and pressed the sole of his brown boot against the wall.

"Looks like a cooler day, today," he observed, looking outside, unbuckling the front buckle on his backpack.

"What?" Aurora asked.

"The day. It's gonna be cool out. Can't you tell?" he scooped some air with his hand, cupped it, and waved it in. "*See?*"

Aurora cocked her head, maintaining a fixed expression. "Doesn't quite work like that. But, yes, I noticed."

The short-haired girl, having only just returned to reading, put her book down. "Is she the one you were telling me about?"

"Yeah, that's her," he said, then looked back outside, nibbling on his lower lip.

"What'd he say?" asked Aurora.

She smirked, lifting her pierced brow quickly and lowering it. "Nothing too harsh," she replied, raising her book and her gaze where it was just skimming above the tops of the pages.

"You're a real jerk, you know that, right?" said Aurora.

"Wow. Now who's being a jerk?" Donovan looked back to her. "Like Cari said, it wasn't anything too harsh, so you should chill."

Blaze looked to her, but Aurora held her gaze on him and wouldn't give in. Elliot watched a few feet from them, amused.

Donovan lowered his boot from the wall, straightening his posture as he took in a deep inhale through his nose. "Is this going to be a problem now? Because if it is, we'll just leave you here. And then—you know—then Blaze and I can do some bonding. And I'm sure he'd *love* that, too, wouldn't you, Blaze?"

"Er—I would?" Blaze questioned.

"Right. See, Aurora?"

"I'm not going to be a problem, I'm not a problem, and I'm not planning on becoming a problem." Aurora shook her head. "I'll stick to my lane, you stick to yours? Deal?"

Donovan widened his chest, squared his jaw. "Well, you're in my group, so we may find that to be a bit of a challenge, won't we?"

Aurora rocked on her heels, crossing her arms across her chest. "Okay, let me simplify it for you this way," she spoke with piercing precision, each word the cut of a freshly sharpened blade, "if you're not a dick to me, I won't be a bitch to you? There, does that clear things up for you? Have I set the ground rules?"

Donovan smirked, nodding in understanding, in admiration, though he'd never admit that; certainly not to her or anyone standing in the room. He looked out the doorway, turning back to face the group. "As a matter of fact, it does. Let's head out."

Cari lowered her book, cleared her throat. "Yeah, Donovan, she's a keeper. Don't mess this one up."

And before Aurora could reply, to really press for what had been said, Donovan was already out the door and Blaze was following.

They stepped down the steps of the school. Blaze pointed to a breakage in the concrete, warning Aurora and Elliot to watch their step. They did so and were on the sidewalk after two steps more. Donovan had leapt, landing with one hand firmly on the ground.

"Who are you trying to impress? Look around. Newsflash, the city's a ghost town. Everyone's dead," said Elliot, looking to him.

Lined down the road, along the concrete walkways, thick-rooted and overgrown trees pressed into the old storefronts of grocery stores, bakeries, barbershops, and gadget stores. The metal fences that had protected them had been ripped down, thrown carelessly aside so looters could claim what was behind them, as if a new television would save them from the Illness, raw meat would last decades after society collapsed, and fresh baguettes would hold over starving stomachs decades later.

Even though Blaze wasn't alive for this, never seeing the desperation, he wondered why people would be so dull. Then he remembered the keyword, here—desperation. Desperation could drive even the soundest minded of people into madness, the most good-natured, kind-hearted into monsters. Somewhere, eventually, desperation took its toll, made its incision, and bled out all the good left in a person.

"How long until things calmed down?" asked Blaze, looking away from the remnants.

Donovan spun around, continuing to walk backwards. He pulled on the straps of his backpack, thumbing the canvas material. "Calmed down? Er—I guess until most of 'em died. Left a shit-storm of a mess, don't you think? *Animals...*"

"A bit harsh for people trying to survive, don't you think?" Aurora asked, her tone still razor sharp.

Donovan's gaze shot to Aurora. "What happened to keeping to your lane?" he asked. "Don't defend them. This—" he pointed, arms now stretched towards both sides of the street: the debris, the destruction—"is their leftovers. They acted like dogs, fought each other instead of working with each other. Between us, it's good they didn't last long. We don't need selfishness in our society. We work for the greater good."

"But can you understand they were scared and needing supplies?" pressed Aurora. "I get it. Greed is an ugly thing, but there's a reason for it. If you—"

"Don't defend the dead, Aurora," Donovan said. "They can't hear you, and the living don't want to hear it."

* * *

The group lost sight of Trent and the others a short while later.

He made sense of the streets. Made sense of the numbers and words associated with the roads, avenues, and lanes. Each had specific meaning and an association of place. At some intersections, the signage had faded, bleached by sunlight and aged by time and the elements.

Blaze had to fight to keep his focus close to him. In the distance, the jungle of concrete and steel—skyscrapers— pierced the sky, much taller than the walls around River Ridge.

Nearby, the buildings were smaller and fatter. As they passed, some windows in the buildings were shattered. Torn and shredded curtains blew outward, like ghosts suspended in the wind.

Aurora pointed towards them. "Have you checked those?"

"Someone has. Not me. Not personally, no," replied Donovan. "Any ideas?" he asked Elliot.

He shook his head quickly. "No clue."

After clearing his throat, Blaze asked, "How do you guys decide where you go next?"

"Whatever hasn't been looted," Donovan replied. "Getting harder and harder nowadays, as you can imagine."

Blaze quickened his step, moving quickly to walk alongside Donovan. He lowered his voice, his tone. *"And society never recovered?"*

Donovan laughed, scratching his chin. "Er—*well*—you tell me. Define recovered. Does this look like recovery? Maybe we have different definitions of recovery?" He motioned around them. "I mean—you know—after the panic, after the death, I guess you could say some sense of order found its way back. Don't get me wrong, it wasn't ideal. The original government tried to regain control, but the people decided they were inept and not to be trusted. A bit brave, a bit reckless. A gamble during a crisis. Not sure if it worked out for the best or not. I guess we'll never know what the alternate was, so it's dumb to even daydream."

"Deal with reality," Blaze replied absentminded.

He pointed to Blaze. "Right," Donovan said. "Exactly. Play with the cards we're dealt, not the ones we wish we had."

Blaze listened to the silence for a moment, steadying his thoughts and trying to be mindful of what he would ask next. He continued, "And the other groups?"

"What about them?"

"Do they get along with everyone? I mean—people help each other out? Try to get through it together, right?"

Taking a breath in, Elliot moved beside Blaze. "We don't really co-mingle," he said. "We do deal with them, from time to time. Trades of information and things, tools, food, you name it. We mostly keep to ourselves, though."

Donovan kept his attention on the mission in progress and the path ahead of them. He started to slow, Blaze noticed.

His stride shrank, footsteps slowed.

He was listening.

Focusing.

The others caught on quickly. Blaze came to a stop, letting Donovan continue forward a few more feet, where Elliot also joined him. The two veterans of the group turned their heads, peered around.

Rising above them, on both sides of the road, was an old apartment building twenty or so floors up. It was the first in a line of tall buildings beginning to mark the edge of the makeup of the city's skyline.

"Anything good?" asked Blaze quietly.

Donovan shook his head, defeated. "Thought I heard something, but no."

"It's very quiet," agreed Elliot, scratching the back of his right arm with curved fingers.

"Isn't that good?" Aurora asked, stepping forward carefully, keeping her gaze surveying the surrounding area. "Don't you normally keep to yourselves anyway?"

"Usually yes," said Donovan, "but—*SHIT!* Get down!"

Of instinct and propelled by adrenaline, Blaze lurched off his feet to the side. In a frozen moment, he felt the air rushing into his lungs and felt himself defying gravity. It was as if he were flying.

But he fell, and he fell hard. His knee smacked into the curb, and he cried out. Blaze squeezed his eyes shut as the sharp ache and numbing throb of pain wrapped itself around his knee.

Then came gunfire. Single bullets, every few seconds, were being fired.

He spotted an old mail drop with splotches of blue still visible. Blaze mustered up some strength, emptying the reserves of adrenaline that hadn't been used, and crawled quickly. Around him, the others took refuge behind one of the dozens of abandoned cars on the street.

But one thing was certain, the gunfire was coming from the apartment complex. He looked over, saw Elliot comforting Aurora. Donovan was digging into the backpack he'd brought along with them.

"Dude, do something!" Elliot hissed.

Donovan shut his eyes, took a breath. He cupped his hands across his mouth. "Elise! It's Donovan."

The gunfire stopped. Silence returned to the city once again.

"*Donovan?*" asked a distant female voice with a smoker's rasp. "Is that you?"

Donovan raised both hands, standing up slowly. "Yeah. Not quite the greeting we were looking for. Didn't know you guys had moved."

Blaze peeked around the edge of the mail drop and saw a few figures standing on one floor of the building behind opened windows—young faces, a few old ones. All of them, regardless of their age or color, were holding rifles. In the center, aiming down a scope was an older white female—late sixties—with bold red hair, streaked pale pink at the roots.

Blaze kept low to the ground, mindful of his surroundings. In this world, trust was something you didn't give up easily, even after it was earned. He kept his sight scanning, looking for any other signs of trouble, if the line of marksmen in the apartment weren't enough.

Stepping forward, Donovan pointed in the direction of the fiery-haired woman. "Elise, mind putting the rifle down?"

"Not wearing my glasses, Donny, so this scope is the best I can do," she said, pulling her eye away momentarily from the sight, leaning back, and rising just a little. "Can't see worth a damn."

Looking up, he saw pots with tall greenery and sunflowers in a few for decoration. Some life in the city was refreshing and much needed. Fresh herbs—basil, thyme, rosemary—lined one of the balconies of the complex. As the tower climbed, so did the variety of plants for consumption.

"How many have you brought?" asked the red-haired woman, Elise.

"Four, myself included," he replied. "We weren't planning on stopping, but I guess we'll have a change of plans."

She leaned her head back into the scope, scanned her rifle downward across the roadway. Blaze leaned back.

"Show them," she called out from behind the gun. "I won't shoot. Promise. If it makes you feel better, just pretend it's a fancy telescope—if telescopes fired bullets—but I digress."

Aurora stood up first, offering a wave. "Nice to meet you," she said, "I'm Aurora. We're friends of Donovan's."

"Yes, I can see that," Elise said, almost drowned out by a gust of wind. "And the other two?"

Elliot stood up next, placed his hands on the hood of the rusted car.

"Why be a stranger? We're friends, Elliot," said Elise. "And the last?"

Blaze pressed off the cement and turned to her. He felt his knees shaking beneath him, and he steadied himself against the mail drop. Looking down the sights of a rifle aimed directly at him wasn't exactly the most comforting. In general, he knew he grew a bit nervous meeting new people. But this time, and only this time, he would give himself a break.

"Name?" Elise called out, still aiming her rifle at him.

"Er—Blaze," he said.

She shook her head, frustrated. "Honey, I can't hear whispers. Say it again. Say it loud and proud!"

"*Blaze!*" he called out again, cupping his hands around his mouth.

"Much better," said Elise. "Unique name."

Blaze shifted on his weight, unsure of what to say next. For his sake, Donovan continued on.

"Mind if we come up?" he asked. "We could use a drink, a snack."

"What do you think this is? A hotel? Bring your own damn food and drink," Elise said, stepping back from the rifle.

"Okay—a visit? Can we stop in?"

"Fine," Elise replied stiffly, waiving for them to approach. "I'll meet you at the entrance. No funny business, Donovan, I'm not in the mood today," she said cautiously, raising a finger. "And I don't like false promises."

Donovan extended a hand and gave a thumbs up. "You bet. We'll behave."

Seemingly satisfied, she flashed a peace sign and stepped back, placing her firearm into the arm of a young male near her. He seemed a bit perplexed, unsure of what to do with his leader's weapon. Blaze smirked, forcing down a laugh.

But he looked to his own group and saw Donovan waiving for him to approach. Blaze stepped away from the mail drop and towards him. But Donovan exhaled quickly, tapping his boot against the pavement.

"A bit quicker, please," he said.

"S-Sorry." Blaze moved into a jog, came to a stop beside the group and put his hands into his pockets.

"She's a bit wacky. Harmless, but wacky. Sometimes we trade with them. I brought a data stick to share information. They may want it, might not. Just be on your best behavior and don't push anyone's buttons."

Elliot folded his arms. "The others are nice. Elise is a bit *off*. She's seen a lot, so we don't hold it against her."

In front of them, Blaze heard the familiar clanging of chains, of opening locks and sliding barricades. It wasn't much longer until the door to the apartment complex was opened, the make-shift overhang still masking much of the door in shadow.

Elise stepped out into the sunlight. A young male stood behind her, hand ready to reach for a pistol on his hip.

"Donovan, good to see you. How's Carl doing? Asking about me often? I always had a thing for older men."

"Er—yeah, daily," Donovan replied. "He's good. A bit tired, but still running the show pretty much. How about you? Your hair—"

"I know," she interjected, "isn't it *fabulous*?" she asked, running a well-lined hand through it. Side-swept bangs blew in the breeze revealing heavily penciled-in brows, raised in excitement.

"It is. Aurora, darling, what do you think?"

"Like a sunset," she offered with a smile. "A fiery one."

Elise continued to toy with her hair, wrapping a curl around her finger. "The secret is to double the amount of Fruit Punch powder-mix. Smells good and gives you that special flare, you know? Take note, Missy, it'll be your turn soon enough. I know this may come as a bit of a shock, but I'm only twenty-or-so years older."

Donovan raised a brow, eyes widened. "Twenty years older than what? Her mother?" he asked.

"Now, now, we're practically sisters?"

It took great strength to keep Blaze from laughing. To do so, he had to imagine the possible danger laughing at someone who was clearly a bit delusional—could bring.

Aurora wisely pressed beyond, pulling Elise's attention back to her hair; something she was proud of, unlike the reality of aging. "But when you wash your hair, doesn't the—uhm—*dye*—come out?"

"Of course, silly girl. That's why I don't wash it. Well, okay—I take that back. I wash it once a week. Don't want you to think I'm some slob." She lowered her hand, looked both ways down the street. "The things we do for beauty, right? Anyway, come, come in. Lots to catch up on and lots to chat about."

Donovan led the way, following the two from the other group into their home base.

Blaze climbed the steps beside Aurora. *"This should be good."*

"Stay vigilant," Aurora said beneath her breath.

At first he thought she was joking, but when he turned to her, she didn't return his gaze, and continued up the stairs. Having known Aurora all these years, Blaze knew she didn't joke like this. It never had been her style, nor was it now.

Blaze dropped the smirk, continued up beside her. He took her hand in his, squeezed it, before letting it go. Out of the corner of his eye, he saw her turn slightly to him and lift the corner of her lips just before they entered the complex.

It took a few moments for his eyes to adjust to the dark. Windows lining the walls were boarded-up with mismatched scrap wood. Slivers of light that snuck through the gaps lit the area in streaks. As they adjusted, his eyes noticed crates built up in make-shift walls, doorways sealed with chains, and old furniture—likely original to the building—arranged to make a narrow corridor to another set of doors. Now, only mere skeletons—shadows of their former selves—the fabric of the couches and chairs had been ripped, the stuffing long-gone, the springs taken and used elsewhere.

"Love the new place," Donovan said.

"It's fine for now," Elise replied coolly, brushing a hand over the top of an old couch. "Still figuring out where I want stuff."

She led them down the hallway, through the narrow furniture corridor. "Mind your head," she said, placing a hand above the crown of hers. "Especially you tall, handsome boys," she said.

Blaze appreciated the warning, bending at the knees a bit. He placed both hands on the walls as he slid through the narrow channel behind Aurora, forcing down a bit of anxiety that was creeping its way up in the confined space.

They slipped through the narrow corridor and entered a dim, open space. In one corner, along empty shelves built into the wall, sat four wooden crates aligned in a circle. On the wall, a large television from the old world was still hanging. The cord that once provided electricity to it had been pulled, dangling along the wall after all these years.

Blaze pointed to it. "Crazy to see one, isn't it?"

"Shouldn't be," Aurora replied, "but it is. Always is a bit trippy seeing any old tech."

Elise turned to them, her face even more gaunt in the darkness. "Oh, that dusty thing? Doesn't work. Hasn't worked since the world went kaput."

"Figured," Blaze said. "That'd be a trick, you know—getting it to run off anything but electricity."

Elise nodded, thumbing her wrist "Yeah, I won't see it. We're moving too slow to catch up during my life. You might see it, but that's a big *might*."

"Optimism isn't your strong suit, is it, Elise?" Donovan asked.

She looked to him, leaned her head slightly. "Never was yours either, was it now?"

"And that's why we get along so well," he said, breaking the facade and cracking a smile. "Mystery solved."

Elise motioned to the corner with the crates. "Sit, please. Make yourselves welcome. Anyone want a glass of water?"

Blaze raised his hand, lowering it quickly when he realized the others weren't. "Er—I'll take one, if you don't mind."

"If I minded, I wouldn't have offered. Zayne, go grab our guest a cup of water. Anyone else?"

Aurora sighed, teetering on the edge of decision. She gave in, raised her hand too, but kept hers up. "I'll take one, too, thanks."

Elise looked around. "Anyone else? Going once...*twice...SOLD!*"

Behind her a short, brown-haired boy nodded and took off without word.

302

"Zayne, do make sure the water is ice-cold." She turned back to them, lifted her brows. "We always offer our *best* to guests."

Bustling away, Zayne raised a thumbs-up before vanishing into what Blaze assumed was a kitchen.

Donovan sat down on the crate closest to the corner as the others took seats. "Making your servants do your job?" he asked, pulling his knee into his chest and double-knotting both of his boots.

"My job? I'm too old to be fetching water," Elise replied. "When you're my age, you'll get it. You'll understand. When you hit forty, you get other people to fetch for you. One of the few perks of getting old."

"So, they've been fetching for you for a while now, eh?" asked Donovan.

Elise's face contorted as if she smelled something foul. "I'll pretend I didn't hear that. So, what do you have for us?"

"Jumping straight to the point. I like it," he said.

She shrugged. "I have no interest in chit-chat. Never did as a girl, and not as a woman with no time to waste."

Donovan reached around and slipped off his backpack. He propped it up between his knees and unzipped it. The room remained silent, listening to the rustling of supplies. He dug for a few still moments until he let out a brief, "Ah."

Withdrawing his hand, held between his right thumb and index finger was a small metal rectangle. Even in the dim lighting, it glistened.

Elise lifted her brows. "Let's see if the saying, 'good things come in small packages' is true. What do you have?"

"Data stick," he replied, holding it out towards her.

"You can't keep bringing those. Last one had duplicates."

"This one doesn't. Checked it myself. Maps, information, top-secret files from the old world," Donovan said. "I think you'll like the material on the Creators."

She sat up in her seat, eyeing the device. "How good is the info? Worth starting-up the generator?"

"I think it's worth the fuel," Donovan replied.

Zayne had returned to the open space, two glasses of water in hand. He stood behind Elise, waiting to interrupt.

But she turned to him, beat him to it. "Well, don't just stand there and look cute. Go on, hand them out."

He did, quickly moving between Aurora and Blaze.

"Thanks," Aurora said, taking the glass from him.

When Zayne reached him, Blaze took the glass. "Thank you."

He nodded, then looked to Elise again.

"Take this, start up the computer, and load it. And do check for duplicates," she said, looking back to Donovan.

Zayne took the data stick and without further word left the space in another direction.

Donovan cleared his throat. "You'll be excited to hear that Blaze and Aurora are from River Ridge—one of the walled cities."

She turned to Donovan, waiting a moment to reply. She took an inhale, then looked back to the two. "Let's drop the act, Donny. We both know I knew that. Carl told me. He also said your group is in trouble, needing help."

Blaze looked to Donovan, wanting answers. But none would be given. Not yet.

Elise smirked, looking over to Blaze and Aurora. "Don't worry, kids. I won't hurt you, since I don't want you," she said. "No, it's the device you brought back that we need. The one from the others—the Council. Now, you'd do well to hand it over if you don't want trouble."

FOURTEEN

Elise's hawk-like eyes focused on Blaze, then to Aurora. "So," she pressed, "which one of you has it."

Aurora looked to Donovan. "You ratted us out?"

Donovan lowered his eyes to the floor, "I didn't, but I know who did. Shit..."

"These two are from River Ridge and your grandfather thought we might be willing to help you out if we met. A former resident meets two younger ones. Tell me, kids, how is Victor Winslow? Still up to his usual tricks? Did he ever mention the girl who escaped the first time the walls fell? The day I found our device?"

"First time?" asked Blaze. "The wall came down only once. When we left."

"Please, don't be naive. It was twenty-years ago. Left on my own, on my own accord. By the time the officials caught on, I was long gone. They figured no one had known about it—the wall opening up—so they closed it with their tool and

BEYOND

acted like nothing ever happened. Eventually, I'm sure they caught on that I was nowhere to be found. I swore I would be no one's prisoner. Now, hand me what you found. I need it for ours."

"Wait." Blaze held up a hand. "How did your grandfather know?" he asked Donovan. "You went through my things?"

"Didn't need to," said Donovan. "I was told."

"By who? Forrest?"

Donovan shook his head. "Someone in this room."

Blaze looked over, and from the moment he caught her out of his periphery, he knew the terrible truth. It was Aurora. Aurora had told Donovan about the artifact.

Blaze's lower lip quivered on the cusp of speech. He bit down on his lip to stop himself from saying something he'd regret. But right now, he sure did feel like saying something that would hurt her and cut her deep.

"Blaze, I'm sorry. I didn't think this would happen. I swear," said Aurora.

"Regardless, it's happening now. Here we are," he replied.

From the doorway behind them, there was a change in light, a shadow making itself seen. Blaze turned, saw Zayne standing there.

"Elise," he said softly, "data stick is good. Worth a trade."

"Get a few others down here," she said, looking over to him finally. "I think our new friends aren't going to part with theirs so easily."

Zayne nodded, left again.

Donovan looked to Blaze. "Look, man, I—I'm sorry. They'll help us all out, but you have to give them yours."

But Blaze wasn't about to reply to him. No, he was past the point of even listening. He could hear nothing over the drumming of his heart. Nothing but the trembling breaths he was taking.

"It doesn't do anything," said Blaze.

"Then surely you won't be missing out when you hand it over," Elise replied.

Three others entered the room with rifles slung on their backs. They kept their distance, standing alongside the back wall.

"So you're from River Ridge?" asked Aurora.

Elise shifted her gaze over to her, focused. She cleared her throat. "I am. Grew up there, left, found this place. It was headed by someone else back then. After a few years, after a few disagreements, he stepped down. The rest trusted me over him. But defeated, he became a traitor, as most men become. Tried to sell our device to a neighboring group. Tried to screw us over. I couldn't let him get away with that. No, I couldn't."

"What do you know about it? Why's it so important?" Aurora continued.

Blaze looked over to her. He wondered if these were genuine questions or attempts at stalling. Was Aurora offering a chance to run. To escape? He looked around the room, careful not to be too obvious about it. Masked by shadow, if his movements were subtle, no one would be the wiser that he was looking for an escape route.

"Alone? Nothing. Just ancient relics of a civilization that no longer exists. Together? Merged? They're everything."

Blaze pulled his attention back to the present, to the conversation at hand. "Ancient?"

"Ancient," Elise repeated. "Advanced civilization—the Council. Think of us as the children that never rise to the greatness of their parents. The Creators made us, but the Council built the walls for the day they'd want to save us, protect us from the horrors out there. I don't know much about them, so don't ask. They don't make themselves known."

Aurora held up her hand. "But what does all of this have to do with the artifacts?"

"Listen, Missy, the devices were planted randomly inside the walled-in sections, only to be found by the inhabitants who'd be saved. Following me?"

"I'm following."

Elise took in an inhale, breathed it out. "How should I say this?" she questioned herself.

"One word at a time," answered Aurora. "We can handle it."

"Thank you for the lesson on constructing a sentence. I really needed it," Elise quipped back. She clasped her veined hands, admiring a few sun spots as if they were tattoos of years gone by. "We don't know much about them, but what we've pieced together—from them, from other survivors—is that the Council are an off-shoot group of the Creators. Think of them like grandparents. Well, the grandparents are pissed at the grandchildren. No birthday money, no extra slice of cake, no gifts. Nada. *Nothing*," she said. "The grandparents want us grandchildren dead. We're the bastards of the family. A screwed-up family of sorts."

"Er—sure, whatever you say," said Aurora.

"Well don't agree if you don't agree. That's just stupid. But we are what we are, so don't disagree. The Council have some connection to us. They want to protect us. They had a feeling we'd be the black sheep, so they planned ahead and planted those walls. Probably with a bit of mind-warping, they had the original founders build the city outward and only to the boundaries of the walls. I'll never know how they got it so precise. But those walls are old. Not seventy-years-old. I mean *old*."

"Hundreds?" asked Aurora.

Elise raised a thumb, quickly moved her hand up and down. "Higher, dear."

"*Thousands?*" Blaze joined in.

"Roughly. Give or take a few centuries. The device you have is as old as the walls, same as ours."

Blaze's brows crossed, and he looked aside, trying to remember what the device looked like. He remembered the smooth plastic, the unchanged white with a soft glisten. It couldn't be thousands of years old. Blaze had seen pictures in his old school books of relics from ancient civilizations. The thing in his backpack didn't look like anything of that. He felt their eyes on him. Felt the piercing intent.

"Haven't all day. Go on," Elise pressured, motioning with a hand.

Blaze nodded once then lifted his backpack from the floor and placed it securely in his lap. He released the latch on the surface, lifted the flap of canvas, and dug his hand in carefully, as if something would reach up and bite him.

His fingers wiggled in the dark depths of the bag, and he shifted his hand around until the back of it graced a smooth, rounded piece of plastic. He took hold of it and held it between his fingertips.

"Blaze..." Aurora said.

"Don't distract him, Missy," Elise spat. "You don't know how it works, so it's of no use to you. We will share it's information."

"Please, you've never shared anything in your life," Donovan said.

"Always a first time for everything," she shot back.

Blaze withdrew the device from his backpack. Even in the dim lighting, it seemed to glow from within.

"Proximity sensor," Elise murmured just above her breath. "Never seen this before. No...Zayne...."

"Already have it," replied Zayne.

"Bring it..." she continued, her voice distant and distracted.

From behind his back, Zayne had a small sphere, about the size of a softball. It appeared as clear as glass; however, from within there was a small blue orb floating freely in the center. As Zayne walked, it seemed to wobble, but held its location for the most part. Getting closer to Blaze's half, the light seemed to burn brighter, filling the space with an ambient light.

"Hand it to me," said Elise. "Alone, they're worthless."

PETER GULGOWSKI

In the light, Blaze saw his escape route knowing he needed to decide fast. The relic trembled in his hands, and he gripped it tighter.

Elise sat back in her chair as she took the orb from Zayne. She held it in front of her face, the blue light illuminating the severe lines and curves across. She gazed into the light, as if able to read something deep within. Her eyes grew watery and reflective.

"You know that man—that *thing*—came back decades after first appearing before Winslow. It came back the first time the walls lowered. It came the time we were supposed to leave and join the other survivors. It took me to this. Raised it from the earth and handed it to me. No strings attached other than to save as many as I could. Protect them until I came across the other pieces."

"How many did you save?" Donovan asked.

She pointed her index finger at her chest and dug it in hard into her breast bone. "Winslow refused to hear it. Called me a liar, and said I was trying to mess everything up. He had everything under control. Famous last words. Knew I was alone, so I fled and here we are."

"So, what is it?" asked Blaze, pointing to the orb.

"Honestly, I don't know. The Visitor only said it would tell us where we go from here. What lies ahead. What's next. That's all I know, I swear," said Elise. "This is the brightest I've ever seen it, though. And I think you know why."

Blaze could feel a slight tremble within the grasp of his hand. Felt it deep and within the tiny bones of his fingers. A torrent of adrenaline surged within his veins and cleared his head. He felt his senses strengthen. His eyesight focused, hearing cleared, and even the slightest brush of air against skin was overwhelming.

"You're making a wise choice. Together, we'll figure this out."

But Blaze could feel the heat rising within, rising from his core. He felt anger towards her and Donovan. He didn't know who to trust, but he felt maintaining the status quo was important. He was taking a risk. A risk so unnerving, he was unsure whether or not it was calculated wisely.

"No," he replied, slipping the relic back into his bag.

"Blaze," Elliot said. "Be smart, man No need to be the tough guy."

"There's no promise that they'll share the information with us," said Blaze. "And frankly, I don't trust you guys either. Not after what you did."

"Blaze-buddy, it wasn't us. It was my granddad."

Blaze shrugged, adjusting the canvas flap of his backpack. "Fine. I don't trust him or you."

"I didn't know, man!"

"Enough!" ordered Elise.

Blaze's attention shot to her. He saw the crazed look in her eyes, the flare of her nostrils, the veins in her neck jutting out, pulsating. She steadied herself, straightened her posture. "Hand it over."

"Sorry. No deal."

Elise stood up. Her eyes grew hot with hate. Blaze was gripped by a cold terror, a sudden, agonizing regret. She held the orb, twisted it between fingers like one would a pencil.

Held in the secure wrap of his fingers, Blaze could feel a striking heat growing from within his half of the relic. It grew hotter, but instead of burning, his skin became numb. He relaxed his grip and looked down at it. From inside, waves of blue light ran the length, illuminating previously invisible designs and symbols.

The more Blaze looked at it, caught off guard by its sudden activation, he could swear that the carvings were pulsing, enflamed with the bright blue light.

Elise came nearer, reached her hand out. "You don't understand how it works."

"Neither do you," said Blaze.

"Give it to me now," she said. "Last chance."

"Blaze—just give it up," Donovan said. "We don't need it, and we're out numbered."

He looked over to Donovan, shook his head. Donovan's lips pressed together as he took in a breath, held it.

"Sorry," Blaze murmured.

And he pressed off the floor with all of his power.

The others—Elliot, Aurora, Donovan—all ran behind him.

Elise, caught off guard, looked around. "Grab it!" she ordered.

The armed others ran forward, swung their guns around and into their grasp. Aiming them, Blaze pressed through the doorway they'd come through.

Locked.

'*Shit...*" Blaze whispered.

Behind him, he turned to see Zayne approaching Aurora. Before he could call out to warn her, Zayne grabbed her and lifted her off of her feet. She began kicking frantically, twisting her body to get out.

Through sounds of struggle, another two of the armed guards ran forward to join in. Donovan twisted into a fighter's stance. He saw an opportunity and seized it.

Donovan swung his leg out, hooked his boot around the back of Zayne's calf, and pulled in.

Zayne fell, pulling Aurora to the wood floor with him.

"Move!" he yelled to her.

Zayne's hands ripped through her hair, wrapped around her mouth. Aurora opened wide and bit down. Hard.

Blaze wasn't sure which came first—the scream or the blood. Flowing free around his grasp was a river of crimson. She turned and spit out onto the floor. With fingers fluttering, Zayne tried repositioning his grip, but Aurora was too quick, and she slipped out from him.

But there were two more armed guards waiting for Donovan now. He leaned down and helped Aurora up, but as soon as he was standing again, and Aurora back a few feet, he took the blunt butt of a rifle to the head.

Donovan fell, raising a shaky hand to the spot where he'd been struck. Zayne slid away, rising to his feet. The two others took over now. The other figure bent down and lifted Donovan up by the collar of his T-shirt.

Still disoriented, Donovan was slow to raise his fists to defend himself when the first fist collided with the side of his jaw. Side-profile facing them, he raised a hand, and begged for pause. He lowered his hands to the tops of his thighs, leaned down, and spit out blood.

Blaze approached quickly. "Want it? Take it. Just stop this."

But Donovan rose, twisting to face him. Blood dribbled from a split lip. "I just took a fist to the jaw for this. Don't you dare hand it over now."

The two others stood still, fists raised. Blaze was unsure why they stopped. Perhaps there was a little human left in them. Aurora hurried over to Donovan, pulled him back. Blaze maintained a careful watch over the others in the room. In turn, they were watching him. Watching how this would play out.

"Are you okay?" she asked, cupping her hand carefully around his jaw.

"Been better," he said. "Watch your hand," he said just before spitting out some more blood. "Elise—"

In that same moment, that same breath, all of Blaze's senses were overwhelmed by an unimaginable power. In one moment, he was standing; the next, he was flat on the ground, eyes clenched shut, fingers trembling, dancing on the wooden floorboards.

Fragments of bricks rained down. Smoke screened the space. Fire illuminated it.

As Blaze came to, high-pitched ringing drowned out the screams. Drowned out the mayhem that had only just been. He raised his hands to his ears, tapped the side of his head. He could still hear nothing but the ringing.

Opening his eyes, he saw the others on the ground. He saw what had come from the blow of the explosion. Piecing together that few moments, he remembered the shattering of glass, the rush of movement, and the sudden blow of fear. It was as if time had skipped forward on the timeline. Perhaps it had.

He looked to his right and saw a huge, monstrous bite had been taken out of the side of the building. Bricks from above continued to fall to the Chicago streets.

Carried by wind, dust entered through the opening in the wall and began settling across the remains of Elise's base. And slowly, bits of sound could once again be heard. He heard whimpers in the distance, a few cries for help.

He looked up and saw part of the ceiling, what had once been solid, now caved in.

Chunks of concrete littered the floor, leaving snake-like piping exposed, weaving through the now-empty space.

"We're okay. It's over. Everyone accounted for?" Blaze heard Elise asking.

Blaze slowly rose to his feet and looked around. Donovan was several feet ahead lifting some debris from a figure lying on the ground. Beneath the debris, there was movement. Hands tried to push up. Tried to lift what lay atop their body. Blaze was relieved they weren't dead.

"Blaze! Quit catching flies," Donovan yelled. Soot coated his hair, blood trailed down his face and arms. "Get over here and help me."

He looked down and saw a familiar pair of boots—Aurora's. Blaze joined Donovan at the opposite side of the debris. He couldn't even figure out what it once was—only that it was heavy and atop his friend. That's what mattered most.

Blaze steadied himself and his breath. "Aurora, we'll get you out. Just hang on."

"On three," Donovan directed, not skipping a beat.

He counted down. They lifted. It didn't budge.

"Again!"

They counted once more. Lifted. Failed.

"Fucking lift, man!" Donovan screamed through blood-stained teeth. "Put your back into it!"

"I am!" Blaze yelled back.

He lifted with all his might. Lifted until he thought his muscles would tear free from the bones. "Someone, please!" he cried.

Elise ran over, stepping over a body struck by concrete—Zayne's. "Where do you need me?"

"Other side," Blaze said. "On three."

"Forget counting," Elise snapped. "Lift, boys, lift!"

They did.

The weight budged and Blaze felt encouragement. Adrenaline was pumping rapidly through his veins, fueling his muscles.

"C'mon, Missy," Elise forced through clenched teeth. "We don't have all day. Move!"

Blaze held the structure, squeezing his muscles, as he looked down. Aurora was pulling herself out.

Donovan screamed a booming yell, lifting the debris another inch. Blaze focused intently, hearing a voice say, "Once more. Just lift."

And he did.

Aurora pried at the ground, sliding herself out from beneath. As soon as she was free, the three dropped it.

"Move aside," Elise ordered, kneeling beside Aurora. "Where does it hurt."

"Ankle," Aurora managed to get out. "I think it's broken."

Elise turned to Blaze. "Fire-boy, grab some wood. Rip Zayne's shirt into strips. We need to stabilize it, if it really is."

Blaze nodded quickly, scanning the area for small bits of wood. He spotted some of the old, narrow floorboards that were broken by the concrete. He bent down, and ripped up one. He took it in both hands, pulled it to calf level, bending it, before stomping down in the center.

"Here," he tossed them to Elise. They scattered around her, and she shot him a look.

"Shirt," she ordered, pointing beyond Blaze.

He looked down and saw Zayne's body lying still. He'd seen death before, but not like this. Lost within the moment, Blaze found himself frozen. Donovan stepped beside him, shook him free.

"Go be with Aurora," he said calmly. "I'll handle it."

"No, I'm—I'm good," Blaze said, swallowing hard. "Just give me—"

"Man, we don't have the time. Go. I'll handle the shirt."

Blaze nodded once and went over to Aurora's side.

Elise looked over, pointed at the floorboards scattered around her. "I need those cut in half. Still too long."

Blaze took them but knew he'd need to get more creative. He couldn't hold them in his hands, because his foot couldn't split them in two again. They were too short for that. He scanned the room, looking for anything that could be a makeshift saw.

He spotted the corner of some fallen concrete. It was a sharp, jagged edge and Blaze ran over. He centered the floorboard on the corner and pressed down. It snapped exactly where he needed it.

'*One more,*' he told himself.

He placed down the second piece and pressed hard. It worked again.

"Here," he said running the pieces to Elise.

"Good boy," she said, nodding in approval. "Place them around the ankle and—er—Donovan—" she called out, voice more cross, "get me that shirt."

Blaze looked over and saw the blood-stained shirt, torn down the middle of Zayne's chest. Donovan was freeing it from around Zayne's arms, pulling the limp hands through the sweat-stained arm holes. Once in hand, he ran it over to Elise.

"Hold the wood there—no, not there—*higher*," Elise directed Blaze. She took the shirt and began wrapping Aurora's ankle tightly.

Aurora clutched her jeans and squeezed her eyes shut, as she fought back a groan.

Elise wrapped it several times, tying the fabric when she had run out, and tucked it within the makeshift splint.

"Not pretty, but it'll do. We have to move."

Elliot had since joined them, keeping his distance as he peered around. "What was that? That explosion."

Elise raised a hand and wiped beads of sweat from her brow. "I think we've been found. We need to get out of here. It's not safe." She rose to her feet and stepped onto a wooden chair. "Everyone!" she yelled out, silencing the room. "If you can walk, we have to leave for now. If you can't walk, stay here and we'll figure something out."

Several of Elise's people walked over to join them. A few remained on the ground, surrounded by the debris that had ended their chances of escape.

Aurora called out. "Blaze, a hand?"

Blaze turned to her and bent down, lifted her by the hands. Immediately, she let out a cry. Tears flowed from her eyes, and she bit down on her lip.

"Damnit!" she said, lowering to the ground again.

"You can't walk," Blaze said. "Not like this."

"Just leave me here. It's safe for now, and once you guys have the others, we can figure out what to do from here," she said.

"I'm not leaving you," Blaze said. "I'll carry you."

"Blaze," Aurora replied, "be serious."

"I am being serious."

Donovan moved in, stopping beside the two. "Blaze, let me. No offense, but you're not exactly built—not like me, anyway," he said.

"She's my friend," Blaze replied.

"Yeah, well she's mine, too," said Donovan slipping his hands around Aurora and scooping her up. He lifted her like nothing, cradled her like a child.

Aurora tried to free herself of Donovan's grasp, but he wouldn't let go. "Let me try to walk. This is embarrassing."

"Honey, at least you're not dead," Elise said, patting her on the cheek with a soft slap. "Let's move."

"The sphere," Blaze said, pointing to it lying on the ground.

"You carry it," Elise said. "I'm sorry about before. I guess, after that, we're in this together, now. Truce?"

Blaze nodded, lifting it from the floor. As he put both devices, both pieces of the otherworldly puzzle, into his backpack, it was here that he knew both sides had agreed there was a greater enemy to face. One far worse and far deadlier than each other.

* * *

Through the streets of Chicago, they made quick progress. There were ten of them left.

Ten survivors.

At no point did Elise mourn the fallen. She took charge of the situation at hand. She'd grieve at a later time. She fought through the emotions, built up a strong wall between them and her. It was time to dig deep and get to safety. The tears could come later, but not yet.

The explosion—whatever it was—had reached a mile away. Small fires burned and shattered glass from skyscraper windows blanketed the roadway.

"Has that happened before?" Blaze asked.

Elise nodded. "The Creators," she said flatly. "They're trying to find us. Close together, they create some sort of frequency. The Creators can pick up on it, register it. I don't know how it works or how they work. Regardless, we've been found."

"How?" asked Donovan.

"I didn't invent the fucking things!" she quipped, breathing deep through her nose, while checking down the next intersection.

"Sorry," Donovan said, still carrying Aurora. "Figured you would know."

"You folks didn't even know about the Council," she said.

The truth was they had. Donovan knew that they were well aware of the Council and the Creators. They didn't understand them. Couldn't point them out, but were familiar with the name, with the terms.

Elise pulled out a folded map from her back pocket. "Which way to your hideout?"

"Why ours?" asked Donovan.

"In case you didn't notice, mine is full of the injured and dead. And full of destruction," Elise replied firmly. "Yours is safe. For now."

Donovan nodded and pointed down the road at the next intersection. "This way to us," he said.

"Then that way it is," said Elise.

They continued down the roadway, through the remains of civilization frozen in time. They passed the countless shops, wove through abandoned cars that hadn't been driven in decades. Blaze scanned the skyscrapers, feeling increasingly small the taller the buildings became. A sensation of unease ran across him. He stopped, felt his head grow fuzzy. Thoughts were unclear. The line they followed became warped and curved. But as he looked forward, it seemed the others had stopped too.

"Something's off," he heard Elise say. "Everyone stop."

Blaze looked past them and saw a large shimmering screen, nearly transparent, a short distance in front of them. He hadn't noticed it until then, not even when they were walking directly towards it. It must have just appeared now.

The others seemed to see it. A few pointed to it.

"Everyone—" Elise said.

But she stopped herself when a watery figure leapt out of it, landing in a crouched position, hands steady on the pavement.

It stood up, one vertebra uncurling at a time, until it stood fully before them.

The figure was massive, and at least nine feet tall. It was built like a machine, strong and powerful. Fully unclothed, the figure was entirely androgynous with no sex organs, no body hair, and a glimmering, translucent casing appearing to have been made of water. Blaze wouldn't call it skin, however. He'd never seen anything like this. The body contained life-requiring organs that appeared to be humanoid in form; however, none of them would consider what stood before them to be anything close to human.

It stood still, slowly scanned each of the survivors before it stepped forward one step.

"Elise—what is that?" Blaze murmured.

Frozen, she didn't reply.

"Elise?" Blaze stammered out forcefully, breaths coming fast.

"They've found us," she said, her voice trembling. "Run!"

And they did.

Blaze was pulled forward by instinct. It took hold of him, held him, and guided him down the street. Feet thumping against hard pavement, he felt he'd never moved faster. His arms pumped beside him, faster and faster.

He turned back, saw Donovan close behind, with Aurora across both arms.

"What are you doing?" he spat. "Go! Go!"

But Blaze felt something holding him still. It was as if blocks of concrete had formed around his feet. The Shape appeared only to walk, but somehow, it kept up with their running.

Standing still, the Shape continued forward. Against the shimmer of sunlight, it's face became clear for a moment. Expressions were firm and unwavering.

Blaze swallowed a solid lump and found himself holding his breath. He felt the power around him. Felt coldness wrap his body. It tightened, moved up to his throat like a thick rope across his neck.

PETER GULGOWSKI

Blood rose within the cavity of his chest, pooling and swirling inside of him. Searing jolts of pain tore through his brain. Blaze lifted trembling fingers and placed them against his temples as he lowered, gasping for air.

Across the pavement, cold air fanned in, carrying a foul odor of death on it.

With his mouth open and gaping, he felt his knees strike the ground, hands still clutching his head. The sensation of pain was his only tie to realty, interrupting the frantic display of apocalyptic scenes.

He saw fire, saw death. He heard the screams of millions, felt the woes of those who would survive long enough to feel death. Blaze wanted to lie down and die himself. The Shape was approaching closer, the watery surface reflecting his anguished face back to him thousands of times, like tiny diamonds. He couldn't take it any longer—the misery gripping at his heart, ready to rip it free from his chest.

But he felt a pull at his collar.

"...Blaze..." he heard on a distant echo.

Another pull, tight against skin.

"Blaze!" he heard again.

He fought to open his eyes. They fluttered, and he felt the muscles in his face twitch beneath his skin.

"Blaze!" he heard clearly. It was Aurora.

He craned his neck, and blocking out the sunlight above, stood Aurora, pulling at him.

Donovan was close behind. "We've gotta go, Aurora. He's stunned. You try and help him, we die!"

"You go! I'm not leaving him," her voice boomed over the chaos.

Aurora placed both arms beneath Blaze's armpits and lifted, letting out a scream. Blaze lowered his hands to the pavement, trying to push himself up. But with Aurora's pull, his hands only scraped alongside him.

She fought through to help Blaze, pushing aside the obstacles of the blinding pain in her ankle, to try and save him. But somewhere within, a solid thought formed. Blaze knew he needed to help himself. Whatever the Shape had been casting out had drained him of everything. But now, a few feet further away, the lure of walking death had weaned. He turned suddenly, looked up to Aurora.

"Aurora, you can't do this. Go with Donovan."

"It's not for you, this is for me, too," Aurora said. "Now help me, help you."

And he listened.

He pressed up, palms against pavement, pushing himself up. He looked forward, his eyes focusing upon the Shape in front of him, only a few feet away now.

It seemed to have stopped approaching, however.

The press of cold air was still strong, but thoughts came clearer now. His body no longer felt limp with exhaustion. Muscles seemed to function, and his eyes could adjust to light and shadow.

Blaze rose to his feet, unsteady at first. He took a full breath, but there was no time for this now. Aurora was already pulling at him, and he moved forward with her.

"Your ankle. It's broken, isn't it?"

PETER GULGOWSKI

Aurora squeezed her eyes shut, shaking her head. "Sprained, not broken," she forced out. "Cleared that up the hard way. I wasn't letting you go," she continued, moving beside him with a bad limp.

Donovan hurried forward and scooped her up into his arms. "One lucky bastard to have a friend like this," he said to Blaze. "You owe her a few favors."

"Never mind that now. Move!" Aurora directed.

As they hurried towards Elise and Elliot, and the others who were waiting, watching ahead. Elise pointed forward, brows lifted in terror.

Blaze turned around to see the Shape standing with its arms outstretched above its head. Against the overhead sunlight, the silvery liquid of its skin glowed bright. And as its arms grew longer, a chill fell across the vacant city.

In mere moments, the sun vanished behind a veil of obsidian-gray sky. The cloud layer dropped, just hovering above the tops of the skyscrapers, swirling around the spires. Then, as the Shape continued to pull forth the energy of the unknown, Blaze saw a sharp point began to fall from the heavens, like a funnel cloud.

The Shape pulled at it until suddenly, it let go. The sharp point of clouds flung back to the sky. And Blaze looked back to the Shape.

But beside him, Blaze sensed motion. He turned to it, seeing Elise step beside him.

"Get back," she ordered, slipping her hand alongside the side of her hip. She lifted the edge of her shirt revealing a holstered pistol.

Quickly she drew it out, raised it up to aim at the Shape. Blaze heard her hesitation within the tremble of her breath.

"C'mon, do it..." Blaze thought to himself.

And she did.

She fired once. Fired twice.

Echoes of gunfire rang again and again through the city block.

And then there was silence.

Blaze looked ahead and saw both shots had struck the Shape. A narrow wound was already bleeding crimson blood. It rolled down the transparent flesh, dripping down to the roadway below.

The Shape stood there, seeming unfazed, and lowered its chin to meet its chest. Then, in one solid movement, its chest rose, as if taking a deep breath. The wounds healed; the bleeding stopped.

And within that same breath, a second figure—one just like the first—stepped outside, joining the first.

And then another.

Beneath the churning clouds, three identical figures now stood.

Blaze cursed aloud.

Donovan began trotting back with Aurora. "Shit! Look what you did, Elise."

"Whatever happens," Elise said to Blaze. "That backpack must make it back."

Blaze swallowed a hard lump, nodded quickly. "Understood. I'm fast."

Elise fired again, striking the original figure in the center. Almost instantly, the wound sealed itself. But it didn't separate. Not this time.

The three figures proceeded forward, steps synchronized and firm with intent. At once, their arms extended outward and sudden purple orbs of light fired from their palms.

Blaze followed the light, frozen by his own frightened reflection in the silvery flesh of the three. He watched as the orbs collided with the skyscrapers towering above the street.

In that moment, debris rained down from massive gashes in the towers. Shattered glass rained upon them like spilling diamonds.

But above, at first, he thought it was an illusion, the towers began to lean in towards each other. Slow at first, then moving faster and faster, splitting from their foundation, the towers suddenly collapsed into each other, sending even more glass raining down over the group. The towers rested against each other, supporting the failing structures.

They took off running, realizing the buildings would come down on top of them, but a bright ball of blue light appeared on the street.

A few flashes filled the air, and then rising from the center was a cloaked figure—the Stranger from River Ridge.

The three shapes stopped. The original one, still in the center, tilted its head, leaning one ear to the other shoulder, while the other two looked to it, as if for direction or an order to be given. The figures stepped close to the original before, in the blink of an eye, merged back into their original basis.

The cloaked figure did not pay Blaze or the others any attention. But it did step around Blaze, cloak dragging behind it along the pavement, to step in front of the group. The Shape maintained its firm facade, but something told Blaze that it was afraid of getting closer.

Perhaps the Stranger held more power than the other entity?

Blaze continued moving back, watching as loose paper fell across the area like big snowflakes. Furniture continued rolling out shattered windows above, falling to the ground with an earth-splitting bang.

Suddenly, twisting steel let out a cry of agony as the leaning towers gave way. Wood split, glass broke, and metal bent and groaned. There was a deafening roar as the mighty buildings began to collapse. Blaze turned left, turned right. Split-second thoughts were too costly now. He needed to run. Needed to move.

Anywhere. Anywhere but here.

The cloaked figure looked up before rushing beside Blaze. It raised its staff, and a rush of orange light shot upward and spread out, engulfing them in a domed enclosure. Donovan and Aurora were contained, as was Elise. However, Elliot and the others from Elise's camp remained outside, too far away to make it in.

He couldn't have been within the enclosure for more than a moment before the thunderous roar of the towers drowned out their screams. The debris fell, raining against the protective enclosure, and the dust engulfed them, pulling them into full dark as the towers came down around them.

PART THREE
HUNTED

FIFTEEN

Blaze grabbed at his chest, clutched the fabric of his shirt, twisting it, as he tried to steady his breath.

"What is that thing?"

"They call them Infiltrators." Elise cleared her throat. "It's what we've been hiding from for years. Surprised it took this long for you to come across one."

He shook his head. "Who sent it?"

Elise pointed to the cloaked figure. "The ones who made them. The Creators."

Blaze looked to the Stranger and stepped aside, making sure he was still within the protective dome. The dust must have been settling, as orange light, slipping through gaps of the debris, cast a fiery glow across their faces.

"Thanks," said Blaze.

The Stranger turned to him, face mostly concealed in shadow. It waited a moment before replying in a thick accent, "Brace yourself."

Without further word, Blaze felt as though he were being sucked down a massive drain. His body stretched and lengthened, the streets of Chicago vanished, swept away from them in a twist and pull. He was spinning, arms and legs flailing, stomach churning, as the world fell dark again.

He squeezed his eyes shut, fighting back the feeling of sickness that surged within his gut. Then just when he thought he would fall into the void, instead, he fell face-down onto sunlit street.

Dizzy and uneasy, he lay there for a moment, sliding a hand back to reach behind him. He felt the backpack and its contents. Blaze breathed a sigh of relief right there. But he noticed a sudden shadow approach, stopping just above him. He turned his head, peered up.

Blocking the sun was Donovan and Aurora.

"You okay?" asked Donovan.

"Help him," she said immediately, nudging him in the ribs.

Still holding Aurora, Donovan shrugged. "Hands are a bit full, if you didn't notice already."

Blaze shook his head and held up a hand of refusal. "I'm good," he said, despite already feeling a bit sore. He turned on his side and sat up. He paused, remaining still, before standing to his two feet. Blaze brushed off his pant legs and peered around.

His brain was still in defense mode. Ready to run; ready to fight. Blaze remained wide-eyed, peering around. It had to be close. He kept a wide-legged stance, swiveling around, unsure of where they were.

Beside him, Elise stood still, for once not rocking on her heels; gaze aimed downward.

Aside from her, it was just Blaze, Aurora, and Donovan.

"Where did it go?" he asked. "Where is it?"

Donovan shook his head. "Guess this was a drop and go. It got us out of there," he said. "Elise, you okay?"

Blaze turned to look to her.

Tears clung to the apples of her cheeks. She raised a trembling hand to her face, covering her mouth. Her fiery red hair streaked across her face. A few strands clung to beads of sweat.

"Elise?" Blaze asked again, stepping closer.

She looked up, looking across them. Her eyes were wide, mouth slightly ajar. "I—I thought they'd be here, too. But they're—they're—*gone*," she said, voice shaking. "All of my people are gone. Everyone is gone. Even some of your people..."

The remaining few walked towards her and wrapped their arms around her, holding her close. And then the tough warrior they'd come to know Elise to be broke.

Entirely.

* * *

In the time that passed, those who remained gave Elise a short amount of time to grieve, to think, to cry. They stepped away, gave her some space, but remained watchful for any signs of the hunter. Donovan held in his own emotions. In a moment, unexpected and even more unprepared, he had lost Elliot.

How would they explain this to Nori?

Blaze stood close to Donovan and Aurora. Carefully, he put his hand on Donovan's back. For once, he didn't flinch or fight it off.

"Sorry, man," said Blaze. "I don't know what else to say."

Donovan nodded once and cast his gaze aside. For a moment, he held his lips in, trembling on the verge of speech. But he held it in and buried it. Buried it deep.

As for Elise, in the minutes that followed, she pulled herself together quickly, combed her fingers through her hair, and took in a deep breath. She held it, counted softly to herself, before releasing. Blaze looked over to her. Now, only a muddled complexion remained as any sign of her crying.

Donovan looked to her, lowered his watery gaze slightly. "Ready?"

"As I'll ever be," murmured Elise softly, nearly beneath her breath. "Where to?"

"Good news is—" He cleared his throat. "—we're close," he said, finishing his thought. He raised his hand and pointed down the long street. "See that building—the one with the wall of balconies?"

She swallowed, squinting her eyes. "Er—yeah. What about it?"

"That's the corner of our street. Just a few buildings in, and we're home. Aurora, do you think you can walk? Arms are getting tired."

"I'll figure it out," she said. "You can put me down."

Donovan nodded, bent at the knees, and put her down carefully. Watching her feet hit the ground, was like watching a NASA spacecraft land on the surface of a faraway planet. Careful and steady.

"If it's too much, let me know," he said. "I'm serious. Don't try to impress us."

"I won't," said Aurora.

"Blaze, you hang in the back. Keep your eyes open. Any signs of anything, you let us know." Donovan turned to the remaining group, smoothed out his shirt. "Okay," he breathed, "let's move."

Together, they made their way quickly down the street. Keeping to the narrow sidewalks, they slipped between abandoned vehicles and across pools of shattered glass. Blaze kept his sight moving, looking everywhere. Feeling so small on the streets, beneath the shadows of the high-reaching skyscrapers, Blaze got the feeling that the Shape could be anywhere, watching from the shadows, planning out its hunt.

Blaze stepped beside Aurora, who's limp was growing more noticeable. "How are you doing?"

She hesitated, looked to him. "Yeah, I'm hurting," she admitted.

"Here," he stepped up beside her, wrapping his hand around her waist. "Let's do it together."

She shook her head. "Blaze, I'm good. The pain makes me feel alive, which after today, I'm pretty freaking grateful for."

"Pain shouldn't make you feel alive. Pain sucks, and if you can fix it, fix it," he replied.

"Let me handle it my way. You handle it your own. I'm good, Blaze. Honest," Aurora said. She took her hand, reached it back and pulled Blaze's hand away. "You're always trying to be the hero."

"No, I'm trying to help a friend," Blaze said.

"I know," she said, turning to him. She smiled lightly. "As always, and as I always tell you when you're getting too protective, I appreciate it. Thanks, but I'm good. Honest."

Up ahead, the building that Donovan had pointed out earlier stood in front of them. The four-way intersection, still and silent, also came up as they approached. Without skipping a beat, Donovan turned, continuing to lead them through the concrete jungle of the city.

Now, on this street, Blaze recognized where they were. The world became a little smaller, a little less intimidating. He felt they were in the home stretch. He'd be able to breathe and relax soon.

"Almost there," he murmured aloud.

He scanned forward, looking over the tops of cars. Several moving figures were approaching. They stopped.

Donovan paused, too.

Blaze looked a bit closer, then saw the familiar mop of hair that Forrest had. He saw the goofy grin, then the unique wave that only Forrest had.

"Look, it's the others," said Blaze.

"Thank God," Donovan said to himself. "Thanks for being my eyes. Vision is for shit."

But Blaze was already darting forward, through the narrow passages between cars. Forrest stood waiting. Trent was pointing Rose and Amelia inside.

"We've gotta get inside. Something found us," said Blaze.

Forrest's expression went solid. "You saw it too, didn't you? That invisible assassin?"

Blaze nodded. "Yeah. It nearly got us, too. Killed some of the others we were with. We found a group. Then it found us."

"How'd you get back?" Forrest asked.

"Winslow's visitor. Seems we have a guardian angel protecting us in him. You?"

"Same," said Forrest. "This doesn't make sense. I don't know what's going on."

Trent stepped forward, standing beside Forrest. He looked past Blaze's shoulder, scrutinizing the approaching group.

"Is that Elise?"

"Yeah," Blaze replied. "Know her?"

"Know her? We hate her group. They think they own the whole city."

"They're all dead now, so we're all she has left."

Trent's brows lifted. "Donovan's grandpa won't be pleased, but he'll have to get over it, I guess."

Without word, Blaze swung the backpack around and lowered it to the pavement. He opened it up and reached in, withdrawing the two relics.

"Well, she gave us this part, so I hope he'll be a bit more welcoming than usual," said Blaze.

When the rest of the group reached the steps up to the old schoolhouse, Forrest looked Aurora over.

"Geez. Always were a bit clumsy, Rory," he said. "We'll get that wrapped up when we get in."

From behind the doorway, the rattle of chains interrupted everyone. A few moments further, and the door opened. Nori stood behind it. She looked down the staircase to the gathered groups.

"Where's the supplies?"

Donovan remained quiet. She hadn't noticed yet.

"Er—"

Her expression went solid. She peered around quickly. "Where—Where's Elliot?"

Blaze looked to his side. Donovan began swaying in place, his chest rising and falling faster. "Nori—He—uhm—"

"Something terrible happened., hasn't it? I just knew it," she said, hurrying down the stairs. "We heard the commotion and knew it was bad." Nori ran onto the street, stopping in the middle. Veiled in the shadows of the skyscrapers around them, she began twisting, turning, looking for any sight of the son she already knew to be gone.

"*Elliot!*" she called out. She cupped her hands around her mouth. "*Elliot!*" she screamed. Tears rolled down her soft skin, as she leaned down, steadied herself on her thighs before calling out once again.

"Nori..." Donovan said, then pressing a closed fist to his lips.

"No...No...No! This isn't right..." She broke. "It isn't fair. This isn't how it's supposed to go!" She fought back tears, pressing her hands to her face. But what came next, he wasn't prepared for.

Grief filled her; consumed her. It poured itself out of every pore, of every crevice in the small-framed woman, as she sobbed.

Blaze squeezed his eyes shut, unable to watch a mother's grief any longer.

Donovan swallowed a firm lump, broke the silence. "Nori, it found us—an Infiltrator. It's still out there."

She turned to him, lip quivering against white teeth. "An Infiltrator?" she asked softly, wiping tear-streaked cheeks with the edge of her shawl.

"It found us," Donovan confirmed. "One of the Hoods saved us."

"And us," Trent added.

Nori looked between the two and nodded once. Only once. Somewhere in that moment, she found her inner-fighter, pushed aside the demons that had found her, and fought back their wicked clutch. She motioned fast with an arm to the entrance. "Go inside. Tell Carl."

"Nori, you can't stay out here."

She nodded. "I know. There is soup on the stove. Serve yourself, get some fuel in your bodies."

They waited as Nori climbed the steps. She turned once, looking across the city.

She had to have known he wouldn't come running, but she gave it once last chance. She took a breath before turning her back to the city, to the fantasy of Elliot's survival, and returned inside the base.

The rest followed. Donovan helped Aurora up the stairs, and they were the last up to go back inside. Blaze waited just behind Nori in the shadows.

"How do we kill it?" asked Aurora, leaning onto Donovan as she adjusted her stance on the cement step. She pushed back a chunk of hair that had slipped out from behind her ear.

Nori breathed deeply, turning to her, then back out to the cityscape. "You don't. You run from it."

Inside, Blaze moved beside Aurora and had her put an arm around his shoulder. Together, with Donovan, they moved her much quicker.

Nori wasted no time locking the door behind the two groups. Chaining the doors, checking for any give, she fiddled with it some more until she was satisfied. She then turned to a portly male who had taken the place of the younger female, Cari who'd been stationed at the door.

Nori cleared her throat. "Anyone tries to come through, you use your imagination, yes? Shoot first, ask questions when they're dead. Understood?" her voice remained shaky, but resolute in the words she said. She meant each and every one.

"Yes. Understood," he replied, gently patting the rifle that lay across the table he sat at.

"I'm serious," Nori pressed. "Anyone trying to come through now is no friend of ours. Do what you need to do."

The rest were waiting in the entrance hall. A few lamps in the corners cast light across the ceiling. Nori moved into the center, where unknowing to the others, they had formed a circle. Immediately, she went into crisis mode. She began calling for others to bring first aid kits, for the rest to gather available weapons.

"Anyone injured?" she asked.

Aurora raised her hand off of Blaze's shoulder.

"Other than you," she said, slightly cross. "Anyone bleeding? Anything broken?"

No one raised a hand.

Nori nodded once, seemingly relieved. "Okay, good. Boys—" she pointed to Donovan and Blaze "—get her upstairs and in bed. Elevate her ankle. Wrap it firmly in rags. If it doesn't hurt her, you're not doing it right."

"What about ice?" asked Forrest

"Without power, we don't have that luxury, and it's not winter," said Nori. "You'll have to go without."

Elise cleared her throat. "I think it's best someone else take her upstairs. Blaze has something you may find interesting in his bag."

"The artifact?" Nori asked.

"Not just one. Two," replied Elise. "I gave him ours. It's a two-part puzzle. Might as well have both parts."

Nori looked to Blaze. "Show me."

Blaze swung his bag around and lowered it to the ground. He reached in and pulled the two relics out, holding one in each hand.

"Not sure how they work," he admitted.

She looked between the small glass sphere and the smooth piece of plastic. Nori lifted her thumb to her lips, bit down slightly as she studied it, pondering how it worked.

"Give it here," said Nori. "Carl will know."

"Yeah, well Carl ratted us out to her," said Blaze. "He offered us up in exchange for supplies."

Nori's brows creased. "He...what?"

Blaze stood taller, pulling back his shoulders. "You heard me."

"Dude, we don't know that," Donovan replied.

Blaze looked to him. "Really? You said so yourself, didn't you?"

Donovan sighed, then pressed his lips together. "Look, Nori. Elise knew about this. Knew about everything. Do you know if my grandfather had been talking outside of the base?"

Nori lowered her gaze. "During supply runs, possibly. But he's no traitor. You know your family, Donovan. He's not a traitor."

"Misguided, maybe? Traitor, I don't think so either," said Donovan.

Nori turned to Elise. "What were you told?"

Elise lifted her gaze up to the ceiling while she thought back, rummaging through the files of a disorderly cabinet. "It was early this morning. Carl came, told me about the River Ridge kids, which he thought I'd be curious about given my history. Told me they knew information and had a relic of the Council. He knew I had one, too. That was it."

"That doesn't make sense. Why'd you threaten us for it? What you're telling us sounds like an honest conversation," Aurora said.

"Because I wanted it. Figured some kids would be terrified into giving it to us."

"You're sick, Elise. You know that, right?" slammed Blaze. "You're lucky we don't throw you out of here for that."

"Relax. No one is getting thrown out," Donovan snapped. "There are bigger enemies to be fighting right now. We'll get them to Carl. He may have an idea of what to do and how they work."

Blaze turned to Aurora. As if reading his mind, she nodded.

"We don't have any other options. To us, they're useless," said Aurora.

Without another breath taken, not one moment, Blaze extended his hands out to Nori. "Here. Take them."

Nori shifted in her feet, afraid to take them, as if they were a deadly animal. She shook her head quickly, turned to another unfamiliar face. The name on his military jacket read, 'Hopper' in bold lettering on a name plate. "Take those to Carl. Like I said, he'll know what to do."

"Oh, trust me, he will," Elise said, her gaze intent on the small, free-floating plume of blue light glowing in the center of her orb. "He's been waiting for these for years. If I'm not mistaken, he should have one himself."

"A third relic?" asked Donovan.

"Lots of important things come in threes," she replied. "I think that's it, though. Other groups have only mentioned three pieces—the remaining few people, that is."

Nori handed them to Hopper and stepped back as he took them, held them close, and disappeared into the shadows leading to the cafeteria. Nori watched him closely, studied each step until she could see nothing further than the tiny speck of blue light fading the further he got away.

"Any idea what they contain?" Donovan asked Nori.

Elise leaned against the wall. "A honing device. That much is obvious."

"Would make sense. Explains how the Infiltrator found us," said Aurora.

"Two relics in one room seemed to do the trick. Who knows what'll show up if there are three in one room. Glad not to be near Carl now," Elise continued.

"But we didn't have one," Trent said. "That thing found us. How do you explain that?"

Elise shrugged once. "Not sure. Bad luck? Short end of the stick. His goofy grin?" she replied, pointing to Forrest.

"Hey, it's my best feature."

"Shooting for the Moon, kid, you are," Elise replied.

"He does have a point," Donovan replied. "Maybe it wasn't the relics that brought out the thing—"

"Infiltrator, Donovan. It has a name. Use it."

"Who named it?" asked Aurora.

"Not sure. Ancient folklore talked about the Shapeshifter that hunted man long ago. Of course, the story evolved, and the more we came to know about the Council and the Creators, the more we learned about their other creations. Now, those stories look stupid, but I guess there were slivers of truth all along."

"Elise, what do you know about them?" Nori asked.

"We already asked," Blaze said. "Not much."

"Is your name, Elise, Blaze?" Elise asked.

"Er-Sorry."

She turned back to Nori. "*Not much.* Learned today they can split into at least three, have abilities to conjure magic. They defy gravity; they can defy physics. Everything about its existence tells me it shouldn't exist, but it does."

"Best case scenario in running from them?" asked Nori.

Elise's eyes lifted to the ceiling as she thought. She paused, waiting, then shrugged. "You live another few minutes," she replied.

"And worst case?" Nori continued.

Elise lifted her brows, then waved with her hands. "Light's out."

Blaze looked to Aurora, then to Nori. "Mind if we get her upstairs now?"

"Of course, get her comfortable," Nori said. "I'll bring you up some soup when you're settled," she said to Aurora.

Aurora smiled to her. "Thanks, Nori, but you don't have to do that."

"It'll take my mind off things. We'll let you know if anything comes of the devices you brought back."

Blaze walked over and put his shoulder beside Aurora. Donovan did the same. Together, they lifted her onto her good foot.

"Forrest, you coming?"

"Eh, I'll check up on you later. Trent's going to show me something. Besides, it could get kind of tight, the more people trying to help."

Blaze flashed a thumb's up. "On the count of three, we'll move."

"I'm not a piece of furniture. How heavy do you think I am?" Aurora asked. "For goodness sake, just lift and go."

And without counting, they did.

* * *

Donovan and Blaze got Aurora to the side of a cot.

She held up her hands. "I've got it. Thanks." She sat down, slid herself back while fighting through a grimace.

Blaze leaned forward, about to help, but she shot him a stern look. He took a step back, pressed his hands together.

Donovan snatched a pillow off one of the empty beds and slid it beneath her leg.

"Probably gonna need another," Blaze suggested.

He listened, reached over, and grabbed another.

"Better?" he asked Aurora.

"Better," she agreed.

Donovan nodded. "Cool. I'm going to go hunt down some pain relievers, see if we have any bandages. I'll be back in a few."

Aurora raised her hand in farewell, before leaning back against the wooden headboard, shutting her eyes. She pressed the bases of her hands gently against her eyelids.

"You okay?" Blaze asked cautiously.

"Yeah, I'm fine. Just a lot to take in for one day, on top of feeling useless and like shit. Not a good mix."

"You're not useless," Blaze said, carefully taking a seat beside her. He kept his focus across the room.

"Blaze, you and Donovan just helped carry me up a flight of stairs. I could've gotten killed by that thing chasing us, had you both not stepped up. Thank you for doing that, by the way.

"Don't mention it."

"What happens next? It comes here, and I'm supposed to expect you to save me? This goes against everything I've taught myself: Be self-reliant, don't expect help from others, be brave, stay strong. I'm brave, but the rest? Can't really count on all of that with a bum ankle."

"Well, you're already healing. We're gonna get you back to normal in no time."

"It takes days for this to heal," said Aurora. "Not hours. We're running on borrowed time. Chances are that thing is looking for us. It's pissed we got away."

Blaze turned to face her. Aurora had lowered her hands, and her arms were now crossed across her chest. She looked to him, seemingly waiting.

"Hear me out, okay?"

She lifted a single brow.

"Maybe the cloaked man, the one that saved us—"

"Not sure about you, Blaze, but there aren't that many cloaked men in my life," Aurora quipped. "I know who you're talking about."

"Right. This is just a thought, but what if he's protecting us?"

"I mean, it did save us from the falling buildings, but shouldn't it have better things to do then make sure we stay out of trouble?"

"I don't know?" Blaze replied. "Does it?"

"Probably so. Look, I'm going to say this once, so I hope you don't take it the wrong way. Don't get your hopes up in something we don't understand. What we do understand is ourselves. We know our strengths. We know our weaknesses. Let's play to the strengths and work on the weaknesses. We've got a fighting chance if we play our cards well. Be smart, be vigilant, and we might be able to escape this nightmare."

Blaze agreed, and he lifted his legs up onto the bed to sit cross-legged. He sat in the silence for a minute, but it felt longer. He wondered if Aurora liked the silence, too.

Softly, he asked, "Do you miss River Ridge yet?"

Aurora paused, perplexed. Her brows shifted movement only just, and she looked back to Blaze with thoughtful eyes. "I miss the idea of River Ridge."

"The idea?" Blaze pressed back.

"You know—before all of this, we didn't know what was beyond the walls or what was waiting for us. We had our families, our friends. We thought we had it bad, but we were the lucky ones. In the end, as much as I hated him—and will always hate him—Winslow kept us safe inside the four walls. Kept us from knowing the truth."

Blaze partially agreed. "But he let the power get to him. He let his cronies start worshiping him, building a full following while he did so. He isn't innocent."

"Yeah, I never said he was innocent. But in the scheme of things, at least we could understand Winslow. We could wrap our minds around him and his ways. These things, out here—" she pointed to the boarded-up window "—trying to kill us? Can't really wrap my head around them or how they work."

"Right, well if—"

Two knocks sounded as the door opened. Blaze turned to see Donovan standing with a small first aid kit in his hand. He walked in, set it beside Blaze.

"Mind giving me some space?" he asked Blaze.

"Oh—er—sure. Sorry."

Donovan unzipped the dusty, red bag. A white vinyl plus-sign was peeling away at the corners, chipping away on the interior of the design. He dug his large hand into the opening, withdrawing a small roll of tan-colored bandage and a sealed packet of a pain reliever.

"Er—shit—forgot the water," said Donovan, setting the packet on Aurora's thigh. "I'll be back."

"No need. I can do it."

"Really?" Donovan asked.

"Everyone has their talents," Aurora said, lifting the packet and tearing across the top. She put the two small, salmon-colored pills into her palm and without hesitation, tossed them both into the back of her mouth, swallowing them both in one gulp. She turned to Donovan and opened her mouth. "Impressed?" she asked with a slight smile.

"I am."

"They raise us tough in River Ridge, don't they, Blaze?"

"Nah, I think just you," replied Blaze.

Aurora tilted her head against her shoulder momentarily. "I mean, you're not wrong."

Donovan cleared his throat. "You want me to do this or do you have it?"

She thought for a moment. Blaze could see the wheels turning. As much as she wanted to say she could handle it, the reality was that she knew she didn't have the flexibility to do a good job.

"Sure," she said. "But don't get used to this, you know. I've gotta get back on the horse myself, so you can't keep helping me."

"This isn't much. Just relax," Donovan said, motioning with his hands. "Tomorrow you can get back on the horse. Right now, let us take care of you."

Aurora sighed. "All right. Thanks. I appreciate it."

Donovan unraveled the bandage between both hands. "I'm sorry if this hurts, but I've gotta do a good job. You heard Nori."

"If you're not hurting me, you're not doing a good job," Aurora repeated. "Do this right, and get it done."

Carefully, Donovan wound the bandage around Aurora's ankle until it was entirely immobilized. She leaned forward, pressed a long finger into the cushion of the bandage.

"Feel anything?" Donovan asked seriously.

"Barely. It hurts, but I'm not screaming. Go tighter."

"Only if you're sure," Donovan smirked. He wound the remaining bandage around, pulling it taut and folding it in on itself.

Aurora squeezed her eyes shut, expelling a breath. She held up a thumb.

"Blaze, let's let her rest. Nori should be bringing up some soup for you." Donovan laid his hand on her shoulder. "Try to relax, take a nap, daydream. Do whatever you want as long as you stay off that foot."

Aurora felt her pulse flutter in her throat. "Thanks, Dr. Donovan. I'll do that," she said.

Blaze looked to Donovan, who flashed a glimmer of a smile through his eyes. "Blaze," he said, "let's go see what trouble we can get into downstairs."

Blaze nodded, looking to Aurora who was still taken by Donovan. "See you, Aurora. I'll be back later."

"Same here," Donovan replied. "I'll check on you in a bit, okay?"

Suddenly, her expression hardened as she rolled her eyes. "Just go. Both of you. Please."

Donovan turned to Blaze. "Hey, at least she said, 'Please'," he laughed.

Aurora rolled her eyes. "Go!"

The two boys exited the room, shutting the door behind them with a firm pull. Blaze listened to Donovan's breath and didn't move.

"Do you know what's her deal? You know, the whole solo gig?"

Blaze turned to him, unable to make out his expression in the dim lighting. "Meaning?"

"Don't get me wrong. I think it's cool and all. But her whole schtick is a bit irksome. She sprained her ankle. She's gonna need help."

"That's just Aurora—"

"I get that it's *her*," he shot back. "I just don't get it," he clarified.

Blaze shrugged slightly. "Just don't overthink it, then. She likes to be independent. It's simple."

Donovan looked to him, and though it were dark, Blaze knew he was shooting daggers at him.

"Right," Donovan agreed stiffly. "No man in the history of the world has ever thought of a woman as simple. Complex? Difficult? Yes. Simple? No."

Blaze didn't wait for Donovan to join him as he started down the wide stairwell, counting the breaks in the quickly fading sunlight gleaming through the narrow cracks of boarded-up windows. Donovan joined a few steps behind, but Blaze didn't pay attention.

"Where you heading?" Donovan called down behind him.

"The cafeteria. You?"

"Same. Not going to start anything, are you?"

"Why would I? I'm just going for soup," he replied, not bothering to turn to him.

"Just making sure," he said. "Just remember, you three are guests, here. You don't have a stake in this place, nor do we in you."

Blaze suddenly stopped on the stairwell, spinning around to face Donovan. His face crinkled in annoyance, as he threw his arms out. "What's this and where's it coming from, man? I'm not the enemy."

"You're the one spewing out the tone," Donovan replied, arching a dark brow in slight amusement.

A flush deepened Blaze's cheeks as he fought to maintain his composure. Fought to keep everything in check. He shut his eyes, breathed in and out for two long breaths.

"You good, now?" asked Donovan, crossing his muscled arms across his chest.

Shit, he saw that.

"Yeah," Blaze replied. "I'm good."

Donovan slid his hand over his hair, pushing some behind his ear. "Convincing. Not."

But without further word, Blaze continued down the stairs, with the heat and tension pulling him down, like a tightly-wound cable yanking him down and away from Donovan.

He may have been calling down after him, but Blaze wasn't paying any attention now. His mind was already in the cafeteria, curious as to what—*if any*—progress had been made towards the artifacts, and if there was, in fact, a third one.

When he reached the ground floor, he stepped out into the entrance hall, where the previously gathered group had long-since dispersed. He followed the gentle lull of distant chatter, walking down the darkened corridors. All around him, paint was peeling away from the drywall, and in some spaces, entire wall chunks had vanished, revealing the skeleton of the building and pieces of aluminum ventilation shafts.

He moved past an old couch missing its cushions, with metal springs sticking out of the worn fabric. And he maneuvered around a drinking fountain that was jutting out of the wall and pulling outward by Father Time.

Ahead of him was the cafeteria. A single door—one of the original two—hung loosely on the hinge. Blaze stepped around it, through the opening and was met by the gentle pull of the scent of homemade soup.

Having had the acrid taste of decay and destruction lingering on his tongue throughout his time in the city, Blaze savored the new smell.

Sitting at tables were a vast majority of those at the base. A few faces Blaze recognized. A few others, he didn't. Elise turned, eyeing him up and down before returning to a solitary game of cards.

Carl sat at another table. Curious onlookers crowded around him, a few tinkering with unknown pieces of equipment on the table. Large pages of sketch paper, drawn with various designs, arrangements, and drawings covered the tile flooring surrounding the table they sat at.

Blaze moved forward, pausing, as if he needed an invitation to join the others. He looked around and did not see Trent or Forrest. The only familiar and youngest face, Aiden, stood behind Carl, with his head peering over his shoulder. Nori stood in the kitchen area, wooden spoon in hand, swirling the contents of the massive pot, lost in thought.

As he approached, he felt a few sets of eyes divert their attention from the tabletop momentarily before looking back quickly.

"...and like that, it should fit," Carl said, voice becoming clear as Blaze approached. "Still don't know why this is in pieces. Should've been together," he continued. "The others said they were, any way."

Nibbling on his thin lower lip, hands trembling, he was inserting Blaze's artifact into a wide, cone-shaped piece of a smooth, glimmering material. Across a small section of its surface, was an inlet just the size of the cylindrical piece Blaze had offered up. Carl pressed it in, and there was a click.

Followed by the rush of silence.

Sure enough, there were three pieces in total.

"Okay," Carl continued. "Next is the orb. Where is it? Anyone?"

"Here," offered the tinny voice of Aiden, who held the orb out to Carl. In his small hands, it appeared massive.

"Ah, there we are," said Carl, taking the orb from him. Now, his hands trembled even more. Blaze wondered if he could feel the great power within. Feel the unknowing and uncertainty, as if both were elements of dark magic.

"This should sit on the base," said Carl, focused and to himself.

As he drew the orb nearer, the glow within burned brighter, illuminating the space in an icy haze. Blaze found himself transfixed upon the bright light, watching the tiny plume rotate and swirl, contained to a small space within the glass orb.

Carefully, Carl lowered the glass orb onto the platform. Three tiny metal prongs reached out of the base, seemingly appearing from nowhere, securing the orb down. And then, after referencing the sketched diagram once more, he pressed the square piece with a firm press.

There was a soft clicking, and within that same moment, a sudden rush of blue burst outward from the device. Blaze ducked. A few others gasped. Aiden slipped beneath the cafeteria table, peering out from above the bench.

The burst of light spread out, grew fast, and enveloped everything in its path until the entire room was illuminated in blue.

Stretched across the ceiling and reaching down the four walls was a grid-system. Bright white lines crossed the new canvas like etchings into the misty blue air. Across the room, something caught Blaze's eye. It was as if they were zooming through the galaxy at light speed when a holographic depiction of the Earth came into view, flying towards them until it came to a hover just above the device.

Blaze felt the hammering in his chest beat quicker, more uneven. As he looked across the awe-struck faces, some bordered on the cusp of confusion. He looked to Carl, whose watery eyes glimmered the reflection of the floating Earth before him.

From the other side of the room, a holographic, triangular-shaped craft, about the size of his hand, flew towards Blaze. A few near him ducked again. He held his ground and didn't flinch for fear he'd miss something.

Much like the Earth, the floating craft seemed to float over the depiction of the planet. It remained there, floating stationary, for a few moments longer, before without any further activity, took off, vanishing into the blue haze of the room.

Suddenly, from the orb, the light within burned brighter, changed to white. It cast a series of numbers onto the ceiling. With a decimal point after the first two digits of the two sets, Blaze knew straightaway what it was.

Coordinates.

Carl was nudging the person beside him. "Write those down. Hurry!"

Beside him, the male who had taken Blaze's relics—Hopper—scribbled them onto paper with a trembling hand and a dull pencil.

Carl asked, "Got it?"

He nodded rapidly without response, at first. "Er—Yeah, yeah. Last few," replied the other as he finished up the line of numbers.

Without further word, without another depiction, the hologram collapsed upon itself and vanished into the device.

"Bring it up again," Carl said.

Hopper reached his hand in and pressed the rectangular button once again.

Nothing.

"Try it again," Carl pressed.

"I did," Hopper replied. He reached forward again, pressed the button. He held it for a moment in anticipation.

Nothing.

"Sorry, boss," he said to Carl. "I got them all, if that's what you were worried about. Was just double-checking. I think we're good."

"You think or you know?" Carl pressed

"We're good. Trust me," he replied, setting the pencil down on the paper.

Satisfied, Carl lifted his brows as he looked to the gathered crowd. "We all know what these are, yes?" he asked, pointing to the written numbers.

A few faces nodded. Others waited, unsure.

Elise cleared her throat softly into a fist pressed to her lips. "Coordinates," she said, voice with a slight rasp. She cleared her throat again. "Something is there. Something they've been planning for a long time. Something big, something important," Elise continued, pointing to the coordinates. "They wouldn't have gone to this trouble for nothing, but we were meant to put the pieces of the puzzle together. Now, our next job is to get to wherever *that* is. Is that what you were expecting this to be?"

"Not exactly," said Carl. "My contacts were close, but not spot-on. I feel something is missing. Even look at this," he said, taking the device. He pointed to a small spot that appeared to be the size of a quarter. Something should go there," he said. Carl reached over and took the piece of paper with the coordinates off of the table. He held it out to Hopper. "Work to find out this location. Hurry now."

He took back the paper, holding it tight in between his fingertips. He understood the gravity of the task. He turned to the others. "I'll be back in a few," he said, before hurrying out of the cafeteria.

Blaze crossed his arms across his chest. "So, what's next? What do we do until we know where we're going next?"

Carl looked up, meeting Blaze's eyes. "We wait, son. We wait. We're not quite done. Not yet."

* * *

Time seemed to slow.

Despite knowing of the horrors outside actively trying to locate the two groups that had gotten away from the Infiltrator, somehow, the wait for the location of the coordinates took precedence and consumed their thoughts.

Trent and Forrest had gone to find some supplies on one of the other floors. Donovan had kept his distance. Elise kept to herself.

Blaze sat quietly. He hated being alone, especially now. He hated the silence. Silence allowed for bad memories to flow freely through his mind, wander the narrow corridors, and consume what little happiness remained for him.

He was proud of himself, however. He had kept his wits about him and was staying positive. Many at this point would have lost both by now.

Blaze sat in a wooden chair, hunched over against his arms. He rested his chin against his two thumbs as he listened to the non-descript, distant noise of the base.

A part of him wanted to see Aurora, but the other part knew she needed rest. Heck, he needed rest himself. He wasn't sure how long he'd been running on fumes. The call of sleep was growing stronger, but he knew he couldn't rest.

Down the corridor, a distant tapping of small feet sounded. Blaze opened his eyes and leaned forward, craning his neck past the wall that hid him in the corner.

It was Aiden.

Within, the clouds that had veiled his soul lifted just slightly. But it was enough that Blaze formed a smile to greet the young child. He extended his hand in a wave.

"Any word?" he asked.

Aiden shook his head quickly. "Not yet. Mr. Carl told me so."

"How long ago was that?" Blaze asked.

Aiden's brow creased. "I just asked," he replied, slightly confused. "I was coming from the cafeteria. That's where all the grown-ups are." Aiden's expression softened as he sat down in front of Blaze, crossing his legs. "I heard what happened. Out there on the streets. I heard about Elliot. He was my friend, too."

"Yeah, he seemed like a nice guy, for the short time I got to know him. I'm sorry for your loss," Blaze said.

"I knew they would find us eventually. No matter how safe the grown-ups try to keep us, the monsters find a way in."

Blaze took in a deep breath, unsure of how to respond. Aiden was too smart to even consider a counter argument to that. He was so young, yet already knew how their messed-up world worked.

Even Blaze didn't know how the world worked until just days prior. But he knew he had to at least try to comfort the child.

"You know we won't let anything happen to you," Blaze said. "Not Nori, Not Carl. Not Me."

Aiden looked aside and stood up, brushing the backside of his jeans off with his palms. "I've seen the pictures. They told me not to look, but I did. The grown-ups don't say much, but I'm not stupid. If it gets in here, the grown-ups can't stop it."

"Aiden—"

"I'll let you know if I hear anything," he said before turning down the corridor once again.

Blaze wanted to follow, but knew Aiden was right. Changing his mind would be impossible.

He sat back and stretched his legs out. He pressed the back of his skull against the cool wall blocks. Sitting there, the visions that the Infiltrator had presented came back to him. No matter how hard he tried swatting them away, they rebounded with even more speed, gripped even tighter.

Aiden had said the word 'monsters'. Were there more out there than just the Infiltrator? Was it a misspeak? Or had the Creators sent down more beings to wipe them out?

Before he knew it, within a smooth transition, he fell asleep. He dreamt of the monsters. He could feel them within, stalking the shadowy corridors of his soul. He could hear their footsteps within the hollow of his chest, within his very heart. He saw his loved ones, but the monsters cast them away before he could recall who they were and their importance to him.

Blaze could feel the fiery inferno against his cool skin and could smell decay rolling down the vacant corridors of the base.

The monsters were there, lurking in the shadows, waiting. Despite hope and optimism clutching onto whatever they could, Blaze knew the truth. He wasn't a fool. The shadows would linger, just as the monsters had for decades.

Waiting.

* * *

"Sweetie. Blaze," murmured a soft voice.

Blaze gasped, sitting up. He could feel his heart thumping against a gently pressed hand on his chest.

"Woah. Easy now," said the voice.

The troubled face before him was that of Nori. Her shawl hung off her shoulders, loose strings sweeping against his thighs.

He was still sitting, and he starred at her for a few moments while he returned to reality. Blaze's thoughts were a mess. Flurries of random memories, some recent, some not. Blaze fought to connect them and tie them together. Exhaustion had a unique way of playing tricks on the mind.

"Sorry," he said breathless. "Bad dream."

"I can tell," Nori said concerned. She stepped back. "You want to lie down?"

Blaze laughed lightly. "And go back to that? I'll pass."

"What was it about?" Nori asked.

"This afternoon, in Chicago, the Infiltrator cast some visions into my head. I—I don't really want to talk about it, but I saw them again.

"It was trying to distract you," Nori said. "It was projecting your worst fears, I'm guessing. Playing with your mind; warping it…"

"The others got me away."

"If they hadn't, you wouldn't be here now. Few escape and live to tell the tale."

"But I've seen this before, these memories."

"Dreams can feel very real—"

"It wasn't a dream. It's an impossible past, but I know it happened."

"Blaze…"

"I know it sounds crazy, but I just know it was real. What do you know about the years following the Illness?"

"Not much," Nori admitted. "Anything shared was passed on by grandparents, our parents."

"And the Infiltrator," Blaze continued. "Are there more of them?"

"Yeah," she admitted. "There are a few types. Some haven't been seen for decades, but I'm sure they've just moved on to different prey."

"How many are out there?"

Nori shrugged. "I'm not really sure. A few dozen perhaps? It's hard to get a count, when the people who come across them usually don't live to tell the tale."

Blaze could feel the frustration in her voice. He needed to back off and take it down a notch.

"Sorry," he said. "Just a lot going on right now."

Nodding once, Nori said, "It's okay. It's hard on all of us. But we've just got to keep going. We need to keep chugging along, right? Stay positive. We're not finished yet. We may have a location for a safe zone, or another piece. Who knows, really? But we've got to keep fighting. It's what makes us human. It's what makes us the enemy to the others."

Nori cupped the side of Blaze's face. He followed the scar across her face with his eyes before meeting hers.

"We've got to fight. For the ones we've lost," Blaze agreed.

"For them," she agreed as her eyes went glassy. "And for us, too."

Down the corridor, there was a rapid patter of feet. Nori stepped back a few feet, turning to the source of the running.

"What is it?" she asked quickly.

Blaze looked down the corridor now, too. It was Aiden again.

"They found it!" he exclaimed. "They found the location," he said between giant gulps of air.

"I'm going to go find Trent and Forrest," said Blaze. "I'll see if Aurora can come down, too."

"Right," Nori said. "If you see anyone on the way up, tell them to report to the cafeteria immediately."

"Of course," Blaze agreed, pressing off of the chair.

His first steps were unsteady, but he found his footing quickly as he maneuvered down the remainder of the corridor and up the stairs.

Passing through glimmers of moonlight lighting the stairs, he slowed his pace. Last thing he needed to do was to trip up the stairs and break his fall with his face. But as he climbed to the next floor, he heard an odd noise up ahead but wasn't quite sure what it was. Fabric against fabric, unsteady breaths. The moment he realized what it was, what he'd likely be coming across, it was already too late.

What he saw next sent nerves through his veins and tightened his throat. He saw their two bodies pressed against each other, obscured heavily in shadow. But he recognized Forrest's boots, heels against the baseboard, rocking slightly. Hands belonging to Forrest cupped the other's face, trembling slightly.

The other figure lowered their hands to the top of Forrest's jeans, taking hold of Forrest's belt buckle to unbuckle it. Forrest lowered his hands, pushing their hands away, revealing the face of the other.

Trent.

"Not now," whispered Forrest, leaning in and kissing him one last time before pulling away again.

Blaze feared his pounding heart would alert them to what he'd seen, but as he turned away. He heard another sharp inhale. This time, not of passion.

Of fear.

"Blaze?" asked Forrest.

Trent backed away quickly, nearly crashing into the wall behind him in the narrow corridor.

Blaze stopped on the step, lowered his head. "Yeah, I—I came looking for you both. They found the location of the coordinates," he continued, trying to give off the impression that it was business as usual. But as he held the railing, his hands were shaking. He tried gripping the wood tighter, but it only made it worse.

Forrest's pupils were wide, and he sunk his teeth into his bottom lip. "Look, Blaze, I think we need to talk."

Blaze shook his head and turned back down. "I'm good. I'll—uhm—I'll see you downstairs. Cafeteria."

"Blaze, wait!"

But he didn't. He continued down the stairs, moving as fast as his feet would allow. The more he tried to erase what he'd walked in on, the more he felt bothered. Jitters ran up his legs, and he was growing lightheaded. He guided his hand along the railing, gripping it when he thought he would faint.

He squeezed his eyes shut, which he realized was a stupid thing to do in a dimly lit stairwell. He opened them to realize tears had formed.

He wasn't bothered by two men being intimate, but rather that it was Forrest—his Forrest. The person he was supposed to know everything about.

How could he have missed this? And after all this time?

Blaze realized he was practically sprinting down the steps, now. He didn't want to discuss it with Forrest. What was there to discuss?

Right now, the last thing Blaze wanted to do was talk to Forrest about this. But he knew he wouldn't be able to avoid him forever, nor would he be able to avoid this forever.

Unless he wanted to rid Forrest from his life entirely, he'd have to talk to him eventually.

Blaze moved down the corridor, realizing he'd forgotten to grab Aurora. He told himself he'd fill her in afterwards.

The cafeteria was bustling with activity. Carl stood at the end of the cafeteria table. He held a battery-powered flashlight in his left hand and was pointing at the map with his other.

Chatter was nondescript and nearly muffled in the great space.

Nori stood behind him, appearing to count those in the cafeteria. Elise sat a few feet away in a chair she had pulled up, arms crossed.

Behind Blaze, Forrest and Trent entered the room. Blaze saw them from the corner of his eye and left them there. He moved in close, stopping beside Elise.

She turned to him before looking back to the table.

"So where are we going?" Elise asked impatiently, tapping her foot as if it would propel a response that much quicker.

Carl turned to her, then looked to the rest. "A place you're all familiar with. A place that isn't too far away, like we feared."

"*Where?*" Elise pressed, in no mood for guessing games.

His brows lifted ever so slightly, and a slight smile tugged at the corner of his lips. "River Ridge."

SIXTEEN

He thought he'd misheard the words at first.

River Ridge?

Home? Really? It couldn't be. Not *that* River Ridge. There was no mistaking the words, however.

Perhaps there were others, in other states.

That had to be it, because it simply couldn't be home—where they'd come from. Why would they be going back?

It just didn't make sense. What was still there? Could it be another artifact? Had they missed one? Was the device telling them to return home where it was safe? Had Winslow been right all along in keeping everyone locked away, keeping the outside world away from all of them? Could they have avoided all of this by just staying put?

There were more questions than answers now, and Blaze found it hard to breathe as he processed all of it.

One of the few people left that Blaze knew he could confide in, Forrest, had betrayed him. He was angry, and he didn't know what for yet. He was hurt, but Forrest hadn't done anything to him. He was sad, and he didn't know why.

The others in the cafeteria continued to talk and discuss their next plans, but Blaze stepped away and left the space. From the corner of his eye, where he'd left Forrest and Trent, he saw them look to him and then exchange looks between themselves.

But he couldn't stop. He maneuvered down the corridors and climbed the steps until he reached the sleeping quarters where Aurora was lying, reading some comic books. Aiden must've come up to visit her.

"I need to talk with you," said Blaze.

Aurora turned to him, expression solidifying with her glance of him. "You look like you've seen a ghost," she said. "Sit down." She pointed to the empty bed beside hers.

Blaze removed his shoes and lifted his feet onto the bed.

Aurora set down the comic book down beside her. "What's up?"

"They found the location of the coordinates."

"Where?"

"River Ridge," he replied.

Aurora shook her head before pressing her hand to her face. "How?" she finally said. "That doesn't add up. Nothing is there anymore."

"I know," Blaze replied. "Doesn't make sense to me either. But I—"

Aurora's expression hardened. "What else?" she asked. "Something is bothering you. Something beyond this. I just know it."

"It's nothing, really."

"Blaze..."

"Aurora, honest."

"Tell me, Blaze. Trust me, nothing bothers me."

"I think I saw something I wasn't supposed to see."

"Blaze, I'm in a lot pain, so let's skip playing twenty-questions. What did you see?"

"I think Forrest is—er—I—" he cut himself off, rubbing his hands against his thighs. "I think he's gay."

"Oh," Aurora nodded. "Did he tell you?"

"No, I walked in on him and Trent kissing."

Aurora lifted her brows. "Well, I guess that's a pretty good clue."

"You don't seem surprised," Blaze said. "What gives?"

Aurora shrugged. "Because I already knew," she replied. "He told me about a year ago, I think."

"A year ago? Why you? No offense—"

"None taken," she replied, not thoroughly convincingly. But Blaze continued past. "He never told me!"

"I feel bad saying this, but he thought you wouldn't handle it well."

"Not handle it well! Why would he say that?" Blaze practically shouted.

Aurora held out her hands towards Blaze, palms to the ceiling. "You're kind of making his case," she said.

Blaze leaned back. "Right," he said softly. "Sorry, I'm just—hurt."

"Do you not accept him?"

It was a loaded question, and Blaze hesitated, took a breath. He wasn't sure how he felt at this point.

"I—I don't know," he admitted. "That makes me a terrible friend. I know how bad it sounds."

But to Blaze's surprise, Aurora shook her head. "It doesn't make you a terrible friend," she said. "It's a lot, and we're going through a lot. You found out in an abrupt way, so I think it's the shock talking through you."

"I feel like I should've known, but it's like—it's—" He sighed. "That isn't the Forrest I know."

She nodded slowly, but didn't respond, lowering her eyes. Aurora sat still, listening.

"I just feel like everything was a lie," he continued.

"What was a lie?" Aurora asked. "Him being gay? Okay, I'll give you that. But everything else? Your friendship? Your brotherhood? You guys were inseparable growing up. You think that all goes away because of this? Does your friendship just fly out the window because he likes guys more than girls? I mean, at the end of the day, you have a choice, Blaze. I like dogs a bit more than I do cats. I don't see you not wanting to be my friend."

"Aurora, it's a bit different than a pet preference."

"How so? Does me liking dogs more than cats impact you negatively?"

"Aurora—"

"Answer the question. This is a teaching moment."

Blaze looked to his hands, where his fingers were moving along the length of his forearm. "No," he finally admitted.

"Okay. See, you can let this ruin your friendship, but I wouldn't, if I were you. But in the end, it's your choice."

He leaned forward and rubbed his eyes with bent fingers. "I just can't get it out of my head. I keep seeing them and feeling this crushing sense of loss."

"Well, you haven't lost him yet," said Aurora. "Has anything actually changed between you two?"

"Yeah, I don't trust him. So, that's changed. Er—he hasn't been honest," Blaze said, counting on his fingers. "You know, those minor things, just to name a few."

"Well, that's your problem, not his."

"My problem?" He felt tightness in his chest again, a rolling heat in his belly. "Why am I the bad guy? Gee, sorry I'm not bouncing off the walls," Blaze said. "I feel betrayed by my friend. You could at least attempt to see it from my side."

"I do see it from your side," Aurora rejected, sitting up.

"Oh, that's a lie," snapped Blaze. He slapped his hand against the pillow to his right. "You don't! I'm the bad guy, I'm the unaccepting friend. You're assigning me the damn role, and you know it."

"What role?" Aurora pressed, narrowing her brows in frustration. "Blaze, I'm not playing this game with you. I'm sorry you feel betrayed, and it may take some time for you to come to terms with this, but guess what—Forrest is still Forrest. He's always been Forrest. He's always been the way he is, and despite what you may think, nothing has changed or will change between you and him as friends, unless you want it to. Not him—you. Sure, maybe if you talk about girls, he may not be as interested as you are, but I'm sure he'll still have those talks with you, just as he did before."

"Yeah, all the girls he lied about—"

"Of course he lied!" she replied sharply. "My God, Blaze. He was playing a role. Guess what, Blaze. No more pretending for him. He won the award for Best Actor, and now he's free. He doesn't have to worry. That's the only thing that has changed, and it's a beautiful thing. I couldn't be happier. He's free, Blaze. He's free. I wish you saw it that way, too."

"I mean, I'm happy for him..."

"You sure have an odd way of showing it," Aurora replied, crossing her arms across her chest. "Again, I get the shock; heck, I even get the hurt. But you have to let go of it."

Biting his tongue, Blaze held back a response. He realized anything said further would be him just talking out of his mouth, with no real sense of direction or purpose. Sure, openly talking helped, but he also knew once something was said, there was no taking it back. Something said now, of anger or shock, would have a lasting impact, long after those feelings had subsided.

Blaze stood up from the bed, stepped beyond the foot of it. He paused, looked at the boarded-up window, to the slivers of light shining through. Focused on the silence, the simplicity of it, he found himself listening to the ambient sounds around him.

"You okay?" asked Aurora, interrupting it.

He nodded, choking on his next words. He swallowed. "Er—yeah. Just a lot to process. I'm probably just tired, too. A lot going on right now."

Aurora slid her legs over the side of the bed, sitting up and standing on her good foot. She hopped over to him, steadying herself with outreached hands on the beds. "You should know that this fucking hurts, but I'm doing it because you need it."

She reached out her arms and pulled him in. "Blaze, you should know I don't think you're a terrible person."

Blaze laughed softly, holding her tight. "Glad to hear it."

She leaned back and looked into his eyes. "Look, this is as big of a deal as you make it. You can make it the greatest disaster or the greatest blessing. It's up to you. It's your call."

"Right," Blaze agreed. He stepped back. "Need help laying down?"

"You trying to get me into bed, Blaze?" Aurora replied, raising a brow. She saw Blaze turn bright red, his lower lip quivering on the cusp of speech. "Kidding. No, I'm good."

She turned and hopped back to the bed, sitting down and scooting back to her earlier position, when there was a knock at the door.

"Blaze..."

He shut his eyes, knowing the voice, and exhaled. He opened them to see Aurora aiming towards the doorway with her eyes.

Blaze turned to see Forrest standing, hands clasped in front.

Blaze straightened his posture. "Yeah, what's up?"

"You know what's up. Can we talk?"

"Forrest—there's nothing we need to—"

"No, man," said Forrest firmly. "There's a lot. Please. For me?"

Blaze nodded. "Yeah, of course."

He took the first steps towards Forrest with apprehension. As foolish as it was to him, he felt as if he were walking towards a stranger—a stranger he couldn't remember ever not being in his life. One he thought he'd known well and everything about.

"Just us?" Blaze asked when he was at the doorway.

"Just us," Forrest agreed. "No Trent. Aurora—you're welcome, though…"

She dismissed the idea with a wave. "No, I'll leave you boys to it. But do let me know how it goes."

Forrest's brows lifted momentarily as he let out a nervous laugh. "Great way to set that up, right?" He looked to Blaze. "I know a place where we can be alone."

"I bet you do," Blaze replied, wishing desperately that he'd bitten his sharp tongue.

Forrest took a breath, pausing to find the strength to bite his better than Blaze had.

"Sorry," Blaze continued, following Forrest down the corridor. "That was low."

Forrest took a turn at the wooden stairwell, starting the climb. "It's fine. You're pissed, I get it."

The remaining steps were taken in silence, in nervous preparation for what was to come. Blaze tried playing the looming conversation out in his mind, the possible the branches that could be taken and expanded upon. He imagined the responses he'd have, reminding himself to listen. After all, his mother had always told him that God gave people two ears and one mouth for a reason. It was all about the ratio.

But the more he prepared, the more nervous he became. He forced the thoughts out of his mind, the words yet to be spoken away. If he were to move past this, he needed to focus on the here and now.

The steps became harder to climb. His heart was beating like a rapidly flashing lightbulb. Ache bubbled in his chest, filled his lungs.

"*Shit...*" he murmured breathlessly.

"*Blaze...you...okay?*" the words came out drawn and slow, sluggish and distorted.

He couldn't hear himself think, couldn't hear anything but the beating of his own heart. Blaze gripped the railing with both hands. He couldn't wait. What needed to be said would be said right here, right now.

"It's—" He felt the tears building, his lower lip quivering. "It's like you died." And the tears came.

The emotions swirled through him like water around a drain. He felt each of them prickling his core with their respective sensations. He felt sadness, felt loss. He felt crippling isolation, and he felt shame—not for Forrest, but for himself. How could he do this to Forrest, but these were his emotions. These were his thoughts.

Breaths were ragged, raw, and deep. He lost the strength in his legs and fell to the step, burying his face in his hands.

The tears felt like fire on his cheeks, burning into his skin and branding him in marks of sorrow.

Beside him, Blaze felt a soft thump. He eyed to his left and saw Forrest sitting beside him, arms bent, chin resting in his hands. He reached out and pulled Blaze into his side.

"I'm still here, buddy," Forrest said gently, nearly in a whisper. "I'm not going anywhere."

And though Blaze couldn't bring himself to respond, he nodded, wiping his eyes.

"So, I'm going to talk, and you're going to listen. Got it?" Forrest said. Without even a moment for Blaze to refuse, not that Forrest thought he would, he continued. "I never told you because I wasn't even sure about me until several months ago. I talked to Aurora because—well—you know, she gets that stuff. She has two moms, so it's nothing new for her. I didn't talk to you because I was embarrassed. I mean, I love myself. I love who I am, but I wanted to be normal. I wanted to be like the other guys."

Blaze lowered his hands, but continued looking down the stairs as he continued to listen.

"I wish I had told you first, but I wasn't ready. Because once you go there; once you say those words, there's no going back. And I guess—to borrow what you said—the Forrest everyone knows goes away. Sure, it's still me, but now there's this new version—an honest version—but a new version. And as much as we tell ourselves, 'Oh, it's the same person,' I get why someone would see me as a whole new person and the old Forrest is gone. But Blaze, don't see this as a sad thing. See it as a rebirth. I'm still the same, crazy, wacky and borderline-insensitive person you know and love. I'm still going to beat you at bike races and be able to climb trees higher than you. That's just me, regardless if I'm Straight-Forrest or Gay-Forrest."

Blaze was laughing softly to himself, shaking his head. "Guess some things never change."

Forrest patted Blaze on the shoulders. "Just give Gay-Forrest a chance. Can you do that for me? Please."

"Just don't change too much," Blaze replied, sniffling and wiping his face one more time.

"Change? Please, I've always been me. What you see is what you get."

Blaze looked over to him and grinned with tight lips, fighting back another wave a fresh tears. "I'll take it."

Forrest leaned over. "And I promise, I'm not going anywhere, buddy. Take your time, but I'll be here."

Blaze shook his head. "I'm fine. I should've been fine to begin with. I'm sorry for that..."

"Don't be," said Forrest. "Not blaming you. You did walk in at an awkward moment."

"Yeah, about that. You need to get a room," Blaze laughed. "Didn't need to see that. With a man or a woman."

"You didn't see anything," Forrest quipped, nudging Blaze in the side with his elbow.

"And I breathe a sigh of relief. Look, let's change the topic. Did I miss anything downstairs?"

"After you left?"

Blaze nodded as he wiped away some lingering tears with the sleeve of his shirt.

Forrest turned back to him. "Nothing really. Just leaving tomorrow, those who want to go."

"Wait, not everyone is going?"

Forrest shook his head, running his fingers down the polished wood of the base of the railing. "Doesn't seem like it. Nori and Carl are hanging back. So is Amelia. A few others I don't know are staying, too. Sounds like Donovan is coming."

"What about the kid—Aiden?"

"No clue. Does he have parents here?"

Blaze shook his head. "Dead."

"Man, that's rough. I mean, do you think it's safe for him to come?"

Blaze shrugged. "Is it safe for any of us? No one knows. It's a risk, but it could pay off."

"Or backfire," Forrest reminded him. "But if we stay here, forever, this is it. Nothing ventured, nothing gained, as they say."

"Yeah, well I'm sure *they* were talking about taking strategic chances, you know, with career moves or moving to a different city. Not about alien technology directing them away from their safe-house. Maybe then *they* would have had a different quote that applies here."

"You think too much," Forrest said. "We're smart people. We have supplies. If it backfires, then that's that. Light's out. But a life spent in isolation, spent hiding, is no life at all. Blaze, if I've taught you anything in our friendship, let it be just that. No one should live life locked away and hiding yourself—your true self. Sometimes you've just gotta take a chance."

Blaze knew what Forrest was getting at. There was truth to what was being said.

"So tomorrow then?" Blaze asked. "We leave?"

"At dawn," Forrest replied. "Sounds like they have a few vehicles still running. They're letting us take one, and that'll take us as far as it can. They've siphoned gas over the years, collected it. Won't go forever, and we'll end up walking some distance, I'm sure, but It's better than nothing. Worst case scenario, it doesn't start and we just walk the whole way."

"A little exercise never hurt anyone," Blaze said.

"That's the spirit," said Forrest. "You want to stay up here, in the dark, or go back down? I think Nori wanted people to put together some travel kits."

"Travel kits?"

"You know—backpack, snack foods, maps, equipment. Anyone leaving in the morning is supposed to make one. You think Aurora's going to come tomorrow?"

"I'm not leaving her here," Blaze said. "I'll carry her myself if need be."

"Right," Forrest said. "I'd do the same. So, I guess we've decided for her. She'll love that," he laughed.

"On second thought, it might be best to run it past her," said Blaze. "In the end, it's up to her whether she comes or not."

Forrest nodded. "And miss all the fun? She'd never miss out."

Blaze pressed off his thighs and rose to his feet. A little unsteady, he gripped the railing. "We should ask and then put together our backpacks."

Forrest also rose to his feet. "Sounds good. I'll catch up with you in a bit. Trent wanted me to tell him how it went."

"Sure," Blaze nodded quickly. "Of course."

"Still a bit a nervous hearing his name, I see," Forrest replied. "He's really cool. Give him a chance, too. I promise Blaze."

"Just make sure you find a keeper," Blaze said, starting down the steps. "You deserve it."

"Thanks, Blaze. That really means a lot." He started down the stairs behind Blaze. "And just so you know, he is. He's a good guy."

Though Forrest couldn't see it, Blaze smiled softly to himself. "Good," he replied finally. "I'm glad to hear it."

* * *

Within the lower corridors, Blaze and Forrest parted ways. Blaze climbed the stairs, entering the sleeping quarters to find Aurora sitting with Aiden, reading a comic book aloud to him. But based upon the number of finished books, Blaze knew she was also reading them for herself and enjoying them.

"Could you wait until she's done fighting the villain. This is a good part, then I'm all ears," Aurora said, looking over the edge of the comic book.

"Only a few more pages!" Aiden added impatiently.

"Sure, take your time," Blaze replied. "I've got all night."

He sat down on the cot beside Aurora's, listening to the story, admiring her with Aiden. Sure enough, Aiden wasn't exaggerating when he said there were only a few more pages in the book. Blaze had hardly settled in before Aurora closed the back cover and set it down in her finished pile.

"These are pretty good once you get started," she said to Blaze. "Addicting, too. They suck you right in, book after book." She looked to him, and her expression firmed up. Blaze realized she must've seen a blotchy, tear-streaked face in lieu of his usual, cheerful self.

"Aiden, can you give Blaze and I a few minutes alone? Then we'll read one more before bed."

"Nah, he can stay," Blaze said. "It went well. A lot of emotions, but we're good. I'm good."

The corners of Aurora's lips curled upwards. "Oh, I'm so glad. I'm sure it was tough for both of you."

"More so for him. But I'm proud of him, and we're continuing along. I'm sure you'll talk with him about it."

"Naturally," she replied. "I'm nosy."

"But I was going to ask, are you coming tomorrow?"

"Where?"

"River Ridge. They're leaving in the morning, at dawn."

She pointed to her ankle. "I'd love to, but—"

"If we have to, we'll carry you, Aurora. I think this is a one-way ticket. There's no coming back. They're preparing supplies for those who are leaving."

"But some are staying?" Aurora asked.

"Some. Yes."

Aurora placed a hand on Aiden's shoulder, pat it softly. "What about you, kiddo? Are you going on the adventure tomorrow?"

"Miss. Nori wants me to stay here until we know what's there," he sighed. "She's being difficult."

"I get it. That makes sense," Aurora replied. "Well, you won't believe this, but River Ridge is where we came from. It's where we grew up."

Aiden's brows lifted, impressed. "But then why'd you leave?"

"Because we thought we were safer out here, away from home. But maybe we were wrong about that. Maybe there's something back home, something we hadn't found."

"If you want my advice," Aiden said, "you should go back and find out. Once you know what's there, then come back and take me there."

Blaze looked to Aurora. He knew she was thinking of what he had said and how this was a one-way ticket, a one-shot deal. There was no returning.

"Aiden," Blaze said. "If I talked it over with Miss. Nori, would you want to come with us?"

"Can I bring my comic books?" he asked after a pause.

Without skipping a beat, Aurora jumped in. "Of course. How else will we find out if Empress Inferno beats the Titanium Falcon? Or—Or what happens after Falcon found Inferno's base in Downtown Shanghai? These are questions I need answering!"

"I know, but I won't tell," Aiden said. "Falcon's a smart villain. He won't give into her easily. He won't go down without a fight."

"Aurora…" Blaze said gently. "Are you coming?"

"It's just a sprain. It'll hurt, but I'm going to give it a shot."

"They have a vehicle that they're letting us use, according to Forrest."

"They've been saving those for a long time," Aiden said. "It sounds like a special occasion."

"It is, buddy. That's why I've got to work my magic and get you to come along," Blaze said. "I'll talk to Nori, and we'll go from there. But Aiden," Blaze said, lowering slightly to be eye level, "Miss. Nori may want you to stay here, you know, to help around and stand guard. Don't be sad, if she doesn't let you come with us. If we can, we'll come back and get you, okay?"

"Promise?" Aiden asked.

"Promise," said Blaze.

* * *

Night had fallen across the city by the time Forrest and Trent met up with Blaze in the cafeteria. Elise stood in a corner, smoking a cigarette as she watched the operation at hand. A small number of backpacks had been set onto the cafeteria tables, with remaining supplies sprawled out across the surface surrounding them. Blaze had selected one made of blue canvas. He took it, set it aside on the ground and began to go through it.

He unzipped the bag and immediately beneath the opened zipper tracks was an old map of the state. Portions of the others were there. He had an idea of where River Ridge was based on the map Carl was looking at earlier, but now, seeing it up close and on his own, it was a bit more of a challenge. He traced outward from Downtown, looking for any cities that began with an "R" near farmland. He'd only seen the town on a map once, as a kid. Winslow didn't like for there to be maps easily accessible. It was as if he'd written off the rest of the world when the walls rose.

He found the town, quite a distance from the big city, then set the map aside. He dug through the bag, finding a first aid kit, a wind-up flashlight, a few bottles of water, and some snack food.

Bare bones and basic.

But it would be enough to get them back home. Forrest stood by Trent as they each went through their own bags. Blaze peered over, saw they had what he had, then looked past them to Nori.

She looked busy, but then again, Nori was always looking for chores and things to do. He'd need to approach the topic carefully, with surgical precision.

Blaze put the map back in his backpack, zipped it up, then slung it onto his back before moving over to her quickly.

"Jesus, child," Nori exclaimed, setting down a container onto the table "What on Earth is so urgent that you needed to scare me half to death?"

"Oh, sorry. For tomorrow, who's all going?"

"Evidently that," she said to herself. "A few. Why do you ask?"

"Are you?"

Nori shook her head. "My son is still out there, on the streets. It sounds crazy, but I can feel it. I know he's out there. It's a mother's intuition, I guess. He may be in his twenties, but he's still my baby. I have to stay here. This is the only home he knows."

Blaze kept his eyes on her, nodded. "And Carl?"

"He's staying too. The man's closer to ninety than eighty. He can't make the trip. He succeeded in uncovering what the devices said. Now that he knows, he can let you guys take the torch."

"What would you say to Aiden coming along?"

"I'd say absolutely not."

"Nori—"

"I said no. That boy lost his parents when they went on a supply run. I'm not sending him to his death, too, just for another adventure that may lead nowhere."

"I know you don't believe that. You saw the hologram. You saw what it said."

Nori lifted the container and began walking towards an open storage room. Blaze followed. "To my knowledge it didn't say anything. It didn't display any words to read."

"Right, but you saw between the lines..."

"You know, I always hated when people claimed one thing meant something, and their reasoning for seeing it was, 'Well, you have to read between the lines.' If it's not there, it's not there. Especially in something as important as this."

"Then why are you supporting some of us leaving?"

"Because you'd do it anyway. At least you're prepared now."

"So what do you think?"

"Doesn't matter what I think," she said, setting the container on a shelf. She immediately reached for another, lowered it to the ground, and lifted the lid. "Damn, wrong one," she said, putting it back.

"Please, let us take Aiden. We won't let anything happen to him. He'll be safe with us."

"Last time I let one of my babies go with you, my son didn't come home. He's safer here."

The words struck Blaze, burned him, but he needed to brush them aside. He needed to continue making his case.

"But Nori, what if this leads to something huge? To something great?"

"Then he missed out, but at least he has his life. We're safe here."

"For now," Blaze replied. He sensed motion behind him and turned to see Forrest in the doorway to the storeroom.

Nori exhaled, looking past Blaze. "Can you tell him to stop badgering me."

Forrest cleared his throat. "Blaze…"

"What? I'm trying to get Aiden to come with us."

"And I'm trying to tell him that it's not safe for a boy of his age to go," Nori said.

Blaze turned back to Forrest, raised his brows. "He doesn't want to stay here anymore. He wants to go."

"Of course he wants to go! He's eleven. Eleven-year-old boys aren't exactly the best at deciding what's best for them. That's why God invented mothers!"

"But you're not his mother!" shot back Blaze. "His parents are dead. He has no ties to this place anymore. Do you want this to be his life? Hiding from the outside world in an abandoned school?"

"Blaze," Forrest said. "Let it go."

"No, I can't, man."

But Nori continued on, too. "It's not the ideal life, but it's a safe life. I need you to stop. He's *not* going. I know your heart is in the right place, and you're trying this whole, older-brother role—"

"It's not a role."

"—but he's too young and we don't know what's back at River Ridge or what's waiting for you. Please don't paint me to be the monster."

"I'm not painting anything." Blaze took a breath, held it in, trying to ease the knot in his chest. It felt like massive, strong hands were clutching the muscles of his chest, twisting them into a tight bunch.

Forrest stepped forward beside him and set his hand on Blaze's shoulder. "She's playing it safe, man. Don't be mad at her. She's not the enemy. Besides, we can't be worrying about him if shit hits the fan, right? It wouldn't be the right thing for him. It wouldn't be the safest option, either."

"I guess so," Blaze agreed, eyes focused on the worn tiling. "But if that thing finds this place like I know you fear it will. Like we know it probably will. When it comes in, starts killing you all one by one, I hope you remember that you had a chance to get out. I wish you'd all come with us."

Nori's brown eyes narrowed on Blaze's. "It's not that simple, but you've said what you've said; said it rather poorly, in my opinion, and now it's time to leave. Be grateful for the supplies we've given you, the food off of our table, the beds you've slept on—"

"I am," Blaze said. "Eternally."

"Sure," Nori replied unconvinced. "Odd way of saying so. Look, I think it's best you go upstairs and rest before tomorrow morning. It'll be an early start."

"Please, Nori," Blaze begged. "Let us take Aiden."

But as he expected, she shook her head. "He's not going and don't you dare try to sneak him out. You can come back later and get him, get us, when you know it's safe."

Blaze shook his head and moved towards the door to the main cafeteria. "You know as well as I do that there's no coming back."

Nori nodded just enough for Blaze to wonder if she'd nodded at all. "Then I suggest you say your goodbyes tonight. It's for the best, Blaze. For all involved."

Though it hurt to admit it, internally, Blaze wondered if she was right.

* * *

"What do you mean she said no?" Aiden shot back after Blaze and Forrest had told him of Nori's refusal.

"She said you need to stay back and help, buddy," Blaze said. "Since we're leaving, you're in charge, and she's expecting you to run a tight ship."

They stood in the sleeping quarters on the third floor. Candle light flickered, illuminating the room with an orange glow.

Donovan had joined them in the room, sitting on the end of one of the beds in the corner. "Aiden, Carl coming either. Someone's gotta keep him company, or he gets real ornery."

"He doesn't even like me, Donovan. I want to go with you guys," Aiden said. "It's not fair."

"I know, and we tried, but like I said, we'll come back and get you once we know what's next. There are too many things up in the air right now and the grown-ups need to work out the kinks."

"You're not grown-ups. You're only a few years older than me."

"Yeah, I know. But—" Blaze looked to Aurora for back-up.

"Aiden, they need you here, close to home. They'd miss you if you left. And Miss Nori needs a helper."

"Well, she can find someone else."

"When we can, we'll come back and grab all of you when it's safe. I promise," Aurora said. "Besides, I need to know what happens next in those comics, so I'll be here the moment we can."

Aiden sighed.

"Keep your chin up, little man. We'll be back," Donovan said. "It's only for a little while." He took a seat on one of the empty cots.

Aiden kept his eyes downcast. "Say goodbye before you leave in the morning," he said, walking over to Aurora's pile of comic books, gathering them in his hands and pulling them to his chest. "Night."

And with that, he moved to the door and slipped out without uttering another word.

The remaining few in the room kept silent. They didn't move a muscle, didn't breathe a breath.

"I feel like garbage," Blaze said.

"Why?" Donovan asked. "He doesn't need to know the truth, man."

"He's old enough to remember us," Blaze replied.

Donovan leaned back on his forearms. "I know. But telling him the truth just creates pain."

"But when we don't come back, he's going to catch on."

"And we'll be long gone," Donovan replied.

"Wow," Blaze replied.

"That's cruel, Donovan," Aurora said.

He sat up, straightening his posture. Hearing the criticism from her bothered him more than if it had come from Blaze or Forrest.

"Truth hurts. Life does too, but we keep living. We have no choice," he continued. "None of us gets to escape hurt. You can't outsmart it. Can't run from it. He needs to be exposed to it, especially in our world. Look," his voice shifted tone, "we better get to sleep. I want to be up by five, out the door before sunrise."

"Which is?" Forrest asked.

"When the sun comes up," Donovan replied stiffly.

"Yeah, that I figured out. What time?"

"A little after six."

Forrest nodded. "Aurora, need anything?"

She shook her head. "I'm good."

"All right," Donovan said. "Everyone get ready for bed, then light's out. Sleep well, all."

A few minutes came and went. The others had crawled into bed, pulled the thin blankets up to their faces. A few others, some that Blaze wasn't as familiar with had joined them in the sleeping quarters, going straight to sleep.

But Blaze lie there in the quiet darkness. He listened to the soft lull of deep breathing in the cots beside his. He stared up at the ceiling, watching tiny shadows on the surface remain stationary.

As he would as a child, he tried to make out shapes of animals in them. He focused on the soft curvature, letting his mind wander and his imagination project. As Nori would disapprove, he sought to see between the lines of the delicate features of the shadows and see something his mind would conjure as familiar and safe.

But tonight, despite his efforts, he saw nothing but shadows.

SEVENTEEN

Blaze woke in the dark, fighting for a breath to breathe.

The hand of paralysis gripped his throat, squeezing tight, as whimpers croaked out, trying to call out to anyone who could hear him. They were mere whispers, raspy and uncontrolled. The dark made his nightmares even worse, and far more terrifying.

As the dream faded, he still saw the figure—the Shape—lingering. It's translucent skin was still glimmering, as if burned into the back of his retinas. He could still see the shimmer of his reflection staring back at him.

'A dream...a dream...' he told himself. This seemed to work.

Still trembling, the tightness in his throat eased, and he found himself able to breathe fully again. He took in deep breaths, focusing on the ceiling just as he had while falling asleep. The shadows had moved slightly, taken on a different shape. But as before, they were still shadows, just as he'd left them hours ago.

He peeled away the moist sheets before raising a hand to his forehead. He let it lie there, strewn across, for a few moments before lifting the blanket to dab his face and wipe away the sweat.

Sitting up, he felt the back of his cotton T-shirt cling to his damp skin. He pulled it away, fanning himself with the fabric up front.

"Bad dream?" asked a voice.

It caught him off guard. "Yeah," Blaze admitted quickly, the word escaping from him without much thought. He swallowed a lump in his throat. "Any idea of the time?" he asked, thumbing the bridge of his nose.

The figure leaned over, took a clock off a bedside table. "A little after four."

Blaze narrowed his eyes, focused a little closer. He realized he knew who the figure was across from him.

"Trent?" Blaze asked in a sharp whisper.

The figure nodded, replied quietly, *"Er—yeah, why?"*

"Just asking," Blaze said hushed. *"Can't sleep?"*

"Bit of a bad dream myself. If you want to talk, we should probably leave the room. Don't want to wake anyone."

Blaze shook his head. *"We have a long trek tomorrow—er—today. We'll talk then."*

And without another word, Blaze lay back onto his pillow, and tried to will himself back to sleep for what little time remained before they'd be getting up.

By the time he sensed movement and heard hushed voices, Blaze wondered if he'd gotten back to sleep at all. Regardless, he felt even more tired now than he had before. He lie in the darkness, bringing both hands behind his head. Beside him, Aurora was sitting up, running her fingers through her hair before tying it back into a ponytail, fastening it with a rubber band.

He sat up slightly to see Trent making his bed, smoothing the sheets carefully with his hands. Forrest remained in bed, having pulled the sheets higher above his head, as if no one would see the large mass beneath the blankets.

In the corner of the room, nearest the windows, Donovan was standing shirtless, stretching a bit longer than necessary. Even at five in the morning, he would ensure that everyone saw the fruits of his weight lifting before putting on a shirt.

"Nice show, Don," Trent said.

Donovan smirked. "Wasn't for you, my friend," he replied, eyeing towards Aurora who, while very aware, refused to give him the attention he sought.

Blaze sat up, swinging his legs over the edge of the bed. Aurora faced him, pulling on her long-sleeved flannel and buttoning a few of the bottom buttons.

"Morning, sleepyhead," she said.

"Morning."

"Sleep well?"

"Eh—I've had better nights of rest."

"Yeah, same here. Good news is my ankle is feeling better. Still a bit swollen, but the pain isn't as sharp."

"That's good. Think you can walk on it?"

"It's possible," she said. "One step at a time, right?"

"Right. They have a car, too, so we've got that going for us." Blaze looked over and saw Trent trying to wake Forrest.

Forrest pulled back the sheets and ran his fingers through his hair, tousled it a bit before rising, and pulled on the pair of jeans that were strewn across the foot of his bed.

Donovan pointed to a few figures who were still in bed asleep—the few who weren't joining them for their own, personal reasons. Raising his index fingers to his lips—the universal sign to be quiet—the group gathered their things, finished getting dressed, and tied their shoes in silence.

Aside from the nerves, Blaze felt it was every-bit as normal as any other morning. He wondered if the others also felt the nerves. He didn't dare ask, but assumed he was in the company of a few others like him.

When they were outside of the sleeping quarters, they slung their backpacks on and started down the steps. They remained quiet in the dark stairwell, and the only sounds made were those of footsteps in sync, as if marching into a battlefield of the unknown.

In the early hour, only candle light lit the space. The generators were shut down before bed, only to come back on after dusk. As the group moved into the entrance hall, distant voices sounded from the cafeteria.

Donovan led them in, approaching his grandfather who was standing near Elise and Nori. Without an exchange, Donovan wrapped Carl in his bulky arms, held him firmly.

Carl pressed his thin lips together, then closed his eyelids. He patted his grandson on the shoulders. "You'll be okay, kid. You've got a good head on your shoulders."

Donovan leaned back, nodded to his grandfather. "Learned from the best," he said.

Raising a hand to his mouth, Carl cleared his throat. "Elise will be coming with. She has some unfinished business back home, and she knows the way." Carl looked over, stepping back another foot, motioned towards Blaze, Forrest, and Aurora. "They're locals, too, but I doubt they could find their way back. Understandably," he added.

Donovan eyed across the group. "No Amelia?" he asked.

Nori shook her head. "She changed her mind. She's gonna wait for the second round."

Donovan nodded. "Her choice, I guess. We'll find a way to let you know what comes of this. If we get another clue, some trail to follow. Anything, really," Donovan said.

"We'd appreciate it," Carl replied quietly.

Donovan took a step back. Now, a few feet separated the two. "Do you have what we talked about? The device?"

"Right," Carl nodded, moving over to the nearby table. He lifted a torn piece of thin fabric, pushed it aside, and revealed the mysterious assembly of artifacts. "Tried playing with it this morning," he said. "Nothing. Probably ran out of juice or whatever it runs on. We didn't have long to experiment with it or figure out how it works."

"If you want to keep it—"

Carl was holding up a frail hand before Donovan even stopped himself. "It's of no use to us now. Take it. You might need it if you come across anything in River Ridge."

"Right," Donovan agreed. "So—er—"

"Nori. Keys," Carl said, dismissive of his grandson. He refused to let himself feel. Refused to let himself deviate from the mission. The time to feel would come later, long after they were gone.

Nori reached into the pocket of her sweater. She held out a set of car keys. The plastic nub on the end had was worn, with a logo nearly unrecognizable in the smooth plastic. "Full tank of gas. Should get you there with no trouble. Started her up this morning."

Elise walked up, taking the keys from Nori's grasp. "I'll be driving. Thank you very much."

Carl crossed his arms. "Are your eyes up for the challenge? Especially in the dark?"

Elise lifted a penciled-in brow. "Better than yours, old man."

Amused, the corners of Carl's lips raised. "Fair enough."

Nori pointed to the table. "Weapons?"

"Ah, yes. Nearly forgot," Carl said. "Pick your poison. Choose wisely."

Donovan shook his head. "Are there enough for the rest of the Reapers? What if there's an attack."

Hand raised, Carl waited a moment before answering. "Relax, son. We have plenty. We're more than ready for a last stand. Besides, when have you ever really cared about the group entirely?" He snickered slightly.

But Blaze could tell the statement struck Donovan hard. Struck him cold. Maybe under different circumstances, he would have seen it as merely playing around, but now—in this moment—it hurt. The reality that they may not see each other again was already planted deep. He didn't want to go out like this.

"Is that really what you think?" asked Donovan.

"About what?"

"About me—that I never cared about the group?"

Carl exhaled a breath, lowered the corners of his lips. "What is this about?"

"This is our last time together, and that's how we're leaving off?" Donovan replied, straining near the end.

"Stop that. Stop that right now," Carl said. "You know I was joking. This isn't about that. This is about us staying back, right? You know that some have to remain back, for the others that can't make the trip."

"I get that," Donovan said, his tone shifting with each word. "I mean, this is crazy. We don't even know what's at River Ridge. They came from there, they never saw anything."

This was the first Blaze had heard apprehension from Donovan. Reality was striking hard this morning. He turned and saw Donovan's eyes turning glassy.

"We didn't know what we were looking for, to start with," said Aurora. "There might be something there."

But Carl was frustrated now. He walked to his grandson, who was perhaps an inch taller than him. But broad-shouldered and wide-legged, Carl still exuded the power. He reached out, graced a thumb across Donovan's face, wiping a tear. "Enough," he said flatly.

Blaze looked closer and saw the tear streaks now. He looked to his left, making eye contact with Forrest, then Trent. Shadows played across their eyes making them unreadable. Reality was continuing to settle in and dig deep.

"Enough," Carl repeated, slowly and with precision. "Pick your weapon."

Donovan's shoulders raised, as he used the back of his hand to wipe away the remaining tears. He cleared his throat, swallowed a lump, as he approached the table.

Without hesitation, he lifted a charcoal-black handgun, checked the magazine, and grabbed a holster for his belt.

Elise approached the table, eyed down the small display of selections. "*You.*" She pointed to Aurora. "This will do you well. I like a revolver. Reliable and chic. A classic."

"I don't really care about being a fashion icon right now," Aurora said, moving slowly to the table.

Elise eyed her up and down. "Yeah, you've proven that." Elise looked down, watching as Aurora moved towards the table. "How's the foot?"

"Better than last night. One step at a time," said Aurora, coming to a stop and leaning slightly more onto her good foot. "I'll take the revolver."

"Good girl," Elise said. "Need me to go over the basics?"

Aurora shook her head. "My mom taught me when I was younger."

"How? Winslow allowed your family to have one? They confiscated my father's back when I lived there," Elise said.

"Unregistered," Aurora said.

"Ah," breathed Elise. "Boys—we haven't all day. Chop, chop! On the double."

Trent moved forward, took a handgun nearly identical to Donovan's. He motioned for Forrest to come.

"I think you'll like this one," he said. "Easy to use. Easy to master." He held it out for him.

Forrest took hold of it, thumbing the edge of the barrel before reaching out for a holster.

"You know how to shoot?" asked Elise.

"The basics," said Forrest, not fully confident. "Aim, pull the trigger."

"I suppose that's all we need for right now. I'll show you more when time allows. Fireboy, you're up next."

"It's Blaze." He walked up to the table, running his gaze across the remaining weapons. They all looked like good choices. A few revolvers and two more handguns. He looked to their weapons. Elise and Aurora both had wood and metal revolvers, and the boys had the black handguns. For simplicity's sake, Blaze went with the handgun. He held it, cupping his hand around the grips. It felt good in his hand. He liked the weight, and he liked feel of the textured grip. In the seconds he held it, it felt like an extension of him. He assumed this was a good thing.

"Good, that's settled," said Carl. "Make your first shot, your best shot. I hope you won't need to use them."

Another silence fell across the cafeteria. They stood quietly, anticipating the next moves. It was clear there was nothing really left to say. Supplies had been handed out, weapons assigned. At this point, it was time to move. It was time to carry on forward.

Elise fumbled with the keys in her hand. "Where's our chariot?"

"Lower-level garage," said Nori. "I'll show you the way." She started forward immediately and Elise followed, then Aurora.

But Donovan remained stationary, feet solid against tile. He stood before his grandfather, lowering his gaze to the floor before meeting Carl's eyes.

"Thanks for everything."

Carl gave a dismissive wave. "None of that, now. Good luck out there. I'm sure you'll have loads of stories." He walked up, took his grandson against his chest, and smoothed his hands across Donovan's back. "They'd be proud of you—your parents. And, for the record, so am I."

Donovan smiled. "I'll see you later, old man."

Carl touched his grandson on the shoulder once more. "Go on. You're holding everyone up."

Without further delay, Donovan followed Aurora and the others. Blaze trailed the group. Before leaving the cafeteria, he turned to see Carl standing in the low-light, hand raised in farewell, posture confident and proud. But Blaze could see through the façade. He knew this was a bereavement, as Carl watched his last family member slip away.

Blaze twisted around to catch up to the others. They moved silently down the corridor, turned at a hallway near the stairwell, then slipped further into inky blackness. Nori grabbed a flashlight hanging from a nail into the wall. She took it, flipped it on.

Illuminated, the stairwell descended to a small, square-shaped landing before turning and descending a bit further. They moved together in the confined space. Blaze held onto the railing, felt it wiggle a bit under his grasp.

"We're not taking the Jeep, are we?" asked Donovan.

"Too small," Nori called back. "You're taking the SUV. Besides, it's the newest one we were able to get running."

The group poured out into the garage. It was small with low-hanging ceilings. Metal shelving units were loaded with wooden crates of food, of supplies. Equipment such as generators and old, manual typewriters—anything they found over the years that could be useful—were stored down here. Blaze figured it was the safest place in the entire structure, too.

Nearest the garage was a dusty, sun-faded, black SUV. Elise walked up to the driver's side door, unlocked it, before unlocking the others. Nori moved to the garage door and pulled aside two steel poles that were serving as make-shift locks to keep the door down. She knelt down, lifted the door from beneath. Slowly, it rose, groaning and creaking the entire way up.

Cool breeze wafted down the concrete ramp into the lower level. Blaze pulled his shirt around him, putting his hands under his armpits to keep them warm as they moved towards the vehicle.

Aurora got into the rear backseat. Donovan took shotgun, while Trent and Forrest also got into the backseat, leaving room for just Blaze. He climbed in, fastened his seatbelt, and shut the door.

Elise started the engine in one try. She lowered the passenger window Nori stood outside of.

"Well," Nori said softly to the group, "be safe."

"You too," said Donovan. "Take care, Nori." He extended his hand out to her.

Nori took it, squeezed between hers, before letting it drop and stepping backwards. She waved and the others did too as Elise backed out of the parking spot and slipped through the garage entrance, climbing the ramp, and exiting onto the street.

As the vehicle accelerated, Donovan pulled out his map from the backpack. "River Ridge," he said absentmindedly, tracing his finger atop the roads he had lined with marker—a route he had planned to take had he been driving.

"I don't need that," Elise said. "Trust me. I know the way."

* * *

From the highway, the darkened Chicago skyline pierced the low-hanging clouds. Swirling around the concrete jungle, the clouds masked the state of disrepair they were in. Sunrise was near, casting a fire-red glow across the thick canvas above. Without word, they watched out the windows, catching glimpses of the abandoned city. Vehicles sat, some spun in opposite directions of travel, others serving as charred remnants of the panic that had set in during the Illness.

Streets were skeletons, stripped of their flesh decades prior. Only concrete structures remained aside from the occasional faded marketing display. In some areas, even streetlights had been taken down, dragged away and used elsewhere. Metal had been cut loose by the other scavengers, panes of glass taken. Blaze wondered where the others—others like the Reapers—were hiding. Were there many groups, or had they died off over the years or been found by Infiltrators?

Outside the city, the highway stretched long and far, pavement charcoal-hued and cold. The vehicle rumbled gently as Elise navigated away. Every so often, they would come across a cluster of vehicles, but it was clear they had been moved, gutted, and siphoned since they originally turned off. They were of no use to them anymore.

Blaze let his mind wander, trusting Elise to deliver them safely. He peered out the window, but after a while, even the world outside couldn't keep him awake. And unsure of the next time he'd be able to get solid sleep, he didn't fight it. He welcomed it and leaned back into the nook between the headrest and the side of the vehicle.

But even as everything around him faded away, merging into a world that was his only, there was still no peace to be found.

Not yet.

* * *

The first crash was the worst.

Then came the second.

Blaze woke to screams. He felt powerful vibrations in his chest, then felt the SUV go inverted, spinning, climbing, falling. Blaze barely had time to react before the airbags deployed, knocking him to the side. The curtain dropped across the passenger window, blinding him to what was going on.

The world was spinning. Blaze clutched the top of his head as the vehicle went inverted. He lowered his chin to his chest, and disoriented, squeezed his eyes shut.

The vehicle tumbled over and over into the barrier on the edge of the road before coming to an absolute stop.

Silence.

Blaze was fleetingly aware of the soft metallic taste in his mouth he knew to be blood. He opened his eyes, and thought it had been a dream at first. Eyelids fluttering, he looked through the air thick with smoke.

There were groans and cries. Blaze looked down, realizing the SUV was on its side. In the front seat, Elise sat still, head angled towards the ground in a sea of glass and pressed-in metal.

Donovan, in the seat ahead, had unbuckled his seatbelt and was now struggling to open the door that was above him.

Trent nudged Blaze frantically. "Get the door open! We have to move," he said. Blaze saw blood trailing down his forehead. "Hurry!"

Blaze reached for the handle, pulled it towards him. He heard it unlatch, then he pushed. He pushed as hard as he could until the door swung open. Unbuckling his seatbelt, Blaze held onto the edge of the doorframe and lifted himself out.

Trent followed, then Forrest.

Blaze jumped down from the side of the SUV, landing on both feet. He ran to the trunk, pulled it open. Aurora was trying to squeeze through the narrow space between the rear-seat and the roof of the vehicle.

"Blaze!" she exclaimed.

"Give me your hand," he directed, pulling the backpacks out of the trunk that lie strewn across the side of the vehicle.

She did so and used her other hand to push herself over the seat. Aurora slid herself through a sea of glass, standing to both feet.

Beside them, Donovan grabbed for his gun and freed it from the holster. "It found us!" he screamed, aiming down the roadway behind them.

Blaze spun around and saw the Shape standing, arms at its side. It tilted its head, as an artist would admire a painting.

How had it located them? This had to be a nightmare. Blaze was really asleep. Had to be. This wasn't real. Couldn't be real.

"Don't shoot!" Blaze yelled. "It'll make two of them!"

Forrest grabbed his backpack, grabbed his gun that was laying in the trunk. "You good to run?" he asked Aurora.

"No choice not to," she said.

"Get the relics!" Donovan screamed back to Blaze.

Blood streaked each of their faces and stained their clothes. Blaze could only imagine how he looked. He bent down once more to look into the SUV, grabbed for what had been Donovan's backpack. Out of the corner of his eyes, and in the midst of chaos, Blaze checked once more on Elise. She remained still.

He cursed beneath his breath as he unzipped Donovan's backpack, spilling the contents out onto the pavement. He saw Donovan's map, but Blaze knew he had his own. They could use that one. Blaze grabbed the device from the debris, shoved it into his own backpack, then stood back up. Donovan was already running forward. Trent and Forrest followed, with Aurora close behind. Blaze made eye contact with the Shape once more before following, running past the wreck of the SUV—the wreck the Shape had caused.

But it didn't follow.

It didn't run. Didn't move a muscle.

Blaze wondered why, but continued running forward and didn't look back. The trek to River Ridge would now be on foot. He had no idea where they were and no time to figure it out.

So, with Donovan at the lead, they ran forward and away.

When the humans were out of its sight, the Shape moved in on the vehicle. It disregarded the one it had killed, not bothering to give her a glance. For it, the human woman was just another tick mark on an endless scroll. Small and meaningless. Another number.

The Shape knelt down and extended a long-fingered hand into the trunk of the SUV.

It eyed the supplies they had left behind, scanning the supplies to see if anything could be useful. It spotted two firearms, but disregarded them. The Shape knelt a bit lower down, spotting the folded map half-opened.

It reached in and pulled it up, wiping away some shattered glass. Its translucent skin seemed to glow beneath the early-morning sun. It illuminated the path drawn on the map. Tracing a finger along the thick line, following the curves and turns with precision, it disregarded the other printed roads. Those weren't important, it had determined.

The line ended on the words: RIVER RIDGE.

Seemingly content, as far as human emotions went, the Shape dropped the map onto the ground and slipped past the burning wreckage, trailing the survivors that thought they were going to get away.

The Shape thought it would let them think that. For now. After all, it liked to play games with its prey.

* * *

"Is everyone okay?" Trent asked.

They had been running for a mile and slipped into an abandoned gas station. The shelves were empty, and light fixtures dangled from exposed wiring. Gusts of wind blew through broken glass, toying with the page of an opened phonebook on the counter.

Trent knelt down between aisles and pulled the first aid kit out of his backpack. Donovan and Aurora had left theirs behind in the wreckage.

"Just a little banged up," Aurora said.

"Bullshit. You're bleeding," he said. "Come here." He opened a paper wrapping of an alcohol wipe. He unfolded it, pressed it lightly to her forehead.

"We have no time for this!" Aurora said. "We have to keep moving."

"When you get an infection, you'll have all day," Trent said. "Blaze, Forrest—get yours out. Check on Donovan."

Donovan was standing at the windows of the gas station, looking outward for any sign of the Shape. Blaze leaned down and took out the red canvas bag, unzipping it and looking inside.

"Donovan," Blaze called. "You okay?"

He flashed a thumb's-up sign. "Fine," he said. "Bleeding has stopped."

"Need a bandage?"

Donovan shook his head. "Save them for later. Thanks."

Blaze turned to see Trent gently smoothing a bandage onto Aurora's forehead. She already looked better with the streaks of dried blood cleared away.

Forrest tapped Trent on the shoulder. "Your turn. Sit down."

He took another alcohol wipe, cleaned up the scratches and cuts on Trent's arms and the side of his face.

"Sorry, sorry," Forrest squeezed out as he dabbed the injuries.

Trent's facial muscles tightened as he fought the stinging.

"All right, all done," said Forrest. Putting a series of flesh-toned bandages onto Trent's injuries. A few were thin scratches, but Forrest wasn't taking any chances. "Good as new," he said.

Within the following few minutes, both Forrest and Blaze were treated, and the remainder of the gas station was checked for any lingering supplies. Coming up empty handed, they exited back onto the street, continuing forward to River Ridge.

There was no time to waste for the hunted.

EIGHTEEN

Partially veiled in clouds, the walls of River Ridge stood out against the vast, desolate landscape.

They had followed the roads and cross-referenced the map every few miles or so, and somehow, by the grace of God, they had made it nearly there.

Crisp air bit into Blaze's skin, but the excitement kept him warm and gave him fuel for the remainder of their journey.

They hadn't spoken of Elise. Hadn't spoken of the accident either. As had become custom amongst them, they spoke to the present. The past, even the near-past, could be dealt with later. It had to be dealt with later.

The Shape hadn't followed them. Blaze, remaining in the rear for most of the walk, had been turning around more than he thought he would. It seemed the Shape had simply given up on them. It didn't make sense. None of it did.

"Any idea what we're looking for once we get there?" Trent asked.

"I never lived there. Only three in this group did. The fourth person who did is dead," said Donovan.

It was the first they'd mentioned Elise.

Donovan spun around, continuing to walk backwards. "Did you guys ever see anything that would fit my grandfather's device?"

Forrest looked to Blaze. Blaze to Aurora.

Blaze cleared his throat. "If there was anything found that could be related to this, it would be with Winslow. Either he's hid it or destroyed it."

Donovan cursed beneath his breath. "We'll have to talk with whoever is still there, show them what we've got. Someone has to know something."

"The only person who would know anything would be Winslow." Aurora said.

Donovan shot her a stern look. "Yeah, I get that. He's the obstacle right now. So we're going to have to press him for information."

"He won't budge," Forrest said. "He'll claim he won't remember or flat-out refuse to help us."

"Oh, he'll help us," replied Donovan. "I can be very convincing."

"You know, you're kind of scary when you're pissed," said Trent.

Donovan tilted his head. "You've seen nothing yet."

They continued forward in silence, following the winding road towards the walls. As they grew closer, Blaze observed the entrance was lowered, just as it was when Nori,

Donovan, and the others had greeted them, welcoming them to the outside world.

So much had changed in the short time since.

But Blaze remembered Winslow closing the wall after they left. Why was it open now?

They moved forward, stopping just on the cusp of the walls. The formerly bright, florescent lights that flowed through the wall like veins and blood had gone dark.

The five looked through the opening into the town. Usually bustling with activity, there was no one around.

"Hello?" Blaze called in, stepping forward one foot into his former town.

Nothing.

He was about to call out again, but stopped himself, unsure if it was the right thing to do.

Donovan reached to his side and put his right hand onto the grip of his handgun. He stopped, motioned for them to be quiet with the press of a finger to his lips.

They stepped into the square, looked around. The houses lined around it were dark and quiet. In the great space, they felt even more insignificant in the silence, in the unease.

Blaze felt for his own weapon. He looked to Forrest and Aurora. They still had families here. For him, he had no ties to the town anymore. He felt Aurora's eyes on him. He could see she was scared. He took her hand, held it tight.

"I think they abandoned ship," said Trent quietly. "There's no one here." He stepped forward, past Donovan. "I wonder if—"

"*QUIET!*" Donovan hissed.

No one moved. No one breathed. Donovan inched forward, pointed a hand towards some tables in the square.

"Look down," he whispered. *"By the tables."*

Blaze tried to follow Donovan's line of sight and the invisible line that he was pointing along. He squinted, struggling to make out anything odd.

But what he saw next, he didn't need to be in the mindset to see. A dead body jumps out whether or not you're looking for it.

Distant, pale, and feminine, the body was strewn beneath one of the tables of the square. Closer to them, a slew of weapons lie strewn across the ground. Blood spatter stained the pavement. He hadn't noticed it at first, but the scene was building itself.

"What happened?" Aurora asked.

Forrest pressed his fingertips to his forehead, covering his eyes slightly. Aurora looked away, her breath fluttering within her chest.

"I'm sorry, guys," Donovan said to the three.

"We can't go back," said Forrest. "We have to look for what we came for. As hard as that may be, right now." He pressed his tongue against his right cheek, as he surveyed the space. "We'll find survivors. Let's stop pretending we won't."

"Yeah, our families are here," said Aurora. "We have to look for them. We have to know for sure."

Donovan's expression went solid and unwavering. "We came here for a mission, to find the next clue—"

"Fuck your clues! Our families are out here," Aurora said. Her voice was trembling and uneven. She dropped Blaze's grasp, wiping a tear from her cheek.

Blaze had never seen Aurora cry. Not once. He held out his arm and pulled her into his shoulder.

"No—I'm good," she tried to force out, "I'm good. Just—I—uh—need a second."

"Blaze, the device," Donovan said.

"Give them a few minutes, will you?" said Trent.

Donovan walked around Blaze and began unzipping his backpack. "I'm not heartless, but every minute we're wasting—and I hate to say that word—is another minute that monster is out there looking for us. We're sitting ducks in here, with one way in, one way out. I don't want us to face the same fate as the people here did."

"But we don't even know if everyone who lived here is dead," Blaze pressed. "Let's not write them off."

"He has a point. The door was open," Trent added. "Likely some of them got out."

"They didn't," said a distant voice.

Donovan shoved the device into Blaze's grasp before pulling out his gun, aiming it at the figure.

As if he'd suddenly appeared, emerging from around what had once been the kitchen building for community meals was Victor Winslow.

"Mr. Winslow?" Aurora said. "It's okay, Donovan, put down your gun."

Winslow was ghost-white, clothes torn and ripped. Blood stained his collar and abdomen. He walked towards them quickly. "I'm happy to see you kids are alive. So much happened while you were gone. They found us—"

"What found you?" Blaze asked.

"The monster," Winslow replied flatly. "We couldn't fend them off. By the time we got to the arsenal, the town had been overrun. There wasn't anyone left to save."

"How many survivors are there?"

"The few who lived left. No idea what happened to them afterwards. I've been burying the bodies myself. As you see, I've missed a few," he said.

"When did happen?" asked Donovan.

Wright turned to him, lowering a brow. "A week or so ago. Why?"

A week. We haven't even been gone a week.

"Just asking," said Donovan.

Blaze could see Donovan's hand remaining close to his gun. He sensed something was off.

Blaze looked to Wright. "We were directed here by the relics we've uncovered. Do you know of any other pieces of technology that have been found? Any you've hidden away?" Blaze asked.

"I have this," said Winslow, reaching to his chest. His hand went for the ruby necklace he wore. He took hold of it, ripping it straight off his neck with ease. It glimmered beneath the daylight, seemingly glowing from within.

He held it out to Blaze. Blaze took it. Winslow's eyes were locked onto his, bright and brilliant.

"Your necklace? After all this time?" asked Blaze.

Winslow stepped back, arms dropping to his sides. "It'll go in the center of your machine. It'll fuel the teleporter."

"We never showed you it," Aurora said. "How do you know how it works? What it is?"

But Donovan didn't wait for Winslow to reply. Instead, jumping in with, "You said this happened last week or the week before, sir?"

Winslow turned to look to him. Nodded slowly with a firmed expression.

"Is this true?" he asked Aurora, though seeming to already know the answer to his own question.

"Er—I don't think it's been that long," she replied. "Might be just confused. Stress can do—"

"Get back." Donovan grabbed his gun, aimed it at Winslow. "That's not your leader," he called out.

"Donovan!" Aurora gasped. "What are you—"

It happened in a solid swoop of movement. The skin of Victor Winslow began to ripple on the surface. The muscles beneath stretched, then tightened. His face was the first to disfigure as skin drooped, losing its grip of his skull. His eyes went dark and then sunk in, vanishing. Winslow's jaw went slack, opening an inhuman amount, as another face—a familiar face—appeared to crawl out of the town leader's former mouth. The face, translucent and slimy, slipped free from the body-suit of Winslow, and then the rest of Victor Winslow simply fell off into a pile of decaying flesh.

"Blaze," Forrest said. "The ruby."

"It came from him!"

"Just try it. It's the right size my grandfather said would be the missing piece. We've got nothing else!"

Blaze twisted the cannister as the Shape began to approach. He reached in, grabbing the jewel from the tiny holder it was set in. Warm to the touch, Blaze swung his backpack off, and pulled out the relic.

Sure enough, there was a spot—a tiny spot—for the ruby. He pressed it in, heard it snap in good fit.

The device began to rumble in his hand. A small button on the top started to glow red.

"Guys! Grab onto me."

Blaze felt their hands grab onto him, and he pressed the button on the relic.

A dome of light captured them. A small screen on the relic was counting down from five.

The Shape ran towards them.

"It's gonna get in. It wanted us to take it wherever we're going!" said Aurora.

"No, it won't," Forrest said.

As if in slow motion, Forrest forced his way out of the dome, slipping back into River Ridge. He ran, full-force towards the Shape and dove forward.

Contact was made. The two collided with the cement ground. Forrest began swinging, fist colliding with the Shape's face. It didn't flinch. It shoved Forrest off of itself and into the air. Forrest fell to the ground, but scrambled onto his feet, as the Shape stood, starting to move towards them.

Three, the number read

"Forrest!" Trent cried out. "Get in!"

But as the Shape was nearly a few feet away, Forrest grabbed onto it, holding it against his chest. The Shape's hands grasped frantically at nothing, just barely skimming the surface of the dome. It's eyes locked with Blaze's.

Two.

"We have to help him!" Donovan yelled.

One.

Crushing force slammed into Blaze's chest. He felt the hollow of his chest press in a bit. He squeezed his eyes shut, feeling the world spin away from them into nothingness. Losing a sense of reality, he found himself disoriented and blinded by bright, ever-changing colors. He wanted it to be over, begged for it to be over.

Even if it meant death.

But as fast as the teleporter had swallowed them, it spit them out.

Blaze's head felt thick and slow. In his ears, there was a high-pitched ringing which seemed to engulf him, ensnaring him in delirium. It made clear thoughts an impossibility.

He lifted his head, glanced upward. His mouth pursed; eyes fixated ahead on a blinding white light. Blaze blinked, refocusing. Turning aside, he saw Aurora sitting up slowly pressing her hands against her temples. Trent was covering his ears, rocking himself on the ground. And Donovan stood hunched over with hands pressed against his thighs. His back was bobbing up and down. It took another blink to see that he was throwing-up.

But within, distant and echoic, a female voice spoke. A thick accent carried itself across a gentle, lilting voice.

"It will pass," she said gently, voice distorted as if spread across time.

Blaze swallowed a firm lump and extended his hands out. Beneath them, he felt icy metal and seeing past the throbs in his head, he finally registered grated flooring. He took another breath before looking back towards the blurry light that had been ahead of them before.

Now, there were three figures standing in what appeared to be a doorway of light.

In the center stood a dark-skinned man with a thick spare lip, appearing fully human. Short white hair had recessed to the top of his scalp, and a thick beard covered much of the long scar running down the left side of his face. Even from this distance, Blaze could see a sharp contrast in his eyes: one dark and the other milky white; blind. He wore a suit of rust-colored, plated armor, with numerous parts making an entire suit. A chocolate brown cloak hung from his shoulders, collecting at the base of leather-brown, buckled boots.

The man to his right, slimmer and taller, appeared even more unnerving. Slicked-back white hair reached mid-neck. Angled cheekbones cast his narrow face in shadow, while bright-blue eyes illuminated around the edges. As he looked across them, his eyes narrowed beneath thick white brows. He wore a black uniform with gun-metal gray buttons up the center and down the lengths of his arms. He too wore a matching black cloak.

And on the far left stood a purple cloaked woman, tall and severe-looking. A bejeweled crown of sorts sat atop bone white hair which was brushed back into an up-do. She appeared to be the eldest of the three—closer to the male furthest than the male closest. Her face was made-up with discrete make-up and deep red lips. A pair of jeweled earrings matched her crown, catching the glimmering light around them.

Blaze had been so focused on the new people ahead of him that he'd looked right past their surroundings. Above and around, the canvas of space wrapped around them. Blooming stars hung stationary in the sea of the abyss. The three figures began moving slowly down a metal ramp, cloaks dragging behind in their wake.

The four of them were on a slightly inclined ramp, Blaze realized. Ahead, there appeared to be another portal behind the three officials. The ringing in Blaze's ears stopped. He looked aside.

"It's taken you long enough," said a deep masculine voice, as it came nearer. "On your feet."

"No need to be rude, Cullen," said the woman. "You remember the first time you traveled via portal, don't you?"

"What?" Donovan said, pressing off his knees. He looked a little unsteady on his feet, but Blaze figured he wanted to face the new figures with the appearance of strength. "Where are we?"

The dark-skinned male in armor approached Aurora, disregarding Donovan. "She's injured," he said firmly. "Cuts and bruises across all of them." He leaned down towards Aurora.

"They'll heal," said the stern-faced man, Cullen.

"Don't touch her!" Donovan said breathless. "Please, we're not enemies."

The woman turned to Donovan. "Of course not," she said. "Do you think you would have come this far, if you were? Would we have helped you? Sent rescuers to you."

"We have to go back. Our friend didn't make it back to the portal in time. He dove out to stop the Infiltrator."

"Infiltrator?" repeated the black-cloaked man, Cullen. "They know the verbiage. I'm impressed."

The other male shook his head. "Didn't know the Creators still had them down there."

"We need to stop it," Blaze said. The others turned to him. "Do you know how we can?"

The dark-skinned man lowered his head. "You don't stop it, son. Even we can't stop the creations of the Creators."

"Then who are you?" Donovan asked.

"The Council," said the woman. "My human name is Winona Neilson. Commander of the *Exodus*."

The pallid man stepped forward, his scarred lip twitching slightly. "I am Lord Cullen Walker," said the man in black. "This is—"

"I can introduce myself just fine, Lord Walker. I am Wikus Brackton. Lord Brackton to you," said the man in armor.

Aurora shook her head. "You're not understanding. We need to go back. We need to save our friend, Forrest."

"I'm sorry," said the woman. "There is no going back. Your friend did a noble deed. He protected you and protected us—the Exodus—from being infiltrated. I'm sure he didn't know the damage it could have inflicted. They've been attempting to gain access for decades."

Tears burned at Blaze's eyes. It had struck him, just now, that Forrest wasn't coming with them, and there was no going back to try and save him. The throbbing in his head was beginning to subside, but the confusion kept him wondering if this was even real.

"Who is the Council?" he asked. "How did we know bits and pieces about you?"

Winona turned to him slowly. "Because we shared your future, your planet's future, with selected few. We dedicated ourselves to preventing our civilization's destruction at the hands of the Creators."

"You went against your superiors?" asked Trent.

"If we hadn't, you'd have all been eradicated in the plague," said Lord Brackton.

Winona stepped forward, leaning down to help Aurora stand to her feet. She reached around, fixed Aurora's hair. "We knew what the Creator's plan was. They felt your species had...lost its way. The Council believed in redemption, so we came up with a number of possible solutions, though ultimately none were fully feasible."

"*Couldn't save everyone,*" Donovan said softly, gaze focused on the stars surrounding them.

"Correct," the Commander replied. "We had differences in opinion on how far we were willing to go to save our species, but this was our final solution." Commander Neilson lifted her arm, pointed above. "The *Exodus*."

Above the ceiling of the dome was a massive triangular-shaped craft. Layered in matte-black octagons, only the edges of the triangle seemed to be reflective. From the center, a metallic cylinder passed through the dome and reached the platform they stood upon. A swirling portal in the base of the cylinder is what Blaze saw earlier and where the Council members had come from. Thin blue lines of light, geometric shapes, and pictographs shone brightly from the metallic surface.

Blaze saw it as piece of home, reminding him of the walls and their patterns. It was clear it was these three who had been responsible for the walls and their design.

"The clusters of survivors we saved from the cities would be taken here, loaded onto the *Exodus*, and taken to a secure space away from the eyes of the Creators."

"The walled-in cities were from you," Aurora said.

Lord Brackton nodded. "My idea," he said. "We planted the tools needed to get here, shared information via our informants with selected individuals. Some have been here for decades. We're still waiting on a few," he said. "Others were breached by Infiltrators sent by the Creators. The enemy you encountered was sent to terminate the survivors of their plague and their descendants. Apparently, they nearly succeeded with your lot, like they have with a few others."

"It got in somehow, weeks ago. It breached the wall, but didn't get in. We escaped with a survivor group. When we came back after seeing the hologram, it was the Infiltrator that gave us the final piece we needed—the ruby."

None of the three seemed bothered by this.

"It could do more damage here than down there," said Lord Walker. "It's a smart creation, indeed. It wanted to get onboard."

"So, this ship, where does it take us?" Donovan asked.

"To a new homestead—a place to start over, start anew," said the Commander. "It's your call. We can send you back down, but you're fully on your own. The Council will no longer protect you. I hope you'll choose wisely."

Blaze looked to Aurora. "Everyone we know is gone," he said.

Aurora nodded, biting her upper lip. "Everyone."

"I have family down there," Donovan said. "They thought it was another clue, so they sent us. Just us. Can you get them here?

Lord Brackton exhaled a breath. "I'm sorry, son. They made their choice not to come with."

"How can you people claim to want to help us and then say that? It doesn't add up."

"Because they had the choice," Lord Walker said. "Unfortunately, they chose wrong."

The space went silent aside from the distant hum of the portal. Donovan lowered his chin to his chest and held it there. Blaze saw that Donovan had his eyes closed, while his lower lip began to tremble.

"He knew, didn't he. Your grandfather?" Blaze asked.

Donovan turned to him.

"He knew all about the teleporter. He even said, back at base, that it should have been together. Did he have friends that had gone through this?"

"Not sure," Donovan replied quietly. "He said something about a portal to me years ago. I forgot about it until now. He knew people from the walled cities. Guessing not everyone wanted to take the leap and stayed back. He should have come with us, if he knew, though. I don't know why he didn't." He took a deep breath, closed his eyes. "I have no one now."

Commander Neilson cleared her throat softly. "We do have to get going," she said. Her voice softened; accent eased. "I'm sorry for your losses. You can talk more once we're secured."

"Donovan," Aurora said, running her hand along his shoulder. "We're with you and you have us. Take your time."

"Didn't you hear her? We haven't all day!" Lord Walker spat.

"No," Donovan finally said, raising his hand, "I'm okay. I said good-bye. I think everyone in that cafeteria knew we weren't coming back. One way or another.

"How do we go on without Forrest?" Blaze asked. "He might still be down there."

"Blaze, he's gone, buddy. He's gone. We've got to press on," said Donovan. "Without him. Without everyone."

"We have to," Aurora added. "And we have to do it right and well. If not, his death was for nothing." Aurora took Blaze's hand. "We have to do it for him and for ourselves."

Trent stepped forward, joining the three facing the Council. "You heard them. We have to move. Ready?"

Fighting back tears, clutching his emotions and holding them close, Blaze nodded.

The Council turned and began to walk to the portal. The clicks of heels against metal echoed in the space. Beside them, the stars seemed to follow them. Blaze couldn't see Earth, but knew it was somewhere. And though it was far away, he could return home anytime he wanted to in his mind.

The portal glowed bright with light. It illuminated all of them, casting brilliant, swirling colors across the space.

"In your own time," said Commander Neilson before vanishing into the light.

Lord Brackton followed, then Lord Walker.

Now the four remained behind in the vast chamber, alone. They looked to each other before looking skyward to the *Exodus*, their future, straight above.

As Blaze knew, the moment you step forward, there is no going back. For now, the future was promising, and though he knew the fight may continue in the days and years ahead, he looked to the future with a sense of hope carried by the winds of those lost before them.

"Ready?" he asked softly.

Aurora looked skyward once more, and then back to him. "For Forrest."

"And for us, too," said Blaze.

He took Aurora's hand in his, running his thumb over the top, and together, they stepped into the void.

CPSIA information can be obtained
at www.ICGtesting.com
Printed in the USA
LVHW091510080221
678719LV00026B/1232/J